STARTING
from
SCRATCH

**Center Point
Large Print**

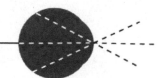

**This Large Print Book carries the
Seal of Approval of N.A.V.H.**

STARTING *from* SCRATCH

Susan Gilbert-Collins

CENTER POINT LARGE PRINT
THORNDIKE, MAINE

This Center Point Large Print edition is
published in the year 2011 by arrangement with
Touchstone, a division of Simon & Schuster, Inc.

The text of this Large Print edition is unabridged.
In other aspects, this book may vary
from the original edition.
Printed in the United States of America.
Set in 16-point Times New Roman type.

ISBN: 978-1-60285-918-0

Library of Congress Cataloging-in-Publication Data

Gilbert-Collins, Susan M.
  Starting from scratch / Susan Gilbert-Collins.
    p. cm.
  ISBN 978-1-60285-918-0 (library binding : alk. paper)
  1. Life change events—Fiction. 2. Families—Fiction.
    3. Mail-order business—Fiction. 4. Cookery—Fiction.
    5. Domestic fiction. 6. Large type books. I. Title.
PS3607.I42326S73 2010b
813'.6—dc22
                                            2010026674

For Ellen

Brookings, South Dakota 1996

1

The afternoon that Olivia Tschetter defended her doctoral dissertation, her mother, Vivian, fell from a step stool she'd placed in the pantry and struck her head—possibly on the nearby kitchen table or the knob of the pantry door, which was propped open. The accident was heard by Olivia's oldest sister, Annie, who had just walked in the house to drop off some Mason jars for the aunts; it was Annie who rushed to the kitchen and found Vivian unconscious. A CT scan revealed that the "accident" was probably caused by a mild stroke, but although Vivian remained unconscious, her condition was stable, and doctors felt there was no reason to transfer her to one of the big hospitals in Sioux Falls. They seemed confident, or at least hopeful—the family were to argue about precisely which, later—that she would regain consciousness at any moment and that her chances of recovery were fairly good. It wasn't until Vivian died two days later that anyone could have known about the second blood clot already forming.

In the meantime, Olivia, immediately after defending "The Use of Flouting Implicatures by Advanced Non-native Speakers of English"—

and almost before she could register sweet, dazed relief at the ordeal being over—found herself taken gently aside by the department secretary and told that something had happened. Olivia was on a plane to South Dakota in two hours. She already had a ticket to fly home the next morning (unbeknownst to everyone but Vivian), and it was only fifty dollars to change the day of departure.

On the flight home, she was grateful for the dull, insulating roar of the aircraft and the bright, stale air. She was still dizzy from lack of sleep, from days and weeks of intense, caffeine-fueled preparations culminating in the gallons of adrenaline that washed through her system sixty seconds before she approached the tabletop podium in a conference room full of committee members and graduate students. For two hours, time had no meaning, then for five delicious minutes she was weightless, months of worry and work lifted from her back. Five short minutes— then the disconcerting news of her mother shunted Olivia onto a kind of plateau, an emotional waiting room of sorts. She was too drained to do anything but let things happen around her.

She tried to doze on the plane. When she found she was too tired to sleep, she rehearsed in her head the story of her defense, which she would tell Vivian as soon as she was conscious. Later she would tell the others. In the Tschetter family, it was important to be able to tell a good story; to Olivia, the youngest of four by a good six years, it was all but a survival tactic. The only thing better than telling a good story was pulling off a good surprise. Olivia had often done the one but not the other. For a variety of reasons (all of which, she felt, boiled down to birth order), she was the only one without a flair for surprises, not counting Charlie, their father. Surprises were antithetical to his very nature. Olivia, in contrast, loved surprises; she was just bad at them.

Until now. No one but Vivian knew that Olivia's defense date had moved up an entire month. And no one *would* know, until she'd told Vivian the end of the story. That was the natural order of things.

Vivian did not regain consciousness the next day. Ruby, Olivia's middle sister, delayed her plans to return to Sioux Falls, and their brother, David, even began to talk of coming all the way from the Black Hills. Great aunts Barbara and Rubina came in from the farm with food and took Annie's daughter, Abigail, back with them so Annie's husband, Richard, could go to work. Vivian's closest friend, Maureen, came to the hospital whenever she could. Olivia still wasn't sleeping; her life was on hold until she could talk to Vivian. The others thought she looked ill, and she thought so too when she caught her reflection in the bathroom mirror of the hospital

11

room. Exhaustion had bleached the color from her already pale skin, and her straight brown hair, which could be coaxed to swing in a curve just below her chin if she bothered to blow-dry, hung in dull strands. Her face was thinner; she touched her cheekbones, ran fingers along the line of her jaw. She heard someone say, outside the bath-room door, "This is terrible timing; she's got less than a month," and smiled at herself.

What with everyone coming and going, Olivia didn't find herself alone with Vivian until shortly before she died. Ruby had run home to take a shower, and the moment Annie and Father headed down to the hospital cafeteria to stretch their legs, Olivia took advantage of the privacy to tell her unconscious mother that she had in fact passed her defense with flying colors, just as Mother predicted, that she'd been far more nervous than Mother predicted (no sleep at all the night before, no appetite the day of, fingers and toes like ice the entire time), that one committee member, Dr. Ogilve—who was inordinately fond of noun-phrase referring expressions—had caught her off guard at one point by pouncing on the indefinite article in one of Olivia's subject's utterances. Wasn't it also important, he said, to consider such referents in light of their cognitive status on the Givenness Hierarchy? For one moment Olivia's mind had gone completely blank, wiped clean of the ivenness Hierarchy, wiped clean of the entire English language, but she maintained a white-knuckled clench on her poise and the next moment managed to say, "I think you've answered your own question," a response that Dr. Ogilve and the other committee members accepted without question. It wasn't the most important moment of the defense, but it made the best story; it would get the biggest laugh. It was the part that the others would always remember. David, Richard, and Father, who all had graduate students of their own to advise, would each retell it in their own time and their own way, for their own purposes. David holding forth in a lecture hall, towering over the lectern and issuing robust pronouncements on the amount of bull to be found in the academy; Richard, good-humoredly stepping in to relieve the nerves of a doctoral candidate about to face his own moment of truth; Father—Father didn't have David's impeccable timing or Richard's natural affinity with students. But Father's students would relish it the most as a rare moment of levity shared by Charlie Tschetter, a professor of few, carefully chosen, widely spaced words.

Olivia, watching the door, had just told Vivian, "You know, Mother, you're going to have to hear this all over again as soon as you're conscious," when Vivian's hand moved the slightest bit, then went limp again. Olivia watched her

closely. She didn't seem to be breathing. Olivi̇
pushed the call light for the nurse, but a code
blue team had already arrived with a crash cart,
and Olivia was shuttled off to the hallway. She
didn't think to go looking for Father and Annie.
The whole thing was over so quickly that Olivia
was back in the room sitting on the edge of
Vivian's bed, shrugging the nurse's hands from
her shoulders before Father and Annie had been
tracked down. It was over so quickly, in fact, that
it almost seemed not to have taken place. Still, it
must have taken place, because Olivia found
herself waving the nurses away, insisting on a
moment alone, with an energy she hadn't had
since she stepped to the podium two days earlier.
There was the danger that the others would be
back before she could finish what she'd been
saying to Mother, and she had the oddest
impression—which she knew to be false but
could not believe was false—that if she could
only finish, Vivian would open her eyes and
everything would seem real again: the defense,
the numbing drone of the aircraft that still
echoed in her head, the doctors' bland assurances,
and especially her mother's limp hand, which
Olivia held between her own.

So Olivia, gripping her mother's arm now,
hurried to the end of her story and got there with
a minute or two to spare, and Vivian still didn't
open her eyes. There was something that

Olivia's mind wasn't grasping, but another part of her was starting to understand, something that operated on a visceral level, because panic was setting in and she couldn't speak. Father and Annie were there then; she heard their voices. Annie pulled her from their mother, pulled her in close, gasping. Olivia clung to her sister, both of them shivering like trapped animals; she saw Father kneeling at the bed, disbelief distorting his features until she couldn't recognize him, and then she felt something cold and damp soaking Annie's shirt. She lifted a hand to her face in surprise, and that was when she realized she was crying, and that was when she knew her mother was dead.

2

Two months later, Olivia sat on the hard piano bench in her father's living room, hands tucked under her thighs, facing Father, Great Aunt Barbara, and Great Aunt Rubina. She was waiting for them to get to the point. So far Aunt Barbara was holding forth on the homemade noodles she'd brought, and Father wouldn't meet Olivia's gaze.

They had entered the room like perfectly civil people, but they might as well have sprung from behind the furniture, because this was definitely an ambush. She visualized it to pass the time: Aunt Barbara vaulting her well-padded self energetically over the easy chair in which she now sat, thin little Aunt Rubina scaling the back of the sofa to Olivia's left, and Father darting out from behind the lacy green curtains that Vivian had threatened to replace for years—all descending upon Olivia and interrupting a perfectly peaceful moment alone. Or if not perfectly peaceful, at least quiet. At least blank.

She was grateful, at any rate, for the piano at her back, glad to have the sheer silent mass of it in her corner, so to speak. She discovered that if she strained her leg back under the bench, her bare toes could just stroke the corner of one of the unopened boxes shoved against its pedals. Father and the aunts did not know that the boxes contained (among other things) marked-up copies of her dissertation, committee members' comments from her defense, and all the necessary papers to submit once she'd made the minor changes they requested. She had not told anyone in the family that she'd passed her defense, and while she knew this was odd, it also seemed irrelevant. She found it fairly easy not to think about.

Now she stifled a yawn and noted with fascination the faintly greenish cast to Aunt Barbara's carefully sculpted blond hair. It must have been

e sunlight filtered through those green cur-
ains; Aunt Barbara was not one to tolerate an
inferior dye job. Olivia made a mental note to
share this observation with Annie, then wondered
again if *she* knew about this little meeting, if
perhaps she'd even been invited. Annie's niche
in the family practically required it. She'd been
ten years old when Olivia was born, with one
foot in childhood and the other planted firmly in
the world of grown-ups (so it always seemed to
Olivia). She spoke her youngest sister's language, but sometimes to adult ends—Olivia's
ally, but in a most unequal alliance. Annie was
useful to Vivian whenever there was a need to
reconcile Olivia to changes in plans or dull trips
to the clothing store. Now, at thirty-six, Annie's
influence was more subtle, less inevitable.
Olivia could resist it, mindfully, in the same
way that it was possible to swim against the tide.

If Annie had been invited today, this meant
that the others knew she would take their side.
The fact that Annie wasn't there told Olivia
nothing: she'd been ill all week again, ill and
irascible, and might have stayed home on that
account.

She could have warned me, Olivia thought—
although she should have figured it out herself
the moment Father called from work to say
he'd be home for lunch. He was home for lunch
every day, and at exactly the same time, 12:15,

and Olivia was always there with lunch ready.

And then Olivia had heard the slap of the bac door at 12:00, not 12:15, and Father walked i. with the corners of his mouth turned down, which meant he had something to say and was preparing to say it. (It might take him ten minutes to begin, if no one was competing for the floor, or two hours, if all the Tschetters were home.) While he and Olivia were still looking at each other, the aunts had pulled up, and Father, watching them approach through the picture window, had looked neither surprised nor dismayed, just tightened his mouth. Olivia just had time to say, "Does Annie know about this?" when the aunts entered.

"Would you believe," Aunt Barbara was saying now, "some of those noodles took over a day to dry? The wide ones, that is. We had them spread out all over the downstairs on sheets, just like usual. It must be more humid than we thought."

"I would think the humidity wouldn't be an issue, what with your having central air and all," Olivia said finally, knowing full well that Aunt Barbara would rather set fire to a stack of fifties than turn on the central air. Central air had been one of the many battles she'd fought with Uncle Emmet—and one of the few she'd lost.

Aunt Barbara snorted. "We haven't had the central air on yet this year."

livia said, "Well, there's your problem."

Aunt Rubina clasped and unclasped her hands, smoothed her cotton skirt printed all over with lilacs. Aunt Rubina was the youngest of Vivian's aunts (and Vivian's favorite), but her hair had been white as snow for as long as Olivia could remember. Today it was piled loosely in a bun, a few flyaway strands escaping to frame her thin cheeks.

"So. Where are these noodles?" Olivia asked. She was trying to send Father accusing looks, but he just stood there in front of the window jingling the change in his pockets, looking at nothing in particular in the center of the room. Even on a hot summer day like today he wore a tie, dark blue with thin maroon stripes. He would as soon have shaved his head as lecture on campus without a tie.

"They're in boxes in the trunk of the car," Aunt Barbara said. No one made a move toward the door. "Do see that Annie gets some right away. She says that's all Abigail will eat for breakfast some days, homemade chicken noodle soup."

"Just like Olivia at that age," Rubina said with her slow-blooming smile. "Your mother always said you had chicken broth in your veins."

Aunt Barbara opened her mouth—Olivia steeled herself—but before she spoke, her eyes dropped to something at Olivia's feet, and she clamped her lips together, sent a short, audible

19

puff of air through her nostrils, and beg
rummaging in her purse. Julia Child, to who
Aunt Barbara was allegedly highly allergic, wa
emerging from behind the boxes under the
piano. J.C. was the show cat Vivian had ruined.
She was brought to the Tschetters years ago
when she was less than a year old and winning
blue ribbons for Cousin Bernice, one of the
Toronto cousins. Bernice was in the middle of
the summer cat show season—she was showing
three or four seal point Siamese that year—when
J.C., whose official name at the time was
Phairydust Phoo, came down with some sort of
eye infection and had to be quarantined. She
asked Vivian if the cat could convalesce at the
Tschetters's and left behind an array of food cans
and equipment that covered the dining room
table. Vivian had looked over the grooming
instructions with horror. "I don't spend this
much time on *my* hair," she'd said. "And what
sort of a name is *Phoo*?"

But she felt sorry for the cat. She was such a
scrawny, ugly little thing, and anyway she was
sick; her crystalline blue eyes were watery, and
she complained a lot. Father tried to point out
that *all* Bernice's Siamese complained a lot, and
they all looked ugly to the untrained eye: skinny
as snakes, with peevish, triangular faces, ears all
out of proportion. Vivian thought J.C. just needed
to fill out a bit. She took the cat to the kitchen

let her perch on the kitchen stool, fed her ~le tidbits as she went about her work. J.C. ~veloped an eclectic and discriminating palate ~ver the next few weeks. She liked goat cheese but not feta, she accepted slivers of toasted garlic but not raw, she ate ratatouille and minced coq au vin and went ecstatic over chicken in aspic. By the end of the month, everyone agreed that J.C. was looking a little more *normal*.

Bernice returned and was horrified. She actually shrieked. "You've given this animal a potbelly," she said when she could speak again. They all looked at the cat, which Bernice held up under its armpits. There was a slight paunch, perhaps, but it wasn't really noticeable unless the cat was walking. "This is not an animal I can show! This will take weeks and weeks to undo. Have you been *feeding* her?"

"Of course, we've been feeding her," Vivian said stiffly.

"I mean, besides her prescription diet? Has she been living on *straight cream?*"

"If she follows me around the kitchen vacuuming up any little crumb that drops, I don't see what I can do about it," Vivian said.

Bernice packed up Phairydust Phoo and her numerous accoutrements and marched out the front door. She marched back in four weeks later on her way home to Toronto and deposited a cat carrier on the Tschetters's living room floor.

21

"You've ruined her," she said. "She won't tc her food. She bit a *judge*." Bernice demand five hundred dollars to cover the loss.

Vivian was sorry to have a cousin angry witr her, and sorrier still about the five hundred, which they could ill afford (Ruby was about to start college in the fall). But she wasn't sorry to have J.C. (as she came to be known) back in the kitchen. Vivian insisted that the cat could tell when pasta was al dente, and preferred it.

Aunt Barbara had thought the whole thing was a lot of foolishness, and still did.

"How old is that animal?" she said now. She was still rummaging. Father handed her the box of tissues from the coffee table.

"Nearly fifteen, I think," Olivia said. J.C. insinuated herself round one leg of the piano bench, considered Olivia's feet with a mildly alarmed sniff, and finally sauntered to the center of the room, where she sank her claws into the carpet and leaned back into a long, low stretch.

"How you can bear to witness that, I'll never know," Aunt Barbara said.

"Olivia," Rubina said suddenly, "something smells lovely. Whatever have you got going for lunch?"

Olivia stifled a sigh. Aunt Rubina was so well intentioned. "Osso buco," she admitted.

Aunt Barbara said, "Olivia."

"It isn't Mother's osso buco; I wouldn't even

22

empt—it's just a sort of experiment I'm trying. om the book we gave her at Christmas, the *ellegrino Artusi*. The 'authentic' one."

"Olivia, you can't continue on this way."

"It's the most useless excuse for a recipe you've ever seen," Olivia said to Rubina, because she'd been indignant about it all morning. "It's not just that he doesn't give amounts—sometimes he gives amounts, in fact —it's that he assumes you're already a chef. It's like he's not so much giving you a recipe as referring in passing to a dish you've already made a hundred times. Maybe that's fine if you're born knowing these things, like Mother, but for the rest of us mere mortals—"

"Olivia, you cannot continue on this way. You cannot sit here doing nothing with your days but making veal osso buco for lunch—"

"Actually I used lamb shanks."

"—and coq au vin for dinner—and—and beef Wellington for *breakfast*."

"I have never made beef Wellington for breakfast," Olivia said coldly. She had in fact *eaten* some for breakfast, just last week—Father had, too (he was looking away guiltily now)— but only because it was left from the night before. They had a hard time finishing all their leftovers these days.

Anyhow it hadn't quite turned out, and there-fore, Olivia felt, shouldn't count. She definitely

23

lacked Vivian's touch with puff pastry. In fa
she ought to have used store-bought; this thoug
depressed her heavily.

"I was just trying to illustrate my point," Aunt
Barbara said. "The specifics are not relevant.
You are doing nothing with your time but
cooking elaborate meals the two of you can
scarcely be expected to finish—not to mention
the expense"—she glanced at Father, whose
money was being wasted—"and not making any
effort to, well, return to your studies. Get back to
normal."

Olivia thought, *There is no normal now.*

Rubina leaned over and squeezed her arm.
Olivia wondered if she had spoken out loud
without realizing it.

"Olivia," Father said. He finally left the picture
window and crossed over to sit on the edge of his
recliner. Father was composed of long, narrow
lines, but he didn't usually seem gangly—unless
he was seated, as now, with his long feet planted
wide apart, elbows resting on high, narrow
knees. He clasped his large, spare hands
together. "No one's suggesting that you should
jump back into things with both feet." He paused.
"No one's suggesting you should try to defend
your thesis next week, or even next month." He
paused again. Even J.C., sitting back on her
haunches now, seemed to regard him with mild
interest. "However, you might think of making

24

tart. You might find it helpful to think about
tting a new defense date."

"Yes," Aunt Barbara said. "That gives you something to aim for. Then you can start looking over your notes, or however you prepare for these things, maybe a little more each day. Ease back into it. You'll feel better once you've made a start."

"Oh," Olivia said. She turned to Father. "Do you feel better?"

Father had gone back to his office on campus the Monday after the funeral.

He took a breath. "I do find that work can be a very good thing."

"Work is salvation," Olivia said.

"No one is saying anything ridiculous about work being salvation," Aunt Barbara said impatiently, pulling another tissue from the box. "Why must you make everything out to be so dramatic."

"Death is dramatic," Olivia said.

Father said, "It's not like you even have to write, Olivia. You've got the dissertation handed in, the worst of it over with. You might make a beginning by just looking through the things Dr. Vitale was kind enough to send." He nodded at the boxes under the piano.

Dr. Vitale had been kind; he'd taken more trouble than Father knew. Some weeks back he'd gotten the graduate school to extend her deadline

for handing in the final signatures. Olivia wa.
sure (she hadn't paid close attention to his rece
spate of emails, and at this point was not eve
reading beyond the subject line), but she had the
impression that she had missed this extended
deadline.

"What's this? Your advisor sent some things?"
Aunt Barbara was looking at the boxes brightly
—as if in all the times she'd been over for
Sunday dinner in the past weeks, she had minded
her own business to the point of remaining
oblivious to every alteration, large or small, in
the Tschetter household. "Wasn't that thoughtful? I thought perhaps Harry—"

"They're not from Harry," Olivia said with a
neutrality she would never have managed before
Vivian's death. Harry, her closest friend from
grad school, had sent a package recently, but it
was best if Aunt Barbara didn't know that. The
package had contained some of his cake mix
cookies (the one thing he attempted in the
kitchen), several episodes of *Mystery Science
Theater 3000* that he taped for her himself, a
stack of bulletins from the church they both
attended near campus, and a small silken brown
bear wearing a tiny University of St. Anselm
sweatshirt. The bear had made her cry.

Aunt Rubina sighed. "Such a nice young man.
Coming all this way to the funeral, and fitting
in so beautifully . . ."

"...'s nice to have one's *good friends* about in ...es of trouble," Olivia said pedantically. "I ...ppreciated all of my good friends who managed ...o come."

"He stayed only a few days, didn't he?" Aunt Barbara said. "I thought it was a shame we never had the chance to give him supper out at the farm. In fact, I've wondered if—"

"He had to get back," Olivia said. "His own studies, you know, and I think it was his girlfriend's birthday. You can't expect someone so thoughtful to blow off his own girlfriend's birthday."

Aunts Barbara and Rubina subsided momentarily, looking a bit crushed. Aunt Barbara rallied first. "These boxes from your advisor, then. I'm sure he's a busy man to be shipping packages off to students who don't bother to open them. Why don't we open them now?"

Olivia said, "They're addressed to me."

She didn't look at Aunt Barbara when she said this, because she knew she was on the edge of what Father would consider civil. She looked instead at the pile of neatly folded, used tissues that Aunt Barbara had stacked on the coffee table. She felt almost a professional interest; her own mounds of wadded-up tissues tended to spill to the floor.

Father persisted. "I for one would be very happy to see your dissertation. You could walk

me through it. I'm not claiming I would un
stand it all, but it can be a useful experience
have to explain your research to someone wl
doesn't understand it."

"She should explain it to me, then," Aunt
Rubina broke in with a small, self-deprecating
laugh. "I'm sure I wouldn't understand half of
it. I still don't understand what an implicature
is."

"It's something that's true even though you
haven't said it," Aunt Barbara told her.

"No, it isn't," Olivia said. She sighed. She
didn't want to get drawn into this. "For heaven's
sake, lots of things are true even though you
don't say them, that's—you've almost got it backward."

"Well, what is it, then?"

Olivia knew what Aunt Barbara thought she
was doing. She watched J.C. stand up again and
stretch—just a small tune-up stretch this time—
and saunter toward the kitchen. Finally she
turned to Aunt Rubina and said, "Here's an
example. Person A says, 'Where's Aunt Barbara?'
Person B responds, 'I smell something burning
in the kitchen.' Now, Person B hasn't actually
answered the question, have they? It sounds like
they've even changed the topic. What is Person
B really trying to say?"

"Aunt Barbara is in the kitchen burning
something," Rubina said helpfully.

Exactly," Olivia said. She hadn't had to think
~~rd~~ to come up with this example; it had been
~~ivian~~'s favorite way of explaining Olivia's
~~work~~ to other people. "Person B didn't say it in so
many words, but we understand it nonetheless
because we assume Person B is being cooperative
and trying to contribute something relevant to
the conversation. So the idea that Aunt Barbara
is in the kitchen burning something—of course,
this is just an example, Aunt Barbara—is an
implicature: you can infer it from what was
said, but it's not a condition for the *truth* of what
was said. That is, it's true that Person B smells
burning from the kitchen, whether or not it's
Aunt Barbara who's responsible."

"My goodness," Aunt Rubina said. She was
smiling at Olivia with real admiration.

"I don't see how that's different from what I
said," Aunt Barbara said.

Olivia shrugged.

Father cleared his throat. "Well, this is good.
You see, you can begin to think about things
again, engage your mind, and little by little it will
get easier to occupy yourself instead of—dwell-
ing on everything. Which I know is very painful."

Olivia began to count the implicatures in his
statement, ending with: *making osso buco from a
vague Artusi Pellegrino recipe doesn't require
thought*. This, from a man who could barely fry
an egg.

29

Olivia said, "I am too doing things. Moth[ ] last newsletter never got finished."

Implicature: Olivia was actively working [o]n finishing *Cooking with Vivian*. This wasn[ ]t entirely false; she had gone so far last night as to crack open the door of Vivian's study and wonder if the final issue was that sheaf of papers sticking out of a manila file folder in the middle of the shelf.

"Well," Aunt Barbara said. "That's something. It's worth doing, I'm sure. I'm not sure it should take priority over a dissertation defense."

"I think it's a lovely thing to do," Aunt Rubina said. She removed her glasses and peered at them—probably so she wouldn't have to look at her sister—then brushed at them with thin, papery-dry fingers. "I for one would truly treasure having that final issue. All the more so if you add your own touches to it."

"Anyway, I'm not ready to think about my dissertation defense," Olivia said, which was perfectly true if misleading. She kept her mind carefully blank as she said it. She felt as if her body were occupied by a perfectly ignorant and impartial observer from outer space: a being that could feel the shapes form at her lips but not take in the sense of them.

"How long could it take to finish the news-letter?" Aunt Barbara asked. "A week? Less than that, if it's all you do?"

"It is a project with a definite ending point," Father said. "You mail it out and it's done. It's a fine thing to do. And in the meantime, you might consider . . ." His words trailed off. Olivia looked at him in surprise. He was a *pauser,* but he was not a trailer-off of words. "Annie has raised the idea of a grief counselor."

The coward, Olivia thought. *Not even showing up to say it in person. Ill, my ass.* "No," she said.

Aunt Barbara said, "I hardly think a *counselor* is necessary, Charlie."

It rankled to have Aunt Barbara take her side. Olivia wanted to say that she actually thought it was a smashing idea, a wonderful, healthy thing to do, something everyone should do—and so she did think, but she'd be damned if she was the only one in the family to go to a grief counselor, and she knew she would be. It was just like Annie to think it was a fine thing for Olivia, but would Annie, practical, ever-competent, multitasking Annie, be caught dead seeing a grief counselor? She would not. Would Ruby? Would David? Father? She could have laughed.

"What about Italy?"

Everyone looked at Aunt Rubina as if she'd just spoken in Greek.

"I mean," she said meekly, "the trip you and Vivian were supposed to take. Maybe you should still go."

"That was supposed to be a graduation

present," Aunt Barbara said. "Here she hasn't even set a new defense date."

Father held up the flat of his hand to Aunt Barbara. "Olivia? Do you still want to go to Italy? We could always change the dates of the Casa Ombuto reservations, instead of canceling. A change of scene—"

"This isn't a Jane Austen novel," Olivia said, aware of sounding irrational. "No, I don't want to go." She had to work harder now to keep her mind blank. She focused on Aunt Barbara's pile of tissues, on the feel of the corner of the box against her toes.

"You wouldn't have to go alone," Father said. "Maybe Annie, or Ruby—"

"You could go, Charlie," Aunt Rubina said, but Father and Aunt Barbara both quelled her with a look. Vivian had been trying for years to get Charlie to take her to Italy.

"It's cheaper for me to stay home and make bad osso buco," Olivia said.

"I can't imagine it's anything but delicious," Rubina said.

"You're welcome to have some," Olivia said politely. "I have to run now, so I won't be having any." She stood. She could think of nowhere to go. The blank mind thing was working too well.

"Where are you going?" Father asked. He stood as well, and the aunts rose in tandem. They all stood there, tentatively.

Aunt Barbara said, "You aren't going to Annie's, I hope. It's my understanding that she still isn't feeling well."

"Exactly," Olivia said, because something had just come to her. "And she was supposed to deliver Meals on Wheels today. She called and asked me to sub for her."

Implicature: Olivia had agreed to sub for Annie. In fact, she had said no.

"So you see I have plenty to occupy my mind," Olivia said. She looked at her wrist, but of course she wasn't wearing a watch. "Father, if you wouldn't mind feeding J.C. She likes the marrow from the osso buco. Be sure to cut the meat up small enough so she doesn't throw it up."

He nodded.

"And if no one else wants osso buco now, feel free to save it for supper, although I really don't know what else there is for lunch. We're nearly out of eggs."

"I'll enjoy the osso buco very much," Father said, and she could feel the look he was sending Aunt Barbara—it was palpable—although by then she was headed for the front entry for her purse and sandals. It wasn't that she never went anywhere, she told herself as she slipped into the sandals—anyone could see that, for here in her purse were the keys to the Oldsmobile. She went to the grocery store. She went to Annie's.

And now she was going to Meals on Wheels.

"You can make whatever you want for supper, Olivia," Father was saying from the doorway to the entry. "I never said I didn't appreciate it."

Olivia shrugged and reached up to peck him on the cheek. She waved at the aunts over his shoulder. "Good-bye," she said, and she headed out into the sun a little too quickly. The contrast with the cool green light of the living room was too great, and she had to stand there blinking for a moment, knowing their eyes were probably on her back, before she could get her bearings enough to move off in the direction of the Olds.

Chicken Broth

Here you go, Jeannie. It's been hard to get this down because I never measure a thing when I make soup. I had to make a pot just to see, and now I'm not sure I did what I usually do because I don't usually think about it. Anyway, throw a chicken in a pot with some veggies and you can't go far wrong.

Place in a pot:

1 whole chicken, 3½ or 4 pounds, cut up or not
2 carrots, chopped in 3 or 4 pieces
2 stalks celery, same
2 yellow onions, quartered
    (leave the skins on for color)
2 tsp. salt
10 to 15 peppercorns
    (forgot to count before I tossed them in)
1 bay leaf
several sprigs of fresh parsley or 1 tbls. dried
a good pinch of thyme
2 cloves garlic, peeled and squashed,
    if you want to
Water

Cover the whole thing with water, about 2 qua.
Bring to a boil, skimming off the foam as t
liquid heats, then cover and reduce heat to
simmer. I usually crack the lid just a little so some
of the steam escapes. Simmer 1½ to 2 hours.

Remove chicken (it'll be falling off the bones
by now) and save for use in the soup, or for
casseroles, tacos, sandwiches, etc.

Strain broth and discard vegetables. Let cool,
then refrigerate. Skim the fat off the top before
using.

Heat broth to a boil, throw in some thin egg
noodles, and you've got dinner. They ought to
outlaw the canned stuff.

3

It turned out that Olivia couldn't remember exactly where the Senior Center was and had to circle the same three or four blocks downtown for ten minutes looking for what she recalled was a low white-brick building.

The entire downtown wasn't much longer than six or seven blocks. She drove north toward the large Lutheran church, the one with the thirty-foot painting of Jesus facing Main Street with his arms outstretched (directing traffic, the kids always snickered). She passed shoe stores, pizza places, a basement-level aquarium store that crept to a new location every few years. Most of the real shopping in town occurred a few miles away at whichever of the two malls out on Twenty-second Avenue was thriving at the moment, but the downtown remained acceptably active. It had a couple of decent restaurants, and clothing stores the college kids couldn't afford. She turned left at the post office.

She wouldn't have minded driving around if she hadn't been trying to get somewhere. And if Aunt Rubina hadn't brought up Casa Ombuto. That was the one thing she had looked forward to before Vivian died, beyond getting her defense

37

over with, and she had had it all planned out. trip would really begin once they'd chang planes in Chicago. First, they would rehash th details of the defense, the reactions of everyon in the family. Once they were over the Atlantic . . . she imagined it now, the endless blue over which they would hover, seeming not to move. In that state of suspension, with all the time in the world, she would admit to the hard things. Her doubts about starting a postdoc. Her self-loathing over the fact that she would sooner risk the appearance of institutional incest than leave St. Anselm for the wider world. Her suspicion that she was no more than a smart, obedient extension of one of the field's bigger names. Vivian had heard it all before, in bits and pieces, mostly over the phone. This would be different. Olivia would listen back. Things would be solved, and resolved upon.

And by the time they had landed in Florence, perhaps she would have admitted to the other reason she didn't want to leave the University of St. Anselm, the one reason Vivian hadn't already heard: Harry. It seemed as irrelevant as anything now. She wasn't even sure if she still loved him. She couldn't gauge anything these days.

Someone behind her honked and the blue sea fell away. Olivia jerked forward and took a left onto Main. Again.

Certain members of Olivia's family had often

professed surprise that Olivia could have trouble finding anything in a town of only sixteen thousand, and the very town she had grown up in; Olivia felt that if anything, growing up there made it more difficult. She knew, of course, how to get to all the places she *knew:* the hospital, the library, houses of old school friends. She could get from Father's office on campus to the Dairy Micro building, where they bought ice cream in the summer, and all around the sprawling campus—where many of the red brick buildings looked alike to her—on foot. But getting around that way, you tended not to think about street names or north and south, and then when someone mentioned some little street named after a tree, or started going on about Fifth Street versus Fifth Street *South,* you didn't have a clue as to what they were talking about.

"Wait a minute," David had said. "You don't know *south?*" This was a couple Christmases ago, when they'd all been home for a few days and Olivia had to admit to not knowing exactly how to get to some church Abigail's school was singing in.

"I know south on a map," Olivia said.

"Point south," David said. "Right now, show me what direction south is."

Olivia looked out the window, but the sky was overcast, and anyway she wasn't entirely sure it would have helped if she *had* seen the sun.

Even when the sun was clearly shooting up from the east or plunking down in the west, she had to stop and mentally place compass points around the horizon—and the afternoon sun, hanging around some vague middle portion of the sky, was no help whatsoever.

"This is amazing," David said to Ruby.

"Oh, we've always known this," Ruby said, but David wouldn't stop grinning at Olivia and nodding as if something he'd suspected for years was finally being confirmed.

"I do just fine in Columbus," Olivia snapped, "which has a bigger population than all of South Dakota. I rely on maps and good directions, and I do just fine." She didn't mention that she left twenty minutes early before venturing anywhere new for the first time. "But who goes around Brookings with a map? I mean, it's not like I could get lost."

"It's a good thing you're an academic," he told her, "and not something requiring actual life skills, because you couldn't find your way out of a paper bag."

It wasn't fair, she thought now, driving slowly past the same antiques store for the fourth time. Half the family were academics: Father, and David, and Ruby nearly so before veering off into television; Annie married an academic. Yet no one else seemed to lack the supposed "life skills" David was talking about. Olivia suspected it had to do with all those years of trailing along after the others, worrying more about keeping up than about where they were heading.

She approached a short alley she was tired of seeing over and over, and in exasperation turned up it abruptly. Halfway up the block the alley opened out into a parking lot before a low building that suddenly looked familiar, although she didn't know where she'd got the white brick from; the building was colorless concrete. *Not a very cheerful place for seniors,* Olivia thought as she parked near the double glass doors. Next to these doors stood a large metal rack on wheels bearing several large, shiny metal boxes. It was probably too late to deliver meals today, Olivia realized, and feeling a little better, she got out of the car and went into the building to make an honest woman of herself.

She found herself standing in a dining hall. Twenty or thirty old folks—mostly women—sat around several round tables, finishing lunch. Olivia hadn't been here in years, but she could swear she recognized the centerpieces of orange and yellow artificial flowers that adorned each table. Her entrance didn't cause much of a stir. One or two people nodded at her, and the cloth covering a deserted table nearby twitched; two young girls peered out at Olivia before dropping the cloth and exploding into giggles.

Olivia crossed quickly to the cafeteria-style

window that opened into the kitchen, her sandal slapping hard on the bare floor. A warming table on the other side of the window held covered dishes; pots and pans littered the counter near the commercial dishwasher across the room. If she leaned forward she could just glimpse several sheet cakes cooling on the counters in the next room and a tiny television silently flashing commercials.

"Can I help you?"

Olivia jumped. A tall, spare woman with a straight line for a mouth had appeared in the hallway next to the kitchen. The woman was wiping her hands on an apron. She looked at Olivia like she might look at a stray cat.

"I was—Annie Huussen, my sister, was supposed to deliver today, with the group from Brookings Christian Reformed. But she was sick, so I thought I'd see if I could help out."

"Little late now," the woman said. "Deliveries start at eleven-thirty."

"Oh well," Olivia said cheerfully. "I must have gotten the time wrong."

"Come on back and we'll sign you up for tomorrow." The woman turned and went off down the hall. Olivia followed.

"Actually, it's possible Annie will be better by tomorrow," she said to the woman's back, although she didn't believe it. The woman didn't respond. She turned into an office where several women and an elderly man were clustered around a computer.

"I don't know, Doris," one woman said when they entered. "It's not doing what it did yesterday when Marjean was here. Marjean just hooked up the new printer, and voilà."

"No, she did something with a disc first," another woman said.

"Don't you kids take tons of computer classes these days?" Doris demanded of a girl who was leaning against the desk, chewing a wad of grape gum that Olivia could smell from four feet away. The girl's gum chewing slowed and her eyes widened. She shrugged.

"What's wrong?" Olivia asked.

"The new printer won't print," the elderly man said.

"Stupid thing," Doris said. "I knew we shouldn't have bought a new one with Marjean in and out all the time. The director," she added to Olivia. "She's supposed to be on maternity leave."

Olivia leaned in to read the message on the screen. "Looks like the printer driver just needs to be reinstalled," she said. "Have you tried that?"

Doris looked at her as if she'd just asked whether Doris had tried to pilot the space shuttle. "All I do is tell it to print," she said. "I don't turn it on, I don't turn it off. I print the labels for the next day's meals, and then I make the changes by hand. I don't trust this thing farther than I ca throw it."

Olivia thought Doris looked strong enough to throw a computer pretty far. She said, "My advisor's printer just did this; it came with a bad disc. We had to download the driver from the website."

The women scattered. The elderly man gallantly held the back of the office chair while Olivia sat. It was an HP DeskJet, same as Dr. Vitale's. She found the site without much trouble and clicked on "Drivers."

"You're running Windows 95, right?" she asked. Doris gaped, but one of the women said, "That's right."

Olivia started the download. She shut off the printer while she was waiting. It was strange, after all this time, to be doing something someone needed.

She turned on the printer again.

"Is this what you were trying to print, 'Labels for July'?"

Doris nodded.

"There we go," someone said as the printer woke up. There was a light scattering of applause.

"I see you've got things going," someone said from the door. Olivia turned and saw a youngish woman with a diaper bag slung over one arm and a tiny flannel bundle against her shoulder. She was patting the bundle and jouncing just a little.

"The computer fairy came," the elderly man said, and the young girl with the grape gum snickered. Olivia stood up.

Doris said, "Plenty to do in the kitchen, people. And could someone corral Lydia and get her going on those boxes that need to be crushed? She and Violet are fooling around in the dining hall."

The others melted away, with Doris issuing orders to their backs.

"I'm Marjean Warren," the youngish woman said. She shifted the bundle to her other shoulder and shook Olivia's hand. She had very dark, thick, shoulder-length hair shot through with threads of gray that gave her an authoritative air Olivia immediately envied.

"Olivia Tschetter," Olivia said. "I just stopped by because my sister was too sick to come in today, but I guess I was too late."

"Tschetter? Ruby Tschetter's little sister?"

"That's my other sister, yes." Olivia nodded with a modest smile. At least she hoped it looked modest, and not like an effort to show forbearance.

Marjean broke into a grin. "I knew her before she was famous," she said to Doris. "We graduated from high school together."

Doris's thin eyebrows rose. She said, "I would never have known you for sisters."

Years of practice enabled Olivia to maintain

45

a neutral smile. "She takes after our father," sh. said, "and I take after our mother."

"Did you know," Marjean said to Doris, "that Ruby Tschetter was the only person in the history of Brookings High School to be elected president of the student council on the strength of write-in votes alone?"

This was true. Good things had always come to Ruby without her bidding them. Good things crawled to Ruby's feet and prostrated themselves before her. Olivia's lips were starting to feel frozen. She said, with a glance at the door, "Well, I—"

"I'm surprised she hasn't been snatched up by a Minneapolis station," Marjean said.

"Sioux Falls'll be lucky to hang on to her," Doris agreed. "Full-fledged meteorologist like her, with those looks . . . But she never acts like she's above herself."

They were both nodding approval and looking at Olivia, who suddenly wondered if she should take a bow.

"Well, we're all proud of her," she said instead. She looked at her wrist, but she still wasn't wearing a watch, so she ended up rubbing the bones of her wrist with the fingers of her other hand, thoughtfully, as if nursing a sprain. "Actually, I should probably—"

"So what do you do, Olivia?"

"I'm—home on a break from graduate school,"

she said, because it sounded better than the absolute truth: *I'm hiding out in my dead mother's kitchen.*

"For the summer?"

Why not? "Yes," she said.

"Would you be interested in picking up a few hours while you're home? For pay, I mean, not as a volunteer. We need someone in here who can handle a computer besides me. I'm supposed to be on maternity leave, but I have to come in every time the computer says 'boo.' I'm never going to get Lizzie into a schedule this way."

The flannel bundle hadn't peeped the entire time; it was hard to imagine her bucking a schedule.

Olivia said, to buy time, "Just doing whatever needs to be done on the computer?"

"Yes, and if Doris needs a little backup now and then."

Olivia glanced uneasily at Doris, who appeared to be a de facto member of the hiring committee that had just formed, and who was looking at Olivia as if she might ask why she had been let go from her previous position.

"Mostly it's printing out labels," Marjean said, "and updating them as necessary—that's easy— and maintaining the volunteer schedule. That's probably the biggest deal, because it changes all the time; the churches are in rotation every one or two weeks—but you could always call me at home. I know everybody. For that matter, Doris here knows everybody. Once in awhile the routes need to be shifted around, and we have to rewrite the directions a little. But you're *from* here." She spread her free hand expansively.

"Well—yes," said Olivia. "You say I could call you?"

"Lizzie sleeps right through the phone," Marjean said.

"Exactly how many hours?" Olivia asked. She had not been on a schedule since the day before her defense; the days had gone by in a blur, made distinct from one another only by the ever-changing ingredients spread across the kitchen counters. Even before her defense she hadn't been on a schedule, come to think of it; for weeks she'd just studied, eaten, slept round the clock. Sometimes she'd eaten at four in the morning; she never knew whether to call it breakfast or dinner, just threw together a meal of fried eggs and noodle soup, whatever was in the fridge.

"Well, say you came around eight, because if Doris is going to need backup that's when she'll need it, and stayed until noon. One at the outside. Twenty, twenty-five hours a week?"

It would get everyone off her back. It would, in addition, be a little money, which she didn't care about, but Aunt Barbara would. Father would like the fact that she was supposed to be somewhere at a certain time doing something.

"I suppose if it's only twenty or so hours a

ek," Olivia said. "I mean, I really couldn't
y all afternoon."

"Oh no, I'd never expect that," Marjean said.
'You'll do it, then?"

She didn't want to commit—but Doris had a
look in her eye, as if she might ask Olivia what
else she had to do that was so important, so Olivia
said, in a brighter voice than came naturally, "I
guess I could give it a try."

"Wonderful! I can train you today on the
office stuff, since I'm here anyway, and Doris
can show you the ropes in the kitchen tomorrow morning. In fact," she turned to Doris, "why
don't we put her with Donna for the rest of the
week? Donna's our star volunteer," she told
Olivia. "We'll send you on a few delivery routes
with her, get you up to speed."

Olivia hadn't realized she'd have to do
deliveries. Her heart sank a little. "I thought the
deliveries were done by volunteers."

"Ideally they are. Once in awhile numbers are
low, and I'll step in and take a route. Doris can't
go." Marjean flashed Olivia a conspiratorial
smile. "She's indispensable. You and me, we're
just office drudges." There was a squeak from
the bundle, and Marjean shifted it to the other
shoulder and commenced patting. "Doris is
amazing. She is a cooking goddess."

"I do a bit of cooking myself," Olivia said,
smiling at Doris.

Doris said, "I'd better see to the frosting," and moved off toward the door.

Marjean leaned in and lowered her voice. "Don't let her scare you," she said. "She just needs to be handled."

Olivia was not feeling in peak form for handling difficult people. She stifled a sigh.

Marjean went to one of the filing cabinets in the corner, jouncing the whole way. "I'll grab you an application. It's just a formality, but I'll need a couple of references. Nonrelatives. Names and phone numbers would be fine."

Phone numbers, Olivia thought blankly. "Can I make a quick call?" she asked.

"Be my guest."

Olivia picked up the phone and dialed home. She looked at the twelve-month calendar on the wall before her while the phone rang and rang. It was a South Dakota calendar, with the usual panoramic view of Mt. Rushmore, and some smaller insets of Custer State Park, Crazy Horse, Wall Drug (ugh, she thought), the Badlands—you would think the eastern side of the state didn't exist. The answering machine went off, and her father's voice said, "You have reached the answering machine of Charlie and Vivian Tschetter. Please speak after the tone."

He still hasn't changed the message, she thought. Then realized—

Of course.

vian was not going to pick up.

ne replaced the receiver swiftly.

This was what came of letting yourself get distracted: you forgot the unthinkable, just for the space of a heartbeat, and then had to realize it all over again.

"You okay?" Marjean said.

Olivia's hand was still on the phone. She removed it. She wasn't sure she could trust her voice, so she coughed instead. "I'll have to get you that number later," she said finally, and coughed again.

"There's a water fountain just down the hall," Marjean said. She was still bent over the baby. Olivia managed to keep coughing while she went down the hall to the water fountain, and then she drank and drank from the cold stream even though she wasn't thirsty. She could hear chatter from the kitchen a few feet away, and beneath the chatter, bursts of sound from the tiny TV. Finally she straightened and wiped her mouth with the back of her hand. She walked back to the eight-by-ten office and, acutely aware of the price she'd pay later, deliberately put from her mind every thought having remotely to do with her mother's death.

4

It took all of two or three days for Olivia to feel that she had always worked at Meals on Wheels, not because she felt at home inhabiting Marjean's office or passing through Doris's kitchen, but because the stark sense she had of being a stranger in these surroundings suited her perfectly. Walking the empty hallway between kitchen and office, she felt she was wandering in a foreign country, able somehow to speak the language and pass unnoticed among the natives but unencumbered by roots or ties to anything in her immediate surroundings. Home, and the nagging issue of Aunt Barbara and Father and the boxes under the piano, even Annie's oddly distant behavior, were all unreal to her while she printed out labels or checked lists of volunteers.

Lydia and Violet contributed to this sense of unreality as much as anything. Lydia was a young woman—eighteen or nineteen, Olivia guessed—from the Step Ahead Center for Developmentally Disabled Adults, which paid her part-time wages so she could gain work experience. She was quick and shy and unfailingly good-natured but had to be closely supervised; collapsing boxes was her passion, and en left to her own devices she would empty the canned goods from a box willy-nilly just or the pleasure of collapsing it. Her other passion was hide-and-seek, and when she didn't have something to occupy her attention, she tended to slip away and hide without telling anyone. If no one thought to go find her, she would jump out at the first person to pass by and yell "Surprise!" in her thin falsetto, even though this invariably frightened her more than her victim. Olivia rather liked Lydia, but she did wonder at first how Doris, of all people, had the patience to deal with her.

Then Doris brought her daughter Violet to work again, and all became clear. Violet was also developmentally disabled. ("Retarded," Doris said, matter-of-factly, causing Olivia to cringe inwardly.) Violet was the tiniest fourteen-year-old Olivia had ever seen. She looked about eight, with a mess of curly brown hair cropped short and a small, pointed face. There was some-thing blighted rather than elfin about her looks: her nose was shorter than one expected, her eyes very round and heavy-lidded. She spoke so seldom that for a week Olivia thought she wasn't verbal at all. Violet shadowed Lydia devotedly, and Lydia treated her as an affectionate, scatter-brained older sister might. Often, traversing the hallway between kitchen and office, Olivia caught a glimpse of brown curls disappearing into a

storage room or heard frantic whispers disso▓
into giggles behind a half-closed office door.

Olivia herself engaged in only two activitie▓
that threatened to disturb the pleasantly blank▓
surface of her workdays: email, which she
checked simply because she had time to do so, and
meal delivery. The former was thus far more
potentially troubling than actually so; she found
she could ignore Dr. Vitale's emails as effectively
at work as from Father's computer at home. The
latter activity she hoped to avoid as soon as her
training with Donna Hansen was over.

Olivia delivered route 5 with Donna for three
days. Route 5 was held to be the least desirable
route by just about everyone but Donna; Donna
didn't consider anything undesirable. Donna
Hansen was capable of facing down the most
depressed and depressing client with the sheer
force of her raw, indomitable cheer, and to
Olivia's amazement, most of the clients thrived
under this rough-and-tumble care. Perhaps it was
because they sensed Donna wasn't afraid of
them, of their undeniable proximity to death. Old
age? Donna barely acknowledged it. Woe betide
anyone who tried to tell her that she couldn't
possibly know what it was like to be old and
alone. Mrs. Carlisle tried.

"Fiddlesticks." Donna said this with such
force that Mrs. Carlisle and Olivia and the black
short-haired cat Olivia was petting all jumped.

y old grandma was ninety-eight when she
ant, and she lived the last twenty years alone,
ad loved it! She was half-blind when she
went—"

(Where did she go, thought Olivia, *Europe?)*

"—and arthritic to beat the band, and all but
lost the use of her left arm, not to mention her
hearing, had just the one functioning kidney by
then—did she complain? No. She was happy and
busy because she made up her mind to be.
Anyway, you're certainly not alone," Donna
said, swooping to scoop up an unsuspecting tiger
cat walking by, "not with these little darlings for
company, you're not. You're a woogums," she
told the cat, burying her face in its fur. The cat
looked too alarmed to move until Donna
relaxed her grip. Then it bolted out of her arms
and scrambled gracelessly up the stairs.

"Well, now, that's so." Mrs. Carlisle was
actually smiling. "I always say you can't beat a
cat for company."

Once back in the car, Donna said to Olivia,
"Don't let them tell you how hard it is to be
old."

"Don't you think—" Olivia tried to sound
thoughtful in an academic way, as if she were
discussing a theory and not challenging
Donna's optimism, "that it must be hard, being
old?"

"Of course it's hard." Donna started up her

car and cranked the radio, which was set
country-western station. "But there's noth.
that can't be made worse by bellyaching abo
it."

Olivia admired this attitude but did not pretena
to understand it. All Olivia could offer was pity,
and what was this kind of pity worth? It wasn't
of any practical use.

And so the three days of delivery passed, Olivia
trailing Donna in and out of clients' homes,
knowing herself to be completely extraneous but
grateful to be so. It wasn't until the second-to-
last delivery on the last day that Olivia was any
use at all. They were at the Walkers' house, the
only couple on the route. Donna went to the bathroom with Mrs. Walker to fix a shower curtain
that was falling down, and a moment later Olivia
heard a thump and a crash. She ran to the bathroom to find Donna lying next to the claw-footed
tub under the shower curtain.

"I don't think you should move," Olivia said,
kneeling and pulling the curtain out of the way.
The fact that Donna lay back again without
arguing frightened her more than the sight of
Donna's leg twisted under her.

"We are not responsible for this," Mrs. Walker
said shakily from the doorway.

"For heaven's sake," Olivia snapped, forgetting
for the moment to feel sorry for Mrs. Walker.
"Where's the nearest telephone?"

ter the ambulance had taken Donna away,
via delivered the remaining meal of the
ute alone. She hoped it would be her last.

For four days her luck held. For four days, there
were enough volunteers to cover for Donna, and
Olivia had the lunch hour to herself, or nearly so.
She learned to keep visits to the kitchen brief:
stride in, grab her lunch from the fridge, stride
out. It wasn't that she minded helping out. She
privately gloried in this amusement park of a
kitchen, stocked as it was with industrial-size
mixers and bottomless stockpots. It was Doris she
wanted to avoid.

"How's the new car working out for Ruby?"
Doris asked one day early on, when Olivia had
paused to watch her spread cake batter across a
baking pan half an acre long. "New to her, I
mean. That Mustang convertible she's having
refurbished."

"She hasn't said much," Olivia said, which
was true. She hadn't even known Ruby had a
new car. She never knew anything about Ruby
unless Annie told her. After a moment she asked,
reluctantly, "How did you know she had a new
car?"

"My cousin happens to be her landlady." Doris
did not look up from her spatula. "Lives two
town houses down, in fact. Says Ruby's the ideal
tenant. Never late with the rent, no loud parties.
Can't seem to keep her garden alive, though."

"I'm not surprised," Olivia said, inching way toward the door. "She's pretty focused work."

Another time Doris said, "She might be over watering those moss roses."

"Excuse me?" Olivia pulled herself out of the fridge, sandwich in hand.

"Moss roses are a great choice for a career gal like her, don't require much in the way of care, but if they're sickly, like my cousin Verna says, chances are she's overwatering. Or they need better drainage. Moss roses like a good dry spell in between waterings."

"I'll pass that along," Olivia said, and left as quickly as she could.

Once in the sanctuary of her office, she would close the door, pull a manila file folder labeled Summer Issue 1996 from her backpack, and riffle gloomily through its contents: recipes on sheets of stationery or gaily decorated recipe cards, recipes torn from magazines, recipes printed out from a computer. Notes scrawled across napkins and scraps of paper. Letters from Vivian's readers, with half-formed answers crossed out and begun again. Vivian had been putting out her cooking newsletter for more than thirty years, if you counted the early years when it was more of a letter to friends run off on a mimeo machine, and Olivia desired to honor her mother's intentions for this issue as closely as possible—which desire of course doomed, and which doom filled with despair. Pork Enchiladas with Roasted ꙩmatillo Sauce, evidently sent in by a reader, but ꙏere was no name. Her mother never printed a recipe without crediting the source. A letter from another reader asking if Vivian had a really authentic recipe for shrimp creole, because her husband grew up in the South and he was just sure his grandmother had used juniper berries, and she didn't even know where to get juniper berries. It was signed, "Stumped in Beadle County." Vivian had penned "W.K." at the bottom of the letter and underlined it twice. Who or what was W.K.? Wild Kingdom? Without Kraut? Wilhelmina Kleinsasser? Olivia felt just barely capable of light copyediting these days, much less sleuthing. Usually she stuffed everything back in the folder without so much as taking the cap off her pen.

Still, it beat delivering meals.

Then on Thursday night, the Cross of Christ Lutherans were struck down by food poisoning at an Interdenominational Softball League and Potluck. This spelled an end to Olivia's relatively peaceful, quietly desperate lunch hours: it was the Cross of Christ Lutherans' week to send volunteers.

"C. of C. Lutherans are flakes," Doris said Friday morning, after Olivia had gotten numerous calls from nauseated Lutherans canceling their services. Olivia leaned into open window of the cafeteria counter and c sidered this slanderous statement while s watched Doris sprinkle the crumble topping o an apple crisp.

"Well, they are sick," she pointed out.

"It was an interdenominational potluck," Doris said, "and the only ones to get sick were the C. of C.s."

"They're the only ones we know about. Of course, we wouldn't know about the others because they're not volunteering this week."

Doris was shaking her head. "Arlys Sorenson, who watches Violet some days? She's from First Methodist, and she was right as rain this morning when I dropped Violet off. She was there."

"Maybe she didn't eat whatever it was that made the C. of C.s sick," Olivia said.

"It's a potluck. Everybody eats everything."

Olivia wanted to argue but wasn't sure where to begin.

"Mark my words," Doris said, "you start calling up some Baptists, ask them to be subs, there won't be a sick one in the lot."

Olivia returned to Marjean's office—her office—and did as Doris said. She was able to reach four Baptists, two of whom could sub, none of whom were sick. She reported this back to Doris, who merely lifted her eyebrows knowingly.

"But we don't even know that these specific eople were at the potluck," Olivia said.

"I hear it was the potato salad," Donna said. She'd arrived while Olivia was calling Baptists and was settled on a stool at the island scooping coleslaw into plastic cups and snapping on lids. Her leg, clad in an enormous cast already covered with signatures and games of tic-tac-toe, was propped up on a folding chair just far enough out from the island to get in Doris's way every time she crossed to or from the stoves. "Marge Pierson loads her salad up with tons of mayonnaise, then lets it sit there in the sun during the entire softball game. If my leg wasn't broken, I would've been pitching last night for Emmanuel Baptist, but I'd have had the God-given sense not to go near that potato salad. I ask you, how hard is it to stick it in a cooler with some ice?"

"Actually, it's not the mayonnaise that goes bad," Olivia said, without any hope of being believed. "It's the potatoes."

"I never heard of a potato hurting anyone. I mean, they're cooked."

"No one ever believes this, but it's definitely the potatoes. Cooked potatoes that sit out too long at lukewarm temperatures are pure poison." She realized with a start that this was an exact quote from an old issue of *Cooking with Vivian*. In the margin, her mother had drawn a mound of potatoes under a skull and crossbones.

The whole family had teased Vivian about th.
illustration, and David had sent a fake lette
from the American Potato Council threatening
litigation.

"Olivia's right," Doris said flatly, stopping in
the middle of the kitchen with her hands on her
hips. "It's the potatoes. Speaking of which, Ruby
feeling any better? Was that food poisoning or a
stomach bug?"

"Oh—" Olivia floundered, loathe to admit she
knew less about her sister than someone who'd
never met her. "She hasn't missed a broadcast,
has she?"

"Took a half day, though. Verna went to let the
plumber in and they found Ruby being sick in
the bathroom."

"She's never sick," Olivia said.

"She's a trouper. She was real nice about
being surprised like that, said it was her fault for
forgetting to cancel the plumber. And she still
managed to go on the air at noon."

"I guess she's feeling better, then," Olivia said
lamely.

"You got how many Baptists?"

It took Olivia a moment to remember what
Doris was talking about. She rallied with an effort.
"Two. Plus Mr. Wilson and Reba Myers are both
coming as usual." They needed, ideally, eight
more; volunteers were supposed to go out in
twos, and there were six routes.

"Try the Catholics next," Doris said. "They're always good in a pinch. Or the Peace Lutherans. The Peace Lutherans could be at death's door and they'd still show up to deliver. C. of C. Lutherans are flaky as a pie crust."

"That's pretty flaky," Olivia admitted, thinking of the cherry pies Doris had made Monday. Doris's entrees were lackluster at best, but she handled desserts with the touch of a true pastry chef. Olivia moved off as several more of the kitchen volunteers showed up.

She fired off an email to Ruby, though she was gloomy over her prospects for a meaningful reply:

You feeling any better? I hope you haven't got whatever Annie's got.

Then she spent most of the morning on the phone, until her ear was mashed and numb, and finally came up with one Catholic, two Peace Lutherans, two members of the Brookings CRC (that was the Christian Reformed Church, Olivia's own), and a Speak the Word charismatic who was willing to take a route alone—as long as it wasn't route 5. Olivia, stifling a sigh, had agreed and expressed her thanks. She knew where this was headed.

At least it's one of the shorter routes, she thought glumly. And she had driven it three days in a row; she should be able to find everything anyway.

It was immediately clear that after just a few days without Donna's robust ministrations, route 5 was already sagging under the weight of its own decrepitude. Mr. Ryerson rendered his opinion of cream-style corn in such strong terms that Olivia, murmuring unheard sympathies, feared he would give himself a stroke. Mr. Reynolds, a large, quiet man who lived in the smallest house Olivia had ever seen, seemed larger, more silent than ever, his house smaller and poorer. Olivia found herself chattering more and more as the colorless walls closed in, until by the time she left she was sure she must have seemed manic to the utterly, desperately mute Mr. Reynolds. One of Mrs. Carlisle's cats wasn't eating properly, and Olivia had to crawl after it in the dust under Mrs. Carlisle's bed with a bowl of cat food to calm the woman down. By the time she pulled up at the fourth stop, she was thinking that perhaps she'd been hasty about the grief counseling. At least it would mean only an hour once or twice a week, and she wouldn't end up getting depressed about other people's troubles that she couldn't do anything about anyway.

She got out of the car and looked up at the house and tried to remember the client who lived here. A nondescript little woman (although Olivia seemed to recall a Southern accent), sandwiched in between the voluble Mrs. Carlisle and the squalid Mrs. Hammond.

But the house was another matter. She'd known this house her whole life. It was a thing of beauty, or would be if one could only sink some money into it: a wide, sagging porch that wrapped around the southwest corner, two-over-two paned sash windows all across the front, leaded glass across the top of the polygonal bay that rose into a small but splendidly staunch second-story turret. Olivia remembered how, growing up, she used to ride her bike several blocks out of her way just to pass this house, and how she had envied the lucky girl who must have gotten that second-story turret for a bedroom.

It had been disappointing, that first day delivering with Donna, to see the inside at last. If one looked only at the outside, and from a distance—say, no closer than the curb—it was easy to imagine restoring it. You would first have to pry the dying tree from the western side of the house; its branches had been given leave to spread over the roof, the roots to invade the foundation, so that the house buckled from beneath and caved from above, and the section of porch caught between these slow, steady pressures cowered like an animal. The tree gone (replaced, Olivia decided, by a stand of purple lilacs), and the porch in good repair, she ripped off the roof, tore down beams and walls and chimneys, and threw them all up again, then stripped the peeling gray paint and replaced it with a fresh coat of white—no, dizzying purples and yellows and bright greens, like a true Queen Anne. She washed the windows upstairs and down until they shone like mirrors. Then there was nothing left but to clear the jungle growth of weeds four feet deep against the house and plant purple hydrangeas and big showy peonies and yellow roses, and anything else old-fashioned she could think of. She let a sweet pea vine twine itself round the porch railing.

But the inside . . . dim, gray, and fusty. She recalled suddenly why it was hard to remember the woman who lived here—little and gray, she didn't seem person enough to inhabit such a house—and as she did, the weeds sprang back, and the house sank once more into extreme disrepair. Olivia took a deep breath.

It was the Cross of Christers' fault she was here. She wished she were home with food poisoning.

She went to the backseat to snap open the hot box. She pulled out the foil tray—Mrs. Kilkenny, the label said—and slipped it into a protective hot pack, reached across to the cooler for the plastic-wrapped cold meal. Next week was Methodist week; she couldn't remember what Doris had said about the Methodists. She shoved car door shut with one hip and started up the acked cement walk.

Donna had simply thrown open the screen door and thumped a couple times on the beautifully grained wood of the front door (hard enough that Olivia had feared for the glazing), and then walked right in. Olivia couldn't bring herself to do more than push the rusty old doorbell. Two tones sounded in the distance, slow and uneasily flat. She waited, then pushed the bell again, tried to recall whether this client was particularly deaf; there was no note on the route instructions. She was reaching for the handle of the screen door when the doorknob of the main door rattled, and a moment later a woman was peering up at her through the fine gray mesh of the screen.

"Meals on Wheels," Olivia said, which was what you were supposed to say.

The woman continued looking at her. At five foot four, Olivia loomed over her.

"I've got your lunch here. It's pork chop today, with mashed potatoes and gravy. And creamed corn," she admitted, thinking of Mr. Ryerson.

The woman brought the fingertips of one hand to her lips, eyes still fastened on Olivia's face. Olivia began to wonder if she had a gaping head wound that she'd somehow overlooked. She finally stacked the hot and cold meals and balanced them in one hand, pulled open the screen door with the other. Mrs. Kilkenny stepped back as she crossed the threshold, and for one moment Olivia thought she was actually alarmed.

"Why, you remember me," she said, trying to laugh lightly. "I was here just last week, with Donna."

The woman said, "After all this time."

Olivia had been right about the accent: slight but unmistakably Southern.

"I'm sorry I'm late," Olivia said, with a token glance at her watch. "I'm still sort of new at this."

"I never thought to expect you again."

"Oh—you didn't cancel, did you?" Olivia lifted the meals in question. Mrs. Kilkenny looked at them in some surprise. She wasn't alarmed; Olivia saw that now. She was almost eager. Whether it was the eagerness or the high rounded forehead, she was younger looking than Olivia had remembered. She had large, wide-set gray eyes, a child's earnest gaze. Her gray hair rose in a springy halo that Olivia suspected formed corkscrews when wet.

"I didn't cancel," the woman said, but she sounded unsure.

"Well, good. Where shall I set these for you?"

They were in a small dark entryway with a staircase that rose directly in front of Olivia; worn cabbage roses spilled down the runner of the stairs and under Olivia's feet, on into the

lor that opened on the right. Olivia could see
ry little in that room; the windows were con-
ealed, floor to ceiling, by heavy green drapes
that damped the light and cast the room in under-
water murkiness. To the left, the cabbage roses
flowed into a living room with the same heavy
green drapes. At least here the windows looking
into the side porch were not covered, allowing
more light into the room.

Olivia would have dearly loved to wander
around for a really good look, if she hadn't
wanted even more to get this over with. Mrs.
Kilkenny raised a hand as if she meant to touch
Olivia's arm, then withdrew it. "Please, in here,"
she said, turning toward the living room. She led
Olivia over the cabbage roses, did not pause by
the little table between the sofa and the wing
chair, which was where (Olivia now recalled)
Donna had left the meals. She moved with sur-
prisingly small, quick steps through the living
room, through two sets of open double doors
that enclosed a small formal dining room, and on
into the kitchen—much farther than Olivia had
gotten all last week, and so quickly that Olivia
barely had time to notice anything about the
dining room besides a heavy mahogany table
and matching breakfront.

Mrs. Kilkenny stopped in the middle of the
large, square room, which was a 1950s dream
gone nightmarish. There was a pink porcelain

stove and a pink double sink and a stubby, blu[
cornered refrigerator in white. Pink ginghe
curtains concealed the lower panes of glass .
the double window over the sink, and a frill o
pink gingham edged the upper. In the middle of
the black-and-white checkerboard linoleum
stood a green metal table with two matching
chairs. There was nothing on the table but a
place mat and an open can of Coke.

"What a pretty room," Olivia said without
thinking, even though it wasn't. It was a wistful
room, a room that was trying too hard. "Well,
shall I set these here?" She slipped the hot meal
out of its pack onto the place mat and placed the
cold meal next to it.

Mrs. Kilkenny seemed not to notice. "It's up
there," she said, pointing to a high cupboard over
the windows.

"Oh. All right." Olivia pulled one of the green
metal chairs over to the sink. "What am I looking
for?"

The woman looked at Olivia in amazement.
"My skillet. Way up there on the top shelf."

Olivia thought of Donna's broken leg and
sighed, tested the chair; it seemed sturdy
enough. She lifted the skirt of her tank dress and
stepped up onto the chair. It wasn't high enough.
"May I stand on your sink?"

"You better had," the woman said, gently and
reproachfully.

livia suppressed another sigh. She slipped off sandals and placed one bare foot carefully to the edge of the sink, braced her hands against the cupboard for support. Before she could hoist herself the rest of the way up, the view out the upper windows arrested her. "Mrs. Kilkenny," she said. "What is out there?"

It was a silly thing to ask—she knew rhubarb when she saw it—but she'd never seen rhubarb like this. Three feet high, almost four in places, the larger leaves spreading nearly two feet across, it had spread from the back northwest corner of the fence across the yard nearly to the shadow line of the great house. Olivia spotted the gray tip of a tail moving along the edge of the patch and thought, *There's probably a whole ecosystem under there.* New species were probably evolving. It was like looking down on a rain forest canopy.

"Used to have a rhubarb patch out back," Mrs. Kilkenny said.

"Well, you've still got one," Olivia said. *With a vengeance.* Mrs. Kilkenny came over to the sink and pulled aside the gingham curtain, peered out. She didn't seem impressed.

"Haven't used rhubarb since Mr. Kilkenny died," she said. "The stalks are toughening, this time of summer. You harvest in June."

"We used to have rhubarb," Olivia said. "I mean, not like you've got rhubarb . . . Our mother used to warn us about the leaves."

She remembered how she used to pretend th were fuzzy green elephant ears. Every year sh used to pull up a stalk and snap it in two anc force herself to take a great bite, even though she knew it would screw her tongue and cheeks into knots and tweak her salivary glands until water rushed in her mouth. She felt a rush of water now, just remembering, and had to swallow.

"Used to make strawberry-rhubarb pie," Mrs. Kilkenny said, "and rhubarb-apricot jam, and sour cream rhubarb cake."

Olivia tore her gaze from the backyard and looked down at Mrs. Kilkenny. "I've had that," she said. "Sour cream rhubarb cake."

Mrs. Kilkenny let the curtain fall and stood back, looking up at Olivia expectantly.

"Oh. Right." Olivia hoisted herself up and jerked at the cupboard—it stuck as if it hadn't been opened in a long time. It finally opened to reveal an ancient cast-iron skillet and a few glass jars at the back. "This?" Olivia said. She pulled the skillet forward carefully. It weighed about eight hundred pounds.

"Of course."

Olivia pulled at the skillet some more, and when it was far enough out to teeter, she said, "Stand back." She braced herself, gripping the edge of the shelf with one hand, and pulled the skillet the rest of the way out. It swung heavily her side, but she hung on to it until she'd gained her balance enough to lower it, on end, to the edge of the sink.

The skillet thus supported, she made her way down to the floor. Her arm ached. She hefted the thing up with both hands and said, "Here it is," as firmly as Donna would have, to bring this episode to a close.

"My old skillet," Mrs. Kilkenny said in wonder, as if Olivia had surprised her with a gift. Olivia went to the stove and placed the thing carefully on one of the large black coils, stood back to catch her breath. It was enormous, like her mother's—twelve inches across? Fourteen? She rubbed her upper arm. Mrs. Kilkenny said, "Chocolate skillet cake."

Olivia looked at her in surprise. "You've made chocolate skillet cake?"

"Best chocolate cake there is," Mrs. Kilkenny said. "We used to call it Chocolate Puddle. Moist like anything."

"Is that the recipe with sour milk in it?"

"Sour milk, or buttermilk if you like."

"And cinnamon."

"I never added the cinnamon," Mrs. Kilkenny said. "It competes with the chocolate. No cinnamon, and no vanilla, just one third cup cocoa powder."

"And whipped cream on top?"

"Instead of icing," Mrs. Kilkenny said.

"What do you know," Olivia said. She co
see the recipe, though it had been years—r
mother had drawn a border of tiny cast-irc
skillets around it, and Father had teased her fo.
once. They look like they're dancing, he had
said. Cast iron's going to break your foot if you
drop it, and you've got them dancing all over the
page like angel wings. It really had been years,
because Olivia could remember standing at the
old speckled yellow kitchen table they used to
have, looking up at him; she was barely as tall as
the table.

She was about to ask where Mrs. Kilkenny got
her recipe when the woman said, "It's unusable."
She was standing at the stove looking into the
skillet. Her eagerness had dissipated; disappointment carved the wrinkles in her face, and she
looked old. Olivia saw this and was suddenly too
tired to be having this conversation. She began
rather desperately to want this to be over.

"Well, that's normal, isn't it?" she said. "It
must be years since this was used."

"Years." The woman repeated the word faintly.
"I don't know what I was thinking."

"Surely it can be seasoned again. Can't we
scrape off the rust and rub it down with oil?" She
wasn't sure how she knew this; her mother's
cast-iron skillet phase had been brief, and years
ago.

"Yes," the woman said. But she looked away

n the skillet as if she were weary of it.

Olivia said, "Mrs. Kilkenny, next time I come e'll see about seasoning it, all right? Don't try .o lift it, just leave it there." She looked at her watch again. "I'm running late. I'd better get the rest of the meals delivered and let you have your lunch before it gets cold."

This time it was she who led the way back through the dining room and living room to the front entry. She turned at the door. The woman looked past her out the mesh of the screen. Olivia wondered how she had ever thought the woman looked young. Somehow Olivia had managed to make everything worse.

"It's terribly heavy," she said again. "Don't try to lift it yourself, okay? I'll be back."

Mrs. Kilkenny looked at her, nodded once, and dropped her eyes.

Back in the car Olivia tossed the hot pack on the seat beside her and let her head fall back against the headrest. She closed her eyes, saw rhubarb leaves, cast-iron skillets, her mother drawing at the old yellow table with the cold metal legs. Tears pricked at her eyes, and she sat up abruptly. She didn't have time for this. There was the rest of the route to finish; there was Mrs. Hammond to face. Nothing terrible had happened, she told herself: just an old woman, a little confused, and her own useless pity welling up and making her promise stupid unnecessary things about a skillet the woman proba̶ couldn't lift, let alone use. Donna would ha̶ said, "This is going right back where it cam̶ from," and shut the thing back up in its cupboard, and that would have been the end of it. Olivia started the car and pulled away from the curb.

The woman probably wouldn't even remember that Olivia had offered to come back. In fact, hadn't she been basically normal last week, before she ever noticed Olivia? Normal enough that Olivia had scarcely noticed her either. As far as she could remember, Mrs. Kilkenny hadn't looked alarmed or eager or disappointed or anything when Donna breezed in and out with Olivia trailing behind. It might be the kindest thing if Olivia didn't return, if this was the effect she had on the woman. She began to feel a little better, and by the time she had reached Mrs. Hammond's, she had also reviewed her words to Mrs. Kilkenny carefully and was quite sure she had never actually promised anything.

Chocolate Puddle

This recipe is reason enough to buy a cast-iron skillet. Be sure to use a large enough skillet, else when the cake rises you'll have a puddle for sure—all over your oven floor.

½ cup butter
1 cup sugar
2 eggs
1 cup light Karo syrup
1 tsp. vanilla
1¾ cups flour
⅓ cup cocoa
1 tsp. each baking soda and baking powder
1 cup sour milk
    (This is milk with 1 tbls. white vinegar
    stirred in; let sit for a minute or two
    before using. Or you can use buttermilk.)

❦ Note: Winnie says some folks like to add
    1 tsp. cinnamon, but I don't think
    she approves of this.

Preheat oven to 350 deg.
    Butter and flour a large cast-iron skillet. To

distribute the flour evenly over the buttered surface, you can tip the skillet and tap it lightly against a <u>sturdy</u> surface. Careful—these things can do some damage.

Cream the butter and sugar, then add the eggs and beat. Add syrup and vanilla and beat a little more.

After measuring the flour, sift it with the cocoa, baking soda, and baking powder. (And cinnamon, if you feel so led.) Alternate between adding a little of the sifted ingredients, then a little of the sour milk, to the butter-sugar-egg mixture, mixing the whole time, until everything has been added.

Pour batter into the skillet and bake for 25 or 30 minutes. The center should still shake a little as if it's not quite done, but a toothpick inserted into the center will come out clean. The edges of the cake will appear more fully baked.

Serve warm with whipped cream or butter.

☙ Winnie claims this recipe serves 8 to 10, but our family of six polished off the whole cake in one sitting both times I made it. Of course, David is 13 and eats like a pack of starving wolves. If he doesn't pace himself, he'll eat us into the poorhouse before we can ship him off to college.

5

In spite of the delay at Mrs. Kilkenny's, Olivia was one of the first to return from her route that noon. She got Mrs. Hammond over with quickly by ignoring the week's accumulation of Meals on Wheels trays; the Walkers had canceled due to a doctor's appointment (bless them, Olivia thought, although she was not on speaking terms with God these days); and at the last stop Olivia just handed the meals through the door to a home health-care worker, barely glimpsing Mr. Wheeler, and the shine of his oxygen cord, on the couch beyond.

It was a relief to find herself back in Marjean's office. Olivia took out her sandwich and started in immediately even though she wasn't hungry, so that if Doris came by with a leftover meal she could say she'd already eaten. Then she settled in front of the computer and checked her email.

There was a message from Dr. Vitale with the subject line "URGENT please read," which she deleted, and a message from Marjean about the new temperature-testing kits, which she answered. Most of the rest were from family. Friends from graduate school wrote occasionally to ask how she was doing, but Olivia was a poor correspondent these days and didn't have regular exchanges going with most of them.

Harry was the exception, of course. She might not know whether she still loved Harry, but she could hardly deny he was her closest friend. As far as Harry knew, everything between them was just as it had always been, except that Olivia was a complete mess. Harry was in Medieval Literature. He was writing about the effect of the grammatical characteristic parataxis in medieval anecdotal accounts of incest. Back before Olivia had to live and breathe her dissertation defense, she used to throw together huge late-night snacks for the two of them—maybe five-spice chicken wings and egg-drop soup, or a pot of pasta with some of the homemade Bolognese sauce she kept in the freezer—and she never worried how things would turn out, as she did when she cooked for other friends. They'd talk until two in the morning, and sometimes he fell asleep on her couch. She'd come out of her bed-room the next morning and see him lying there unconscious, breathing deeply through his mouth (he seemed to be allergic to the couch, which Olivia had inherited from a former roommate), and she would long for something to happen that would make it inappropriate for him to sleep over anymore. (Good Christian Reformed Church members did not sleep over.) But Harry would have laughed at the notion of anything platonic going on, would have joked about putting it in his chapter on sibling incest. And anyway, much of what they discussed late into the night was the state of Harry's relationships, most recently with a political science postdoc named Penelope.

Olivia sometimes thought she should take full advantage of her lack of hormonal activity while it lasted and let the entire friendship wane, let him pursue all the lanky blond postdocs he wanted. What did she care? At the moment she could have thrown him a bachelor party without feeling a thing. But it was hard to get out of the habit of communicating with him, and Harry emailed several times a day whether she replied or not. Today he wrote:

> **Haven't seen Penelope all week—she's prepping for her talk at Kalamazoo. She forgets to eat when she's busy so I wish I could take her a vat of your bolonaise sauce but can't even spell it.**
> **Have you told your family yet? If you could try to explain why you won't tell them maybe I could understand. Wouldnt it get them off your back?**

Olivia reread the first paragraph several times. She had never in her life forgotten to eat because she was busy. Her finger hovered over

the delete key, but she finally hit reply a̶
wrote:

**So go to the Olive Garden and buy a vat
of _their_ Bolognese sauce. How hard is
that?**

She hit "Send."
Next there was a message from Father,
characteristically brief:

Thoughts on supper?

Olivia hadn't cooked in days. In her first week
at Meals on Wheels, Father had offered to get
takeout after they ran out of osso buco. So far
they had had fried chicken from the Arctic
Circle, Chinese from Jade Palace several times,
pizza and wings, and meatloaf from the Hy-Vee
Deli. Mealtime had developed into a game of
chicken, and Olivia was determined to wait it
out until Father broke down and at least hinted
that he missed home cooking.
She replied:

**Haven't had Arctic Circle in awhile. Shall
I pick it up or will you?**

David had written. The message was addressed
to his "kinfolk" mailing list, as usual. David

ely saw anything as personal enough to warrant writing exclusively to any one person, and he apparently figured most of his messages were of interest to the whole clan anyway. He sent updates on his mountain lion relocation program at Black Hills State, editorials on why Governor Janklow was an idiot, unsolicited thoughts on whether Ruby should aggressively pursue the Minneapolis market instead of waiting for the idiots in Sioux Falls to move her up to the evening slot (she should). Today it was Olivia's turn:

Dad says youre working for some community thing. What the hell are you doing? Do you need to be reminded what ABD stands for? All But Dissertation. Thats what you're headed for if you dont get off your butt and get back to graduate school.

Olivia found that she was able to feel something, after all: extreme irritation. She hit "Reply to All" and wrote:

Thanks. I've been harassed by Dr. Vitale quite enough for the time being. I'll let you know when I'm ready for more.

She hit "Send."

. . .

Doris was in the doorway. "Leftover lunch from route 2," she said grimly. "The Moberg forgot to cancel. You'd better mark their sheets, and if it happens again you'll have to send a warning."

"The deaf couple? Are we sure they really aren't home? Last week—"

"Reba Myers had to call me from her next stop to say the Mobergs weren't answering, and I called them myself from here. No answer. That daughter of theirs probably breezed into town and took them to lunch again." Doris stared disapprovingly at Olivia, as if she were personally responsible for this shameful spontaneity. "You want one of the lunches?"

"Oh—" Olivia held up her half-eaten sandwich regretfully. "I guess not, I'm halfway through this. What about Lydia and Violet?"

Doris lifted her chin and turned away without comment.

A message from Ruby had just appeared:

I haven't been sick. Sorry to hear Annie's not any better. She should see a doctor.

Olivia stared at the screen for a moment, then replied:

My sources tell me otherwise. Your land-

84

dy apparently sends daily reports to
ier cousin the cook here at Meals on
Wheels. I'm learning more than I wanted
to know about the state of your moss
roses.

So yesterday, sick at home with a
stomach thing? All better today, I pre-
sume?

It was always wise to keep things light with
Ruby. Nonchalance rather than concern. She
hit "Send," and then that was it for messages.
Nothing from Annie, of course. Annie claimed
she was too busy these days to check email very
often, which Olivia didn't believe for a second.
Annie had never been too busy for anything
she wanted to do. Annie managed a house, a
child, several committees, and ran 2.5 million
errands a day. She did it all in clean-cut tees and
jeans that gave her the lean look of an athlete,
wholly undeserved; even her hair, short and full
and naturally wavy, moved with a sense of purpose. Olivia felt her irritation at David morphing
into irritation at Annie. David you expected to
be an unreliable communicator: he was vague,
spontaneous, forgot what family news he'd been
told about whom, was the last to communicate
his travel plans for the holidays. He had the
fastest email turnaround in the family because

he didn't bother with thorough answers. Annie you were supposed to be able to count o

And in the first weeks after Vivian died, that how it had worked: important information wa now routed through Annie, a shift that occurred seamlessly without anyone questioning it, even though Annie, naturally, was having as hard a time as anyone. At the end of the church dinner after the funeral, when emotions had spiked wildly between tears and laughter and were now quieting again as the time neared to leave for the burial, Annie had leaned across the table and said to Father, "Remind me to send a thank-you note to Jeannette Vander Horst. She arranged this whole dinner."

Father had nodded, and Olivia knew that he would not bother reminding her: Annie never forgot anything once she'd asked to be reminded of it. She not only sent the thank-you to Jeannette but coordinated the family in writing notes of thanks and acknowledgment to everyone who'd sent condolences. She'd broken down as often as Olivia and Ruby while rereading the sym-pathy notes, but she'd also been the one to say, "We'll order in tonight—I've got a coupon for KFC."

Then she'd started to feel ill, which dragged on for weeks, and Olivia was the first to urge her to slow down. One day when Olivia had called to ask if she'd like another pot of chicken p, Annie had snapped that she would drown the sight of one more bowl.

"Anyway I'm mostly better," she'd added, without even apologizing.

Olivia had backed off and waited for Annie to call. She used to spend nearly every morning at Annie's; the two would watch Abigail playing through the kitchen window and cry and talk and drink coffee or Coke until it was time for Olivia to go home and make lunch, and even then Annie and Abigail had come home with her most days that Richard ate on campus.

Annie rarely called now. Olivia was glad that she hadn't told her about her defense.

She printed the labels for the next day's meals and took them to Doris in the kitchen.

Doris was alone at the moment, cutting an enormous pan of green Jell-O into squares and watching the news on the tiny television. There was no sign of Violet and Lydia; they had taken to hiding in the bushes around the side of the building this time of day, when the returning volunteers could supply a number of opportunities for Lydia to jump out and yell "Surprise!" Olivia laid the labels on the counter and said, "Any leftover milks?"

Doris nodded, not taking her eyes from Channel 5 anchorwoman Harriet North.

"Up next, meteorologist Ruby Tschetter with some weather you'll want to keep your eye on."

It went to commercial. Olivia went to fridge and took a milk.

"She's going to talk about that thunderstor they're expecting later today," Doris said. Sh washed her hands at the sink, then rinsed a huge dishrag in a bucket of hot soapy water and wrung it dry. She began wiping down the counters. "But then, you probably knew that."

Olivia forbore to comment that her sister didn't have time to phone everyone in the family with daily weather updates. She finished her milk but couldn't resist lingering to watch Ruby. She had a compelling, unsentimental beauty, with a mane of thick, dark hair, strong, perfect facial bones, and reddish-brown eyes that looked directly at you, and you couldn't help looking back even if you'd known her your whole life, even if you used to share a bedroom with her and knew that she snored lightly and kicked in her sleep.

"—and look what's headed our way," Ruby was saying. She moved her hands over a storm system roiling over the midsection of South Dakota. "This upper-air disturbance has been brewing for days, picking up lots of moisture over the Rockies and gathering speed over the western part of the state. Folks, they got pounded but good out west, and we are next."

She never coddled her audience.

"You don't look anything like your sister,"

is said for the zillionth time while Ruby
played the satellite photos.

"She takes after my father," Olivia said automatically, "and I take after my mother."

What did people expect, that you wouldn't be
insulted when they told you that you in no way
resembled your beautiful sister? Once a class-
mate had even asked Olivia if one of them was
adopted, after seeing Ruby. People were idiots.

"—will probably become a warning by late
afternoon, which could last into the night.
Things should clear up tomorrow, though, with a
welcome drop in temperature giving us a break
from this heat. Let's look at the five-day."

"She's named after one of my great-aunts,"
Olivia said, now that Ruby had gone to commer-
cial. Doris was slicing cheese efficiently, fiercely.
"But she doesn't look anything like her."

"I look exactly like my father," Doris said
briskly. "Or so they say."

That, thought Olivia, *explains the moustache.*
She threw away her milk carton and returned to
the office.

She looked over the list of Methodist volunteers
for Monday: things were in good shape. Assum-
ing that potato salad poisoning or typhoid or
leprosy didn't sweep through the Methodist
Church over the weekend, there should be no
need for Olivia to deliver next week. She printed
the list and looked at the clock. It was just shy of

one o'clock. Olivia hated to leave before c
not because Marjean would have cared t
because Doris gave her these looks as she wave
good-bye through the cafeteria window, look.
that plainly said some people didn't feel obliged
to put in an honest day's work. It would have
taken more energy to talk herself into walking
past that window a few minutes early than to
stay at her desk another five minutes. Olivia
sighed and pulled the summer 1996 issue of the
newsletter from her backpack on the floor.

She had called Wilhelmina Kleinsasser
(Vivian's second cousin once removed) a couple
of nights ago on the off-chance that she was in
possession of a really authentic shrimp creole
recipe and learned instead that Wilhelmina had
never had shrimp creole in her life, let alone
sent Vivian a recipe for it. She had also checked
her mother's recipe box, skimmed through her
mother's circulation list to check for other
W.K.s, and reshuffled the recipes and notes into
different piles several times. Looking through
things now, she could not remember her rationale
for the current set of piles, or if she even had a
rationale. Gringo Tacos, Unusual Meatballs,
Scalloped Cheese Tomatoes. Risotto with
Tomatoes and Mushrooms (her mother's recipe).
Tempting Tomato Salad, Corn-stuffed Tomatoes,
Baked Penne Rigate—her mother couldn't have
meant to present menu plans, anyway, not with

matoes in practically everything. This struck
r suddenly, and she looked through the rest of
ie recipes. Tomatoes everywhere. Of course.
Vivian had been fond of featuring a Guest
Ingredient on occasion. In fact, hadn't Vivian
issued a call for tomato recipes in the previous
issue?

This was progress. Olivia sat back and took a
breath. She spotted the plain white sheet of
paper bearing the recipe for Pork Enchiladas and
pulled it from the pile idly.

It was a pleasure to look at. The recipe was
presented in two columns in a sans serif font,
something sharp and neat and very black, a list of
ingredients on the left and instructions on the
right. The instructions were numbered and stated
clearly and simply. There were no typos. There
was (still) no name on the paper, which was
creased as if it had been folded up with a letter;
Olivia had looked for but not found any accompanying letter. She read the recipe again, and her
mouth watered. She would hate to print it with
no name, although of course the Ladies would
understand. They were a most benevolent reader-
ship.

The family had long referred to Vivian's readers
as "the Ladies" with a capital *L*. A typical newsletter Lady (according to Vivian's children) was
middle-aged, usually but not always married,
with short, permed brown hair, a gentle pudgi-

ness, and a true and keen interest in discove[...]
new varieties of hot dishes. A typical Lady w[...]
interested in your children and shared too wi[...]
ingly about her own, had been to California o[...]
Texas to visit relatives but would never want to
live there, and had never had seafood fresher
than what the Sioux Falls Red Lobster could
offer. She had gone to college in the Dakotas (or
possibly Iowa, Nebraska, or Minnesota) and perhaps returned to a job in an office or a school
after her children had left home. She was steadily
involved in a church—Protestant—where she
was known for some specialty that she was
always urged to bring to potlucks. And she
looked upon Vivian Tschetter as a visionary on
the cusp of the culinary world, because it was
Vivian who had urged the Ladies to try olive oil
back about twenty years ago when all their lives
they'd used corn oil; it was Vivian who talked
about Parmesan cheese that didn't come in a
canister. Vivian had very possibly been the first
person in South Dakota to realize that sun-dried
tomatoes were on purpose. But for all her wild
and worldly ways in the kitchen, and in spite of
the fact that she was known to subscribe to *Food
& Wine,* they trusted Vivian as one of their own.
She had the South Dakota pedigree, she had
married a Mennonite boy with a sensible civil
engineering degree, and she knew the value of a
good honest meatloaf.

Annie and the others had gone so far as to list these qualities on paper one Thanksgiving night while everyone was milling around the kitchen picking at the leftover turkey. The turkey carcass was perched on the wooden chopping block surrounded by bowls of leftover mashed potatoes and orange-cranberry sauce and bread stuffing with wild rice, because the kitchen table was spread with the Christmas issue of *Cooking with Vivian*. David read the list out loud for everyone's edification, and Vivian had laughed and swatted at them with her circulation list, which was somewhere up around three hundred.

"You're absolutely the most narrow-minded little—" She swatted David hardest of all. "Here you all go off to your fancy-schmancy eastern universities—"

"East?" Ruby said incredulously. She had gone to the University of North Dakota.

"Champagne-Urbana is hardly fancy," David said, "let alone schmancy."

Olivia said, "Nobody at Oberlin thought Ohio was the East."

"And you're mouthy, every one of you. The point is, you go off and get these big ideas that you're educated, that you've broadened your views, and it's nothing but common snootiness. Listen."—she righted the pages of her circulation list and began to recite from it—"Mrs. Abigail Andersen. Mrs. Andersen isn't even from the

93

Midwest, she's from New York—yes, she is!" Mom swatted again at David. "Her family moved here from New York when she was growing up, and she certainly knows what fresh seafood is all about because she goes to Maine every year or so. Mrs. Sarah Anderson, now she is also not from the Midwest originally, and she is anything but pudgy. She even plays tennis. She could give you a run for your money, missy," she said to Ruby, who was shaking her head. "Celia Betrelle, she is a CPA and has always worked, even when her children were small. Nora Brandt has been overseas—"

"Oooooh!" they all chorused.

"—overseas more times than I can count. Chloe Darnell—"

"Cousin Chloe? She's a classic Lady," Annie said, and the others nodded. Mom pointed her circulation list at Annie triumphantly.

"Chloe does not perm her hair!"

David asserted that this somehow proved their point. Vivian asserted that they were full of malarkey. Then she threatened to suspend rights to the turkey carcass (which she wanted to make into soup anyhow) unless they destroyed the list. She was afraid it would fall into the wrong hands—Aunt Barbara's, for example. Richard finally wrestled it away from David, set it aflame at the stove, and threw it into the sink, where it curled into cinders.

livia now pulled the circulation list from the ck of the file folder in case glancing over it ould help her figure out who could have submitted Pork Enchiladas with Roasted Tomatillo Sauce. Her mother's readers were in fact a pretty diverse group—housewives, college professors, even a violinist with the Minnesota Orchestra— in spite of there being some truth to the infamous list of characteristics. Several of the Ladies weren't even women, including a West River rancher who liked to send recipes like Venison Chislik and Crock Pot Pheasant. But the stereotype of the Ladies had held firm. Probably this was because of staunch Ladies like Bertha Carlson, who went to the Brookings CRC and had been a friend of Vivian's for years. Bertha was a prototypical Lady. One of the recipes for this issue—Baked Cheese and Tomato Pie—was from her. Something in every issue was from Bertha.

Bertha would never have submitted Pork Enchiladas with Roasted Tomatillo Sauce.

This was really the sort of thing Annie might know, Olivia told herself; Vivian might have mentioned the recipe at some point. She dialed her sister. The machine picked up.

"Livy here," Olivia said. "I'm just wondering if you happen to know which Lady sent in a recipe for Pork Enchiladas with Roasted Tomatillo Sauce. Give me a call, I'm at work."

She hung up and regarded the phone for a moment, then picked it up again and redial[ed]. She strongly suspected Annie of screening ca[lls] these days. "Hi, Livy again. Do you remember Mom ever making something called Chocolate Puddle? Would have been ages ago. I think it's a Southern thing. And speaking of Southern, do you know anything about a shrimp creole recipe?" She paused in case Annie decided to pick up; she was sure she was screening. "You know what?" she said, not trying to hide the irritation in her voice. "You're impossible to get ahold of these days, so I'm just going to come over there. See you soon."

What was Annie going to do—lock the door?

She shoved the papers back into the file folder and stuffed it into her backpack along with her purse. Then she fired off another email to Father:

Instead of Arctic Circle, let's go with Cancun Cantina. I'll have the Chicken Enchiladas with Mole Sauce, side of rice and beans. Can you pick it up?

Father hated Mexican takeout. But he could just live with it if he was too proud to admit he missed real food. She was about to shut down the computer when an email from Ruby appeared:

Oh that. That was nothing. I'd already forgotten about it.

>My sources tell me otherwise. Your landlady
>apparently sends daily reports to her cousin the cook
>here at Meals on Wheels. I'm learning more than I
>wanted to know about the state of your moss roses.
>So yesterday, sick at home with a stomach thing? All
>better today, I presume?

She must be online right this second, Olivia thought. Her heart began to hurry for no reason, and she wrote, fingers clattering across the keys:

What do you mean, you forgot? It was yesterday. And it's unusual for you to be sick. People don't forget unusual things.

She hit "Send" and immediately regretted it. She'd been too earnest. Ruby didn't respond to earnest except with annoyance. And it was a generally held tenet among her siblings that Olivia flailing her arms could be safely ignored.

97

She waited anyway, just in case. She sent anoth
note:

On the other hand I imagine you're so busy you don't know if you're coming or going, most days.

Again she waited. Nothing. Of course, that last note was just a comment, not a question. Ruby would certainly not bother replying to something that was just a comment.

Vivian had been gone over two months. Olivia wondered if this had already increased the gulf between her and her second sister, but it was impossible to tell. And if she couldn't even tell, what could she do about it?

If she *could* tell, what could she do?

She shut down the computer and hit the lights.

" 'Night, Doris," she called through the cafeteria window as she wended her way through the departing seniors in the dining room. She saw Doris turn to look up at the kitchen clock, which said 1:12. "Good night, Violet and Lydia," she said as she passed the table with the long tablecloth.

The tablecloth fluttered wildly. "Surprise," Lydia said, poking her head out. "And it's afternoon, not night." It was the longest speech she'd ever made to Olivia.

Olivia, pleased, said, "Good afternoon, then," and strode out into the heat. It was muggier than it had been, and Ruby's thunderclouds, greenish and menacing, were already piling up in one part of the sky. The rest of the sky was still so bright it was almost white.

Annie and Richard's house was a split-level in a new development on the edge of town, a sunny, grassy neighborhood, open and unrelieved by shade except that which was cast by the houses themselves. A bike path wound through the backyards; the sidewalks were strewn with bicycles and Big Wheels. Olivia had grown up in the heart of town: six blocks east of downtown, six blocks west of the hospital, a mile north of the high school, a mile south of the university. The trees within those boundaries were large and old and all but voting members of the community. They shaded the sidewalks in summer, shed slips of brown and gold and brilliant red in the fall, and in winter looked darker than they were under their edging of snow. Occasionally city workers had to be called in to negotiate with some old-timer grown too large or too close to power lines or too far past its prime, and when one had to be gotten rid of, limb by limb and branch by branch, it was missed. The swath of sunshine left behind by one of the elms in their own backyard always seemed to Olivia foreign and sad.

But the trees in Annie's yard, and in her neigh-bors' yards, were young and slender, some still tied to training sticks—trees that you had to take care of, before they could grow up and take care of you. The lawns had been rolled out by hand, lush and perfect, good for tumbling around on. Few violets or weeds had yet intruded.

Olivia parked in the sloping drive beside Annie's van and went inside.

She paused in the split foyer and listened. She could hear the television from the family room downstairs. "Hello," she called as she headed down. Annie was stretched out on the family room couch propped up against three pillows from someone's bed, the remote in one hand and a can of 7-Up in the other. A small plate of saltines rested on her stomach.

"Hey," Annie said, without rancor but also without taking her eyes off the television.

"What are you watching?"

"Well, here on Animal Planet the vet just removed a mass the size of a tennis ball from this German shepherd," she flipped the channel, "and on AMC we've got the tail end of *All About Eve,* very creepy," she flipped again, "and on A&E they're playing the biography of Hugh Hefner's daughter, who runs the *Playboy* empire, even creepier. Other than that, nothing."

"Where's Abby?"

"Down the block, playing at Sue's."

100

"Did you get my messages?"

"I have no idea who sent the enchiladas recipe and I really don't want to think about Mexican food right now."

Olivia let her backpack slip to the floor, moved a pile of laundry off the chair next to the couch, and sat down. "I thought you were feeling better."

Annie flipped back to the German shepherd. He was coming out of the anesthesia, big soulful eyes watching the vet mournfully. Olivia studied her sister. It was easy to tell she hadn't showered yet. Her lips were pale, her hair still tousled. (In the years they were growing up it had swung to her waist. Of all the things Olivia had adored about her oldest sister, she'd adored that dark curtain of hair the most.) Annie wore a T-shirt of Richard's that looked slept in and a pair of panties.

And Annie had thought *she* should go to grief counseling.

"You know, if you're still feeling this lousy you really ought to go to a doctor. Ruby thinks so, too."

Annie flipped to the *Playboy* magnate, who was wearing a very conservative tailored suit and standing in front of a wall of *Playboy* centerfolds.

"I've been to a doctor."

"You have? What did he say?"

"How sexist."

At first Olivia thought Annie meant the *Playboy* woman, but then Annie flipped to *All About Eve* and said, "I'm disappointed in you. This doctor's a she, not a he." *All About Eve* went to commercial, and Annie flipped back to *Playboy.* "Well, what would you do if you were Hugh Hefner's daughter?"

Olivia sighed and tried again. "So what did the doctor say?"

"Nothing I didn't already know. I'm pregnant. Ten weeks."

A&E went to commercial. Annie flipped back to the dog.

"You know what you could do?" Annie held up the can of 7-Up. "Get me a glass of ice."

Olivia rose immediately and went up the stairs to the kitchen. She had trouble finding a glass; dirty dishes cluttered the counters, and the dishwasher hadn't been run. Finally she found a plastic Little Mermaid cup at the back of one shelf and put five ice cubes in it.

There was a low rumble in the distance. Olivia felt it through the floor, as if the storm were brewing in the earth and not the sky.

It was impossible to grasp a baby happening now. An entire person starting from scratch since Vivian died.

She went downstairs, took the can of 7-Up from Annie, and poured the remainder of it into the cup.

"Well, gosh," Olivia said. "You and Richard must be so excited. I'm so happy for you. You've been trying to have another one for years—"

"Well, we weren't trying now, I can tell you that."

Olivia sat again. They were bringing the owner in to see the dog, which thumped its tail a couple of times but didn't rise.

"The one time we sleep together since the funeral—actually it was the night of the funeral." Annie took a sip from the glass. "Really weirded Richard out that I wanted to. And I haven't wanted to since. Anyway, one time and we're pregnant."

"I suppose, well, after all those years of trying, you wouldn't think to use protection."

"We don't even own protection anymore. We own ovulation kits."

"Does Father know? Does anyone else know?"

"No."

"Why didn't you tell us?"

Annie just sighed and flipped to *All About Eve*. Olivia already knew the answer anyway. She thought of her defense, and for the first time felt a little panicky instead of merely numb. Things were piling up: the things that would remain forever untold to Vivian, and hence forever incomplete. But a baby—something that would eventually assert itself as a real person, no matter how you tried not to think about it . . . the thought of it was almost offensive. Olivia remembered a

cliché from a few of the sympathy cards they'√
received: *Life must go on . . .* She'd had to read
those words, and hear them from stupid kindly
people, almost before she'd grasped that Vivian
was gone.

"Is there anything I can do?" she said finally.

"I will give you our firstborn if you clean up
the kitchen."

Olivia stood. "As long as Richard's okay with
that."

She headed for the stairs, but Annie called her
back at the last minute. "Livy? You know what
would really help? If we could do Sunday dinner
at Father's this week. I know it's my turn, but I
can't face having everyone over here right now,
and I'm not about to ask Aunt Barbara to take
two weeks in a row. She'd ask too many questions."

Olivia hesitated. Against all instinct, she had
managed to keep herself from cooking anything significant for a week and a half, and she
was fairly sure Father was close to swerving.
She hated caving in now. The room darkened
suddenly; rain splatted at the window over the
couch where Annie lay. "Sure," Olivia said
finally. "We'll take care of dinner this week."

By the time she left the house forty-five minutes later, Ruby's thunderstorm was pounding
the earth steadily, and the dash to the car was
enough to soak Olivia and her backpack.

6

It was possible that Olivia went a little overboard for Sunday dinner.

She called Annie Saturday morning to ask what she could eat these days.

"Nothing *sweet,*" Annie said immediately. "And please no scrambled eggs with cut-up hot dogs in them."

"Richard's been cooking a lot, huh?"

"When it isn't scrambled eggs with hot dogs, it's macaroni and cheese with hot dogs."

"When do I ever use hot dogs?"

"I seem to do well with soy sauce," Annie said. Her voice became a little dreamy. "Really salty soy sauce. Last night I had a big plate of spaghetti with soy sauce all over it, and nothing else."

Olivia felt a little sick imagining this. "How about actual Chinese? I can never eat Chinese when I feel iffy."

Her tone became fervent now. "Chinese sounds great. But nothing at all sweet—no sweet and sour anything, no lemon chicken. Wonton soup?" she said hopefully. "Some of your wonton soup, and I could add loads of soy sauce and sesame oil—"

"Wonton soup it is," Olivia said.

Saturday afternoon she deboned chicken breas
and put the raw meat aside; then she simmere
the bones with green onions and squashed garlic
and ginger. She mixed ground pork with diced
water chestnuts and green onions and soy sauce
and sherry, stuffed the wonton skins with this
mixture, and froze them to be boiled the next
day. Then she made the stuffing for Richard's
favorite egg rolls. It was poor menu planning—
Vivian would never have served wontons and
egg rolls at the same meal—but she felt sorry for
Richard, living on hot dogs as he'd been. Anyway they all liked her egg rolls, even Aunt
Barbara.

Sunday morning she stayed home from church
and started the tea eggs simmering (another
source of soy sauce for Annie). She slivered the
raw chicken breast left from yesterday—dangling
the occasional tidbit for J.C., who sat on her stool
and cried "Yeow!" whenever she felt neglected—
and slivered carrots and bamboo shoots and
Napa cabbage and more green onions and set it
all aside to stir-fry at the last minute with rice
stick noodles. This was her favorite dish, simple
though it was, and Aunt Rubina's favorite; it had
been Vivian's favorite of Olivia's recipes, too.
(Vivian had never dabbled much in Chinese
cooking herself.) Then she sliced the beef and
asparagus and chopped the fermented black
beans for her father's favorite dish.

Olivia liked making Chinese when the aunts were around because they were even less familiar with Chinese cooking than Vivian had been and could never take over. When they arrived from church, Olivia was able to get them to finish setting the table instead. When everything was finally ready, Olivia went upstairs to tap on the bathroom door and tell Annie they were all sitting up to the table. Then she went downstairs to wait with the others.

They sat looking at one another over steaming bowls of wonton soup.

"Quite a feast," Father said.

Aunt Rubina said, "Everything looks just delicious, Olivia."

"Everything does," Aunt Barbara said, "although I hate to think you missed church just to make dinner."

"I didn't," Olivia said.

"Why can't I have an egg roll?" Abby asked Richard.

"Wait until we pray, honey," he said. He turned to Olivia. "Is she coming?"

"She said she'd be right down."

"*You* had an egg roll," Abby said.

"That was in the kitchen," Richard said solemnly. Since Abby's birth he'd had a dark, close-cut beard that made it hard to tell when he was hiding a smile. "That doesn't count."

"That hardly seems fair," Father said. "Why

don't you bless just one egg roll so Abby can it?"

Richard picked up an egg roll and held it aloft. He closed his eyes; so did Abby. "Lord, we ask You to bless this egg roll and this egg roll alone for Abigail's use. Amen."

Abby took the egg roll, giggling, and began to chew on one end of it.

"Now do my soup," Olivia said to Richard, but Annie had finally appeared.

"Still under the weather?" Father asked.

"I'm fine," Annie said. "Starving."

Aunt Barbara said, "Naturally we assumed you were still ill when you weren't in church either."

"You missed church, too?" Olivia asked.

"I'm much better," Annie said, with a hard, short laugh, "but I'm going to pass out if I don't eat something soon." There was a ferocious look in her eyes. Olivia looked at the others surreptitiously and wondered how they could keep from guessing right that moment—although she wouldn't have either, she supposed, if Annie hadn't told her. They were all so used to Annie not being able to get pregnant, for years now.

Father prayed.

Olivia took the covers off the dishes and began to send things on their rounds. Annie took an egg roll from the platter, shuddered at the little dish of sweet and sour sauce perched in the ddle, and began to shake soy sauce into her up and over the egg roll.

"So I could have just made a plate of spaghetti," Olivia murmured to her.

"Why doesn't Olivia have to go to church?" Abby asked.

Aunt Barbara looked at Olivia expectantly. Olivia looked at Annie, but she was eating as if she'd just fasted for a week, and Richard was watching *her* with something between dismay and fascination. Father set his soup bowl aside thoughtfully and reached for the beef with asparagus and black bean sauce.

There was no help forthcoming.

"Sometimes the hymns set me off," Olivia said finally to Abby.

Abby squinched her nose. "They do *what* to you?"

"They make her sad," Richard said quietly. He leaned over Abby's plate and cut up her rice noodles. "They make her think of Grandma."

"Hymns are very hard," Aunt Rubina said sympathetically. "Remember, Barbara, how you never liked to hear 'In the Garden' after Emmet died? It seemed like every time Barbara came to Huron to visit me, they played that hymn in the MB Church that day." She meant Mennonite Brethren. All of the Tschetters—and the Hofers, too, on Vivian's side—were raised in the MB Church, where Low German could still be heard

109

before and after the services. But there were MB churches in Brookings, and as long as they lived there the Tschetters had attended the CRC which was heavily Dutch. Charlie had been a deacon and an elder, Vivian had cooked for most of the funerals and weddings for years, but they were still considered foreigners until Annie married Richard, who was a Huussen.

Barbara pressed her lips together and did not look at her sister. "I never used it as an excuse not to go to church."

Olivia said, "There is the eeriest old woman on one of the delivery routes."

Everyone looked up at this abrupt change in topic except Annie, who was swabbing soy sauce with the remaining end of her egg roll. "This the woman who lives in total squalor?"

"No. This one lives—well, client information is confidential, but you'd all know the house if you saw it. She's this little, soft-spoken lady with a Southern accent, really quiet most of the time. The day I went there alone she was sort of weird. She took me out to the kitchen and made me get down this huge cast-iron skillet that she probably can't even lift. If she were able to lift a cast-iron skillet, she wouldn't be getting Meals on Wheels, would she?"

She looked across at Father just in time to see something like apprehension flit across his face and dissipate. She lifted her eyebrows in sur-ase, but he was looking down at his food.

"She's probably going senile," Aunt Barbara said gloomily. Aunt Barbara had a horror of going senile. She did crossword puzzles every day and read a large quantity of informational nonfiction in the belief that this would help her maintain her viselike grip on reality.

"She could be," Olivia said, still nonplussed by Father's reaction. "She was sharp enough to recognize that the skillet wasn't in usable shape, though. She seemed absolutely crushed about it, which was very sad and eerie. I can't even explain. I wonder if she's really up to living alone at this point."

"What did you say her name was?" Aunt Rubina asked. Olivia looked at Father again, but he was just winding rice noodles around his fork, innocent of any more interesting expressions.

"I didn't," she said. "It's all confidential, who the clients are. If you were to guess—"

"Good heavens, how would we ever know who you're talking about," Barbara said. "May we please discuss something more cheerful than the mental state of your poor declining clients?"

"Maybe Aunt Barbara or Aunt Rubina knows who sent in that recipe," Annie said to Olivia. "Is there more soup?"

Olivia rose and reached for Annie's bowl. "Someone sent in Pork Enchiladas with Roasted

Tomatillo Sauce, but there's no name on recipe."

Aunt Barbara said, "Isn't David seeing Mexican woman?"

"What?"

"That's right," Annie said. "I should have thought of that. I don't know where my head is these days."

Olivia was always the last to know these things. This was irritating in spite of the fact that no one tried very hard anymore to keep up with David's latest girlfriends. Even Father didn't bother learning their last names. Only Vivian had hung on, though it broke her heart every time to find out all about someone who seemed just right only to have David act mildly amnesic the next time she asked after her. "How can you be fond of someone you've never met [or only met once, or only met twice]?" Father would ask, exasperated. But they all knew what Vivian was really fond of: the idea of David settling down with one of these women and not being alone anymore. Olivia had never understood why Mother seemed so concerned about David when she'd never pushed her daughters to get married. David, Olivia felt, was the most independent, the most self-sufficient (not to say self-absorbed), the least vulnerable, even least *marriageable,* of them all. And certainly the least concerned. "That's just it," Vivian had tried to explain.

"He's so *alone* and he doesn't even know it."

Olivia had never shared an ounce of her mother's pity for David. He was an inveterate serial dater, and far better looking than he deserved: almost as tall as Father, with thick, dark blond hair, a pleasantly sharp profile just shy of rugged. He was completely without female friends because he ended up dating most of the single women he knew and liked at all, and when it was evident that he was not serious, they became sad, or bitter, or determined, but never friendly. Time after time David evinced mild surprise at their inability (or unwillingness, as he thought it) to move past it and just be friends. The ones who eventually married didn't even care to have their new husbands socialize with David. He claimed that the only friends you could count on these days were the ones who were already married when you met them—and these, all too often, had children.

"So how long has he been going out with this one?" Olivia asked finally.

Annie shrugged. "A couple months?"

"It has to be longer than that. Vivian had mentioned her once or twice, not long before—" Aunt Rubina hesitated. "Well, I just wonder if she got David to ask her for recipes."

This had been one of Vivian's favorite ways to gain access to David's girlfriends. He had never seemed to see through it.

"Janet somebody," Annie said to Olivia.

"That doesn't sound Hispanic."

"The last name was," Annie said. "We'll call him after lunch. We'll see if *he* remembers her last name."

They didn't have to call David. He called while they were in the kitchen cleaning up.

"Speak of the devil," Olivia said. "We were just going to call you."

"Put him on speaker," Annie told her. Annie tossed her dish towel over the back of a chair and sat down on J.C.'s stool, bit into another egg roll. Olivia hit the speaker button.

"All Tschetters present and accounted for?" David was saying.

"Not quite," Olivia said. "No Ruby today; she's working this weekend. And Father and Richard are out back playing croquet with Abby."

"Hello, David," Aunt Barbara said very loudly over her shoulder from the sink.

"Hello to you, Aunt Barbara."

"Aunt Barbara still refuses to use the dishwasher," Annie said. "The dishwasher's open, and there she stands at the sink washing up."

"Good for you, Aunt Barbara," David said. "Never let technology push you around."

This was completely hypocritical, coming from David, who never did anything a machine could do for him, and Olivia and Annie rolled their eyes at each other.

114

"Look, David," Annie said. "Olivia's finishing the issue of Mom's newsletter that—the one that was in progress, you know, when she died. Anyway. We were wondering who sent in a recipe for Pork Enchiladas with Something Sauce. Would this have been Janet Somebody?"

There was the slightest pause. "Indeed it would," David said. "Janet Rodriguez."

Olivia grabbed the pen perched near the phone and wrote this name on a paper napkin.

"You still know her last name," Annie said. "I'm impressed. Does this mean you're still seeing her?"

"Indeed it does."

"Does she speak Mexican, David?" Aunt Barbara asked. Olivia rolled her eyes at Annie again.

David was laughing. "Her Spanish is about as good as my German. I understand her husband spoke Spanish, though."

For a moment there was only the sound of water running into the sink. The women all looked at one another, but mostly they looked at Aunt Barbara. Aunt Barbara looked at the phone.

"She's—divorced?" Annie said finally.

"Widowed."

Something like a collective sigh went through the room. Aunt Barbara slowly rinsed a glass. Rubina went back to handing her dishes from the table. Olivia, for no reason she could think of, sat in the nearest chair and wrote the word *widowed* on the napkin, under the name *Rodriguez*.

"Did I scare the aunts?"

"Oh, David," Annie said.

"I don't scare that easily," Aunt Barbara said, but they could tell she was trying not to smile. David had always been her favorite.

"Well, it looks like a great recipe," Olivia said. "Tell her thanks."

"Tell you what. I was going to bring her along next weekend anyway, so if you need to ask her anything about the recipe, you can do it then."

"What's next weekend?" Annie asked.

"Didn't I mention that I was coming up next weekend?"

"No, you did not," Olivia said.

"Thought I did. Anyway I'm bringing Janet."

"David, this isn't the best time for me to be getting the house ready for company."

"Olivia's working now, you know," Annie said.

"That isn't even full-time, is it?"

Olivia wrote *jerk* on the napkin and under-lined it.

"A little notice might be nice," Olivia said.

"What are you talking about? This is a whole week's notice. What's the big deal?"

"Mom isn't here anymore to just do every-

g. *I'll* have to get the house ready, *I'll* have
figure out meals—"

"Hey, we can get Janet to cook. She's a terrific
cook. Throws together these Mexican meals—"

"We cannot ask a guest to cook."

"So Annie'll help. Aunt Barbara will help,
right?"

"I'm sure we can work it all out, David," Aunt
Barbara said. "We'd love to meet your young
lady." She turned off the water and stood with
her hands dripping, looked around for the cloth.
Annie tossed her the cloth from the chair,
shaking her head at Olivia the whole time as if
to say, *What did we expect?*

"Annie's been sick," Olivia said, "and we're
all just kind of making it day to day—"

"Really? You still sick, Annie?"

"Off and on."

"Look," David said, "it's no big deal. We're not
even bringing the kids."

The women looked at one another again, all
eyes finally resting on Annie, who mouthed, *I
had no idea.*

"What *kids?*" Olivia said.

"Janet's kids. They'll probably stay with her
mother. You'll hardly know we're around. You
don't have to clean house for me, Livy. You
overreact to everything."

"You're dating a woman who has *kids?*"

"Only two," David said. "They're good kids.

117

Look, I have to get going, I'm supposed to
them swimming this afternoon. Call Ruby a
tell her I'm coming up, okay? Get her to con
for the weekend. The more the merrier."

"The more *work*," Olivia said. "So that's three
rooms I'll have to get ready."

"For heaven's sake, it's just *Ruby*. And Annie,
tell Richard to give me a call if he still wants
me to bring up my new router."

"Tell him yourself," Olivia started to say, but
Annie waved her down.

"Look, David, are you and your squeeze
showing up in time for supper Friday night?"

"Sure, we can shoot for that."

"You better not just *shoot* for it, if Olivia's
going to go to all the trouble of cooking—"

"I never said I'd cook," Olivia said.

"Takeout's just fine," David said. "But I'm sure
hungry for some of Aunt Rubina's pink dessert."

Olivia would not risk hurting Aunt Rubina's
feelings by throwing up her hands in disgust at
this blatant schmoozing. She underlined *jerk*
several more times and drew stars around it,
tearing the napkin in several places.

"I'm sure I can manage," Aunt Rubina said,
smiling.

"You all take care. See you Friday."

Annie hit the speaker button.

"Nice to know some things never change,"
Olivia said.

Aunt Barbara said, "This business of taking on someone else's children—"

"This is David we're talking about," Annie said. "He's never taken on anything in his life, and I doubt he's starting now. He's probably run out of single women without kids. I mean, the entire population of the state is only what, seven hundred thousand? Eight?"

"Not eight," Rubina said.

"I should make Father order a bucket of chicken and be done with it," Olivia said.

"Yes, you should," Annie said. "Look, I'm just going to run to the bathroom. I'll be back to help finish up."

"I suppose I could do Chinese again," Olivia said.

"You know what would be lovely?" Annie said. She was poised in the doorway. "That lasagna Mother used to make, with the Italian sausage. And lots of garlic bread."

"I hate trying to duplicate Mother's lasagna; I've never gotten the sauce right. If I went French, I could make a cheese soufflé."

"For Pete's sake, your lasagna's fine. David's right, you should have your own cooking show: *Cooking with the Insecure Chef*."

Olivia had heard this before and didn't bother protesting. "Or Greek! I could do stuffed grape leaves ahead of time, and make a big pan of spanakopita. Or stifado. And Greek egg-lemon soup."

119

"I'll bring my marshmallow salad," Aunt Barbara said. She rinsed out a dishrag and handed it to Rubina, who started wiping down the counters.

Olivia widened her eyes at Annie, but Annie fled, and the best Olivia could do was say, "Maybe if I'm making Greek we should have a *Greek* salad."

"This has fruit," Aunt Barbara said. "It goes with everything. Anyway, it's one of David's favorites."

The whole situation made for an inauspicious beginning to the week. Olivia slept poorly that night, vacillating between annoyance at Aunt Barbara and her everlasting marshmallow salad and annoyance at herself for capitulating (as she had known she would) and planning a dinner party for ten instead of setting a bag of McDonald's hamburgers in front of her brother as he deserved. The only constant was annoyance with David. He had only bothered to come home once since the funeral. Now, when it suited him, he would breeze in as if nothing had changed, actually bringing this woman with him and getting everyone stirred up in his usual fashion, and the aunts would *thank* him for it, Ruby would rearrange her work schedule if she had to, and Father would have more to say to him in ten minutes than he said to Olivia all week. She remembered, suddenly and without wanting to, her seventh birthday: David had sauntered into the kitchen where Olivia was finishing lunch and asked if she'd go on a bike ride with him. Too thrilled to question why her fourteen-year-old brother would actually seek out her company, Olivia had gone. They'd raced toward the railroad tracks and flown under the viaduct where it flooded during downpours, then rode way over to Pioneer Park and all around the band shell. When they finally got home, Olivia panting and glowing, she walked in to her own surprise party. Friends shrieked under the rainbow of streamers and balloons Annie had hung, and Vivian brought out a chocolate cake shaped like a castle with a Hershey bar drawbridge. But nothing could quite mitigate her small, private disappointment at the realization that David was part of the ruse—hadn't, after all, just wanted to ride bikes with her.

He was coming Friday, Olivia would be expected to wait on him hand and foot, and the slightest protest would be taken as overreaction. Tossing in her bed, Olivia finally fell asleep in the wee hours and woke five hours later with a stiff neck.

Facing Doris first thing in the morning was never Olivia's easiest moment of the day. Facing Doris first thing on a *Monday* morning, when Olivia was feeling emotionally and physically bludgeoned, was daunting, and she had to force herself to pause at the cafeteria window to say hello on her way through. Doris in her wrap-around full apron, with her hair back in a tight, ponderously large bun under a hairnet, sometimes reminded Olivia of the pioneer women she had had to study growing up: large-boned, spare-fleshed women with humorless lips and the grim light of survival in their eyes, with gaunt cheeks and big strong hands that could build log cabins and beat out prairie fires and toss rattlers out of their babies' beds. Women who could do anything, as long as it was hard enough: shoe a horse, or shoot one, or eat one, as circumstances demanded.

This morning Doris was looking particularly humorless and capable as she presided over the morning crew while saucing several large trays of Swiss steak.

"Good morning," Olivia said at the window, leaning over the counter in an effort to appear friendly and relaxed, which was difficult without a working neck.

Donna Hansen, perched on a stool at the end of the counter with her leg off to one side, was snapping lids on small plastic cups of canned pears. "You look like death warmed over," she said cheerfully.

"Stiff neck," Olivia said. "I slept wrong."

"I could take a crack at your neck," Donna said. "I've snapped my husband out of a bad back once or twice in my day."

'It'll be fine." Olivia stood up hastily. "It just ~eeds a little time. Let me know if you need ne, Doris."

"We're in good shape," Doris said darkly, "so far."

Olivia nodded, winced, and moved on to her office before Donna could renew her chiropractic offer.

Bless the Methodists. No one had canceled; nearly every route had two volunteers today, and the other routes could be manned by a couple of regulars who wouldn't mind going it alone. Her only voice mail was a message from a Leroy Wheeler canceling his father's meals. Olivia thought of Mr. Wheeler's oxygen cord with a pang and dialed the son.

"Dad had another stroke," Leroy Wheeler said heavily. His voice was surrounded by the crackle of movement; Olivia got the impression of a truck bouncing along a gravel road. "Looks like this time he may not make it out of the hospital."

"I'm sorry," Olivia said. She wished she could say more; you would think that losing Vivian— to a stroke, no less—would give her some clue.

"I've got a call coming in from the station," Leroy said. "Just wanted you to know in time to take him off today's delivery."

Olivia thanked him and hung up. The station, she thought: Wheeler Amoco. This was the first time she'd connected old Mr. Wheeler with the gas station Wheelers. Olivia went to the kitchen to peel his name off the hot meal labels. She felt a little sad as she folded the sticky side of the label to itself and tossed it into the garbage can. Then she went back to her office and checked her email.

There was a message from Ruby, replying to Olivia's reply to David on Friday:

> Hate to say it, Livy, but David's right on this one. Whatever else you do you need to finish grad school.

Olivia punched in "You always take his side" but immediately backspaced over it. How many times over the years had she used that line? Had it ever worked? Instead she wrote:

> Speaking of David, he's coming up this weekend. He's bringing his latest girl-friend and get this, she has kids. Your presence is requested.

She hit "Send," found herself thinking again about how David could hijack an entire weekend without even trying. Something occurred to her then for the first time. She hit "Reply" to a new message from Harry without even reading it:

may tell them this weekend. In fact, I'm planning on it. Friday night. My brother is coming. The entire galaxy actually revolves around him, in case you didn't know. I'll wait until he starts to pontificate about graduate school and how I'm going to end up ABD, and then I'll tell them I already passed my defense. That should drop a few jaws.

She hit "Send." Harry would be pleased; she was pleased that she didn't care what Harry thought. She leaned forward now and read his original message. All about Penelope and her state of readiness for the conference in Kalamazoo, and her fear of commitment, and how she was talking about maybe needing another break to think things over. Poor Harry. Olivia was glad she hadn't responded to any of it. If she told him the truth (anyone who says they're afraid of commitment just plain isn't interested), he wouldn't accept it anyway, and the kind of bland, hang-in-there encouragement that she typically felt she owed him, as a friend, made her feel like an accessory to a crime.

She spent the rest of the morning fantasizing about Friday evening.

She would go Greek, for one thing. Dolmades were chic, not to mention impossible to ruin, and would make a perfect starter along with the egg-

lemon soup. Then the spanakopita—but t.
would have to be something else: David I
no respect for meatless main dishes. She'd do
stifado of beef and pearl onions simmered in
red wine sauce. And if by Aunt Rubina's pink
dessert David was not yet harping about her
dissertation defense, Olivia would mention
Meals on Wheels—that would get him started.
Olivia would wait for him to pause, then casually
say, "Oh, that. I passed my defense the day Mom
had her stroke. Thought I mentioned it."

They'd stop talking, all right. And Olivia
would say, "There's more spanakopita."

She worried a little about what she'd say if
they asked why she'd waited to tell them—it
wasn't something she'd even articulated to herself. But this concern dissolved when she
remembered Annie would be there. Annie, who
had not yet announced her pregnancy. Annie
would know what to say. She would probably
reach out and draw Olivia in close; maybe the
two of them would cry. People would understand, even Father. Everyone but David. And
they'd all, including David, fall over themselves
congratulating her.

She thought about the box under the piano, and
the many emails from Dr. Vitale. She'd worry
about that come Saturday. One thing at a time.

By noon, Olivia was in a good enough mood to
admit to Doris that she'd forgotten to bring a

dwich, and was there any extra Swiss steak? ris handed her a meal without a label on it: r. Wheeler's. Olivia pulled a stool up to the ounter and together they watched the news while the volunteers started trickling in from their routes.

"That's a new outfit," Olivia told Doris during Ruby's forecast. "She found it with my sister when they were shopping at some outlet store in Minneapolis."

"An outlet store," Doris said, looking pleased.

"Oh, she's very frugal," Olivia said. She was feeling generous with the world. "You'd never know it because she always looks like a million bucks, but she hardly ever pays full price for anything. She's a shrewd shopper. Both my sisters, really. I'm terrible."

Two volunteers approached the cafeteria window, a youngish middle-aged woman and an oldish middle-aged woman. They were still carrying their hot packs, which were supposed to go in a basket just outside the kitchen door. The youngish one spoke. "Are we supposed to do the same route all week?"

Olivia slid off her stool to approach the window.

"You were on . . ."

"Route 5."

"Usually people like to stick to the same route, so they get to know the directions and the clients," Olivia said, but she knew what was coming.

"That one woman was really upset—Mr. Kilkenny? We thought you might want to send Vivian again. If Vivian's one of your regulars."

A rush of warmth flooded Olivia's chest. "She asked for Vivian?"

"We don't have any Vivians," Doris said. She turned to Olivia. "Do the Methodists have a Vivian now?"

"Then this lady's losing it," said the youngish woman. "First, she practically worked herself into tears about how Vivian said she'd return this time, and then she was almost angry. 'I might have known,' she kept repeating. We promised we'd at least ask."

"Well," Olivia said, "I'll look into that. Maybe I'll take that route tomorrow myself." She was amazed that her voice wasn't trembling; she even sounded quite professional. Doris turned away to check the ovens. "I'll let you know tomorrow what route you'll be on."

They thanked her and left.

Olivia looked at her half-finished meal on the counter. She wasn't hungry anymore but couldn't bring herself to throw it away in front of Doris.

She took the meal to her desk—narrowly avoiding tripping over Lydia and Violet, who skittered across the hallway from one empty n to another—and pulled "Stumped in Beadle nty" from the manila file on her desk. She red down at the initials "W.K." for a long noment. Then she closed her office door and stood before the small mirror that hung on the back of it. She studied her image. Her skin, always either too pale or (as now) too flushed, betraying every strong emotion. The strong line of her jaw—a little too rounded to be elegant like Ruby's—and the straight nose, a little too long, and the way the skin over her eyelids slanted down to the corners, making her green eyes look smaller than they were. She'd never seen the resemblance herself, though everyone else claimed to. Just the eyes, and that distinctive slant over the eyelids, which in her mother had been even more pronounced. The least little smile had always told in her eyelids first, deepening the slant and crinkling the corners, making her look as if she would burst out laughing. Olivia wondered if that was what Mrs. Kilkenny had seen. She wondered if there was anything Mrs. Kilkenny could see that Olivia had always missed.

Aunt Rubina's Pink Dessert

Yes, I have printed this recipe before, but David wants an updated version now that everyone's fussing about raw egg whites. I thought I'd print it here, and then we'll see if he really reads the newsletter like he says he does. Those of you who know David: no fair prompting him.

Mix and place in a lightly greased 9 x 13 in. pan:

    1 cup butter, softened
    1 cup chopped nuts
        (Aunt Rubina says to place the nuts
        in a baggie and take a rolling pin to them)
    ½ cup brown sugar
    2 cups flour

Bake at 350 deg. until mixture starts to brown, about 5 minutes; stir into fine crumbs. Bake about 7 minutes longer or until brown, stirring often; cool. Remove half of the crumbs and save. Spread the rest to cover the pan.
    For the filling, mix in a large mixing bowl:

130

10 oz. frozen strawberries, partially thawed
2 raw egg whites, pasteurized
1 tsp. lemon juice
1 cup sugar

• Buy pasteurized eggs, or get a carton of
those raw liquid pasteurized egg whites
they sell nowadays. That's what I used
and it worked beautifully.

Beat at high speed until well mixed and fluffy.
(You're not going for meringue here, so don't
expect it to whip up real stiff.)

For the topping:
2 tsp. vanilla extract
1 cup whipped cream (Cool Whip works well)

Add the vanilla to the whipped cream and fold
into strawberry mixture. Pour into crumb crust;
top with reserved crumbs. Freeze for 24 hours
before serving. Keeps for at least 2 weeks,
frozen.

7

Olivia intended all evening to ask Father if her mother had ever known a Mrs. Kilkenny, but it almost became just one more thing to avoid doing, along with preparing for David's visit and working on Vivian's newsletter.

She didn't succeed in entirely avoiding any one thing, actually. Regarding David's visit, she went so far as to hunt down clean sheets for all the beds she'd need to change. She first placed a clean set of queen-size sheets on the dresser in her room, formerly Annie's room—and for the coming weekend, Janet Rodriguez's room. This was the biggest bedroom next to Vivian and Charlie's, a large, light, square room at the far end of the upstairs hallway, and it had always belonged to the oldest daughter still living at home. Annie had had it the longest, especially since she attended the local university and lived at home for the first year or so. Then it was Ruby's for a scant two years until Ruby went off to college, and finally Olivia's through all of high school and now whenever she was home. Ruby, when she visited, used one of the twin beds in the room down the hall that she and Olivia had shared long ago; she used to complain about Annie and livia getting the big room for more years than he had. It was, in Olivia's opinion, the only way in which life had not favored Ruby, and she felt no compunction at continuing her claim on the big room. But this triumph was shadowed by the fact that even in high school Olivia would have preferred to be back in the old room with Ruby, both of them in their twin beds. It was never what Ruby would have preferred. Olivia never told anyone she felt this way.

At any rate, she and Ruby would be in their old room this weekend, and she placed two sets of twin sheets on one of the beds in there. Janet Rodriguez might be just one more name in David's litany of girlfriends, but let it not be said that she had received less than the best hospitality the Tschetters could offer.

David's room, by far the smallest, would be the most work to get ready. For years now it had doubled as Vivian's office, but as Olivia opened the door and stood in the doorway with one remaining set of sheets in her arms—extra-long twin—David's room as it had been years ago flashed before her eyes, and Olivia was again eight or nine years old. She never entered this room without the fleeting sensation of trespassing on forbidden ground. David's room, to his youngest sister, had always been holy.

Not in the polished and carpeted way of the sanctuary at church, where the hymn books waited upright and orderly in the pew racks f[...] organ music to fill the hush. No: David's roo[...] was holy and *terrible,* like the altar room of one of the ancient and primitive cities Tarzan was always running across in the books on David's high shelf. The room was dark in those days: the lone window had been boarded up and painted black. A wide homemade shelf, also painted black and then lined with black linoleum, ran the length of the south wall, turned the corner, and ran along the east wall over David's single bed, which was always such a mess of blankets and tangled sheets that David might have been in it, or an encampment of Huns, or then again no one. On the south shelf were jugs of vile chemicals, trays, tongs, film reels, lenses for the enlarger. The enlarger itself sat in silent state under a dust cover; Olivia had been warned never to touch it, on pain of becoming a human sacrifice. There were scraps of photo paper everywhere: on the shelves, on the floor, on the clothes strewn about the floor, even on the bed itself. And hundreds of black-and-white photographs. One wall displayed those photos deemed worthy by some set of standards known and subscribed to only by David himself: an eight-by-ten-inch blowup of David's biology teacher holding a frog before pursed lips; a series of closeups of bicycle spokes; Ruby, wild-haired and bare-footed, chasing Annie through the backyard with garden hose. And his most prized series, ntitled *Tschetters After Dark*: portraits of every family member asleep, followed in each case by a shot of that family member opening bleary eyes and reaching out in protest. He had caught Mother with her mouth open and her eyes half-closed so that she looked completely plastered (which a good Mennonite never was); he had so clearly captured a swear word forming on Ruby's lips that the photograph had been admitted as evidence in an assault case David brought before their parents. The case was dismissed on the grounds that David had entered Olivia and Ruby's room without permission at two in the morning and woken her with the camera flash, garnering great sympathy for Ruby among others of the family who had similarly suffered. Ruby was finally forbidden to use that word or to club people over the head, and David was forbidden to take pictures of people when they were asleep. David broke this rule only once to complete his collection with a portrait of Olivia, curled up like a snail in her Snoopy nightie, mouth open and drooling on her Snoopy pillow. Olivia not only didn't wake; she didn't get angry later when she saw the picture. She was still young enough to want her picture taken as much as possible—especially by her older brother.

Of course, this was ancient history. The photo-

graphic equipment had long ago been clear
out and the black paneling removed from th
window, which had a southern exposure and le
in a good deal of sunlight for the houseplants
that sometimes convalesced on the wide black
shelves. The upper shelves, thanks to Annie's
organizational efforts, had been cleared of
Tarzan and John Carter of Mars and Jules Verne
and now held three-ring binders containing
final drafts of every issue of *Cooking with Vivian*.
David's bed, neatly covered with one of Aunt
Rubina's crocheted bedspreads, was pushed into
the northeast corner, and a file cabinet had been
added under the shelves opposite.

In spite of these changes, the room wasn't any
less cluttered than it had been in David's day.
The lower shelves were stacked high with files
and papers and cookbooks and recipe cards.
Vivian always intended to clear enough space to
work on the newsletter's layout up here; the wide
shelves, just the height at which she could work
comfortably while standing, would have been
perfectly suited for the way she worked. In spite
of having learned word processing several years
ago (under considerable pressure from David),
Vivian had never been comfortable cutting and
pasting and designing on the computer. Instead,
she'd printed out individual articles and recipes
and then cut and pasted by hand, onto the backs of
used computer paper—cut and taped, actually.

When something didn't work, she printed it out again in a different font (she did like to play with the fonts) or a different size or with different margins, and tried until it worked. David found out she was doing this and practically foamed at the mouth.

"You are defeating the entire point of desktop publishing," he said through the phone so loudly that Olivia, home on a break, could hear him clearly. She leaned over to the mouthpiece.

"That's what I told her," she said.

"I like doing it my way," Mother said, moving the phone out of Olivia's reach. "I like adding those little doodads and doohickeys around the recipes." She was looking fondly at some of her doodads as she spoke: little curlicues framing a title, tiny ink sketches of carrots and peas and potatoes. A tiny perfect saucepan, a stock pot with a ladle hovering over it, a whisk of the finest interlacing loops. And the occasional outline of a tiny cook, barely more than a stick figure wearing a chef's hat. Only the mouth and eyes of the cook ever changed—and sometimes she had eyebrows—but her mouth and eyes and eyebrows captured perfectly the tone of the captions below them: *Don't over salt!* the eyebrows said, puckered into concerned *V*'s. Or, *This is the easiest frosting recipe you'll ever try!*, with eyebrows high and enthusiastic. Or *Are you afraid of your pressure cooker?*,

rounded and sympathetic, over-round, gentl
eyes and a small encouraging smile.

"You can still do the doodads," David said, "no
one's saying you shouldn't. I love the doodads,
I find them charming. Why can't you just add
them onto a perfectly finished printout of a
whole—"

"I tried that once and it was uninspiring,"
Mother said. "I couldn't get myself to mar that
perfect page. See, I use the doodads to cover up
mistakes, or balance out something crooked; the
way I do it, they're an improvement. If I listened
to you, they'd be an eyesore."

David even at his most exasperated was no
match for Vivian. *Cooking with Vivian* continued
to be a hand-placed labor of love, and the only
sign that the newsletter ever saw a computer at
all was the greater variety of fonts introduced.

Vivian could have spread an entire issue out
on David's old shelves and cut and pasted to her
heart's content; sometimes she even started out
this way. But every issue eventually migrated to
the kitchen table, where for a week or so it would
interfere with the usual business of life. As
Olivia stood now at the threshold of David's
room, the sight of Vivian's life's work super-
imposed on David's weirdly altered bedroom
almost drained her of the will to take another
step. They would have to tackle this someday;
they would have to go through every stack, decide

hat to keep (and where, and why) and what to throw away, dismantle the entire creative efforts of her mother, reduce it all down to a few more binders on the top shelves.

"Yeow?" J.C. said from the doorway. She had paced the hall outside this room off and on for days, protesting as she always did at any closed door. Now she entered slowly, nose lifting in the musty air, ears back. She leaped to the nearest shelf, lowered her nose to barely brush a stack of papers, drew back as if she'd been stung. "Yeowwwww?"

"Oh, it hasn't been that long," Olivia could not help saying. "You always overreact."

She crossed the room and pushed briefly at the window frame but gave up. Father would have to open it. She'd get him to pull the bed out while he was at it, so she could make it up properly. And she'd have to dust around all the stacks on the shelves. Even David would notice *this* amount of dust.

Having mentally listed all the things she would have to do, she was more drained than ever. She left J.C. neatly skirting the clutter on the shelves and without deciding to, wandered down to Father's office, where she was confronted by the stack of her mother's notes and recipes next to the computer. She had barely made a start. It took a great effort not to turn around and leave.

At least now she knew that Janet Rodriguez

was the author of Pork Enchiladas et cetera, ar
since she was forcing herself to return to Winni
Kilkenny's, she might as well ask for the shrimp
creole recipe. And she had gone so far as to set up
a new document for this issue on the computer,
although all it contained thus far were the letters from readers for the "Ask Vivian" column
and a few headings based on her mother's usual
features: "Casserole Corner," "Just Desserts."
Olivia planned to do the entire issue on the computer. As much as she would have liked to
continue in her mother's idiom, Olivia knew that
she did not have the artistic flair to pull off a
homemade layout. She would ask Ruby to fill in
with a few sketches, and if Ruby didn't have
time, then she'd pull in some clip art. It saddened
her. But it was better than putting out a newsletter that looked like something her niece's first-
grade class would do.

She supposed she could start by blindly entering all the tomato recipes—pure data entry. Or
she could work on "Ask Vivian," which she
dreaded most in the entire issue. Vivian had
finished replies to only two of the letters. Olivia
wasn't sure which would be worse, typing her
mother's words or coming up with replies to the
remaining letters. (She would have to fight the
instinct to apologize over and over for not being
her mother.)

Get it over with.

he put "Stumped in Beadle County" at the bottom of the pile and pulled out her mother's handwritten reply to the next letter, "Down-rodden Daughter-in-Law." She looked at the words for a moment without reading them. Vivian tended to begin with hastily printed letters— her concession, no doubt, to a lifetime of complaints about her handwriting—but after a few words scrawled into handwriting for the rest of the sentence or paragraph. Olivia waited until the familiarity of each shape had hurt her as much as it could, until there were no surprises left in the generous bottom loop of a *g* or the sight of all those *f*'s and *h*'s, *t*'s and *l*'s leaning like top-heavy trees over lesser letters that crouched below—the vowels especially vulnerable, flattened in the breeze, utterly dependent on context for their identity. It took about five minutes before Olivia could begin to type:

Dear Downtrodden,

No, I'm not going to give you my own personal recipe for apple pie. From what you've said about your mother-in-law, there is no apple pie on earth worthy of her little Donald but her own. You dazzle her with a chocolate soufflé instead. She has probably never made one because most people are

scared silly of soufflés. You are no going to be scared, because I am going to tell you exactly what to do, using the recipe my youngest daughter, Olivia, uses. She is remarkably insecure about her cooking abilities (for no reason that I can see), but this recipe has never failed her.

She sat back and reread the line she had just typed. *She is remarkably insecure about her cooking abilities.* Her mother had written this. She had felt it necessary to tell three-hundred-plus Ladies that her little Olivia was remarkably insecure, Olivia aged twenty-seven years, holder of the Esther Parker Fellowship in Applied Linguistics (last time she'd checked) at the University of St. Anselm—a grown woman working on a PhD who incidentally might object to personal notes about her being printed up and shipped off to a bunch of old biddies. Mother had let the occasional indiscretion slip past her editing, and she seemed to feel that each issue of *Cooking with Vivian* was a warm personal letter to a close friend even though she'd never met half the subscribers. Her family had all learned the hard way that the only way to make sure that no *remarkably insecure* comments got printed was to actually be there in the final stages of an issue, read every word, and then mand that Mother not include the information at Annie had just enjoyed her first date with he nicest young man and they were all hoping he called again. In addition to being there and reading every word, you had to actually *be* Annie, of course, because if you were (for example) Ruby and David, you might see the remark about Annie's nice young man and keep quiet so that when the issue had gone to print and returned, all three hundred copies, collated and stapled and folded by machine (but not yet mailed, this was very important), the nice young man could be pointed out to Annie with considerable fanfare. There was a good chance that Annie would then storm about in a rage worthy of Ruby herself, demanding that the nice young man be deleted and the newsletter reprinted and the old copies ritually burned, but would run herself smack into the hard cold brick wall of Financial Reality, and all of Mother's sincerest apologies could not change the fact that each issue cost (in those days) about $1.12 per newsletter to copy (rates had gone *down* in recent years), and that was *with* nice Mr. Langstrom's generous discounting, and reprinting was therefore out of the question—out of the question, echoed David and Ruby sagely from the couch where they watched with a bag of chips. (Olivia, in her corner of the couch, was greatly torn. Annie was the last one she wanted to torment—yet it was so rare to

y

143

be allowed in on an enclave of Ruby and David's, and here they were, even passing h the chips . . .) After a fairly long scene in whic it was at last pointed out in no uncertain term: that Annie would *not* shout at her mother regardless of the nice young man, since after all it had been thoughtlessly, not maliciously, written—after a fairly long scene and most of a bag of chips, Mother and Annie had at last sat down, exhausted, with the three hundred newsletters and two permanent markers and blacked out two sentences from every copy. The article then read:

> **We enjoyed these irresistible Grasshopper Brownies (thanks to Clare Beasley for the recipe!) for the first time the other night when our oldest, Annie, returned from a movie date.** ~~with Richard Huussen, the nicest young man and a new freshman at SDSU. He had four brownies, and we all hope he will call again for Brownies with Toffee Topping~~.

Annie still maintained (though she was down to a sniffle) that people would try to see through the black marker, driven wild with curiosity about what had been censored. "Nonsense," Mother said, "they'll just think there was a typo."

One of those paragraph-long typos," David
.id, passing by the table.
"That's not helpful, David."
It was simply not possible to catch every
reference to yourself, even if you *were* around
during the final stages of an issue, because the
final stages were a mess. Loose pages and tape
dispensers and cookbooks and snips of paper
and Wite-Out bottles and clippings littered the
entire kitchen and dining room tables, and once
the final draft was stacked and ready to go, you
had a narrow window of opportunity in which to
try to skim the whole thing before Mother left
for Langstrom's Printing and Office Supply. And
since comments about any one person were
sprinkled here and there over a number of
issues, it was easy enough to be lulled into a
sense of security until Annie called you at college to say, "I see you've—wait, let me find it
here: you've, quote, *learned what too many
starches can do to the digestive system, now
that she's eating in a dining hall every night.*
Unquote."

They had all simply taken to saying, whenever it occurred to them, "There's nothing in
there about me, right?" Mother tried her best to
remember, and sometimes it helped.

**She is remarkably insecure about her
cooking abilities (for no reason that I**

can see), but this recipe has never failed her.

Olivia highlighted that sentence and paused with her finger over the backspace key. But it was more difficult than she'd expected, finally having the power to edit. It was fair and square to talk her mother out of something, but sometimes, fair and square, her mother had won. She could hear her now. *Think how this Downtrodden Daughter-in-law person will find it reassuring: if someone insecure about cooking can make a perfect soufflé every time, then maybe she can, too. You can see what this mother-in-law is doing to her.*

Why is it necessary to use my name? You can make the same point by—

For heaven's sake, anyone who reads the newsletter knows you're a very good cook, I mention it all the time. The worst thing anyone will think is that you're modest.

Or neurotic.

Nobody thinks things like that except you.

Because I'm neurotic.

You think about things too much.

Vivian might have relented; she might not. Olivia didn't know. It didn't seem fair to delete something if she didn't know. She clicked on the mouse and returned the cursor to the end of the sentence. Fine. Downtrodden Daughter-in-

146

jolly well better appreciate it, too. She con-
~ued typing.

The next time your mother-in-law
comes to dinner, follow these instructions exactly:

1. Invite your best friend and her husband to the meal. The husband
should be prepped in advance to
rave about your food. (If your
mother-in-law is of the old school,
and I suspect she is, then the raving
of any male will carry far more
weight than ten females. I do not pretend to understand this but there it
is, life isn't fair.)
2. Prepare a good, simple dish that you
know you can count on, like a roast
with vegetables, or a casserole.
3. Just before dinner, prepare the
chocolate sauce for the soufflé. (See
recipe below.) Cover and keep
warm . . .

Olivia typed steadily to the end of the meal:

. . . And here's the best part,
Downtrodden: It does not matter what
your mother-in-law says. I tell you the

truth, there is scarcely a woman aliv⟨ ⟩ who does not find a chocolate soufflé enormously desirable.

Olivia considered the merits of *enormously seductive* but discarded the idea. Her mother would never have *said* "seductive," let alone written it.

She can sit there as impassive as a hippo, but I promise you that her heart will quicken and her mouth water at the sight of your soufflé. You enjoy your portion and tell yourself that you have this day shown your mother-in-law what it means to serve dessert.
P.S. Some unsolicited advice: before your mother-in-law leaves for the night, ask for one of her recipes. You can afford to be a little kind after your triumph.

Olivia inserted a textbox for the soufflé recipe but found herself too exhausted to do much more. She was playing around with various borders when Father appeared in the doorway.

"Popcorn?" he said. "Would you eat some if I made it?"

"Yes," Olivia said, though she wasn't hungry.

o you want me to make it? Parmesan pop-
rn? Or sugar corn?"

Father paused. "There's microwave popcorn,"
he said finally. "I can handle that without
bothering you."

"I'm done for the night." Olivia shoved the
papers back into the file folder and shut
down the system. She followed him out to the
kitchen.

"Parmesan, I guess," Father said, and he
brought the wedge of cheese from the fridge
while Olivia got out Vivian's popcorn pan and
rinsed off the dust.

"Making good progress on the newsletter?"
he asked.

"Yes," she said, although she wasn't. Here it
was, nearly ten o'clock, and what had she
accomplished? One reply to a reader entered.
But Friday night Father would learn that she
had made progress far beyond anyone's imagining—had actually defended her dissertation—
and it wouldn't matter whether she'd done squat
on the newsletter. This revelation should buy
her the rest of the summer at least.

"Glad to hear it," Father said. He was trying to
sound hearty, she could tell, which only highlighted his weariness. "It's a good thing you're
doing, finishing that newsletter. I didn't like the
idea of an issue going unfinished."

"It won't be like Mom would have done it,"

Olivia said. "But I guess everyone will un stand. I might get Ruby to do a few drawings.'

"That would be good. Does she know abo David coming?"

The pan was starting to heat up; a drop of oil reached a leftover droplet of water and sizzled. Olivia added the popcorn and put on the lid.

"I sent her an email."

"We can keep it simple," Father said. "It doesn't need to be a lot of work for you."

Olivia shrugged. She knew that he knew it *would* be a lot of work; there was no more point to complaining. She said, "It's easiest to just go ahead with what I've got planned. Greek. I can do a lot of it ahead. I might be able to get off work early on Friday, too."

Father nodded. He was grating the Parmesan, using the side of the grater with big holes. Olivia took the grater from him and turned it so the fine holes faced out, handed it back. She gave the popcorn pan a shake. "Do you think I take after Mom? Physically, I mean."

Father paused, then continued grating without looking up. He never brought up Vivian himself; he also never refused to talk about her. His grief was private, measured, another door through which Olivia could never walk. She did not mind not seeing the depths of it—sinking in her own as she was—but had to fight the urge to judge him harshly for containing it so well.

've always thought you take after your
ther."

"Not *very* much, though," Olivia said. "Not like
Ruby takes after you."

"There's a strong resemblance around the
eyes," Father said, "and the way you carry your
head."

Olivia had never heard this before. She could
not remember anything distinctive about the
way Mother carried her head.

"Did Mother ever know a woman by the
name of Winnie Kilkenny?"

Father stopped grating and looked up. After a
moment he said, "That was a long time ago."

"Were they friends?"

The first few kernels were popping. Olivia
turned the handle of the crank on the popcorn
pan while Father went back to grating. The
kernels were popping steadily before he replied,
and Olivia had to turn the handle swiftly.

"They were getting to be friends, after a
fashion. Mrs. Kilkenny was sort of a sad case,
and you know your mother. She couldn't resist
trying to take care of her."

"So what happened?"

"She was an unstable person. Or in an unstable
situation, anyway. Under the thumb of a rather
severe husband." He lifted the plate of cheese
for Olivia's inspection.

"That's plenty," she said, raising her voice over

the pinging corn, trying not to sound impati
"I meant, what happened to their friendsh
Did something—stop them from being friend
Like the husband?"

He was rewrapping the cheese in its plastic, as thoroughly and neatly as he'd always wrapped presents. Vivian had always rushed that sort of thing and so delegated it to Father. By the time he was done with a present, it looked like a professional job, each edge sharply creased, the exact optimal amount of wrapping paper used, little evidence of tape in sight. He didn't fuss with bows. Vivian added them later.

"Was there a fight, or did they just drift apart?" Olivia persisted, although she knew from experience that she wasn't going to get much further. "Mother never drifted in her life. Something must have happened."

His reply came to her from the depths of the refrigerator, where he was replacing the cheese. "Your mother tried to help. She reached a point where she felt there was nothing more she could do."

Olivia gave a short laugh. "When did Mother ever reach that point?" she said. "When did she ever stop interfering? Anyway, I think she was going to contact her again—was thinking about her, at least. She jotted her initials on one of her letters from readers."

Father turned from the fridge, face red from

152

bending over. "I take it Mrs. Kilkenny is one of your clients."

"I'm not supposed to say," Olivia said. He nodded. "She might be losing it," she added. "I think—she may have thought I was Mother, the other day."

He looked at her gravely. "I'd better melt the butter," he said at last. Then he nodded at the pan. "That sounds done."

He was right: the popping had nearly stopped, and Olivia lifted the pan hastily from the burner and turned off the gas.

"Well, what do you think of it?" Olivia asked, lifting the lid and looking in at the popcorn. She gave it a shake, looking for old maids. "What do you think of her, you know, confusing me with Mother?"

"I think it sounds like she's getting old. She already seemed old way back when."

"Really? I thought she seemed younger than she was, somehow. Not that I know how old she is."

Father brought the little dish of butter from the microwave. Olivia dumped the popcorn into the large ceramic bread bowl and added the Parmesan, then poured the butter over. She salted it generously. She wondered as she salted if they should have worried about this sort of thing—salt content—before Vivian's stroke, if it could have been prevented by something so

153

simple. But Father was known to have excellent cholesterol and excellent blood pressure, and as for herself, Olivia felt far too young to worry or care about her own health. She had years and years ahead of her, a tiresomely long life before she would join her mother, unless God saw fit to arrange it otherwise. It almost angered her, thinking about how He probably wouldn't, probably wanted her to survive a whole array of Learning Experiences here on earth before she'd be allowed to see Vivian again. She'd be fine with dropping dead tomorrow, if it wouldn't be so terrible for the rest of the family. She added a couple of extra-vigorous shakes of salt.

"It's strange," Father said, and Olivia started. He was standing just behind her, looking into the bowl of popcorn. Just standing there, not doing anything with his hands. "You realize there are—events you underwent with the person who's gone, shared experiences, and then once they're gone, you're it. You're the only one who has those memories."

Olivia wanted to look away to give him the privacy that so often frustrated her but could not. She couldn't speak.

"If you remember inaccurately, no one will know. You won't even know yourself." He frowned at the bowl thoughtfully. "I suppose one should write things down more."

He moved away then, toward the napkins,

nd then Olivia was able to move as well. She picked up the bowl and followed him to the living room and watched the news with him without hearing it, and when the news was over she surfed around until she found an old rerun of *M*A*S*H*. When that was over they watched a *Cosby* rerun. They watched late into the night, long after the popcorn was gone, long after they could even pretend to find anything remotely interesting, even though Father's head kept jerking awake and Olivia herself was so tired she could have fallen asleep in her popcorn bowl.

8

The next morning, Olivia fought to awaken from a rambling, troubled dream that seemed to have lasted half the night. For a few moments she lay panting, her eyes half-closed. She was going to be late for work. She imagined herself in a coma—no, mistaken for dead and buried alive. That had been one of her most horrific fears as a child, but it didn't sound so bad now, if one could only fall back asleep for the duration. You couldn't, of course, because as the air ran out, your lungs would wake you in a panic. She opened her eyes all the way and realized then

why she felt she was suffocating: she'd bee~
hyperventilating in her sleep, delirious on too
much oxygen. She unwound herself from the
damp sheets and craned to look at the clock.

She was definitely going to be late.

She dragged herself to the cafeteria window
to receive Doris's look of displeasure, but Doris
barely glanced up. She was kneeling in front of
one of the freezers trying to jam several cases of
Polish sausage into the already-full interior.

"Anything I can do?" Olivia said to Doris's
back.

"Yes," Doris said. "Find Lydia and Violet and
tell them hide-and-seek is over for now. I got
four boxes of canned goods blocking the supply
closet. Tell Lydia that's four boxes that'll need
collapsing, but she has to empty them *right*."

Olivia looked in all of Lydia's usual hiding
places, even knocked on the men's room door
and poked her head inside, said "hello" in the
echoey chamber. Nothing. She was going to have
to check the bushes by the side of the building.
She stopped by her office first, plunked her
purse down on the desk without bothering to
turn on the light. Lydia jumped out from beside
the filing cabinet in the corner and yelled, "Surprise!" Olivia nearly fell over her chair. Violet
sidled out belatedly from the other side of the
cabinet, eyes shining, two fingers in her mouth.

"Well, you two got me good," Olivia said,

once she'd caught her breath. She made her way to the light switch and flipped it on, and they all stood there, breathless and blinking in the bright light, and Olivia felt again that she was just waking up. "Well. Guess who gets to collapse boxes this morning?"

As soon as they left, Olivia shut the office door and sat, eyes closed, head in her hands, thinking how much she didn't want to deliver route 5 today.

She roused herself enough to check her voice mail.

Warren Wheeler had died. Olivia emailed Marjean to ask about sympathy card protocol.

There was an email from Harry:

> **Bully for you. I'm glad to hear you're finally going to tell everyone—wish I could be there to see their faces! If you need moral support I could be induced to come . . .**

The words blurred together, and she had to force her tired eyes to focus. She reread the message a couple of times and finally replied:

> **We wouldn't want Penelope to get the wrong impression, would we?**

She was dissatisfied with her reply; maybe the

sarcasm didn't come through. Or maybe it di
and she didn't want it to. She deleted the whole
message. Then she shoved the keyboard aside
and put her head on her desk until it was time to
let Doris know the final count for the day.

Delivering route 5 was exactly as painful as
she'd feared it would be. She barely had the
strength to drag the cooler and the hot box into
the backseat of the car, which of course she had
forgotten to park in the shade. The car had
trapped so much heat that she sat with the doors
open and the air-conditioning on full blast (and
she knew Father's opinion on *that*) for several
minutes before pulling away.

Mr. Ryerson was in fine form, claiming
cryptically that it was too hot to eat cauliflower.
Olivia was too tired to argue. She handed him
his hot and cold meals, crawled back into the
huge refrigerated car, and drove the five blocks
over to Mr. Reynolds's house. It was a small,
pea-green, weather-beaten one-story box with
one square window on either side of the door.
Usually it filled her with despair, how Mr.
Reynolds's gentle, hulking frame in the doorway
made the house appear even smaller, but today
she barely noticed because Mr. Reynolds
answered the door in a shiny pink nightgown. It
was a tasteful, unrevealing garment, neck and
sleeves edged demurely in white lace, but it was
a nightgown nonetheless. It was pulled tight

across his shoulders and came to his knees.

Olivia said, "It's cauliflower today, so I do hope you don't mind cauliflower."

"This was my wife's," Mr. Reynolds said, turning the same shade as the gown. "It's just so hot today."

"Oh, it's terrible," Olivia said, nodding and looking Mr. Reynolds squarely in the eye and *only* in the eye as she set the meal down on the coffee table. "It's about the hottest yet, and some people don't like cauliflower when it's this hot."

Mr. Reynolds looked a bit confused at this, or maybe Olivia was projecting her own confusion; at any rate, neither of them tried to prolong her stay.

She gained the sanctuary of her car and lay back for a moment against the headrest while cold air blasted her neck and face. She suddenly realized that she had left her hot pack on Mr. Reynolds's coffee table. Not for anything would she have gone back for it.

By the time she'd put Mrs. Carlisle behind her—the cats all languishing under various pieces of furniture—and was picking her way up Mrs. Kilkenny's broken sidewalk, she was thoroughly annoyed with herself for delivering route 5 when it was completely unnecessary, wasting, in effect, all those lovely Methodists. She didn't know what she was supposed to do if Mrs.

Kilkenny *did* think she was her mother—pretend that she was? Explain that she wasn't Vivian, and Vivian herself was dead? Perfect: upset the woman on top of confusing her. There were no good options, nothing to do but alert Marjean so she could notify the proper authorities. Which Olivia could have done without putting herself through this.

Still, she needed that shrimp creole recipe, and recipes were a harmless enough topic. "Stumped in Beadle County" lay folded in her pocket. She'd have fingered it for support if her hands hadn't been full.

Mrs. Kilkenny looked up at her through the screen door.

"Meals on Wheels," Olivia said. The hot meal was carefully perched on the cold; her fingers stung. She could feel the heat radiating up toward her chin, her flushed cheeks, the damp roots of her hair. She forced a smile into her voice. "Turkey burger today, and I'm sorry to say cauliflower."

Mrs. Kilkenny said nothing. Her lips parted; her eyes searched every inch of Olivia's face and then, apparently unsatisfied, started again.

Olivia said, "I think you may have gotten me —that is, you may have known my mother. Vivian Tschetter."

Mrs. Kilkenny's eyes widened. She nodded the merest bit. "One of the daughters," she said. She

160

ut a hand to her chest, which made her look slightly out of breath.

"That's right."

"But not Ruby."

Accustomed though she was to being in Ruby's shadow, this took her aback. "No— Olivia. Vivian's youngest."

"Olivia." She barely breathed the name. She collected herself and said, with something more than politeness, "How is Ruby?"

"She's great," Olivia said, feeling more and more off balance. She barely listened to her own reply. "She's always—she's great. You must watch her on the news. She's doing very well."

Mrs. Kilkenny nodded. "I don't watch the news," she said faintly.

Olivia nodded and smiled.

Mrs. Kilkenny looked away. She opened the screen door and stepped aside so Olivia could enter, then nodded toward the living room. "You can put them on the side table, please," she said.

"Certainly." Olivia went into the living room to the little table between the sofa and the wing chair and set the meals down carefully. "There you go," she said, turning, but the air next to her was empty. Mrs. Kilkenny had not followed her; she still stood at the screen door, her hand on the cross-piece, looking outside without interest. Olivia came forward uncertainly.

161

"Shall we take another look at that cast-iro
skillet I got down last time?"

Mrs. Kilkenny's eyes darted to her briefly, then
dropped. "I won't be needing it after all, thank
you."

"I'd be happy to put it away for you."

"It isn't necessary."

She turned to stare out the door again, waiting,
presumably, for Olivia to leave. But Olivia stood
rooted: did she already understand, then, that
Vivian was dead? It had been in the paper, of
course. Olivia had the impression that all elderly
people read the obituaries as religiously as her
great aunts. Mrs. Kilkenny must know, and didn't
want to upset Olivia—or perhaps she didn't want
to be upset herself, in front of anyone. Olivia
fingered the edges of her pockets nervously; her
left hand slipped inside and found the letter,
and she drew it out in relief.

"I do have a favor to ask you, Mrs. Kilkenny,
if it's not too much trouble."

The old woman was surprised enough to look
at her again.

"My mother wrote your initials on this note
about a shrimp creole recipe. I thought, since
you're from the South, there's a chance you
gave her the recipe, maybe a long time ago."
She gave a little laugh. "Or I could be completely
off-base." She unfolded the letter and held it
out.

Mrs. Kilkenny reached out, took the letter with tentative fingers. "You found this . . ."

"Yes, but I can't find the actual recipe anywhere. It would have juniper berries in it. I was hoping you'd share it again. It's for her newsletter. You maybe remember about her newsletter?"

Mrs. Kilkenny looked up in disbelief, then down at the letter once more. She stared at it for another long moment and then held it out to Olivia, trembling. Her eyes looked straight into Olivia's, two blue-burning flames.

"If Vivian wants anything from me, she can come ask for it herself."

She pushed open the screen door and pointedly flattened herself against the door jamb so Olivia could pass.

Olivia couldn't think. She went cold, then hot She wanted, suddenly, to hurt the woman.

"Vivian can't. She's dead."

The blue flames flared--for a moment the woman's entire face was wild, and Olivia thought she would cry out—and then the door fell shut. Olivia felt triumphant and guilty, dimly aware that she had used her mother's death.

"Sorry to have troubled you, Mrs. Kilkenny," she said stiffly. She pushed the letter into her pocket and moved to the door. Mrs. Kilkenny took Olivia's wrist.

"How?" she asked.

"Does it matter? There's apparently no love lost between you."

"But there is," she breathed. "A great deal. She was my second friend. And my last. She can't be gone, she's far too young. When?"

Her hand tightened, but Olivia pulled her wrist free and took a step back, put her arms around herself. "About two months ago," she said.

"I can't believe it." There was a cedar chest across from the door, and Mrs. Kilkenny made her way to it and sat. She looked around as if finding herself in the middle of a forest, alone. "I suppose I would have forgiven her, if I'd ever thought she could really be gone."

Olivia said, "*Forgiven* her?"

"I almost lost my Stephen because of her." She looked up at Olivia, and Olivia wondered who she was seeing. She went cold again. The woman stood unsteadily and took a few steps toward Olivia, who stepped back. "Whatever else happened, she never lost Ruby. She never came close to knowing what that was like."

Olivia, appalled at what she was hearing, at what she might hear, said, "Why Ruby? What about Ruby?"

But Mrs. Kilkenny showed no sign of hearing. She sagged, and in spite of herself Olivia started forward and helped her back to the chest, where Mrs. Kilkenny sat heavily. Her hands were open and lifeless on her lap, her eyes dead as slate. "She's really gone."

Olivia said, "She really is." She turned and pushed through the door and fumbled her way down the steps. She did not look back at the house, and when she gained her car, she did not put her head back to bask in the cool blast of air. She jerked into gear and hit the gas.

Back at the office Olivia pulled the next day's list of volunteers and put the Methodists back on route 5. Then she closed the door to her office and sat at her desk, but only for a moment before she thought, *No*. She would not think about this—the ramblings of a woman who was probably losing her mental faculties. Olivia got up again, opened the office door, and spent the rest of her short afternoon entering a few minor adjustments Marjean wanted her to make to the route directions.

When she did think about it, she was angry with Father. She was angry in spite of remembering the look on his face last night. But it was the thought of anyone angry with Vivian that sat like a stone in her stomach. She didn't want lunch. Around two o'clock she left work and went home and fell asleep on the couch, where she slept hard without dreaming.

Hours later the phone woke her. She stumbled to the kitchen feeling as if she'd just been peeled off a steamroller. It was Father. He'd gotten caught up in an important meeting regarding the gravel roads manual he was writing for the state, and that's why he was so late. Olivia sighed and said she supposed she could wait supper for him. She replaced the phone but hung on to it for a moment longer, planted her forehead against the wall. She *had* no plan for supper.

She rooted in the fridge and found the remains of the wedge of Parmesan, half a carton of eggs, and some leftover bacon. Then she pulled out her mother's ancient Betty Crocker cookbook, the one with all the sketches of merry, wasp-waisted housewives bearing platters of meat, to look up white sauce.

She'd managed to avoid this book the last few months. It was beyond dog-eared; the front cover was long gone, the spine broken and the fine mesh of the binding exposed. You could open the book to just about any page and it stayed open, perfectly flat. Some pages were falling out, some splotched with spilled ingredients. Her mother's handwriting scrawled down the margins: dates, comments, family reactions. She'd overhauled many of the recipes, changing the amounts, substituting ingredients. Olivia paged through the book, mesmerized. "Prize Coffee Cake": *Charlie's first Father's Day! Sprinkle w/ streusel, walnuts.* "Sweet Roll Dough": *Old faithful*. "Eskimo Igloo Cake," over a black-and-white photo of an iced "igloo" surrounded by sugarcube blocks of snow: *Ruby's bday disaster —looked like a Quonset hut.*

The "Cookies" chapter was completely falling apart.

Olivia started flipping backward through Main Dishes. "Noodle Ring with Creamed Chicken": *Everyone thumbs-up, David thumbs-down.* "Delmarvelous Shrimp": *Consensus: delmediocre.* "Lumberjack Macaroni": *quick + all kids like.* She happened across the meatball recipe that Vivian had marked up with changes and renamed *Annie's Meatballs*. At the bottom of the same page there was one short comment in red ink next to "Spaghetti, Italian Style": *Ha.*

It was the *Ha* that made her eyes well and her nose run, and she turned quickly to the index to look up white sauce: page 398. She scanned the recipe and started melting the butter in a heavy saucepan.

She wondered (pushing the butter disconsolately around the pan with a wooden spoon to hurry things) how much her mother had really used the Betty Crocker in recent years. Most of the recipes she'd probably outgrown or memorized —Vivian hadn't had to look up Annie's Meatballs for years—and the fact that the book retained its place of honor on the first shelf over the microwave may have signified mere force of habit. Vivian couldn't be bothered to reorganize anything unless Annie goaded her into it. Olivia added flour to the pan, salt and pepper, a pinch of dry mustard—compelled for some reason to pass the vial of mustard under her nose although she found its flat, bitter scent distressing. A dash of cayenne, and then she stirred and stirred while the mixture bubbled. A vision came to her—rooted in memory, or imagination?—a vision of Vivian poring over the pages. It might have been yesterday: Vivian standing over the table, hands planted on either side of the open Betty Crocker, reading glasses perched on her nose. The dark hair that fell forward was streaked with coarser gray hairs but still thick, even flattering in the blunt bob Annie had talked her into. She turned a page, shaking her head and murmuring. Olivia thought, *Why is an old woman angry at you?*

The vision poured like salt to the ground.

Olivia slid the pan off the burner, blinking hard, and sloshed in the milk. She returned the pan with a small crash and cranked up the heat.

Vivian would have shaken her head at that, anyway. Olivia was too impatient, she'd said more than once; it was her one real weakness as a cook. She was impatient, and she was emotional. *Emotional?* Olivia had cried out. *There was the pot calling the kettle black!* Vivian talked to her sauces the way some people talked to their ints. She crooned, she coaxed, sometimes she ently, sorrowfully reproached. Olivia mostly begged. Occasionally she threatened. "Thicken," Olivia said now to the white sauce, stirring furiously, "thicken, and don't you dare burn, or I'm pouring you out, I swear I'll do it."

The thing began to bubble, and soon thereafter to spit. Olivia, chastened, turned the heat back down to where it should be and stirred faithfully for another minute before taking the pan off the burner for good. She grated the Parmesan directly into the sauce, tried to grate too close to the rind and sheared off a small, delicate scallop of her own flesh. She swore and carefully scooped the flesh and a drop of blood out of the sauce with a teaspoon. She put on a Band-Aid (she kept the box on top of Vivian's spice rack) and separated the eggs. She set the mixer to beating the egg whites while she beat the yolks by hand.

The pain from the new divot in her finger, raw and intense, worsened her mood.

J.C. entered, ears back at all the commotion, and took her place on the step stool.

Olivia dumped the yolks into the cheese sauce and took it over to the table to stir. She regarded the Betty Crocker gloomily. She'd made a hundred white sauces for a hundred soufflés but still second-guessed herself, still looked up the proportions just to be sure. *She is remarkably insecure about her cooking abiliti* Well, Vivian was right, but what did she kno about it? *She* hadn't grown up in the shadow o someone like herself; her own mother had been indifferent at best in the kitchen. Olivia, still stirring, flipped back to Main Dishes absently and began paging through, watching the upper left-hand corner of the pages for the cheese soufflé recipe she could picture with her eyes closed and didn't follow anymore anyway (more egg whites, fewer yolks). She'd only gone a few pages when a folded-up piece of paper slipped out. She was replacing it when a heading on that page of the cookbook caught her eye: "Creole Shrimp."

The short recipe that followed was credited to Mrs. R. E. Smith of Jeanerette, Louisiana. (Olivia had always loved the credits and the corny, homey anecdotes that popped up here and there throughout the old edition.) In the white space was a note penned by Vivian: *Summer '76: Winnie says not authentic. Need juniper berries etc.*

Olivia opened the piece of paper tentatively.

It was a "recipe" for friendship, the same maudlin sort of thing that certain of the Ladies were apt to send in from time to time. Vivian always published these saccharine offerings in some corner of the newsletter with a hand-drawn border of ivy leaves or chili peppers because, she said, if sentimentality were the worst crime

170

neone ever committed they were doing pretty ell. It was signed "your friend W.K."

Olivia folded up the paper, slipped it into her pocket, and closed the book. She put the book back on the first shelf over the microwave and checked the egg whites.

She was just sliding the soufflé into the oven when Father walked in, still carrying his brief-case. "Twenty minutes," she said.

He looked at J.C., who was eating the last morsel of bacon Olivia had placed on the stool's edge.

"There's bacon?" he said hopefully.

"It's in the bottom of the soufflé."

Father nodded.

"I'll bring you something to tide you over," she said, and when he was settled in his recliner with his newspaper open, she brought a glass of lemonade and a small plate of pickles and radishes. She was angry with him, but what was the point? Everyone knew you didn't go to Father for this sort of information. You went to Annie, and failing that, Aunt Rubina.

Father looked up from the radish he was about to bite into because Olivia was still standing there.

"I was thinking of going out to the farm," she said, although she hadn't thought of it until just now. "Take the aunts those Mason jars they asked for."

"You're not eating?"

"I'll have some when I get back."

Father looked a little lonely, but Olivia hardene her heart. He wasn't making it easy for her either She reminded him to pay attention to the timer while he loaded a carton of jars into the trunk of the Olds.

"The soufflé will have fallen by the time you get home," Father said.

Olivia slid behind the wheel and slammed the door, rolled down the window. "Long before I get home," she said. "It'll taste the same."

Father nodded. As she pulled away, she could hear cicadas and a lawn mower starting up in the distance. The sounds made her more and less lonely at the same time.

9

Mason jars were a natural excuse for a visit to the aunts. Jars made the rounds between the two homes with the regularity of mail. Sometimes they bore ruby red tomatoes, sometimes peaches glowing like a sunrise; sometimes, like now, they were empty and waiting to be filled. The same seventy or so jars had probably been in circulation for thirty or forty years, Olivia figured. Her favorites were the pale blue ones with the d *Ball* inscribed on the side in raised script.

Olivia headed out of town on Medary Avenue and turned at the first county road past Sunnyview. The white gauze that had muffled the sky all day was thinning to a pale blue, but Olivia could still see heat on the horizon. She never drove this route without remembering what Harry had said when he was here over the funeral, how few trees there were. She'd been surprised and pointed out a shelterbelt. He'd laughed. "Yes, a few brave stands of trees here and there, and the rest of it sky." She remembered miles of thick woods on road trips in Ohio, Pennsylvania, New York. But she'd always thought of it as an excess of trees there, rather than few trees here. *Here* was the default, the norm. Probably everyone felt this way about where they grew up. It was hard to see one's home as others did.

She turned in at the shelterbelt on Aunt Barbara's farm—it would always be Aunt Barbara and Uncle Emmet's farm, even though Emmet had died and Rubina moved in upon retirement—and pulled up to the house. Aunt Barbara's car was gone; Olivia hoped she was out running errands. She hoisted the box of jars from the trunk and slammed it shut. Aunt Rubina was already opening the screen door when she started up the steps.

"This is a nice surprise," Aunt Rubina said.

She stepped back to let Olivia inside. "~ timely. We're canning the strawberry preser tomorrow."

"Then I've brought the wrong ones," Olivi said, setting the box down on the kitchen counter. "These are quarts. I don't think we have any pints right now."

Aunt Ruby frowned into the box. "I'll check with Annie. She did all those jars of salsa last year."

Olivia saw a plastic container of store-bought lasagna, half-eaten, next to the box of jars. "Aunt Rubina," she said in surprise.

Aunt Rubina followed her look. "Oh—Barbara won't like it if you know," she said. "You didn't learn it from me. It's just so easy, and one of them lasts us half the week. And truthfully, I think Barbara misses your mother's lasagna." She sighed. "Of course, this is nothing *like* your mother's lasagna."

"Can I have some?" Olivia was suddenly light-headed from hunger.

Aunt Rubina was already carving out a large square portion and sliding it onto a plate, which she then put into the microwave. "You sit," she said, waving Olivia to the table, so Olivia sat.

"Aunt Barbara's out?"

"She had women's auxiliary at the hospital." She poured a glass of milk for Olivia without asking, brought the plate of lasagna, a napkin, a

174

Olivia sighed and sank down a little in her r. She hadn't realized how tired she was of ver being served. She pulled Mrs. Kilkenny's cipe for friendship from her pocket and nfolded it. She waited for Aunt Rubina to pause in one of her treks across the kitchen and handed it to her.

"What do you know," said Aunt Rubina, scanning the paper. "Winnie Kilkenny. Where did you run across this? The newsletter, I guess."

"It was folded up in Mom's old Betty Crocker. Did you know her?"

"I met her a few times." Aunt Rubina handed the paper back and brought a pan of strawberry-rhubarb crumble to the table, and Olivia picked up her fork and began to eat the lasagna. The tomato sauce was too heavy and sweet and the noodles overcooked, but it was just what she needed, an infusion of pure salt. "Winnie Kilkenny and your mother were friends years ago."

Olivia swallowed. "She's on my Meals on Wheels route," she said, realizing that route 5 had become, like it or not, her route. She felt no guilt at revealing a client's name to Aunt Rubina. "She actually confused me with Mother the day after I delivered once, although she didn't seem confused today. I was wondering what happened to their friendship. Nobody moved away."

Aunt Rubina put two slices of rhubarb crumble

175

on two plates and finally sat across the wooden table from Olivia. She squinted a littl she paused. "Now, *that* I'm not sure of . . remember how things started, that was quite story. I don't remember why they lost touch. suppose people get busy and drift apart."

Olivia said around a mouthful, "How did things start?"

Aunt Rubina set down the fork she had just picked up and leaned against the back of her chair. Olivia chewed and felt almost happy. Aunt Rubina was not normally a great talker, nature and necessity having selected her for listening, but with some slight nudging from an interested audience, and in the absence of her sister, she could be persuaded to yield up wonderful stories of detail. Now she was smiling a little.

"Your mother felt so responsible for the woman," she said. "From the day she smashed into her car."

"*Mother* smashed into her car?"

"Well, it was a fender-bender. Nothing really. It wasn't the accident so much; she just felt . . . I'd say she felt called."

"Called?"

"Called as to a mission," Aunt Rubina said. "She was going to save Winnie Kilkenny."

"From what?"

Aunt Rubina looked at Olivia and raised her eyebrows. "Utter loneliness."

• • •

accident—if you believed in accidents, which Vivian didn't—had occurred just after noon that day. Vivian was driving west on Third Street, heading downtown to pick up some curtains at Sears and stop at Snyder Drug to survey party goods for David's twelfth birthday. David was off skateboarding on campus, and Annie was home with Ruby and Olivia; Vivian would always be grateful none of the children were with her. But it was ironic, too, that she should have a lapse in driving judgment *that* day of all days, when for once there was peace and quiet in the car, no arguments to mediate, no one complaining that David was giving them Indian rubs or that Olivia wouldn't stop singing—and ironic to have a lapse just after she and Charlie had impressed upon Annie that her training permit was a privilege, not a right. Vivian, humming to herself, was thinking about David's birthday cake. David always asked for chocolate, which they had just had, and it would be lovely to try something different—but children were not big on *different*. She might be able to get away with *German* chocolate, with a rich coconut-pecan filling . . . Some part of her brain briefly noted the Cadillac Seville nosing up to the stop sign on Fifth Avenue in that diffident manner of huge cars driven by little old ladies, and dismissed it. All of the children,

thank heavens, liked coconut, and as lon[g]
they didn't *tell* Olivia there were pecan[s]
suddenly it registered that the Seville had ne[ver]
really stopped and was arcing into a furtiv[e]
right-hand turn, and Vivian threw her weight o[n]
the brakes as her fender slammed into the back
driver's side corner of the Seville with a terrific
crunch.

She sat with her eyes closed, transfixed by
horror, then forced herself to look in the rearview mirror. Thank God—no cars behind her.
She put the car into park, right there in the
middle of Third Street, because maybe you
weren't supposed to move anything until the
police arrived, and closed her eyes again:
passersby were gathering, a couple of men from
Langstrom's Office Supply trickled out onto the
sidewalk, and she didn't think she could face
them or the occupant of the Seville. She thought
wildly of gas tanks, thought, *Help Jesus help
help help.* A child's wail rose from somewhere,
and for one awful moment—the worst yet—she
wished she were dead rather than to have hurt,
perhaps killed, a child. *Jesus take me now.*

But the onlookers did not sound hysterical. In
another moment she realized that after all the
child couldn't be dead or even unconscious if it
were wailing, so she breathed a few more
Jesuses and opened her eyes again. Someone
helped her from the car, and she forced herself

walk shakily to the Seville. Mr. Langstrom himself was trying to calm the driver, who seemed unable to unclench her hands from the steering wheel.

"Ma'am," he was saying, "we've called an ambulance, which maybe wasn't even necessary. Let's calm down."

By now the child was standing—not lying paralyzed, thank God!—standing by the car being inexpertly dabbed at by the younger Langstrom's man, the one who always ran her newsletter copies. Vivian recognized in an instant that while the boy's nose was very bloody, half his hysteria was due to the woman's. He looked to be about Ruby's age, maybe a little younger; he was built along slighter lines than David. She was on surer footing now. She exchanged looks with Mr. Langstrom and stuck her head in the driver's side window. "You *must* calm down for the sake of the child," she said firmly. The woman gulped and looked up at Vivian, who pressed her advantage: "My goodness, I'm sorry I hit you, but if I've seen one bloody nose I've seen a thousand."

She turned to the boy then, pulled the scarf from her hair, and began dabbing at him herself; the younger Langstrom's man relinquished him in relief. "You're just fine," she said to the boy, who began to slow to a sob. She *hoped* he was fine; he looked terrible from the blood. The first rule of calming children was to be complete matter-of-fact so they believed you.

The ambulance had had an easy shot straigh down Third and now pulled up smugly with a final whine of its siren. Vivian said, "What my boy wouldn't give to ride in an ambulance! Aren't you lucky!"

The boy began to look interested.

Two policemen had arrived. One tried to get the older woman's story, but she fell apart almost immediately, and he turned to Vivian. She took a breath and told him as truthfully as she could that she was pretty sure it was *mostly* her fault, although she didn't think the other car had come to a complete stop. Several passersby confirmed this and emphasized that the Seville had acted unexpectedly; they seemed to want Vivian to be less guilty and the hysterical woman *more,* to pay for her hysteria. Vivian ended up going along in the ambulance. The boy clung to her now, and the older woman still had said nothing but was pleading with her eyes. "Maybe she has a concussion," the policeman said to Vivian before the ambulance doors closed, as if she were his colleague and not the perpetrator of an accident.

At the hospital they examined Vivian cursorily, but she waved them off. They found it best to examine the two "victims" in separate spaces, divided by a curtain, Vivian staying with the ɔoy to keep him calm. She told the nurse what had happened. The boy confirmed that he had smacked face-first into the back of the front seat, a well-padded front seat, and when the nurse questioned him about some marks on his arm, he started to cry and said his nose hurt.

Vivian, truth be told, was only half-listening to this. She was straining to hear what was happening on the other side of the curtain. The nurse *there* would only say that Mrs. Kilkenny (that was her name, Winnie Kilkenny) *may* have had a very *slight* concussion. The doctor would have to say for sure.

The doctor didn't know for sure. He didn't seem too concerned. How fast had they been going? He could assure them that the boy had almost certainly not broken his nose. They were both to be released immediately, at which news Mrs. Kilkenny grew upset and spoke up for the first time. Her husband would be very angry about the car, she said, and she did not calm down until Vivian stepped in again and insisted on accompanying Mrs. Kilkenny home to explain about the accident. The policeman, who had met them at the hospital, tried for several minutes to dissuade Vivian from doing this. Let the insurance companies sort this out, he said, and he would take Mrs. Kilkenny home himself. But Vivian knew her duty and would not be swayed. At last she and Mrs. Kilkenny and the boy all rode with Officer Lewis to 181 Oscar Howe Drive in a squad car—another stroke of good luck, as Vivian pointed out to the boy.

The residence at 181 Oscar Howe Drive was a largish, turreted house with a wraparound porch and leaded glass windows that flashed in the sunlight. Mr. Kilkenny was home even though it was the middle of the afternoon, and Vivian guessed from his age—he looked to be at least ten years older than Mrs. Kilkenny—that he was retired. (She later learned she was wrong about this.) He was a large, beefy man with a silent red anger that spread from his neck to his face and looked all the redder under his thatch of white hair. He listened while the policeman explained, and Vivian apologized sweetly and said how glad she was that the boy wasn't seriously hurt. He barely glanced at the boy, who melted away up the stairs as soon as Vivian turned her attention back to Mr. Kilkenny. She was waiting for him to burst out shouting, that's how tight and red his face looked; but he only barked one question about where the car had been taken and thanked the policeman for his trouble. Vivian asked if she could drop off supper that night since Mrs. Kilkenny might have a concussion; at this, the policeman ran his hand over his face and turned aside in a gesture of defeat. Mr. Kilkenny said that it wouldn't be necessary. Something in his refusal made Vivian straighten her back, and she said, in a deceptively cheerful voice, that it certainly *was* necessary, and she would drop something off at five. She turned to go before he could argue further.

She remembered after walking out that she had not said good-bye to Mrs. Kilkenny; when she looked back at the house, she saw the woman hovering like a ghost in one of the front windows, looking out at Vivian but not returning her wave, as if she were watching through a one-way mirror and did not believe she could be seen.

The policeman told Vivian as he drove her home that it would have been just as well not to involve herself further with the Kilkennys. Vivian told him, more lightly than she felt, that they might well say the same about *her,* since she was the one who crashed into their car. He looked at her sideways and she knew, uncomfortably, what he meant. There was something unsettling about Mrs. Kilkenny's behavior and the anger that Mr. Kilkenny would not release.

She scratched her plans for cold macaroni salad for supper and used tomorrow night's chicken to make buttermilk fried chicken even though it was ninety-two degrees out, because she was sure she had detected a Southern accent in the few words Mrs. Kilkenny had spoken. She had David hang an old blanket in the doorway from the dining room to the kitchen, using the nails above the door frame around which they strung ropes of tinsel at Christmas. This confined the heat to the kitchen fairly well even though the children ran in and out all afternoon looking for lemonade, asking to go swimming, asking for popsicles. They were properly impressed when she finally admitted, in the middle of tossing together a potato salad, that she had been in a small accident, and she used the opportunity to give Annie a lecture on the dangers of letting one's attention wander even for a second. David's fascination with the accident waned when she told him that the car was barely crumpled (having taken the impact square on the bumper) and she could have driven it to the shop herself, if she hadn't been needed in the ambulance. Annie's interest centered around whether she would be allowed to practice driving with Father's car. Vivian finally told her to run up to campus herself to ask him, so she left, allowing Ruby to tag along since none of Annie's friends were handy.

Olivia stayed behind in the hot kitchen and begged to help with the potato salad. Vivian sighed and set her up mashing the hard-boiled eggs with a potato masher and stirring them into the salad along with the mayonnaise and vinegar. She had to watch Olivia's stirring: the salad was too stiff for a five-year-old to manage, and Olivia concentrated her efforts on one nall corner of potatoes until they were nearly alling apart. Vivian finally asked her to sprinkle the sweet peas with salt—just the *merest* bit—and while she was thus distracted took the wooden spoon, gave the salad two or three deft turns, and thanked Olivia for doing such a fine job.

She arrived on the Kilkennys' doorstep at five o'clock promptly, the car running at the curb with Charlie at the wheel, and handed over a basket filled with the buttermilk fried chicken, the potato salad, minted sweet peas, sourdough biscuits, and a rhubarb-strawberry crumble that was to have been the Tschetters's dessert. Mr. Kilkenny took the food at the door. Mrs. Kilkenny, he said, was lying down upstairs. Vivian said that she would return for the basket and other things at Mrs. Kilkenny's convenience; her phone number was on a piece of paper inside the basket.

She breathed a sigh of relief that the encounter had been quick and uneventful. The red had gone from Mr. Kilkenny's visage, but the tightness about his eyes and mouth remained.

Mrs. Kilkenny did not call that day, or the next. Vivian looked in the telephone directory, then called the operator, but the Kilkennys were not listed. Finally, she elected to return to the white house, unasked and on foot, bearing twin loaves of banana bread. She pushed the doorbell and was thinking what a pretty sound it made, like chimes, when Mrs. Kilkenny's startled face appeared in the curtains at the front window. I another moment the door opened and Mrs. Kilkenny was standing at the screen door.

"Good afternoon?" Mrs. Kilkenny said. She wore a neat housedress covered by a half-apron, which she fingered nervously. Vivian had forgotten how petite the woman was. Somehow she looked even smaller and more helpless, now that she was carefully put together and not hysterical.

"Good afternoon, how are you? May I come in?" Vivian smiled radiantly and remarked on the loveliness of the doorbell, the wide porch, the sunny day, and then she was inside. Either she or Mrs. Kilkenny had opened the door and let her in, she wasn't even sure herself which, but this was often the effect she had on reserved people: they gave way to her with resignation or relief.

Vivian handed her the banana bread as if of course they'd both known she'd be dropping them by, and asked after the boy. Mrs. Kilkenny held the cellophane-wrapped loaves to her chest, her shoulders slightly stooped.

"He's going to be fine," she said tentatively.

"That's so good to hear."

Mrs. Kilkenny turned and called up the stairs. "Stephen!" The stairs were a grand affair, with raised velvet roses on the walls and scattered roses on the carpet runner. Vivian gazed at the

ses, the gleaming banister, with real apprecia-
tion for this luxury that was beyond her own
means.

"What a lovely home," she said while they
waited. "Interior decorating is not my forte. Of
course, it's just as well, with four children at
home trying to wear out every stick of furniture
we own. Just last week they managed to break
the hide-a-bed sofa by trying to fold up our
youngest in it."

Mrs. Kilkenny looked a little alarmed at this
but was spared having to respond by the
appearance of the boy at the turn of the stairs.
He came toward them reluctantly, as if drawn
by invisible strings to Mrs. Kilkenny. He was
quite nice-looking, now that Vivian saw him
cleaned up.

"Well, your nose got a good bruise, didn't it?"
Vivian said cheerfully, because David had
always liked to brag about his scrapes. The boy
touched his nose in some alarm, stopping in the
middle of the staircase, and Vivian added
quickly, "Much better, though. Anyway at your
age I imagine you're always getting something
banged up."

He looked quickly at Mrs. Kilkenny, then down
at his feet. Mrs. Kilkenny looked from Stephen
to Vivian helplessly, as if she couldn't find anything to say. Vivian plowed ahead bravely. "My
boy's a couple years older than Stephen, and if

he's not wiping out on his bike and chipping tooth, he's falling off the roof of the garde shed. How old are you, Stephen? Nine? Ten?"

He looked up in mild surprise. "Almost ten."

"My middle daughter is ten," Vivian said, "but she's at Hillcrest Elementary, and I imagine you go to Central."

Mrs. Kilkenny had recovered herself under Vivian's apparent assumption that all was well, and now she spoke in the soft Southern accent that struck Vivian as so much more gracious than a plain old Midwestern one: "Thank you so much for the delicious supper. I have your things in the kitchen."

The boy turned and disappeared up the stairs, and Vivian followed Mrs. Kilkenny through the living room, past a heavy mahogany dining room table already set for three with china (more roses), and into a large, light kitchen with shining pink appliances—even the sink—and black-and-white accents. The floor was a black-and-white checkerboard scattered with pink and black and gray braided rugs; the curtains were crisp pink and white gingham. Vivian was not such a fan of pink—yellow was her color, and she'd tried in vain all summer to talk Olivia and Ruby out of wanting an all-pink bedroom—but it was undeniably charming, this kitchen, and the long white counters were gleaming and bare. Vivian's picnic basket sat primly on one counter, s lid closed and containing, no doubt, her ishes, as clean as every inch of that kitchen.

"Would you like some iced tea?" Mrs. Kilkenny asked uncertainly, adding, "My husband is out."

"That would be lovely." Vivian seated herself at the small kitchen table, a bright spruce-green metal table that set off the surrounding pink rather nicely. "And please call me Vivian. What a pretty kitchen."

"Call me Winnie," Mrs. Kilkenny said unhappily from the cupboard where she was retrieving glasses. Vivian felt a rush of sympathy all over again. It was not easy to be on the receiving end of so much goodwill when one had not had much practice, as evidently Winnie Kilkenny had not. Her manner, so ill-at-ease, so furtive, would have protected her effectively against being befriended. Well, she would just have to get used to it.

"Is Winnie short for Winifred?"

"No, it's not."

"Is Winnie a popular name in the South? You have the loveliest Southern accent, if I'm not mistaken."

"Thank you," the older woman said faintly. "I don't know whether Winnie is especially a Southern name." She brought tall iced tea glasses and long thin spoons and hovered uncertainly at the corner of the table.

"I've never been to the South. I have no ide[ ]what it's like. Do you go back often?"

"It's been a long time." Winnie Kilkenny spotted the sugar bowl on a far counter and went for it gratefully.

"It's one of the only areas of the country where we don't have relatives, so I have no excuse to go there. A lot of our people are either in California or Kansas, somehow."

"I've never been to either," Winnie said, and her expression lightened.

"Do you miss the South?"

"I haven't thought about it," she said. She sat at last, across from Vivian, who picked up an empty glass and held it up.

"I think we've forgotten something," Vivian said, and Winnie burst out, "Oh, how silly of me!"

"Please," Vivian waved this off with a laugh. "Last week we forgot one of our own children at church. We'd taken two cars and both thought the other had Olivia. We didn't figure it out until we sat down to dinner half an hour later!"

Mrs. Kilkenny actually smiled. She rose and went to the refrigerator, bringing back a glass pitcher of tea that glowed amber in the afternoon sun. She poured, smiling shyly as Vivian continued her story. "Olivia didn't even know she'd been left. She was playing with some children in the fellowship hall, happy as a clam, while the deacons were counting the offering.

hen Charlie—my husband—showed up and told
her what happened, thinking she'd find it funny,
and she burst into tears!"

Mrs. Kilkenny made a sympathetic little sound
through her smile.

"You'd have thought we'd left her in a forest
for hours, the way she carried on. We don't know
about that one—so sensitive, too sensitive really.
None of the others gave us any experience with
that."

"You say you have how many?" Winnie
Kilkenny ventured to ask. She sat again, watch-
ing Vivian raptly as if she were the Queen of
England.

"Four," Vivian said happily. "Annie's the
oldest, she's just starting to drive—if *she'd* had
an accident, we'd have grounded her for a
month, but who's going to ground me?" They
laughed together. Winnie was pretty, Vivian
realized in surprise. The lines on her face
lightened when she laughed, and her fair skin
flushed a delicate peach. She had petite, wistful
features. "Then there's David—he's twelve—and
Ruby, two years younger than David. She's got
to prove she can do everything the older ones
do. Anything to keep from being lumped in
with the baby—that's Olivia."

Winnie smiled and took a sip, as if she didn't
know what to say. She added several teaspoons
of sugar to her glass and stirred.

"Is Stephen an only child?" Vivian final[ ]
asked, adding sugar to her own glass. She'[ ]
never been a big fan of iced tea, but she would
sooner have walked on coals than deny someone
the pleasure of seeing their hospitality received.

"Yes, he is." Winnie hesitated. "As far as we
know. He's my daughter's son."

"Ah."

"She was only fifteen," Winnie said, looking
down into her glass. "She left soon after. We
don't know where she is."

"I'm sorry; that must be difficult. Fifteen is
such a difficult age," she added, although the
thought of *Annie* ever being in such a predica-
ment was unthinkable. "I'm sure Stephen is
truly blessed to be raised by such loving grand-
parents."

Winnie glanced up furtively and looked down
into her glass again.

"Is that a cast-iron skillet?" Vivian said suddenly. "I've inherited one from a great-aunt, but
I don't have a clue what to do with it. It's all
rusty. I suppose I'll have to throw it out."

"Oh, don't do that!" Winnie sat up. "You can
easily fix that with a little steel wool."

Winnie spoke almost with confidence for the
first time since Vivian had met her, and Vivian
felt her sympathy give way to genuine interest.
She asked Winnie where she'd learned to cook.

"My parents had a diner. The best in Vidalia,

eorgia. I used to work there in the summers, rowing up. My mother did just about everything n cast iron—flapjacks, hash, fried chicken, even chocolate cake. Her fried cheese grits . . . she had a way with fried grits."

There was a light in Winnie's eyes, a smile at her thin lips. Vivian said, "And you've followed in her footsteps."

Winnie seemed to see Vivian again. The light faded, then the smile. She said, "Oh, no. I became a secretary."

She stood and began to clear the iced tea things.

"I only meant—you're carrying on everything she taught you about cooking."

But Winnie would not smile again, not with her eyes, although she sounded sincere at the door when she thanked Vivian for the banana bread.

"May I bring my cast-iron skillet sometime? Perhaps you'd tell me whether it's really salvageable. We've been using it as a doorstop in the garage."

Winnie hesitated and looked round, as if seeking permission from some invisible source. Then she said that yes, she would be happy to take a look at Vivian's skillet. And then, after another pause, she wrote her phone number down on a piece of paper and handed it to Vivian. Vivian took it smiling and went on her

way, her basket of things in her arms, feelir
that surely it was a good thing for Winnr
Kilkenny that she had crashed into her—wha
was a minor accident compared to unremitting
loneliness? For Winnie was a lonely woman, as
surely as if she'd been living alone in that house
for a hundred years, surrounded by rose briars.
Of that Vivian was certain.

"They were friends for several years at least,"
Aunt Rubina said. "I remember Winnie coming
with Vivian to one or two things at church, the
Annual Women's Tea perhaps."

The lasagna was gone, and they'd finished
their rhubarb crumble. Olivia balled up her
napkin.

"Mrs. Kilkenny mentioned Ruby a couple of
times," she said. "I wondered why Ruby, and
not—" but Aunt Rubina interrupted.

"Come to think of it, I think there was some
sort of problem with Mr. Kilkenny. Some sort of
falling-out between him and Vivian. I don't
know if I ever knew the details, but I wonder if
that's why the whole friendship fell off."

"It seems odd," Olivia said. "Mother was never
one to let things go unresolved."

"Vivian wasn't always happy with how things
were in that home," Rubina said slowly. "She
had her suspicions. I don't even remember why I
think that . . . I don't recall her saying anything

specific. It was just so long ago. Does it matter now?"

Olivia didn't know how to answer. It mattered to Mrs. Kilkenny, but why should that matter to Olivia? "I suppose not," she said. "I suppose I'm just interested because . . . here's this old woman who knew Mother and maybe knew things about her that I don't. Anything anyone can tell me about her—"

She had to stop.

Aunt Rubina said simply, "I know."

They heard a car door slam shut.

Rubina jumped up. "Barbara mustn't see this," she said. She began tossing Olivia's dishes into the sink and swathing the lasagna pan in tinfoil.

Olivia gave her nose a hasty wipe with her wadded-up napkin and stood, too. "Won't she realize there's a lot of lasagna missing?"

"I'll just say I was extra hungry."

They heard the screen door slap shut. Olivia whispered, "I'm allowed to know about the rhubarb crumble, right?"

Aunt Barbara sailed in—as she always did—with the force of a minor weather front. She dropped her handbag on the nearest chair and came forward to accept a kiss on the cheek from Olivia.

"Rhubarb crumble? Betty Sloot brought rhubarb pie tonight with a cardboard crust like somebody kneaded it all day." She was pulling

195

her large rhinestone clip earrings from her ear and tossing them on the counter, inspecting the jars Olivia had brought. As lovely as it was to sit and be served by Aunt Rubina, Olivia was strangely glad to be stirred by Aunt Barbara's brisk gales. She let the torrent of hospital news wash over her, and felt for the first time that perhaps living with Aunt Barbara was not the *constant* trial she'd always imagined it to be for Aunt Rubina.

"I'm off," she said after a few minutes, when the torrent let up. "I'll leave the jars. You'll need them in August for the tomatoes, anyway."

The aunts followed her down the steps and out to the Olds.

"Let us know if there's anything else we can bring Friday," Aunt Barbara said.

Olivia waved through the open window as she drove off. At the turn in the gravel drive, she paused to look back and watch the two old ladies make their way up the steps again. They were slow but steady and looked no older than usual. For now that was enough. She drove home under the big fading sky and tried to hold on to that thought.

10

Winnie Kilkenny could not possibly be the only person in the world who made an authentic shrimp creole.

In spite of the slab of lasagna in her stomach, Olivia finished off the soufflé at home (which, after all, was mostly air, she told herself) and spent the evening looking through Vivian's cookbooks for shrimp creole recipes. When that yielded nothing, she lugged a stack of back issues of *Food & Wine* and *Bon Appétit* from Vivian's office down to the coffee table. She worked her way through the stack while they watched the late news. Ruby was subbing for the usual evening weatherman—things were quiet, no fronts coming or going, just hot days and cloudless skies—and Olivia wondered why. Doris was right: she should have had the evening spot by now, but still she was the noon person, still she was filling in here and there for whomever needed it. Did she even have an agent? Olivia asked Father, but he didn't know. The news ended, and they watched a Western while Olivia flipped through every issue, scanning the tables of contents, the indices.

She dragged more issues to work the next day,

but her first order of business was to email D.
and ask whether Janet Rodriguez had any fc
allergies or extreme dislikes that Olivia shou
know about. She gave him a list of prompts (gree
peppers, peanuts, garlic, red meat, olives, dairy
products) based on past experiences when he'd
failed to tell them of a girlfriend's lactose
intolerance or aversion to stuffed peppers or
moral objections to veal. Vivian had always been
able to deal with these last-minute revelations
gracefully, tossing together a gourmet dinner
salad with whatever was on hand or doing
something elegant with a simple chicken breast.
Olivia was not up to such improvisations. She
had to make this clear to David, and she had to
do it without sounding alarmist, or he would
disregard her entire message and tell her to
calm down. Nothing made her foam at the
mouth like being told by David to calm down.
He wrote back midmorning:

Anything goes.

She spent the rest of the morning playing
around with the Crossword Creator on Marjean's
computer, incorporating avocado trivia into a
puzzle for National Avocado Day. (The seniors
who ate on site loved crosswords.) After lunch,
when Olivia was sure the last of the volunteers
had trickled back in from their deliveries and

e their merry ways, she went to the kitchen to
her ginger ale from one of the refrigerators.
verything fine on the routes today?" she
sked Doris.

"Jim dandy," Doris said, without looking up
from her daily record book. Olivia left quickly
before she could give in to the temptation to ask
Doris if she knew whether Ruby had an agent.

By the afternoon's end she had found three
shrimp creole recipes that looked promising,
although none that mentioned juniper berries.
She would try them out next week because the
weekend was already booked: tomorrow night
was Greek, Saturday dinner was at the aunts' . . .
Sunday she couldn't remember. She might be
able to swing this on Sunday. If she skipped
church again, she could get all three creole
recipes going at once and have a taste test that
noon, with everyone voting for their favorite
recipe at the end of dinner. Olivia would then
publish the winning recipe, and "Stumped in
Beadle County" would have to be satisfied.

She spent the evening reviewing tomorrow
night's menu to get Greek back into her head,
and after watching Ruby on the late news again,
she headed out to do the grocery shopping. She
stood in the produce department, hefting the
garlic bulbs one by one, fingering the pearl
onions in their papery skins, and felt herself
slowly relax.

She remembered that tomorrow she w~~
leave work at noon, and with that thought
bagged and weighed the pearl onions gratefully

Marjean had been very nice when she'd aske~
for Friday afternoon off. "I'm making a huge
family dinner," Olivia had said, adding, to give
weight to the event, "My brother is bringing his
new girlfriend home for the first time." She
didn't add that they'd met so many of his girlfriends over the years that the names were
being recycled. (This would be the second Janet,
to the best of Olivia's recollection; at least it
wasn't another Karen. There had been four
Karens, or actually two Karens, a Caren, and a
Karyn.) No, the real importance of the event,
aside from her plan to announce that she'd
passed her defense, was that it was the first time
they would all be together for a meal since the
week of the funeral. She didn't want to go into
all that with Marjean.

"New girlfriend, huh? Pretty serious?" Marjean
asked.

"Well, that's hard to say." *Serious for the girlfriend, maybe,* but the stab of sympathy that
normally would have followed this thought
didn't come. She just didn't have the energy to
feel sorry about the heartache some woman
she'd never met was inevitably going to endure.
Caveat emptor, as Harry was fond of saying.

She finished up in produce—fresh dill, fresh

ley, what seemed like a bale of spinach—
worked her way over to feta cheese. Olivia
d always liked grocery shopping late at night
a deserted store. The aisles seemed wider, the
ighting brighter, the selection infinite. She
could take her time and compare every brand of
olive oil if she wanted, stand transfixed before
jars of artichoke hearts, traipse back and forth
between the cans of chickpeas in aisle five and
the tubs of hummus in the refrigerator section
until she'd decided to her satisfaction whether to
make the hummus from scratch or buy ready-
made. (She'd chance it and go homemade, though
that meant adding tahini to the list. Maybe this
time she'd get the consistency right.) She found it
calming, the whole experience, no matter how
tired she was, and sometimes back in graduate
school she'd taken thirty minutes at midnight to
buy one package of pasta.

She'd taken Harry on these late-night grocery
expeditions once or twice, but he'd proven too
impatient. He wanted to make every trip to the
grocery store a surgical strike: get in, get out.
Eyes on the prize. Just grab the pasta in the green
box because he'd seen it before a million times,
didn't matter if it was imported or domestic,
didn't matter if it was overpriced. Could the
difference of twenty cents be worth the time she
put into scrutinizing the entire pasta section?
Was not her time more valuable than that?

"You mean *your* time," she'd said. "I'm perfectly happy to scrutinize."

"It's one o'clock in the morning, and I'm *starving*," he finally said, plaintively, and after that she usually left him watching videos in whoever's apartment she was going to be cooking (generally hers) while she made the grocery run herself. This worked well because he was willing to start the video over once she arrived. He said he liked knowing what was going to happen and watching her reaction.

He'd sounded plaintive today, in his latest email. He was still asking to come to the family dinner Friday night. If he caught a flight out of Columbus after his last tutorial and changed planes in Chicago, he could be in Sioux Falls by four. She'd forced herself to respond:

Please, not this time. It's the first time David's been back since the funeral, plus we're meeting his flavor of the month . . . it's already giving me a headache.

Soon though, okay?

Now she tossed two packages of pita bread into the cart and strolled over to the meat department to console herself among the cellophane packages of raw beef. An instrumental arrangement of "Girl from Ipanema" played over the sound system. Stores always seemed to play such random things late at night, old-timer songs that nobody listened to anymore, but Olivia found them pleasant in a bland, powder-blue, Lawrence Welkian sort of way. It freed her up to think about beef chuck versus round. She was just deciding to go with the chuck and thinking how Harry would love this meal, if only he were invited, which he wasn't, when a voice behind her said, "Isn't it past your bedtime?"

It was Annie, pushing a cart full of cans of chunk chicken, hard cheeses, a head of iceberg lettuce. A long loaf of French bread was sticking out of the child seat. Annie's face was pale and a little puffy.

"What on earth are you doing here?"

"Late at night's been good this week. The nausea left from supper sort of wanes, and I get really hungry starting around ten o'clock."

"Hungry for a sandwich, I take it."

"Hungry for a bottle of Italian dressing, and if there happens to be a sandwich around it, that's fine with me."

Olivia said, "Iceberg lettuce has no nutritional value whatsoever. If you got a head of green leaf, or some spinach—"

"I know how to feed myself," Annie snapped. "I just wanted a lettuce that's crisp and functional and won't add a lot of distracting flavor. There's plenty of nutritional value here. See the tomato?

And the cheese, that's dairy, and then there's all the protein from the chicken. You get pregnant and everybody acts like you've lost your brain."

"Sorry, I just—"

"The doctor said that I should eat anything I can keep down," she said. Olivia realized with some alarm that Annie looked near to tears. The puffy flesh around her eyes flushed pink; the rest of her face seemed paler than ever. "She said even potato chips were better than nothing, if I could just keep them down."

"Of course, you're right," Olivia said, trying not to sound placating. "You're right, of course. And a sandwich is actually a very good choice. You know, pizza can be very nutritious."

"That's true." Annie sniffled just a little and looked thoughtfully off in the direction of the frozen foods. "Those little mini pizza snacks aren't half bad . . ."

She sniffled again, and Olivia was relieved to see that the tears shining in Annie's eyes had receded. Olivia was all for venting, but not in a grocery store, and especially not in a deserted one late at night. It would violate the strange combination of public calm and private errand that she found so soothing. "Are you going to be able to eat tomorrow night?" she asked. "At dinner, I mean."

Annie shrugged. "Probably. If I can't, you save some out for me and I'll scarf it down later."

She looked into Olivia's cart for the first time. "I'm not being very useful," she said.

"Well, you just take care of yourself," Olivia said, because that was what she was supposed to say. Frankly, the whole pregnancy thing still seemed unreal to her. Unreal, and irksome. It was almost hard not to believe that if Annie would just put her mind to it, she could set the whole pregnancy aside for a while and then take it up again when everyone was better equipped to deal with it.

Annie was watching her face a little unsurely, and for one moment Olivia feared that she had read her thoughts.

"I might tell everyone tomorrow night," Annie said.

"Oh, that's wonderful," Olivia burst out, relieved. Her next thought was that pregnancy probably trumped a dissertation defense. "But are you sure? In front of David's girlfriend and all? She's a stranger."

"I stopped taking David's girlfriends into account years ago. Anyway, if I wait any longer Aunt Barbara will figure it out on her own, which I can't stand. Remember when I was pregnant with Abby?"

Olivia barely heard her. Even a *second* pregnancy? she was thinking, and a *first* dissertation defense? Guilt immediately oppressed her. Annie and Richard had tried for so long.

But even *Annie* hadn't wanted this now; it was almost cause for consolation, not rejoicing.

Annie was saying, "I should probably tell Father first, alone. I don't know. I don't have the energy for all this, but it's time to get it over with."

"Does Ruby already know?"

"Just you. You and Richard. And Abby. We finally talked to Abby. That's one reason to tell everyone else: she's not going to be able to hold out for long."

It was so rare for Olivia to be the first and only one to know anything (Richard and Abby didn't count); usually she was the last. She should have been enjoying it the past few days, going out of her way to be the supportive one for a change, perhaps even reciprocating by sharing her news with Annie. It was too late for that now. Annie might feel obligated to do something to make the evening a celebration for Olivia, and Annie had precious little energy for that sort of thing these days. Olivia realized for the first time that she herself was making her own celebration dinner (now destined to be shared with Annie's pregnancy). She looked down at the list in her hand, and suddenly the task of trucking about the store finding tahini and bottled grape leaves seemed both insurmountable and superfluous.

"You look done for," Annie said unflatteringly. "Are you coming? I'm heading to the checkout."

"Just a few more things. You better go on without me."

"Look, I'm not up to cooking, but we could pick something up. What about dessert?"

"Aunt Rubina's doing her frozen pink dessert."

"Oh. Of course. Well, if you think of something, let me know. It's not fair for this all to be on you."

But Annie looked distracted even as she said this, and Olivia didn't feel it was necessary to offer assurances. She had an impulse to give Annie a hug—not because she was feeling at all close to her sister, but because she wished she were—but Annie, perhaps on a prescient impulse of her own, gave a wave and pushed off.

Olivia returned the hummus ingredients she'd gathered thus far and bought two ready-made tubs from the refrigerator section.

By the time she slogged home and put all the groceries away, she was wondering how she'd have the energy to make dinner for ten tomorrow night, let alone three batches of shrimp creole later in the weekend. What was she thinking? Half the family didn't even like spicy-hot foods, and anyway "Stumped" must have tried a zillion creole recipes over the years trying to satisfy her juniper-berry-obsessed husband. One more wrong recipe was going to mean nothing. Olivia lay awake for a long time trying to compose a reply in her head:

Dear Stumped:

While I'm afraid I can't lay my hands on the recipe Vivian had intended to publish, I can offer the following completely unrelated recipe for Greek Stifado.

When she awoke the next morning, it was with the distinct impression that she'd been arguing with Annie's baby all night. All she could remember was the disembodied line, "I am merely advocating for Annie"; she didn't even know whether these were her words or the baby's.

The rest of the morning jerked along in an equally disorienting vein, mainly because of the walkie-talkies. Leroy Wheeler, son of the deceased Mr. Wheeler from route 5, had donated a whole box of them in case the volunteers found them useful on the routes. The guy from Wheeler Amoco who brought them by said they were upgrading to cell phones anyway. Everyone—Doris, the volunteers, a couple of seniors who always arrived early for lunch—spent a good deal of time experimenting with them. Even Lydia learned how to press the talk button and speak into the walkie-talkie, although she kept forgetting to release the button when it was her turn to listen. Random utterances crackled from

unit perched next to Olivia's computer
roughout the morning until she felt as if she
were stationed on Mars, listening to communi-
cations from Earth that had nothing to do with
her.

She tried to start a new crossword puzzle for
the seniors but was not inspired, so she checked
her email instead (nothing).

She pulled out the summer issue 1996 file,
thought better of it, and put it away without opening it.

Still no email.

The list of volunteers for next week was
already printed out.

Just before the volunteers were due to start
arriving, Olivia picked up her walkie-talkie and
went to the kitchen.

"You know, maybe I should deliver a meal
today," she said to Doris, "just so we can—"

"Wait." Doris wiped her hands on her apron
and picked up her own walkie-talkie nervously.
"Go down the hall and tell me. I need to practice
if I'm going to be home base whenever you're
out."

Olivia obediently turned and walked down the
hall toward her office, pushed the call button.
"Maybe I should deliver a meal today just so we
can try out the walkie-talkies in the field, so to
speak. Before we let the volunteers loose with
them on Monday."

There was a momentary lag, then a burst static. "Sounds good. Just one meal?"

It should have sounded like a voice from telephone, Olivia thought, *but it did not.* It wa. hollowed out, perfectly rendered but distinctly distant. Olivia imagined Doris crouched at the end of one of the concrete culverts Father wrote about in his gravel manual, herself at the other end, bent over, eyes and ears straining.

She pushed the button. "Yes, just one. The routes are really well covered today."

Another lag, less static. "Whose meal do you want me to pull?"

Olivia waited a moment in case she could talk herself out of it. She couldn't. "Give me Winnie Kilkenny's."

In the kitchen, Olivia slid the lone meal into a hot pack and picked up a cold meal sack. All the way to the hardware store—where she picked up one item—and on to Mrs. Kilkenny's, Olivia listened to Doris give Lydia another lesson on the walkie-talkie. She pulled up to the curb at Mrs. Kilkenny's.

"Doris? Olivia here. Can you hear me?"

"Loud and clear."

"I'm going in to the client now. We probably shouldn't use the walkie-talkies unless we really need to."

"Roger that."

Olivia wondered how she could say that with-

laughing. It made her like Doris a tiny bit
~re than she had. She gathered the walkie-
~kie and the hot and cold meals and her small
~aper sack from the hardware store and went up
~he walk to the house.

The door opened before she could ring the
bell. Mrs. Kilkenny looked up at her, silent, sad,
unsurprised. She stood back while Olivia
opened the screen door and stepped inside. Olivia
watched her face for permission before
moving past her to set the meals down in the
living room. When she turned back, she found
Mrs. Kilkenny just a few steps away, holding her
elbows.

She held up the paper sack, cleared her throat.
"I've brought the steel wool for your cast-iron
skillet."

She expected Mrs. Kilkenny to demur, to say
she shouldn't have; instead she simply led the
way to the kitchen. Light streamed in from the
window over the sink, but it seemed to Olivia
that nothing could brighten those sad pink
fixtures. Olivia dropped the sack and the hot
pack and walkie-talkie on the table and crossed
to the stove, looked into the massive skillet. The
thing could easily kill an ox.

"Do we do this in the sink?"

Mrs. Kilkenny nodded. Olivia carried the
skillet with both hands to the sink and pulled
the steel wool from the paper sack.

"You'll need some salt," Mrs. Kilkenny s<del></del>
She went to a nearby cupboard over the coun<del></del>
and rummaged. "This is all I have. I don't kno<del></del>
if it's still salty, even."

Olivia took the container of Morton's and
shook it to no effect, whacked it against the
counter a few times to loosen the salt inside. "It
doesn't matter if it's salty, does it? Just that it's
abrasive?"

"That's right."

She handed it back to Mrs. Kilkenny, who
poured a measure of salt into the skillet and ran
a little water. "Good and sludgy," she said.

Olivia began to scrub. It was strangely satisfying work. She could bear down and scour as hard
as she liked. The iron was hard, pressure couldn't
damage it, friction couldn't—only rust. And
under the rust it was a good strong pan. She
wondered how it had come to rust in the first
place: just years of lying dormant, or had Winnie
Kilkenny, usually so vigilant, put it away damp,
failed to dry and oil it? She scrubbed, relished
the gritty feel of salt and steel excoriating the
iron and the iron pushing back, imagined the salt
burning through the rust until the iron was pure.
Mrs. Kilkenny stayed at her elbow, peering into
the pan. After a time Olivia spoke.

"The other day I left so abruptly, and right
after giving news like that. I guess I was upset
myself."

ne felt Mrs. Kilkenny's eyes on her face, just a second. "Of course, you were."

"It was very wrong of me, and I'm sorry."

"Of course. There's no need to apologize."

Olivia ran the water, rinsed out the skillet, then poured in more salt and water. The hardest part was around the inside edge. She dug in. "I don't know what happened between you and my mother. I'm not used to anyone being angry with her, outside the usual family stuff. That doesn't mean—" She bore down on a stubborn patch. "For all I know, you had good reason to be angry. My mother was certainly capable of—she certainly knew how to interfere."

Mrs. Kilkenny actually laughed a very little bit. "She did interfere. She did do that. And I welcomed it, up until the end." She let out a small sigh. "Then she did what I should have done myself. It's hard to forgive someone for that." Olivia rinsed out the pan again. Mrs. Kilkenny went to a nearby drawer and pulled out a flour sack towel. Olivia hauled the dripping skillet up by the handle with one hand, resting it on end against the edge of the sink, and wiped it down.

"Can I ask what she did, Mrs. Kilkenny?"

Mrs. Kilkenny watched while Olivia turned the towel to find dry spots. They both studied the pan.

"Beautiful," Mrs. Kilkenny said, and Olivia

was foolishly proud. "Take it to the table. get the oil." She brought a bottle of vegetable and another clean rag, then dragged one of t. green metal chairs out from the table and sa Olivia, still standing, poured a little oil into the skillet and began to rub it down with the rag, slowly.

"I had a daughter," Mrs. Kilkenny said at last. "Long before Vivian came along. I had a daughter named Samantha, named for my best friend growing up, Samantha Fairchild. So long ago." She was smiling down at the skillet, and Olivia suddenly wondered if dipping into the past like this would confuse Mrs. Kilkenny, if she would again forget who Olivia was. The prospect was both frightening and alluring: in her confusion, Mrs. Kilkenny could do what Olivia could not, and summon Vivian herself. "I lived with that Samantha for a time, you know, after she was married and living in Macon, and I was in secretarial school there. And then . . ." She was no longer smiling. "Then I was in Atlanta, working for a lawyer. And after I left Atlanta, I never saw her again. That first Samantha."

"I'm sorry," Olivia said.

"It was my own fault," Mrs. Kilkenny said. "I went to New York to have a baby. I wasn't married. A lot of things—so many things seemed to happen in those days that I didn't choose, but they happened anyway. I have always wondered

's just as bad *letting* them happen as if I
1 chosen them myself. I think that it is just as
.d."

"Mrs. Kilkenny, I'm sure that's not true."

"I didn't know how to stop things, you see,"
she said, looking up at Olivia earnestly. "I have
never known how to stop things. My greatest
sins have been sins of omission."

"We're all guilty of those," Olivia said, but Mrs.
Kilkenny folded her hands and looked away.
Olivia began rubbing the skillet again, grateful to
have something to look at other than Mrs.
Kilkenny. A black patina shone around the flat
patches where Olivia had removed rust.

"I named the baby Samantha. She even looked
a little like Samantha, silvery-blond curls. She
was more like Samantha than she was like me,
that's the truth—a big, beautiful baby, so strong."
Winnie gave another low laugh. "Those who talk
about taking candy from a baby, they never tried
it with my Samantha. She had a strong little grip,
and she knew her own mind from the start. I
always thought that would be a good thing. She
wasn't afraid like me. She wasn't shy." Winnie
sighed. "I married a man in New York. He
thought I was a widow; he thought I had a husband killed in the war. I suppose that was one
bad thing I did that didn't just happen." She
looked up at Olivia and nodded. "I lied about
being a widow. I couldn't bear for anyone to

215

know the truth. He found out, a while after w
moved out here. He was a salesman, you kno
traveled a lot to Omaha, out to Rapid. But eve
year he'd go down to the national conference i.
Atlanta. Once when he was there, he went to
Vidalia to look up my people. That's how he
found out. And he never forgave me."

"I'm so sorry."

Mrs. Kilkenny lifted the fingers of one hand
dismissively. "I could live with that. I deserved it.
But he never forgave my Samantha either, just
for being. Just for existing. The sins of the
mother." She looked across the room at nothing;
the lines on her face had deepened. "The two of
them, my daughter and my husband, they were
not compatible from the start, and then after he
found out it was much worse. He was so strict. I
thought for a time maybe she needed that,
maybe someone strong needed strong rules. That
it would keep her safe from what happened to
me. But now I look back, it was all wrong, even
before—" She looked into Olivia's face again,
put a hand on Olivia's forearm, and gripped it
with a sudden strength. Olivia stopped rubbing.
"I didn't know what was going on," she said.
"Under my own roof, and I swear I had no idea."

Olivia went cold. She forced herself to nod.

"I've gone over it a thousand times, how I
could have missed it. Did I *choose* to be blind?
Was I that weak a mother? Or just stupid,

criminally naïve . . . All I knew then was, suddenly she was different. She was sullen instead of strong, she wasn't rebelling anymore, she wasn't—anything. She wasn't even going to school most days. But then she would run off two, three days at a time, come back cowed. Those were practice times, I think. And then she was pregnant. Suddenly she was my baby again; she was sick, and I cared for her. Mr. Kilkenny left her alone then. Of course, I didn't understand what that really meant. I just thought, he knows he doesn't have to be strict anymore. There's no point. All those months she didn't talk much, but she let me take care of her; she seemed to be getting better. I thought maybe we were over the worst of it. I thought, we can raise this baby together. One day when the baby was a month old she left him sleeping in her room while I was out back picking rhubarb. I came in, my hands all stained from the rhubarb, found the baby crying and Samantha gone. I knew she was really gone this time. That's how I lost my second Samantha." Her blue eyes looking into Olivia's were so bright Olivia felt stinging in her own. "But I still had the baby. She trusted me that much, anyway. It was more than I deserved."

Olivia nodded. Somehow she had come to be sitting, still clutching the rag.

"Wait here." Mrs. Kilkenny rose and left the room, returning with a framed photograph of a young man in a blue cap and gown. She handed it to Olivia. "Stephen," she said.

"He's very good-looking," Olivia said. He was, in a pale, slightly pretty way. His smile was tentative, his shoulders leaned forward a little under the heavy gown. The tassel on his cap was yellow.

"Engineering?" Olivia asked, trying to remember Father's regalia.

"Biology. He's a health inspector for the state now." Olivia glanced up and saw that Mrs. Kilkenny was smiling tremulously at the photograph, her eyes still full beneath a furrowed brow. The woman took a breath, and when she spoke again her voice was steadier. "Goes around to restaurants, cafes; they call him in for all manner of food safety incidents. He's done very well. He got a promotion, had to move to Pierre. Now he supervises I don't know how many others."

So that's a good enough ending, Olivia thought. At least for Stephen. She let out a breath herself and handed back the picture.

"I have a more recent one, something he just sent." She disappeared into the dining room again and returned with a loose photo of Stephen and several other men and women in hiking gear, against a backdrop of pines. "He hikes in the Hills every chance he gets."

He was older in this photo, a little more solidly

t, and Olivia remembered he was about
rty-two, Ruby's age. The smile this time was
onfident although not lighthearted. Still study-
ng the photo, Olivia asked, "What did my
mother—how did you almost lose him?"

Mrs. Kilkenny sat again.

"My husband was strict with Stephen, too, but
things weren't as bad by then. Vivian couldn't
have realized that. Stephen was never rebellious,
he knew to lay low until things got better, and
some of the time they even got along. Did things
together. My husband always disciplined physically, mind. But it wasn't enough that most
people would notice. Vivian wouldn't have
done anything if she hadn't been so upset about
Ruby."

"Ruby?"

Mrs. Kilkenny turned her face away for a
moment, as if out of a sense of delicacy. "That
was right when your parents found out what
happened. And of course, they couldn't do anything about it; those things can be so hard to
prove. If I hadn't known what was going on in
my own house . . ." Her voice trailed off
momentarily. "Vivian was beside herself when
they learned the charges would be dropped."

"What are you talking about? What did Ruby
do?"

Mrs. Kilkenny looked at Olivia in surprise. "Not
Ruby, that coach. The one who molested her."

Olivia couldn't move, couldn't even shake head.

Mrs. Kilkenny's eyes widened. "Surely you—but I assumed you knew all about that."

The walkie-talkie on the table crackled to life, and Olivia started as if it were a snake. She forced herself to pick it up, fumbled for the right button. "Yes?" she said.

Doris's voice pierced the airwaves. "Olivia? Are you coming back soon?"

Olivia could hardly think with Mrs. Kilkenny watching her with that expression on her face. She wanted to turn away. "Is there a problem?" she said finally.

"No problem, but your sister's here waiting to see you."

"Annie?"

Even the static couldn't distort the excitement in Doris's voice. "Ruby Tschetter."

"Ruby's there? What does she want?"

"I don't know, but she's been in your office for twenty minutes."

Twenty minutes was longer than Ruby had ever waited for anything. Olivia looked at her watch, dazed. It was after twelve. She was supposed to be home stuffing grape leaves by now. She was still waiting for Mrs. Kilkenny's words to sink in and make sense.

"I'll be there as soon as I can, okay? Tell her to wait. Make her wait."

ll try."

The walkie-talkie fell silent.

They looked at each other. Mrs. Kilkenny's lips moved for a moment without sound. "If I've said anything I shouldn't have—"

"Of course not," Olivia said, a little too loudly. She stood, swayed for a moment. She dropped the rag on the table and lifted the skillet, welcomed its heft. It grounded her, and she bore it to the stove. When she put it down she felt weightless again, unmoored. "It's just that I'm the youngest, you know. They tend not to tell the youngest anything. I could be eighty and they wouldn't tell me anything. I'm sorry, I have to go." She gathered the things from the table awkwardly and held them against her chest, went through the kitchen, the dining room, the living room. She was conscious of planting her feet hard to cover her unsteadiness. She stopped at the front door, which was still open, and stared out through the screen. "And then I suppose it was so long ago . . ."

"It was. It was a long time ago. Please don't be upset."

The worst thing would be if Mrs. Kilkenny tried to touch her. Olivia would not be able to keep from pushing her away. She forced a smile and turned.

"Now, don't you worry about a thing, Mrs. Kilkenny," she said. "I'm sorry I have to run off

like this. I'm sure I'll see you next week,
added, though she had no intention of
returning.

"Please do come back. You've been so kind.
hate to think what I've done."

Olivia turned away and pushed through the
screen door. "Not at all. You have a good
weekend, then."

She made it into the front seat and found that
she was clutching, along with everything else,
the oily, blackened rag and the photograph of
Stephen Kilkenny hiking. She dropped everything on the seat beside her. She jerked into gear
and pulled away from the curb but had to slam
on the brakes to avoid hitting a passing car,
which blared its horn. Olivia slammed her fist
against the steering wheel, looked back to see if
she was about to slam into anyone else but
couldn't see, had to swipe at the water in her eyes.
She looked again through a blur and finally
pulled into the street.

11

Olivia sped the whole way back to the Senior
Center, then suddenly slowed when she was one
block away. Instead of turning in at the drive, she
went around the block, as slowly as the minimal

c allowed. It would look as if she had come
ning. She *had* come running. She'd come
ning her whole life. Olivia drove around the
ock a second time, at normal speed, then pulled
ito the parking lot, and found a spot under a
tree. Checking herself in the rearview mirror, she
saw that her eyes had dried out and she looked
fairly normal, if disheveled.

She climbed out of the car. There were no
refurbished Mustang convertibles parked in
sight, nor did she see the ancient sky-blue Skylark
Ruby had kept going since her grad school days.
Maybe Ruby had given up and left. Olivia half
hoped so. She was afraid she'd see something in
Ruby's face that she'd never noticed before but
that had been there all along—something that
bore witness to the truth of what Mrs. Kilkenny
had divulged.

And yet she was barely able to restrain herself
from breaking into a trot as she passed the
kitchen and turned down the hall. She was
nearly as well trained now as when she was
eleven, when the older ones had allowed her the
privilege of waiting on them when they had
friends over. By the time she stepped through the
doorway of her office, she was filled with self-
loathing. The sight of Doris standing there
chatting with Ruby—Ruby sitting in *her* office
chair, of course, balancing a napkin of brownie
crumbs on one bare well-shaped knee—did

nothing to mitigate her irritation. Since v
did Doris *chat?*

"Hi, Livy." Ruby folded the napkin, stood, a
accepted the quick hug that Olivia automatical
gave. She sat again immediately, crossing he
long legs in one fluid motion.

"I was just telling your sister how much we
enjoy her weather reports," Doris said. "None of
this pussyfooting around."

"Isn't that nice," Olivia said.

"I'd better be getting back to work." Doris
smiled once more at Ruby. "I'll get that recipe
written out for you; don't forget to stop by the
kitchen on your way out."

"Perfect," Ruby said, smiling back warmly.

Doris backed out, pulling the door shut with a
quiet, respectful click.

Olivia tossed her purse and the walkie-talkie
and the rest of her ungainly armful onto her desk
and dragged a straight-backed metal chair over
from the corner. "Have a seat," she said flatly.
Ruby rose and switched chairs without comment. "You're getting her brownie recipe?
What's wrong with Mom's?"

"Doris's recipe serves fifty. Sometimes we
have these get-togethers at the station."

"You can't double Mom's recipe?"

"People like sharing recipes," Ruby said.
"Anyway, it was a good brownie." She brought
the folded-up napkin to the corners of her mouth

more, then balled it up and tossed it into
wastebasket three feet away.

livia studied her sister's face. She saw
thing she had not seen before, no haunted
hadows in her eyes, no taut nerve barely visible
along the line of her jaw. *Of course,* she
thought, *it was all so long ago,* but she was
reassured. She wondered if there was any way
Mrs. Kilkenny could have been wrong. "I was
in the middle of a very important conversation
with a client," Olivia said. "Am I supposed
to drop everything because you show up
unannounced?"

Ruby didn't answer; she was paging through
Marjean's Triple Crown Page-a-Day Trivia
Calendar from the corner of Olivia's desk. She
was wearing a long sleeveless top over matching
shorts, all in taupe—a cut that would have hung
utterly without shape on Olivia, and a taupe
that would have been colorless. On Ruby, the
garments draped themselves gracefully over her
slender form, the taupe fairly glowed next to the
rosy tones in Ruby's golden skin. Olivia, wearing
the same khaki skirt for the third time that
week, immediately felt that she'd gained twenty
pounds.

"What is that, silk?" she couldn't help asking.

"Linen. Perfect for humid weather."

"Of course. Aren't you working today?"

"Evidently not."

"In David's honor, I suppose. He's not g——
in until dinner, you know."

"Of course, I know." She was still look——
through the calendar, which drove Olivia cra——
"I just thought I'd drive up early and surpris——
you at work."

"Well. Mission accomplished. To what do I
owe the honor?"

Ruby set down the calendar at last. "My gosh,
you're in a mood." She uncrossed her legs,
stretched, and narrowed her eyes at Olivia
thoughtfully, as if about to continue. Then she
looked past Olivia at something across the room.

Olivia said, "Is this about graduate school, or
grief counseling? Because it isn't necessary
to . . ." But Ruby had risen and was walking
past Olivia to stand before the mirror on the
back of the door. She leaned in, studying herself.
It was odd: in spite of Ruby's looks, or more
likely because of them, Olivia could not
remember ever seeing her study herself in a
mirror. It made her seem vulnerable. Olivia
shifted uneasily. Now Ruby placed the middle
finger of her left hand at the corner of her eye,
massaged the area for a moment, then removed
the finger. She leaned in a little more. "What?"
Olivia said, too loudly. "Do you have something
in your eye?"

"I don't know," Ruby said absently, still
looking.

ivia waited. She was afraid again. Quieter ↴, she said, "Do you want me to take a look?"

Yes," Ruby said, surprising her. Ruby didn't ⨪ove from the mirror, so Olivia rose and went ⨪o her sister.

"Well, look at me already."

Ruby turned to face her, but instead of leaning over took a step back.

"How old would you say I look? I mean, if you didn't know me."

Olivia stared. "You've got to be kidding."

"How old? Be honest."

"I'd say you look six years older than I do, and always will."

Ruby's eyes darkened; Olivia instantly regretted her words. "Seriously, though—"

"Graduate school," Ruby said, crossing her arms.

"What?"

"This is about graduate school. If you don't go back and finish, you'll regret it the rest of your life."

Ah. Of course. Yet—the act of Ruby bothering to give her advice was so unusual, Olivia was intrigued, almost touched. Should she be touched? "Why are you here?" she asked finally. "Why are you telling me this?" *Because I care,* Olivia prompted mentally. *Because you're my sister and I don't want to see you ruin your life.*

227

"Annie asked me to have a word with y[ou,]" Ruby said blithely.

"You idiot," Olivia said. "Annie didn't w[ant] you to *tell* me that. You're doing this all wrong."

"I told her it wouldn't work," Ruby said with [a] shrug.

"Not if you don't do it right. You don't even care that you're not doing this right. You don't even care enough to try to manipulate me like everyone else does. Okay, so let's finish this so we can close the book on Ruby's pathetically transparent attempt to give Olivia somebody else's advice. Regarding graduate school: I don't want to talk about it," she said. "I do not want to talk about it. Maybe, oh, tonight in the middle of dinner I'll want to talk about it, but I do not want to talk about it now. Just because David says—"

"Just because David says something doesn't make it wrong." Ruby spied her purse on the floor next to Olivia's chair and went to retrieve it. "Anyway, you don't want to talk about it, we won't talk about it. I'll let you get back to work."

"Wait—why are you leaving in such a rush? You said you came to town to talk to me."

"And I have talked to you. And now I'm going to see if Annie wants to have lunch."

"Annie doesn't have lunch these days. She has midnight feasts of orgiastic proportions."

"Well, she'll have lunch today."

228

by was at the door, hand on the doorknob.

Why don't *we* have lunch?" Olivia said in spite herself, in spite of almost hating the person standing before her. "I'm almost done here. I'll tell you what I would like to talk about. There's this old lady on one of the routes who Mom used to be friends with, and she keeps asking about you, and I'm wondering if you have any idea why that might be."

"Don't you have a lot of work to do, getting ready for tonight?"

Olivia did not try to resume her train of thought. "Yes. And it might've occurred to you to offer to help." She went back to her desk and sat, pulled up the mouse, and began clicking. Ruby followed. Olivia did not look at her.

"Look," her sister's voice said over her head, "I'll come over this afternoon if it works."

"Whatever."

Out of the corner of her eye she saw Ruby bend toward her. Instinctively Olivia flinched, although it had been years since Ruby or David had knuckled her on the head, and then she felt a hard, quick peck on her cheek—so pointed and unpracticed that it almost hurt. By the time she looked up, Ruby was out the door.

The walkie-talkie on her desk crackled, and Lydia's voice, bright and tinny and faraway, said, "Surprise?"

Olivia reached over and turned it off.

229

• • •

She had told David six-thirty, hoping he'd there by seven, and when by seven-thirty still had not arrived, Olivia caved in to family pressure and peeled the plastic wrap off the platter of hummus and pita bread and stuffed grape leaves that she'd placed on the coffee table. She wouldn't have minded except that for once her presentation had turned out well—the dolmades circling the bowl of hummus like spokes on a wheel, the triangles of pita bread piled casually at either end—and here the guests of honor weren't even around to see it. Not that David would have noticed, she told herself. She perched on the arm of the couch and took a dolmade for herself, eating it over a cocktail napkin. She couldn't stop thinking about Ruby and about how she could find out if what Mrs. Kilkenny said was true. Annie would be the answer, under any other circumstances; she couldn't trouble her now. Other disquieting thoughts surfaced in no particular order, again and again: the spanakopita drying out in the oven, Harry and his precious Penelope, the dissertation news she was still planning to spring at dinner. Annie and Ruby and David and the spanakopita drying out in the oven. Olivia shook her head and tried to turn her attention to Richard, who was giving Abby the ear lecture.

The ear lecture had become a necessary

...iminary to any but the most informal
...netter gatherings. (Tonight was formal, as
...denced by Aunt Barbara's seed pearl neck-
...ce.) Abby possessed the unusual and dubious
...bility to stuff her entire outer ear, from the tip
to the lobe, *inside* her ear. The small nubbin of
flesh that was left where the ear should be gave
her a deformed and forlorn look that could be
most effective on people who had never met her
before, until the ear popped out again ten or
twenty seconds later. She could do it with both
ears, although the right ear always popped out
first.

"You will leave your ears alone," Richard said
now. He had planted Abby between his knees
and hooked his feet together behind hers so she
couldn't get away, which she always loved.
"There will be no ear tricks until and unless the
evening should take such a turn as to render ear
tricks appropriate. Which isn't all that unlikely,"
he said to Annie, who sat beside him looking
studiously away from the platter of appetizers.

Abby asked, "How will I know?"

"You will ask. You will whisper in my or your
mother's ear."

"What if David *wants* me to show my ear
trick?"

"He usually does," Olivia said.

"Then it's fine."

Ruby said from the piano bench where she

sprawled, "David knows how to show a g[...] good time."

"I don't know why such tricks are necessary all at the dinner table," Aunt Barbara said. "The[...] don't do much for my appetite."

Annie shot Aunt Barbara a dark look, but Richard said, "That's a good point. We won't even think about ear tricks until after dinner." He was always more patient with Aunt Barbara than Annie was. He said it was because he wasn't a blood relative. Annie said it was because Aunt Barbara preferred males and he was unconsciously encouraging the favoritism.

"There's a guy at the station who can dislocate both his shoulders at once," Ruby said.

"Who?" Olivia asked, in spite of herself. (She would rather not have shown any interest. Ruby had not shown up to help that afternoon.) "One of the anchors?"

"No, a cameraman. Once he did it at the end of a commercial break and one of his arms got stuck. The station manager had to step in and operate the camera while he flopped his arm around in the background trying to pop it back in. Everyone on air was trying not to laugh—"

"I agree with Aunt Barbara," Annie said. "This sort of conversation doesn't do anything for the appetite."

"Are you still not feeling any better?" Aunt Barbara asked.

"I'm fine."

Aunt Barbara's eyes narrowed, and she was about to speak when Aunt Rubina said at the window, "There's his car."

Olivia headed to the kitchen and everyone else headed to the front door.

It was evident from the start that things were going to go hard for *this* Janet. She was more earnest, though less talkative, than any of David's girlfriends that Olivia could remember, and that was saying something. Almost against her will Olivia began to feel badly for her. The fact that Janet was very petite made her seem even more vulnerable; her head barely came to David's shoulder. Her dark hair was pulled back in a simple ponytail that emphasized the cleanness of her profile, and her entire appearance was unstudied enough that Olivia instantly forgave her for being so pretty. She said sensible enough things, and Olivia was sure she would have liked her if she hadn't had to feel sorry for her.

The others noticed it, too, Olivia was sure. They were just bending over the bowls of egg-lemon soup that Olivia had ladled from Vivian's soup tureen (carefully avoiding a few bits of solidified egg white) when Janet blurted, rather out of the blue, "You're all being so warm and welcoming. It means a lot."

There was an almost palpable disturbance in the air as the conversational flow skipped a beat.

Ruby and Richard ate their soup thoughtfully; Annie sent a slight eyebrow lift Olivia's way.

"We're pleased to have you here," Father said finally.

"Thank you." Janet looked around at everyone, then took a spoonful of her soup as if she'd just remembered it was there.

"David tells us you're a technical writer," Annie said. "I can think of at least two engineers in this room who could use a little help in that department."

"Don't you listen to her," Richard said. "I may not be the best speller in the world, but that's what spell check is for."

"We thought it might be a bit much if we brought the kids, this first time," Janet said. "They're at my mother's for the weekend."

Another ripple. Ruby stood and began to collect empty soup bowls. Olivia said, "Janet, would you like to start the spanakopita? I'm afraid it might be a little dried out."

"Livy thinks there's something wrong with everything she makes," David said, not looking at Olivia. He wrestled with the pie server to loosen a square of spanakopita. It finally came loose, and he placed it carefully on the edge of Janet's plate. Then he began working away at one for himself.

"It's not supposed to be in the oven so long," Olivia said shortly. Annie gave her a look.

avid's always late," Olivia added, so Janet
ould know she wasn't blaming her.

"I've noticed." Janet gave David a dark look
hat was rather more severe than anything his
girlfriends usually allowed themselves. "I didn't
even know we were expected for dinner until he
explained why we weren't stopping to eat on the
road."

"David," Annie said. "You might fill your
guests in on what's happening, you know."

"There was an awful lot to remember today,"
he said. "You should have seen the amount of
stuff two kids need to pack to get through one
weekend."

"How old are your children, Janet?" Aunt
Barbara said politely.

"John is nine and Maria is eight," Janet said.
"David's just wonderful with them, of course."

"There's no 'of course,' " Ruby said. "It must be
a testament to your kids. We've always assumed
David was allergic to children."

Abby said, indignantly, "He's not allergic to
me."

David leaned across Richard and Annie to
look at his niece. "John is going to love that thing
you do with your ears. He's got this thing he
does with his toes."

"Later," Annie said sharply.

"Abby, Maria cannot wait to meet you," Janet
said. "She has six other cousins, but they're all

boys, so they just don't count as far as she's c
cerned."

Another pulse. Aunt Barbara actually froz
with her glass halfway to her lips.

"Livy, everything's delicious," David said, but
he still wasn't looking at her. He was looking into
his water glass and swishing the ice around. "I
don't know why you're wasting your time in
graduate school when you can cook like this."

"Janet," Annie said, "what do you mean when
you say—"

"Now you're telling me *not* to go back to
graduate school?" Olivia could not help raising
her voice. She took a deep breath and stood, but
it didn't have the desired effect; no one turned
to her in hushed expectation. Why should they?
She got up a million times during any given
meal to go to the kitchen.

She cleared her throat. "For your information—"

"I'd like to make an announcement," David
said.

"*I'm* making an announcement," Olivia said.

"Janet and I were married last weekend."

Someone's fork clattered against a plate. It was
Janet's fork, Olivia realized numbly. Janet—
David's *wife?*—was looking at him in absolute
horror. "You hadn't *told* them?"

"I thought we should tell them together."

"You hadn't *TOLD* them?"

was standing. Half the family were stand-
although Olivia couldn't remember how
y got that way. Annie said, "You got married
thout bothering to *tell* us?"

"You said they were all excited to meet me!"
Janet stood over David, flinging her hands wildly
as she spoke, and petite as she was, she looked
dangerous, her dark eyes wide and flashing.

David said, in a voice that was not quite the
calm voice that drove Olivia mad—in fact, a
voice she could almost believe to be (if it hadn't
been David) *nervous*—"They *were* excited to
meet you. They just didn't know yet that we—"

"I think I'd better go wait in the car."

"Now then," Father began, but it was apparent
that she didn't even hear him.

"I'm so sorry, all of you—what you must be
thinking!" Janet rushed from the room in tears.
They watched her go in stunned silence—the
very silence Olivia had hoped to elicit. She was
still trying to take it in: *David was somebody's
husband?*

David stood without a word and started after
Janet, but Annie caught his arm as he passed.
"You couldn't bother telling us this was going
on in your life? This is how we find out?"

Even Olivia was surprised at Annie's vehe-
mence. Her face was scarlet.

"Let's all calm down," Father said.

"This is insane," Annie said. "This is not how

237

adults behave! You would never have p[...]
something like this if Mom were alive, trea[...]
us like—"

"This has nothing to do with Mom," Dav[...]
said. "Leave her out of it."

Annie made a choked noise, like a sob. "It is
impossible to leave her out of it; she hasn't been
gone four months. She's—she's behind everything, she might as well be standing in the
corner."

"It's nobody's business if I want to get married," David said loudly.

"Mom dies and you're suddenly absolved of
—of every sort of consideration, you can just
treat us however the hell you want—"

"Shut up, Annie."

"David, *be silent,*" Aunt Barbara said in a
terrible voice—*to her darling David,* Olivia
marveled. "Your sister is pregnant and you will
stop upsetting her *this instant.*"

Everyone gaped at her words. Annie's face,
blotchy and red, was the most incredulous of
all.

"Annie?" Father said finally. "Is this true?" He
started to make his way toward her through the
maze of pushed-back chairs.

She burst into tears and fled to the kitchen. A
moment later they heard her footsteps on the
stairs.

No one moved as David left the dining room

headed through the living room to the front
ry. It was as if they were allowed to move
ly one at a time, Olivia thought, or something
ould break. They heard the door open and
close.

Olivia sat.

Abigail had begun wailing at some point; they
only now all seemed to realize it. Richard picked
her up and carried her to Father's office.

"I'll see if Annie's all right," Aunt Barbara said.

Olivia pulled at Ruby's hand. "Shouldn't we
stop her?" she whispered, but Ruby looked as
dazed as anyone. The two of them finally crept
up the stairs after Aunt Barbara, and down the
hall to Olivia's room—the room that used to be
Annie's, the room with the big bed. They peeked
in the door. Annie's head was in Aunt Barbara's
lap and she was hanging on as if Aunt Barbara's
waist were a life preserver. They could just make
out the sound of Aunt Barbara's voice over
Annie's sobs.

"Now I've seen everything," Ruby whispered
to Olivia as they crept back downstairs.

Father and Aunt Rubina were sitting at the
table, not eating. Ruby and Olivia sat, too. They
all four looked at one another helplessly.

"Nobody's even tried the stew," Olivia said
finally.

Ruby took the lid off the stew and passed it
down to Father, who put some on his plate. Olivia

sent down the bowl of feta cheese to sprink[l]
top. She wondered desperately what Viv
would have to say about all this.

"That poor girl," Aunt Rubina said.

"I think I'll make up a plate for her," Olivia said
She added a couple of stuffed grape leaves to
Janet's plate and a little beef from the stew,
several perfect pearl onions rolling in the savory
sauce. Ruby brought a clean knife and fork and
wrapped them in a clean napkin. Olivia handed
her the plate to take to the car.

"What about David?" Aunt Rubina said.

"He can get his own damn dinner," Olivia said.

Ruby started laughing.

"What's so funny?"

"Our brother has two children," she said.
"*That's* something to think about." She left.

The three of them started eating, slowly. Father
closed his eyes and sighed between bites.

"Unbelievable," he said.

"Which?" Olivia said. "David being married,
or Annie being pregnant, or David having two
children all of a sudden?"

Father shook his head. "I just meant, this is the
most tender beef I can remember eating."

Olivia said, "Thank you." It almost made up for
not getting to say that she'd passed her defense.
She couldn't even think about that now. It
sounded boring even to her.

Greek Egg-Lemon Soup

I can't do an all-soup issue without including this recipe from Olivia. It's become a family favorite and she claims it's the easiest soup to make. She says the amounts below make a small batch serving 2 or 3 as a main dish or 1 grad student who wants leftovers.

2 eggs
juice of ½ a large lemon, or to taste
about 4 cups chicken broth
2 cups cooked rice, white or brown

Beat the eggs in a small bowl. Add lemon juice and beat well. Set aside.

Heat broth until it's almost boiling. Add rice and stir for a moment to heat rice through. Heat soup to boiling, then turn heat to very low.

Slowly drizzle several tablespoons of the hot broth into the egg-lemon mixture while beating well with a fork or whisk. (This tempers the egg.)

Pour egg mixture into the soup while stirring the soup well in a figure 8 pattern. Continue stirring for a few minutes until soup thickens slightly. (If the temp is too high, or you don't stir, the eggs can solidify—still delicious but attractive.) Serve with parsley and/or fr ground black pepper sprinkled on top.

- ❧ It's a very forgiving recipe. Use less egg and rice for a thinner soup, more egg and rice for thicker. Homemade chicken broth is always best, but you can get away with canned because of the lemon juice. You can even cook the rice in the chicken broth before adding the egg-lemon mixture, although this adds a little starch.

12

The beef and onion stew went over well, even if it was eaten in shifts. David came in from the car around eight-thirty, and Aunt Rubina heated some up for him in the microwave; shortly after that, Annie crept downstairs and out to the car herself, and Aunt Barbara joined the rest at the dinner table and asked if there was any more of Olivia's soup—a real concession, as she didn't always hold with foreign soups. At nine o'clock Father took a plate of food out to the car in case Annie was hungry.

"She might be, by now," Richard told them, consulting his watch. He himself had two helpings of stew. He kept scooping it up with the pita bread. Abby sat next to him and had pita bread and played with her ears distractedly, and no one said a thing about it. It had ceased to be a formal dinner.

"The spanakopita's actually very good," Ruby said to Olivia. "Heating it in the microwave sort of softens it."

Olivia didn't reply. It wasn't her fault it had dried out. When she stood to stack the dishes, the aunts insisted that she let them clean up.

Olivia and Ruby went out to the car for the of the evening.

When Olivia woke in the morning in one the twin beds in her old room, Ruby was st asleep in the other twin across the room. Olivia crept out to the hallway and peeked into David's old room to see if the single bed there was in use; things between Janet and David had barely warmed up to frosty by the time everyone had said good night the night before. But the bed had not been used.

Down in the kitchen, Father was scrambling eggs for Janet and himself. The burner was too hot; Olivia turned it down automatically, and Father handed her the spatula and stepped aside.

"I'd be happy to help," Janet said, "but he wouldn't let me."

"Well, you're still sort of company," Olivia said. "Enjoy it while it lasts. Next time we'll have you out here scrubbing pots and pans."

Janet smiled and took a drink of her coffee. Olivia wondered what she was like under normal circumstances. At first there had been that too-earnest manner—completely under-standable now, of course—and then the rest of the evening she'd been alternately upset and apologetic. She talked with her hands when she was excited. This morning she seemed peaceful enough, or at least worn-out. Her hair was pulled back in a clip and she wore no makeup.

avid says you're a really good cook," Olivia
1. "He says you make incredible Mexican
od. Do you do your own tortillas?"

"Me? No way. My husband's—my *first* husband's mother, I mean, sometimes makes tortillas.
She's taught me a few things, but mostly I stay
out of her kitchen as much as possible."

Olivia nodded. Janet's first husband had died
five years ago of leukemia; David told them this
last night after Janet had gone up to soak in the
tub. Olivia divided the eggs between Father's
and Janet's plates and then broke a couple of
eggs into the pan for herself.

"Does your own mother make tortillas?"

Janet laughed, a pretty waterfall of a laugh.
"My mother makes meatloaf. I'm not Mexican,
you know. I'm a complete mutt—Irish and Welsh
and whatever else thrown in. My husband was
Mexican American, and everyone who met me
after we got married assumed I was, too. I guess
it's the dark hair."

"Are you keeping the name Rodriguez?" Father
asked.

This was the first time it had occurred to
Olivia to wonder.

"We're all hyphenating," Janet said.
"Tschetter-Rodriguez. It takes me half an hour
to sign a check now."

"The kids are hyphenating, too, you mean?"
Olivia asked.

"And David."

"*David* is hyphenating?"

"Yes, it was his idea. One of the reasons I k▓ putting him off, for a while, I was worried abo▓ things like the kids losing what they have o▓ their father's identity, but I also didn't want to be one of these families where everyone has a different name."

"*David* offered to hyphenate his *own* name," Olivia said, for clarification, and to make herself believe it.

Janet nodded. Father took a sip of his coffee; Olivia saw the tiny smile at one corner of his mouth that you would miss if you didn't know to look for it. Olivia herself had to suppress the urge to give Janet a hearty slap on the back.

"I was just asking Janet," Father said now, "before you came down, Olivia, if she would care to accompany Rashid and me on our tour of gravel roads this afternoon."

Rashid Al-Zahrani was one of Father's graduate students. "Father, Janet doesn't want to do that."

"It's right up my alley," Janet protested. "It's the sort of thing I do all the time. Lately I've been working mostly on software-related documentation. Gravel would be a nice change."

"But you're not here to work."

"It's a lovely day for a drive," Father said mildly. "We're just going to take a few pictures the manual. Rashid wants to try out his _w digital camera. We'll be back well before _ich."

On the other hand, Olivia thought helplessly, *_t would probably be easier for Father to visit with his new daughter-in-law while looking at gravel roads than staring at each other in the living room.*

Olivia waited until they walked out the door and immediately called Annie.

"*Da*vid," she said, pronouncing each syllable distinctly, "is *hy*phenated. David Tschetter-Rodriguez."

Silence. "Get out of here. David?"

"Janet says they're all hyphenating, and it was David's idea. *David Tschetter-Rodriguez.* How's that strike you?"

"That's not even *her* name," Annie said. "That was her first husband's name. David's taking some other guy's name!"

"I hadn't thought of that," Olivia said. "That's even better."

"This Janet must really be something," Annie said.

"She does seem like a good catch, doesn't she?"

"Definitely. I mean, given that I've had all of one evening to form an impression. Did, uh, they use my old room last night?"

"I guess so. David's room was empty this morning."

"I wasn't sure how that would play out. was still pretty mad at him when we left."

"How about you? You still mad at David?"

"Sure. You?"

David walked into the kitchen, eyes barely open. He was wearing green and blue plaid boxers that looked brand-new, and his hair stood on end. "I'm always mad at David," Olivia said clearly.

"Is that Annie?" he said.

Olivia nodded, then said loudly into the phone, "Guess who's up? Mr. Tschetter-Rodriguez himself!"

David took the carton of milk and went into the dining room without a word.

"So dinner at the aunt's tonight, right?" Annie said.

"I'm sure not cooking again," Olivia said.

"Say, you and Ruby should bring Janet over here this afternoon. We need to figure out when and where to have the reception."

"I thought you were still mad at David."

"Sure, but he's married. We have to do *something.*"

"Do we have to invite him?"

"Nah," Annie said. "We'll have a life-size cardboard cutout of him that Janet can stand next to."

"At least a cardboard cutout wouldn't saunter in an hour late."

ne of many advantages, my dear," Annie
.

Olivia hung up the phone and wandered into
the dining room. David sat at the table, the
carton of milk between his hands, looking
hungover.

"You look like death warmed over," Olivia
said.

"Thanks."

"Didn't get enough sleep?"

"We were up sort of late," he said, rubbing
the back of his neck with both hands, "talking."

"I'll bet."

David took a drink straight from the carton.
Olivia hadn't seen him do that in years.

"Bet you're not allowed to do that in front of
the kids," Olivia said.

David looked around dazedly. "Where is she
anyway?"

"Father took her to look at gravel roads."

David nodded. They seemed to have run out
of things to say. Olivia finally said, "Feel free to
scramble yourself an egg. Everything's still out."
She returned to the kitchen, resisted the urge to
scramble his eggs herself, and went upstairs to
shower.

Father and Janet were not back by lunch. Ruby
and David and Olivia lounged around eating
sandwiches, David looking at the clock every
five minutes. Olivia herself wasn't able to relax;

she felt that she had to be on the alert so t‍
David said one thing about graduate school‍
could quell him with the *don't-you-even-start lc*‍
she'd been imagining all morning. But he didr‍
bring up graduate school. He and Ruby played ‍
game of gin rummy on the coffee table, then
some complicated version of double-solitaire
that Olivia had never heard of.

"So how long's Annie going to keep me in
the doghouse?" David said once.

"The sooner you start apologizing," Ruby said,
"the sooner it'll be over."

David sighed and flipped over the two of dia-
monds.

The phone rang, and Olivia went to the kitchen
to answer it.

"Hello," said Harry on the other end.

Olivia looked at the clock automatically. Harry
generally stayed up until four in the morning
doing research and writing, then slept until noon.
But it was nearly one o'clock already. "Good
morning," Olivia said. "Morning to you, anyway."

"So how'd the big announcement go last
night?"

"What's that noise? Are you drinking coffee?"

"I am." She heard another slurp, exaggerated
for her benefit. "Come on, how'd it go? Give me
the scoop."

It took Olivia a moment to remember what he
was talking about. "Oh. That. It didn't happen."

hy not?"

Olivia looked around the corner of the kitchen doorway into the living room, then stretched the cord across the kitchen in the other direction to sit on the bottom stair of the steps. She sighed. "I never got around to telling them. My news was trumped by bigger, better news."

"What could possibly be better than successfully defending one's dissertation?"

Olivia said, "It's possible that having your own defense looming ahead has clouded your judgment."

"I suppose this is about Annie being pregnant."

"Did I tell you about that?" Olivia couldn't remember telling him; sometimes he seemed to know things through osmosis. "It was only partly that. David announced halfway through dinner that he and the new girlfriend are married."

"Oh." There was a respectful silence. "All right, that is big."

"Everything hit the fan, of course. Annie was the most upset, and Aunt Barbara had to tell David . . ." But Harry was speaking to someone else. She could hear his muffled voice though not make out the words. "Harry? You there?"

"Sorry—Penelope just showed up with lunch. Wow, she made a quiche."

Olivia said, "What kind?"

More muffled tones. "Asparagus and Gruyère. Amazing. And these twisty sesame bread sticks she makes herself. This spread's worthy of Olivia."

"It's a damn shame I'm not there," she sa— adding nastily to herself, *I bet Penelope thin, so, too.* "I have to run—I think everyone's bac for lunch." Harry was asking her something, but she pretended not to hear and hung up.

Janet and Father *were* back, to Olivia's surprise, along with Rashid, whom Olivia had met once or twice before. Everyone stood around the living room watching while Janet punched buttons on her cell phone distractedly. David's arm was around her, but when he saw Olivia he came forward. "Are you finally off? We need the phone."

"I've been on for all of ten seconds," Olivia said, but David pulled Janet past her to the kitchen.

"Janet's kids are sick," Ruby told Olivia. "Throwing up."

"Well, *John* is sick," Father said. "Apparently Maria throws up if she sees anybody else get sick, so hers may just be a sympathetic reaction."

"Does this mean they have to go?"

"Janet wants to leave immediately," Father said. "Understandably. And I need to drop Rashid off."

"I can walk," Rashid said. He lifted the camera hanging around his neck. "I'll take pictures on the way."

via wasn't sure what he intended to take ures of, but he was trying to be nice, so she led. He smiled, too. He was barely taller than e was, very dark, and almost handsome. Olivia ad had quite a few Saudi students when she first started teaching ESL composition in grad school, and she wondered what Rashid thought of Father suddenly having a daughter-in-law he had never met before, let alone endorsed.

"Let's throw together some lunch for them to take on the road," Ruby said, so Olivia followed her to the kitchen. Janet was standing in the middle of the room, holding the phone with one hand and gesticulating with the other.

"Don't even *offer* him more 7-Up," she was saying. "He'll throw it right up. Just get him in front of the TV and distract him. Look in that stack of videos from the library . . . why's she doing that? Well, put her in my bed if she wants . . ."

David steered Janet out to the dining room and said over his shoulder, "Some of that turkey on white would be great. Or she likes tuna."

They made one of each. Olivia wondered the whole time if this meant Ruby would be leaving immediately, too—the reason for her visit having ended abruptly—but she didn't want to ask, in case that put the idea into Ruby's head.

Annie and Richard and Abigail arrived in time to say good-bye.

"I'm so sorry," Janet said to everyone for the tenth time while David loaded the trunk of the car. "When John gets sick, he gets really sick. When Maria even *thinks* she's sick, which she's not, she gets weepy. First, we sweep in here and drop a bomb—" shooting a dark look toward David, who was slamming the trunk, "then we sweep out and disrupt everyone's plans for the weekend." She looked around at the others. "Will someone say good-bye to Aunt Barbara and Aunt Rubina for us?"

"They'll understand," Annie said. "And the next visit will be normal."

Ruby said, "Until further notice: nobody marries, nobody gets pregnant, nobody dies."

Everyone laughed. Then everyone hugged Janet, which felt, if not completely natural, like a good start.

It was Olivia who remembered to ask, as David started up the car, "Hey! How do we reach you? Whose house are you going to be living in?"

"Mine, of course," David said. "Once the kids have a little more time to adjust. For the time being we're still at Janet's."

Olivia felt compelled to punish him for the *of course*. She raised her voice as he pulled out. "Drive safely, Mr. Tschetter-Rodriguez."

David leaned out his window. "That's *Dr.* Tschetter-Rodriguez to you—at least until you've landed your own doctorate."

re's an opening, if ever there was one, Olivia ~~~ght, watching it slip away as David honked ~e and drove off. It was just as well. She didn't ~ve the energy for anything but status quo.

It was a restless afternoon. Aunt Barbara called ~o move dinner that night to the next night. Father went into work for some papers, and Ruby left to have coffee with an old friend who was in town. Olivia wandered around the kitchen and thought about changing the sheets in Annie's room. Eventually she settled herself in front of the computer in Father's office, but she couldn't concentrate; she was listening for the front door. She figured Ruby would announce she was leaving as soon as she returned from coffee. After a while she put her head back and dozed.

"Dad still not back?" Ruby said from directly above and behind her, and Olivia jolted awake.

"I'm not sure," she said.

"I'm running downtown for a minute, then. There's supposed to be a shoe sale at Allen's."

"I might change the sheets," Olivia said. "In Annie's room."

"Go nuts."

She went out to the kitchen and made herself a sandwich out of boredom, then took it to the living room and turned on the Saturday afternoon matinee. It was an old sci-fi horror flick called *Island of Terror*. It was exactly what she needed: reclusive scientists, bubbling test tubes,

British accents, and sweeping, percussive
music. The acting was acceptably workmanli:
the actors having apparently agreed to make
best of things—and the scientist who dared
flout nature by trying to cure cancer was suitab
punished by having his bones sucked out by the
tentacled spawn of his own cancer-fighting cells.
Father wandered in and sat on the couch, since
Olivia had taken his chair, linking his hands
behind his head in the way that meant he was
content to settle in. Ruby returned and perched
on the arm at the other end of the couch as if
about to leave, but she didn't. During one of the
many bone-sucking scenes, Olivia went and
made popcorn, and when she returned, Ruby was
in the corner of the couch, her bare feet curled
under her.

They were watching the end credits when Annie
called and suggested they get takeout and come
over. Olivia was glad to have something concrete
to offer Ruby, something involving Annie. "You
pick the takeout," she said to Ruby, to close the
deal. Ruby called Arctic Circle and ordered tubs
of fried chicken and fake mashed potatoes and
about a gallon of beef gravy.

At Annie's, everyone fell to eating as if they'd
been fasting for a week, and as if it weren't
really too hot for fried chicken and gravy. After
dinner Father and Richard withdrew to the
family room downstairs, where Olivia, descend-

nce to offer drinks, found them watching the news. The three sisters played a desultory ne of Scrabble at the kitchen table. Olivia membered too late that the batter on the fried hicken, for some reason irresistible to her, always made her stomach queasy and her head muzzy afterward. Annie moved about restlessly, filling the dishwasher, wiping counters. From time to time she looked into a sack of tomatoes bearing Aunt Rubina's handwriting, but she couldn't seem to decide what to do with them.

"At least take them out of the sack," Olivia said finally, as Ruby played "oasis" off Olivia's "spool." "They're so ripe I can smell them over here."

"Put them in the fridge," Ruby said. "That'll stop the ripening."

Olivia was aghast. "You can't do that. The second you put tomatoes in the fridge they lose their flavor. How many times have you heard Mom say that?"

Ruby was drawing her replacement tiles. "You know, Livy, sometimes I just don't care how things taste."

Olivia couldn't think of a thing to say. She couldn't think of any possible reason Ruby would say such a thing. She looked at Annie, but Annie, bending briefly over her letters, said only, "I wish I didn't care. Right now that's *all* I care about. Livy, put down 'shalt' on the bottom *s* for me." She went to the oven and switched then pulled a box from the freezer. "I'm ha some pepperoni pizza mini-rolls; you g want any? I'm hooked on these things."

Ruby shuddered visibly. Olivia said, "I'. have a couple," because she knew she would, once they were in front of her. "Annie, you have to draw your letters."

"You draw them for me." She pulled a cookie sheet from the drawer beneath the oven. "So what can we surmise about a woman with two kids who's willing to get married without any sort of ceremony involving family or friends?"

"Well, she's not pregnant," Ruby said. "I asked David."

Olivia was again aghast. The possibility honestly had not occurred to her. She tried to imagine asking David such a thing herself but could not.

Annie stood over Olivia, a roll of aluminum foil in her hands, and looked at the letters Olivia had just drawn for her: two *o*'s, an *e,* and an *i*. "Good hand, Olivia, couldn't you do better than that?"

"Draw your own letters next time."

"The only thing I can figure is that Janet's very practical," Annie said. She ripped off a section of foil and lined the cookie sheet. "And I get the feeling she knows who she is. Like being through one whole marriage already, having her

and die so young and all, she's already
 ned more about herself than some people
 rn in a lifetime."

"She seems pretty grounded," Ruby said.

"More grounded than David," Olivia said. She laid an "ex" beneath an *h* and an *a* to also make "he" and "ax." She hated playing this way. She would rather have made one interesting word like "oxygen" (but she didn't have a *y*) or even "exit" than little cheater words like "ex" and "ax," but that was the way to make points. "Is Janet going to mind being the grown-up in the relationship, do you think?"

Ruby rolled her eyes. "David's not that bad."

"I don't think you can do that," Annie said, pausing as she passed the table. "Isn't 'ex' just a prefix?"

"People use it alone all the time. As in 'Last week I ran over my ex with the car.' "

"Can you use slang like that?"

"Yes, yes, I've used it before," Olivia said. "I've even looked it up."

Annie slid the cookie sheet into the oven. "Did you know David first started proposing to Janet the week after Mom's funeral?"

"Was he already planning to before Mom died, do you suppose?" Olivia asked, but no one could answer her. Ruby built "axiom" off Olivia's "ax." It was worth only fourteen points, but Olivia had to admire it.

"Well, David's settled down, anyway," [...] said, and sighed. Olivia looked at her in surpri[...]

"I thought you were happy for him. I mean[...] sort of had that impression, in spite of how [...] went about it."

"Sure I am. We're all happy for him, right, Annie?"

"Sure. He's an inconsiderate jerk, but I'm happy for him. Janet seems *right* for him."

"If she's so grounded in reality," Olivia said, "what's she doing marrying someone a couple months after his mother dies, before even meeting his family? They always say you shouldn't make any big decisions for two years after losing a loved one."

"Two years?" Annie said.

"Janet's been through a lot of grief herself. Maybe it doesn't scare her," Ruby said.

"But she should know all the better what a stressful, awful, unreal thing it is to be grieving. You can't—you can't think straight; you can't make decisions when you're still trying to wrap your brain around the fact that someone's *gone*."

"Maybe *David* can think straight," Ruby said. "Just because *you* can't . . . I mean, maybe he's got enough distance to have some perspective. I myself—I live way too close to home." She rubbed her eyes suddenly and vigorously, as if something had gotten in them. When she lowered her hands, her eyelids were red and she looked

she was just waking up. "I should've moved
s ago. You get in a rut—"
"Since when are *you* in a rut?"
Annie said, "I still can't believe he didn't tell
s. There's just no way he would've done that if
Mom were alive."

"It's like the glue is gone," Olivia said, "and
we're all flying off in a million—"

"At least he married someone who overlapped," Ruby said.

"What?"

"He married someone he was already seeing
before Mom died—Mom knew about her, she
knew Janet Rodriguez existed, she even got a few
recipes out of her. He didn't marry someone he
met *since*. If anything, it's the opposite of flying
off in another direction."

"Are you saying he married her *because* she
'overlapped'?"

Ruby shrugged.

Annie was leaning on the edge of the table,
staring down at the Scrabble board. "It's something, anyway. It's the things that don't overlap
that are hardest."

The oven timer buzzed, but nobody moved.

"Your turn," Olivia finally said.

Annie turned away to pull the cookie sheet out
of the oven. "What am I supposed to do with all
those vowels?" she said. "Can I make 'anemone'
or something?"

"I'd say he was just lonely," Olivia said, even I don't mind the lonely part as much as y think. I mean, not to the point of wanting replace Mom with someone else. The loneline is the only way I can be close to her now."

Annie pushed a plate of pizza mini-rolls over to Olivia and sat down for the first time since they arrived.

"I know what you mean," she said, picking up a steaming pizza roll with her thumb and index finger and immediately dropping it. "I can handle the lonely part, too—it's all the other things interrupting it that I can't stand. I just want to *concentrate*."

"Well, maybe David couldn't handle the lonely part," Ruby said. "Maybe he didn't want to sit around *concentrating* on feeling lonely all the time. When you say that, it sounds so weird. So selfish."

"You're one to talk about selfish," Olivia said. "You in your own little world."

"Livy," Annie said.

Olivia raised her hands. "I take it back. It's not what I meant anyway. Ruby's not selfish. Ruby's never *had* to be selfish; she gets everything handed to her on a silver platter before she even knows she wants it."

Ruby stood. "You don't know what you're talking about," she said.

"Please enlighten me. Tell me what I'm missing

ll understand. Is there anything you'd like
ell me, Ruby? No? Well, business as usual."

Livy, shut up. Ruby, sit down."

But Ruby turned and walked through the open
kitchen to the living room, where her purse was
tucked into a corner of the sofa. She was shaking
her head. "See you tomorrow, Annie," she said.
"Maybe."

Olivia stood. "How are Father and I supposed to
get home?"

The front door slammed.

"Richard will give you a ride," Annie said. She
sighed. "Livy, did you *have* to?"

"She was saying it to both of us," Olivia said.

Annie picked up a pizza roll and blew on it.
"Just sit down," she said, "and help me eat these
so I don't polish them off myself. Not everyone
goes through this the way we're going through it,
Livy."

Olivia knew what Annie was doing with that
"we," but even knowing this, she was helpless
to keep it from placating her. They threw Ruby's
letters back in the sack and Annie finally played
"phooey" on a triple word. They ate the pizza rolls
without letting them cool and scalded their
tongues on the hot tomato sauce.

13

Olivia slept in the big room that night. It had a deserted air since David and Janet had left; the bed wasn't made, and half a glass of water sat on one of the windowsills. Olivia thought once more about changing the sheets but then crawled into bed without bothering.

The next morning she got up as soon as she heard Father moving around in his closet next door. She went down the hall and knocked on Ruby's door gently, opened it a crack. Ruby was rolled in a sheet, her back to the door. Her tangled dark hair was splayed across the white pillow. Even from the back she was beautiful, the line of her neck curving into her shoulder, the sharp, perfect wing of a shoulder blade. Olivia's throat constricted with envy and awe.

She said finally, "You need a wake-up call?"

There was a groan. "You two go without me."

"I don't usually go these days," Olivia said. "The hymns set me off, and I don't want to deal with all those people noticing I'm still home."

Ruby rolled over onto her back and viewed Olivia through half-closed eyes. "Father has to tell all those same people David got married. You can't make him go alone."

nnie will probably be there," Olivia said, but felt guilty enough about last night that she nt. Anyway, no one would ask why Olivia was ill home when they heard the story of David and Janet.

As it was, she barely had any contact with anyone; she and Father arrived just a few minutes before the service and sat in the back. They used to sit far to the front on the piano side because Vivian had played whatever hymns the organ didn't. Back here, Olivia felt like a visitor. She studied the backs of everyone's heads. Mrs. Bruinsma in the next row had gotten a perm. The Spoelhofs two rows ahead allowed their four-year-old to fidget, and Maureen, sitting with Lennie farther down the Spoelhofs's row, sent several severe looks their way. Mr. Hegg several rows up had a small round Band-Aid in the exact middle of his round bald spot.

With such observations as these she got through the opening hymns, the call to confession, one of Mrs. Leuwen's characteristically painful children's sermons ("How Is This New Pencil Like a Christian?"), a much *better* sermon on Psalm 137 ("Singing in Babylon"), the offertory, and a congregational prayer in which David's marriage was lifted up, and during which Olivia squeezed Father's arm to show support. Then she saw what the last hymn was, "Jerusalem, Jerusalem," a particular favorite of Vivian's, and whispered to Father, "I'm walking home."

She slipped out as soon as everyone stood sing, slipped into the foyer and through the do and across the parking lot of pink gravel. As soc as she gained the far sidewalk she took off he sandals, which were pinching her feet, and went barefoot.

It was a nice enough day for a walk. She wondered the whole way home if Ruby would still be there or if she'd have gone back to Sioux Falls by now. She hoped she'd be there. She had decided during church that she was going to apologize, and it would be easier to do it in person. Ruby detested apologies and always tried to head them off.

Ruby's car was still there, and Olivia went inside gratefully, but the downstairs was deserted except for J.C., who was stretched out illicitly in the middle of the dining room table. She cracked an eye at Olivia, who decided to pretend not to notice. Olivia walked up the stairs very quietly so as not to wake Ruby. She set her sandals down on the top step and went to the bathroom, turned the glass knob without even thinking about the fact that the door was completely closed, and for a moment the sight of Ruby sitting on the edge of the claw-footed tub in a tank top and underwear smoking a cigarette seemed like a crazy apparition, even seemed to disappear for a split second when she blinked. Then it was back, both

y and the cigarette. Ruby was blinking, too. made a choking sound and started coughing.
"What are you *doing?*"

Smoke drifted in the light breeze from the open window.

Ruby stood and stubbed out the cigarette in the sink, still coughing. She filled a toothpaste mug with water, sloshing a little in her haste, and took a drink.

"I mean, what in hell are you *doing?*" Olivia said. "You don't smoke."

Ruby wiped her mouth with the back of her hand. "No, of course I don't. Shut the door."

"Well, when did you *start?* How long has this been going on? Are you completely *insane?*"

Ruby's voice rose. "*I said I don't smoke.* This is not a normal thing. Now shut the stupid door."

Olivia slammed the door and backed herself against it, so there would be no question of anyone leaving, and crossed her arms. Then she had to uncross them to wave at the smoke that was drifting her way.

"Oh, there's not that much," Ruby said, which was true. She sat on the edge of the tub again. Her eyes were red. Olivia looked around, located a crumpled pack of cigarettes sitting on the radiator. She reached for it nervously and looked into it.

"How many have you had?" Olivia asked. "There's less than half a pack here."

"That pack is probably ten years old. I pror
you it's not something I normally do. Now co
you please—"

"You can't possibly *enjoy* it, if you're not use
to it."

"No, I don't."

"Then—what the hell are you doing?" She
peered into the pack again. "These are just plain
cigarettes, right?"

"Oh, for crying out loud. *Yes*."

Olivia didn't care that Ruby had maybe been
crying, or that she sat slumped, looking utterly
defeated. She felt her own eyes fill with tears.
"David goes off and gets married without a word,
you start *smoking* . . . Mom dies, and we all
become people I don't recognize."

Ruby sighed. "Mom knew about this."

"*Mom* knew?"

Ruby licked her lips. "It was sort of her idea. We
had this—agreement." She gave Olivia a sudden
stern look, more like the old Ruby. "And that's
all I'm telling you. This is none of your business. It was something between Mom and me."

"I already know things you don't know I know,"
Olivia said. "Maybe this'll turn out to be one of
them."

Ruby shot her a sideways look. "What do you
already know?" Suddenly her long fingers
couldn't stop moving, pushing the hair from her
forehead, tucking a long lock behind her ear.

o's talking about me? That cook at Meals on eels? God, I hate being talked about."

Olivia stared at her sister for a long moment, nally let out her breath. Even when she could win, she couldn't win. "I know you let your moss roses die," she said finally. "I know you ordered pizza the other night, and it came really late and you tipped the guy anyway."

Ruby let out a breath, too, something between a snort and a sigh. She closed her eyes and tipped her head back, massaging the back of her neck with both hands.

Olivia stood there holding the pack of cigarettes, trying to gather the energy to turn and walk out of the bathroom. Then a thought came to her, as clearly as if someone had whispered it in her ear: *There's one thing Ruby doesn't know.* "I had a secret with Mom, too," she said. "You want to know what it is?"

Ruby frowned. "Is it a bad thing?"

"Do you want to know or don't you? No one else in the family knows."

"Is it about Harry?"

"*Damn* it," Olivia said. "*No.* Nothing is about Harry."

"Is it big?"

Olivia nodded. Her eyes filled again, and this time she let a few tears fall. Ruby put her head in her hands and groaned.

"Yes, I guess you'd better tell me."

"You first."

"Olivia—"

"I'm serious. Why should you know everyth. about me when you won't tell me the least litt thing about yourself?"

"All right already," Ruby said. "For crying out loud." She pulled the toilet paper roll off the dispenser and tore off a wad, blew her nose hard. She threw the wad at the wastebasket and missed; they both let it lie there. "We're going to have to back way up," she said. "I was fourteen. Freshman year of high school."

The year everything came together.

What that mostly meant was that Ruby finally got her period. She was one of the last of her friends to get it, and of course she'd become convinced it was never going to happen. Then one morning she woke up to several bright red blots on her sheets, and just like that, she was normal; God had not, after all, doomed her to eternal prepubescence. The only annoying thing was having to lie there waiting for Olivia, who was nine, to finish poking around the room getting dressed. As soon as Olivia went down to breakfast, Ruby called for Mother, who helped her change the sheets and set her up with the necessary accoutrements.

She never had a minute's trouble with her periods, either: no cramps, no heavy flow.

ing that would get in the way of sports. ngs were coming together that way, too. She ally felt comfortable with last year's growth urt, and she made varsity girls' soccer even nough she was just a freshman. She was one of the best passers; Miss Batty had her start every game. The head coach of the whole athletics department, Mr. Sutter, knew her name.

The other parts of her life fell into place like pearls rolling on a fine silk strand. She maintained the same high grades she always had; she joined journalism club and science club, in spite of an already daunting schedule, and found the increase in activities stimulating. The more that was expected of her, the more she had to give: the sharper her mind, the keener her skills. So much of it was easy.

As if all that weren't enough, she who had always been well liked found herself becoming increasingly popular. Upperclassmen noticed her looks; her classmates liked her for her unsnobbishness. Teachers prized her intelligence and liveliness and had to struggle not to show favoritism. The coaches were more obvious, regularly held her up as a yardstick for others. A few of her teammates resented this, but most of them got over it when they got to know her. Ruby genuinely liked people, and in spite of all her accomplishments—or because of them—felt no need to exclude anyone.

By the time volleyball season rolled arou
Ruby almost believed she led a charmed life.

*Are you sure we're talking about yo
freshman year? Isn't that the year you wer
always breaking something? Your thumb, your
foot, your collarbone . . .*

It was the week of tryouts. Miss Lindstrom,
assistant coach for girls' volleyball, was going to
lead them in several days of practice before she
and Mr. Sutter started making cuts. On the first
day, Miss Lindstrom couldn't find the crank for
the volleyball net. She asked for a volunteer to
go to Mr. Sutter's office to ask if it had gotten
stored with the boys' net. Ruby was one of several
whose hands flew up immediately. Mr. Sutter
had wavy brown hair and narrow, light blue,
laughing eyes, and unlike the other male coaches,
he hadn't gone soft around the middle yet. Miss
Lindstrom chose Ruby, who made a face at her
jeering friends and skipped off on her errand.

*Remember when there used to be a coach's
office off the swimming pool?*

Mr. Sutter found the crank in his office, but he
didn't hand it over right away. He sat on the edge
of his desk and asked Ruby how high school
was treating her. He talked a little about her
performance in soccer, chatted a bit about the
boys' basketball team's chances to go to State
this year. She replied to his questions but hardly
knew what she was saying; it was the most

d ever talked to him. Margaret and her other
nds were going to be sick with envy.

Some boys outside the office were making
ise in the pool, and Mr. Sutter got up to push
he door shut. On the way back to his desk he
accidentally brushed against her, and she apologized, blushing. He laughed it off, set down the
crank, and put his hands on her shoulders. He
said nobody that pretty should ever worry about
being in the way. Ruby said she guessed she'd
better be getting the crank back to Miss
Lindstrom. Mr. Sutter gave her shoulders a gentle
shake and said hey, he hoped he hadn't embar-
rassed her; he hoped he had a daughter like her
someday. Her parents must be very proud. Could
she give him a smile, show that they were
friends? Ruby couldn't bring herself to look up
but managed a smile, and he said that's my girl
and gave her a hug. He gave her a gentle kiss on
one temple, brushed back her hair very tenderly.

Later she would not be able to remember
exactly how things progressed, how she ended
up sitting on his lap. One unformed thought
raced in her head, that if she could only get her
heart to stop pounding, she wouldn't shake so,
and she would be able to move her limbs again.

*So it went from there. Not completely—that is,
he didn't . . . it could have been worse.*

It was odd, what she noticed at the time. It was
like she'd never seen a human face up close

before. His skin repulsed her, his huge pores, the warm, stale smell of coffee on his bre made her want to retch. She heard herself say ir shaky, unrecognizable voice that she was afrar she was going to throw up. He rubbed her back, spoke soothingly, helped her stand; he even helped straighten her clothes. She said, voice trembling, eyes on the floor, that she was quitting volleyball, quitting all sports. He squeezed her shoulders gently and said that if she quit sports everyone would think it was because she was pregnant.

She was so shocked she looked up again for the first time since he'd put his hands on her.

That kind of talk, he warned, forever changed how people looked at you, even if it proved to be completely wrong. He told her to think about that very carefully. Then he smiled and patted her shoulder and handed her the crank for the net, which she could barely hold because she was still shaking so hard, and sent her on her way.

It was only the smell of chlorine that kept her from throwing up the second she left his office: that stinging, stringent smell, pure chemical, rising off the surface of the water. It scrubbed the scent of coffee out of her nostrils, made her head buzz. The pool was the most beautiful thing she'd ever seen. She wanted to be at the bottom of it.

She didn't know what to do, so she told Miss

dstrom she was sick and left practice. She
school and walked home. She ended up at
e sand and gravel piles by the railroad tracks.
*You know the ones—where we used to cut
through before that development was put in?*
She climbed up a pile of good clean sand and
sat on the top, where she could have seen anyone
coming, but there was no one around. She sat
very still, not thinking, just watching the rivulets
of sand that she'd set in motion race down the
pile, finally slow to a trickle. She tried to sit so
still that not another grain was disturbed. Mother
had always told them not to play there; she
didn't want them so near the railroad tracks. No,
that wasn't the only reason: a neighborhood boy
had broken his arm there, horsing around. And
then she knew what to do.

She broke her own thumb.

On purpose?

It seemed like the only way out, the only alterna-
tive she could live with. She couldn't play
volleyball under Mr. Sutter, risk being alone
with him; she couldn't bear even to face him.
But she also couldn't bear to think of the rumors
he might start if she simply quit.

*But Mother and Father—why didn't you go to
Mother and Father?*

She could never tell a soul. She'd never been so
ashamed. Worst of all—a thought that she didn't
allow herself to fully articulate for years—was

275

the fear that it was somehow her own fault. A
all, hadn't she been attracted to him at fi.
Hadn't she wanted him to notice her? Had:
she volunteered to go to his office, *alone?* At th.
slightest approach of this thought, her viscera
churned again, surged into nausea that left her
panting and swallowing hard. Surely only the
guilty could feel such shame.

No one would ever, ever have thought that!

Another possibility presented itself, one that
was easier to think about, so she grabbed hold of
it and hung on: she'd gotten too proud, too confident. Things had been going too well, and
somehow she had to be punished. Her mind told
her this was nonsense, but she didn't trust her
own judgment anymore. What did she know
about life, about anything? Six months ago she
hadn't even had her period yet. (How she was
homesick for that time.) Maybe if she hadn't
started menstruating . . . and then been so success-
ful, so easily, the center of so much attention,
none of this would have happened.

All she knew was that if she had a broken
thumb, she couldn't possibly play volleyball, and
everyone would know why.

*For future reference, it's a lot harder to break
your own thumb than you might think.*

It took her about half an hour. She slid down
off the sand pile, and first she kept trying to fall
on her thumb. She couldn't bring herself to fall

enough, so she fell over and over, hoping eventually something would snap.

Thank God, no one was around. I must have looked like an idiot.

How can you laugh?

Finally, she put her thumb between two flatish rocks and picked up another, bigger rock, the biggest she could reach, and before she could think about it anymore she threw it down as hard as she could. It only took once. Her thumb was so bruised when she was done that it looked like it had been in a barroom brawl. She went home and said she injured it in practice.

They believed you?

They had no reason not to believe her. The *doctor* wondered; he asked if she'd been scrimmaging with the Minnesota Vikings. She told him she'd dived for a volleyball and gotten stepped on. That broken thumb got her out of volleyball for seven weeks—four because of the initial break, and another three because she managed to keep it from healing properly. That part was worse than the original break.

At any rate, seven weeks was as good as a season. Then it was basketball season. Miss Lindstrom and Mr. Kuipers were in charge of girls' junior varsity, but after the first day they wanted Ruby to go out for varsity—coached by Mr. Sutter. He stopped her in the hallway in front of her friends and said he was looking forward to seeing what she could do with the ba

By now she knew how quickly a break co
heal. Sprains were the way to go; torn ligame.
were even better. So this time she twisted h.
ankle. She went back to the sand and gravel pile.
and made a little pile of rocks and gravel and
jumped on it with one foot until she finally fell
off in the right way and felt something tear. Then
she forced herself to put as much weight on it as
she could bear, all the way home. She was on
crutches for nine weeks.

*I remember. I played with the crutches when-
ever you were on the couch doing homework or
watching TV.*

The first time Mr. Sutter passed Ruby on her
crutches in the hallway, he stopped to ask how
her ankle was. He said he couldn't believe her
rotten luck, having another accident like this. He
shook his head. It was a real loss for the team, a
real loss. Good thing she was only a freshman.
She had three full years as a high school athlete
ahead of her—so long as she could keep from
breaking her neck. He patted her on the shoulder
and headed off down the hallway.

You are so lucky, Margaret breathed in her ear.

After that he pretty much ignored her.

For weeks she focused her thoughts on track.
Girls' track was headed by Miss Lindstrom and
Mr. Hortness; Mr. Sutter would be safely busy
with golf and swim team. She even told herself,

never talks to me anymore, he never looks me the eye; maybe it's safe. Or maybe next time e would have the courage to stand up to him, ell and scream, even strike him. She began to fantasize about it, for practice. Sometimes she overpowered him, cracking his head with the volleyball crank. Sometimes she just looked him in the eye in the hallway, before he tried anything else; he'd see that she wasn't afraid, and then *he* would be afraid. She would laugh at him. She would make allusions to his wife, and he would beg for mercy.

Then just before track season was to begin, Miss Lindstrom had to leave school unexpectedly to take care of a family emergency. Someone would have to take her place as head coach of girls' track. Ruby's stomach surged in fear when she heard the announcement; the brave fantasies melted away, and the memory of them only showed her how weak and foolish she really was. Some nights she felt so nauseous it was all she could do to lie very still taking deep breaths. The only thing worse than the nausea was the thought of one day losing control and throwing up. She dreamed about it, and in her dreams she would vomit until her insides spilled out and she was empty, and then slowly she would begin to implode, sucked into the black hole that had been created, waking just as the pressure began crushing in her face.

She gave up any thoughts of track. By the
Miss Lindstrom's replacement was announc
Ruby knew it didn't matter who it was. Her an
was pronounced healed, and only one thing wa
going to make her feel safe again.

*So you did it—you jumped off Aunt Barbara's
old quarter horse and broke your collarbone.*
The ironic thing was, she intended to jump, she
really did, but before she could bring herself to
do it that old horse gave her a good honest
throw—like a gift from God. The last thing old
Piper had in him. Ruby would've kissed him on
his big velvety nose, if she'd been able to stand
without help.

But this time, Dr. Wiems didn't believe her
story. He looked Vivian straight in the eye and
said, *Mrs. Tschetter, did your husband do this?*
Ruby saw the shock on her mother's face and
spilled everything. She said it was all her own
doing, everything but the collarbone, and that she
did it because of what happened with the coach.

It was easier than she'd thought possible, thanks
to Dr. Wiems—wonderful, unemotional, clinical
Dr. Wiems. She looked in his direction the whole
time she was talking, even after she started
crying, and he nodded, sympathetic but always
and blessedly *detached*. He wasn't going to
collapse in tears or throw his arms around her; it
wasn't going to hurt him the way it would have
to hurt Mother. She ignored the sounds her

ner was making and pretended Dr. Wiems
s the only adult in the room, right to the end
her story.

And then she threw up in front of both of them.
After all those months. That was the best part.
Instead of sucking her into nothingness, the act
of vomiting was almost cleansing: just a few
moments of helplessness while the spasms
wrung her inside out, and then afterward the
emptiness was so good, so safe. She felt like a
blank slate ready to begin again—a newborn. As
if God had just created her and nothing had
come along and ruined her yet.

Olivia wasn't sure how long they stayed that
way: she backed against the bathroom door as if
pinned there, Ruby motionless on the edge of the
tub, both of them staring at the tiles on the floor
between them. It might have been the longest
moment of silence she'd known with any family
member other than Father. Ruby wasn't crying,
or even on the verge of it. Her face was calm and
very pale.

When Olivia finally forced herself to speak,
her voice cracked as if she hadn't used it in
hours. "Whatever happened to Mr. Sutter?"

Ruby shrugged. "There were lawyers involved,
at first. I had to go along once—he wasn't at that
meeting. There were meetings with the principal
and the superintendent; they didn't make me go

to those. I know that Mother and Father were
not to contact Mr. Sutter themselves, and
they did anyway. I don't know exactly what th
said or did. I think there was a lot they didn't te
me. In the end they had to drop the charges. 'He
said, she said,' you know. Mr. Sutter resigned at
the end of the year to take a position in Missouri
or somewhere, and nothing about any of it ever
got out at school. Which is amazing. That was all
that mattered to me."

Olivia said, "So. Are you okay and everything?"

Ruby looked at her. "Sure I'm okay. I mean . . .
It could have been a lot worse, like I said."

"Oh—I know. I'm glad."

"The thing is," Ruby said, and stopped. She
massaged her temples with the long, elegant
middle finger of each hand, then wrapped both
hands around her neck and hung them there,
elbows in front of her chest. "It's just that every
once in awhile, over the years . . . Sometimes I
remember how it felt when I finally threw up after
months of holding back. I slept like a baby that
night. I felt safe again. I had *done* something, I
had done the thing I dreaded most, and everything
was better. Like I got to start over. And sometimes
when I'm under a lot of stress—good stress, bad
stress, it doesn't always matter—it's been
tempting. The last few months—"

"You mean—are you talking about bulimia or
something?"

No. No. It's never been about food. It's more— don't know, Mom just dying like that, and all ese offers I'm getting from the Minneapolis nd Chicago stations, and David showing up married—"

"You're getting offers from *Chicago*?"

"I mean, he's got the guts to just *do* it, just walk into all that commitment, kids and the whole nine yards, *David* of all people, and here I can't bring myself to stay in a relationship long enough to exchange phone numbers."

"I didn't know you were getting offers from Chicago. That's huge."

"Well, success isn't all it's cracked up to be."

"Because of what happened with—way back then?"

Ruby tipped her head back and looked up at the ceiling. "You know why I dropped out of grad school? Not because grad school wasn't going well; because my first audition tape for TV was awful. *I* was awful. I did it for the campus show, the weekend weather spot, almost as a joke; everyone said I'd be a natural. And I was awful. I'd finally found something that didn't come naturally, and I couldn't resist having to *try*. Meanwhile, my advisor was going to nominate me for a research fellowship, and I knew I'd get it. I'd get it, and then it would all start again. Wondering if things were going too well, if I was asking for trouble."

"But that's ridiculous."

"Whatever. I couldn't stand the suspen Eventually it was just too tempting, that feeli of starting over that I knew I'd get, and I gave a few times. Really just a few times. But Mon found out. She showed up at my apartment half a day earlier than expected for a visit, and I had just thrown up. I tried to tell her I had the flu, but she knew I was lying. You know how she used to look in our eyes and then tell us if we were sick or not?"

"I know."

"So she got it out of me, what was going on, and I guess it really scared her because she did the strangest thing. She left the apartment without a word and returned a few minutes later with a pack of cigarettes and some matches. She took me to the bathroom and then she lit a cigarette—I remember her hands were shaking—and she smoked it in front of me."

Olivia couldn't even picture this.

"She was coughing the whole time, and I was pleading with her to stop—I can't tell you how disturbing it was. I mean, it doesn't seem like it should be a big deal, but it was awful. *Our mother* smoking a cigarette. She had me in tears. I knew it was my fault she was doing it, even though I didn't know *why* she was doing it. Finally, when she reached the end, she was feeling pretty sick herself. I remember sitting down next to her on tub and telling her to breathe slowly and ply, which was hard for her because she'd rt coughing again. And then she said, 'Every me you do that to yourself, I'm going to smoke a cigarette.' "

Olivia realized her mouth was open. She closed it. She slid down the length of the bathroom door and sat with her back against it, hugging her knees to her chest.

"I said, this is ridiculous, Mother, not to mention *sick;* if I could not throw up, don't you think I would? And she said, then you better get yourself a counselor, missy, or figure something else out, because *you don't treat my baby that way.* That's the number-one rule, she said: You don't hurt my baby. You don't make yourself sick. And if you really can't stop yourself, I want you to promise me to smoke a whole cigarette first, and think about what a stupid thing you're doing that whole time. At least then you'll have an honest reason to throw up."

"Good Lord."

"I know. And then she took half the cigarettes with her." Ruby started laughing. "She put them in a Ziploc baggie so she could leave me the pack."

"You've got to be kidding."

"And then she hounded me every day. I'd try to lie—you'd think I could lie on the phone—and she'd say, there's something I have to do, I'll call

285

you back. And I would know what was goin,
and would stand by the phone gnashing
teeth. It drove me nuts. I would think, what
she gets hooked? What if my Mennonite mothe
gets addicted to cigarettes?"

"Did you smoke one, too, like she said to?"

"Not at first. First, I got a counselor and told her
everything."

"What did she say about Mom?"

"She said it was a desperate, manipulative, con-
trolling thing to do."

"Yeah?"

"Then I asked which was worse: forcing myself
to throw up or smoking a cigarette. And she
couldn't answer. She said it was maybe a toss-up.
They were both self-destructive. So the next time
I wanted to throw up I smoked one cigarette, just
to see. And by the time I was done, I was trying
not to throw up. I took a half-hour shower to get
the smoke out of my hair and clear the air in the
bathroom. I can't bear that smell. You have to
wash absolutely everything, towels, curtains, even
the stupid toilet seat cover." Ruby looked round
the bathroom now, gloomily. "You have to scrub
down the walls. Talk about a cleansing experience. It's cleansing, all right. It's a goddamned
pain in the neck."

"Couldn't you—instead of replacing one self-
destructive behavior with another, replace it with
something constructive?"

Vell, gee, Olivia, you should have gone into chology." Ruby crossed her arms and looked her sister. "What do you think the counselor uggested? Of course, we worked on that. Actually she was a really good counselor. She got me to take a few broadcasting classes before I left school, told me it might be good for me to have to really work at something. She was right. TV's the only thing I feel like I've ever really earned."

Olivia hesitated, turning the pack of cigarettes around and around in her hands. The plastic was gone, the lettering faded. She said, "You were sick recently. You missed half a day of work."

"Yeah, well, after that I dug out the cigarettes, for the first time in a long time. Mostly I just look at them." Ruby uncrossed her arms, clasped her hands between her bare knees. She looked as if she were shivering, even though it was another steamy day and the air-conditioning did nothing for this part of the house. "When I look at them it feels like . . . she's about to walk into the room."

Olivia knew that sometime in the next few sentences Ruby would decide Olivia had crossed a line, but she said very carefully, studying the cigarettes, "And today you were going to do it again."

Ruby was silent for so long that Olivia finally lifted her eyes. Her sister was staring across the room at her own reflection over the sink. just . . ." She stopped. "She keeps not walk into the room."

Olivia heaved herself off the floor, half-blind but before she took a step Ruby had slid off the edge of the tub and crossed to the mirror, leaning against the sink. By the time Olivia got to her she was wiping the last of the water from her eyes with a careful thumb. "Things aren't really bad," she said, more strongly now. She pulled one of her lower eyelids down, then the other, looking at something. "Other than Mom being dead. Things are just changing."

Olivia watched her sister's reflection. "Chicago."

"There would likely be this clause in the contract," Ruby said to the mirror. "I get my face done whenever they say. Within reason."

Olivia looked at her sister, as if the mirror might have lied, but saw that she was serious. "Your *face?* What is there to *do?*"

"Probably nothing for a few years. Maybe take care of any wrinkles around the eyes, that sort of thing."

"You're perfect *now*. And you're only thirty-one years old—which isn't even relevant: you're a meteorologist."

"I'm an extremely minor TV personality who dropped out of grad school."

"So . . . get out of TV and go back to grad

ol. I promise you won't find it easy to finish
octorate. You *will* have to try. Maybe you'll
lucky and blow it completely."

Ruby's eyes met Olivia's in the mirror, for one
econd. Not long enough for Olivia to read her
expression. "That's one option," she said briskly,
and she took the pack of cigarettes out of
Olivia's hand. She bent and shoved it into a
toiletries bag under the sink, then went to the tub
and started the water running.

"I'm serious," Olivia said. "That's it. Go back to
grad school."

"It's not that simple," Ruby said. She bent to
place the stopper, ran her hand under the water.

"I know it's not simple, I'm a grad student,
remember? I know whereof I speak. You just
need—"

"What I don't need is advice from you." Ruby
stood and picked up an ancient box of bath salts
that had been sitting on the shelf over the tub for
years. She sniffed it, frowning, poured some into
the running water.

"I'm just trying to help."

"If you want to help, take all the towels out of
here and throw them in the washer before
Father gets a whiff."

"We are not done here," Olivia said.

Ruby gave a sigh and turned to Olivia. "I
know. You have to tell me your thing. The thing
that Mother knew."

"That's not what I meant. You're stresse̶
enough that you were maybe about to f
yourself to vomit again—you *did* vomit, v
recently—which is a pretty clear sign of how y
feel about this Chicago offer, and I want som
reassurance that that's not going to start happening again."

"I'm fine," Ruby said, a little loudly. "We're
done discussing this, Livy. You know more than
you need to and now it's time to drop it. Tell me
your thing."

Olivia knelt at the sink, furious, and dug the
pack of cigarettes out of Ruby's bag. She shook
out several cigarettes and retreated to the door.
"I'm keeping this many," she said.

"Oh, for crying out loud. Don't be an ass."

"I'm keeping this many, and unless you convince me you're okay, you know what I'm
going to do with them."

"So go ahead. Enjoy."

"I have an obsessive personality, you know. I'll
get addicted. Remember when I was up to four
cans of Coke a day in college and the caffeine
made my heart race, and when I quit I got those
massive headaches? Remember when I was in
middle school and I borrowed your ABBA
record and listened to "Chiquitita" over and over
until it wore out the record in that spot?"

"For crying out loud—" Ruby tried to grab the
cigarettes away from Olivia. Olivia stepped

. against the door. "If you're going to act
. a child every time I tell you something, I'll
ver tell you anything."

"That's nothing new."

"Give me those." Ruby pinned Olivia against the door with one arm across her chest.

"*Ouch.*" She tried to hold the cigarettes out of reach, but Ruby was taller. Olivia threw the cigarettes down, scattering them over the floor. She pushed at Ruby while covering the cigarettes with one bare foot, but Ruby dropped and grabbed her ankle. Olivia almost fell, caught herself against the doorknob, and shoved Ruby in the shoulder with her other foot hard enough that Ruby fell sideways and landed on an elbow, nearly striking her head on the tub.

"Livy?" Father's voice came through the door. "You in there?"

Olivia and Ruby both froze. "I—yes, we'll be out in a minute."

Pause. "You're both in there?"

"We'll be out soon, Dad," Ruby said. "We're just—finishing up."

"Is everything all right?"

Olivia said, "Of course. Could you get the rice started? I'll be down in a minute."

Another pause, and they heard his footsteps depart.

Ruby said, "You little brat." She sat up and pulled a strand of hair out of her mouth.

Olivia picked up a cigarette with her toes looked at it. It was squashed, and there wa tiny piece of pink gravel embedded in it tl must have been between her toes the entire wa home.

"It's not like I can't go buy a pack," Olivia said, but she knew she wouldn't, and she knew Ruby knew she wouldn't, too.

"Look." Ruby pulled her legs under her, Indianstyle. "Now tell me your thing. Get on with it. I have to take a bath and get this smell out of my hair."

"Thanks for caring."

"Is it a good thing or a bad thing?"

Olivia said reluctantly, "Good thing." She felt her nose start to run. Ruby handed her the roll of toilet paper, which had rolled under the tub, and Olivia grabbed a few sheets. "It would normally be a good thing, anyway. I don't really care anymore, except that I almost wish it hadn't happened. I keep thinking, if it hadn't—"

"*What* already?"

"You don't have to snipe at me."

"Well, get to the point."

"If you're not going to stop treating me like your younger idiot sister, at least try to be a halfway decent *older* sister for a change."

"I can't *be* halfway decent if you don't ever get to the point."

"I passed my damn defense," Olivia said in a

voice. Her eyes and nose welled, and she
⁓ into the wad of toilet paper. "The day Mom
⁓ her stroke was the day I defended, and
⁓body knew it but her. It was supposed to be this
ig surprise. Then I came out of the defense and
they said there'd been an accident—I never got
to tell her how it came out." She was crying, and
mad at herself for crying in front of Ruby.

Ruby said, "Livy," and stood, came toward her,
but Olivia wouldn't look at her. She stiffened
when she felt Ruby's arms around her. Then she
realized Ruby was crying too, maybe for Olivia,
maybe for herself. She locked her arms around
Ruby's waist and stood there rocking with her
and thinking subversive words of comfort that
Ruby would never let her say—words for what
they'd both lost, words that would keep Ruby
from ever hurting Vivian's baby—and making
silent promises to their mother.

14

That night everyone—Father and Olivia, Ruby,
Annie et al.—congregated out at the farmhouse
for what the aunts called a light summer supper,
composed of leftovers from the meal they had
planned to serve David. There was Aunt
Rubina's Picnic Macaroni Salad and Aun

Barbara's Company Potato Salad, cr coleslaw, hot German slaw (David's favorit pan of brown sugar baked beans, and an er mous maple ham with warm pineapple sauce because you couldn't expect men to sit down to meal without any meat at all and feel that they'c had a real meal. On the side there was Aunt Barbara's Marshmallow Salad, Aunt Rubina's 7-Layer Jell-O Surprise, deviled eggs dusted with paprika, fresh zwieback rolls, and pickled everything: cucumbers, beets, cauliflower, watermelon.

Olivia knew she would eat too much, and she did, remorsefully and steadily. She looked up toward the end of the meal and met the same dazed expression in the others' eyes that she knew she had in her own—all of them awash in sour cream and mayonnaise, starches and vinegars.

After dinner, as soon as everyone could walk again, they followed Ruby out to her car to say good-bye. The top was down; Olivia leaned down over the driver's side window and whispered, "Are you sure you're okay?"

"If I don't explode," Ruby said, looking past her with a smile.

Olivia gave her a look that went unreceived. "Email me," she said loudly as her sister pulled away.

Back at home, Olivia and Father took a long, slow walk around the neighborhood to try to down the dinner still distending their .achs. They didn't speak much; it was nearly ossible to be heard over the rasping of the adas. Olivia had always loved the sound— e quintessential sound of summer—but she couldn't remember when the cicadas had been louder. Each buzzing voice crescendoed tunelessly to a jerky, insistent fortissimo until an entire chorus buzzed at full blast, comfortably off pitch from one another. It was a relief each time the chorus died down for a few moments, but also a relief not to have to talk.

Olivia went to bed while it was still light out, as soon as she could lie prone without reflux. Then she stared at the ceiling, thinking about Ruby. Her stomach roiled. She thought about Psalm 137 from church that morning, and then she tried to think about anything else at all: what David's stepchildren might be like, Annie's pregnancy, although not Harry. She heard the clock downstairs strike ten, eleven, twelve. When it struck one, she got up and slipped on some sweats and went down to the kitchen. The bottle of Tums still stood on the counter. Olivia shook out four tablets and popped them in her mouth, poured herself a ginger ale to wash down the chalkiness. Then she made her way to Father's office in the dark and turned on the green banker's lamp and the computer. She pulled up her mother's newsletter, which she hadn't touched in nearly a week, and went to blandest, most innocuous section: "Casse Corner." She pulled a recipe card from the ne letter file and read, Elegant French Pork a Beans, by Carmine Grosz of Huron, South Dakot

She tried to imagine her mother smoking a cigarette but couldn't.

Elegant French Pork and Beans, by Carmine Grosz of Huron, South Dakota.

Olivia could remember the first time she'd ever heard Psalm 137. Vivian used to read a Psalm every day as part of her scripture reading, and sometimes she'd read it out loud to Father. One evening she read Psalm 137. Olivia must have been just five or six years old, because she was playing around the footstool with her Upsy-Downsy dolls, only half-listening, when the last line struck her. She looked up and said, "Does 'little ones' mean babies?"

"Yes," said Vivian.

"*What* does it say to do to them?"

Vivian sent Father a look, then recited the last line again: " 'Happy shall he be, that taketh and dasheth thy little ones against the stones.' "

Her mother always read from the King James Version, so Olivia was familiar enough with "taketh" and "dasheth" and thees, thys, and thous. But she thought she must have misunderstood. "So what is he doing to the babies? He's throwing them against *rocks?*"

'He's talking about the babies of some people, the Babylonians, who were very mean to the people of Israel. He's very upset with all these Babylonians. He says they've been so bad that anyone who throws their babies against the rocks is doing a good thing."

"But you can't blame the babies," said Olivia, who was very interested in babies. "Couldn't they just take the babies away and adopt them and teach them to be nice?"

"Well, it was different in those days. They believed that if people were very, very bad, *everyone* had to be punished, even little children and babies, or the badness wouldn't stop. These babies had very bad parents."

Olivia was shocked. She was shocked at the thought of *parents* who were *sinful*. She tried to think of the most sinful thing anyone could do. There were many things to choose from, but once on *The Six Million Dollar Man*, a man chased someone with his car on purpose and would have squashed them if Steve Austin hadn't shown up. Olivia had had nightmares and wasn't allowed to watch *The Six Million Dollar Man* anymore. But that man wasn't somebody's *parent*. Olivia tried to imagine her friend Kathy Myers's mother doing the same thing, chasing someone down the block with her station wagon, her pudgy face determined beneath rows of prickly pink curlers, but Olivia couldn't make

Mrs. Myers look sufficiently upset to actua[ly] run over her victim, who Olivia had decided w[as] her teenaged son Brad. Mrs. Myers kept pullin[g] over and yelling at Brad to get home and take out the garbage. It was easier to imagine *Mr.* Myers murdering someone with a car. Sometimes Mr. Myers drank a beer while watching football, neither of which activity Olivia's father ever engaged in. Still, even when Olivia played this scenario out in her mind, a policeman would just show up and take Mr. Myers off to jail, and it was very hard to imagine the policeman dashing Kathy's baby sister against the gravel driveway. Maybe *both* parents had to be equally sinful . . .

"Jesus loves the little children," Olivia quoted to her mother at last, to get back on surer footing.

"Yes, but this was long before Jesus."

"Didn't God the Father love little children before Jesus was around?"

"Of course. God even loved the Babylonians. In fact, God *let* the Babylonians be mean to Israel, to teach them a lesson."

Olivia stood there for a long time trying to understand this. "Then he should have warned them about their babies," she said finally, feeling a bit put out with God. He seemed to be getting people in trouble himself.

Vivian turned to her husband. "I wouldn't mind having one child who wasn't quite so

cocious," she said, closing her Bible and
:ding Olivia off for her bath.

But the Babylonian babies returned to bother
Olivia at bedtime, and she was allowed to crawl
into Annie's bed. "Of course, God loves all little
babies," Annie told her.

"Little sisters, on the other hand . . ." Ruby
said suggestively from the doorway.

"It's sinful to tease," Olivia said in tears, but
that only made Ruby laugh harder. Ruby was
often sinful. Ruby slammed doors and talked
back, and if she had candy she felt no obligation
to share.

After that night, Mother was more careful to
screen the Psalms she read out loud, and Olivia
forevermore had the King James Version of
Psalm 137 verse 9 burned in her brain: *Happy
shall he be, that taketh and dasheth thy little
ones against the stones.*

She sighed hard and shook her head, realized
she was still staring at the same recipe card in
her hand. She propped it against the monitor and
read again, Elegant French Pork and Beans, by
Carmine Grosz of Huron, South Dakota. She
scanned the recipe, which called for haricot
beans—a not inelegant bean, Olivia thought. Two
kinds of sausage, two cuts of pork. Leeks. Well.
This looked like a midwesternized cassoulet—
definitely better than the usual "Casserole
Corner" fare, which was largely made up of

recipes containing endless and minute variati
on the same hot dishes, issue after issue. Fo.
couple of years there, chicken and broccoli ha
been all the rage: Chicken Broccoli Divar
Chicken Broccoli *Divine,* Chicken Broccoli
Supreme ("Them's fightin' words," Ruby had told
Vivian). Chicken Broccoli Surprise, Chicken
Broccoli *Rice* Surprise (David: "Where's the
surprise? You've just listed all the ingredients in
the title"). Elegant Company Chicken-Broccoli
Casserole. "Which is the elegant part," Olivia had
asked over the phone from college, because she
was studying ambiguous reference in her
Linguistic Description of Modern English class,
"the company or the casserole?"

"The Ladies are sharing their favorite recipes,"
Vivian had said at last (she had given up and
started capitalizing the Ladies years earlier; you
could hear it in her voice), one Sunday dinner
when everyone was home on break but David.
"And anyway most of them are quite good. I
don't recall any complaints yesterday over that
Chinese Chicken Broccoli Hotdish."

"It was delicious," Father said, his voice
barely rising on the last syllable, so that they
knew he was not done. He picked up his glass,
took a sip of water, set the glass down. "But it
was about as Chinese as you and I."

Anything with water chestnuts was Chinese.
Anything with a can of green chilis was Mexican.

Anything over which you passed a carton of sour cream could be called Stroganoff, as in Oven Tuna Stroganoff. David had called over that one, too. "This could start another cold war," he said.

"Why do you even read my newsletter?" Vivian said. "If you're only going to read it to be critical, I'm taking you off the subscription list. You don't even cook."

"I'm just glad you didn't draw a little Cossack dancer in the margin."

"I think that would be adorable," Vivian said, "and if I knew how to draw a Cossack dancer, maybe I would have."

Olivia had to smile at the memory of David and Vivian going round and round, David presenting his linear arguments, Mother always wriggling off in another direction. She thought, *Well, Mother, he's gone and gotten himself married. What do you think of that?*

Then she pulled the keyboard closer and typed:

Thanks to Carmine Grosz of Huron, South Dakota, for the following recipe.

She keyed in recipes until her head grew sufficiently heavy and she knew she could go to bed and sleep. But she didn't, not yet. She pulled up her email and hit "Create New Message" without checking to see if there were any new messages in her inbox. She'd had enough new messages for one weekend—enough painful disclosures. The mere thought of secrets wearied her. She entered the email addresses of everyone in the family, and after thinking about it for a moment, copied in Harry, Dr. Vitale, and Maureen. Then she typed:

On April 22, the day Mom had her stroke, I defended my dissertation and passed. Mom knew I was defending that day. We were going to surprise the rest of you. If you don't mind I'd rather not talk about it for a while.

The aunts didn't have email; someone would have to fill them in. She wondered in passing who would get to them first. Almost certainly Annie. She hit "Send."

Unburdened of one secret at least, Olivia powered down the computer and went to bed.

The next morning at Meals on Wheels, Olivia tried to make it past the kitchen window with a simple wave but was waylaid by Marjean, who'd apparently stopped by on one of her occasional random visits. The morning volunteers were handing the baby around, and Marjean, leaning against the counter, asked how the visit with David's new girlfriend went. Olivia tried to think of an unsensational way to describe David's announcement but soon realized there wasn't one: the less one said in preamble, the more surprising the news that David was married. She tried to build to it a bit by saying how much they all liked Janet from the start, how impressed they were that David was dating someone with small children . . . When she finally admitted that it turned out they were already married, everyone gasped. And it was interesting even to Olivia to realize that the true climax of the story was not, as she'd expected, the moment of that announcement, but the subsequent revelation that Janet thought everyone already knew.

"I bet she had a few things to say about *that*," said one volunteer, and everyone nodded in satisfaction.

"What did Ruby think of the whole affair?" Doris asked.

"She's happy for him," Olivia said, smiling blandly. "We all are. We all like Janet very much."

Pans of cornbread were coming out of the oven, and Olivia used the distraction to slip away.

She was not ready to check her email. She spent the rest of the morning typing up a brief set of instructions on walkie-talkie use. The delivery volunteers for the week were from Speak the Word Church of the Spirit, the Methodists having done their duty for another six months, so at delivery time every pair of Speak the Worders received one walkie-talkie and a set of instructions. Olivia hoped privately that the Spirit would not move anyone to speak in tongues on the air.

She did not check her email.

Olivia left Meals on Wheels at three o'clock that afternoon, went home, and lay down on the couch. J.C. walked up her leg and stood on her hip for a minute, her small feet pressing four painful points into Olivia's flesh, before finally settling into a roosting position right there, paws tucked neatly out of sight. After that they both slept, Olivia quite hard, and when she opened her eyes a couple of hours later, the cat was gone and Father was standing over her. He was actually grinning.

"We don't have to talk about it," he said. "But I'm taking you out for dinner."

They went to Jasper's Downtown Café. Jasper's had been around only one or two years but had so neatly created a niche for itself, a casual-but-white-tablecloth niche, that its patrons could not remember what they had done before. (They had settled for the grill at Sorley's Pub. Some of them had gone to Sioux Falls.) Olivia had lunched there with Vivian and Maureen once or twice. Sitting in that cool interior surrounded by sea-foam green with shell-pink accents was balm to the nerves, even if, mere moments before, you hadn't known you needed soothing.

It was unfashionably early, and the hostess led them to one of the coveted tables for two that sat on a dais against the back inside wall. A long plate-glass window in this wall allowed you to see into the kitchen, so if you wanted to watch Dan Jasper's station chefs assembling salads and slicing cheesecakes, you could. It was the only restaurant in Brookings—possibly in all of eastern South Dakota—that let you look into the kitchen, and many people felt that the playfulness of it, the irreverence, was quite chic. Olivia personally disliked the window (she became self-conscious if anyone watched *her* cook), but she agreed that the food was good, gourmet with a local twist: Dakota Cobb Salad, Very Berry Tiramisu.

Father accepted a menu without opening it. When their waitress arrived, he asked, "What would you recommend along the lines of meat?"

"There's a peppercorn steak with gorgonzola sauce."

He looked vaguely troubled. Father's palate had been broadened by years of marriage to Vivian, but he was a purist where steak was concerned.

"Or the Pork Saltimbocca is very popular," she added quickly. "With polenta on the side, but you can always substitute roasted potatoes."

"Then that's what I'll have," he said, looking relieved and handing her the menu.

"Tortellini in a roasted red pepper sauce," Olivia said. "With the Italian wedding soup, please."

"And a bottle of champagne," Father said. He smiled at Olivia, a bit awkwardly.

"You don't even like champagne," Olivia said.

"What are we celebrating?" asked the waitress brightly.

Father looked at Olivia, who hardened her heart and closed her mouth. Father had always let Vivian do most of the interacting with the wait-staff, with strangers in lines—any situation in which socializing was not strictly required or even, in his view, desirable. After Olivia looked back at him long enough, he said, with a bigger, more awkward smile, "My daughter's finished her doctorate in linguistics."

"Congratulations," said the waitress to Olivia. "Of course, you should have champagne."

"At least make it something we both like," Olivia said to Father. "Maybe just a glass each of the house red."

The waitress gathered the menus and left. Olivia and Father both looked at their water goblets. Olivia remembered that there was a kitchen to look into, and did. Maybe the window wasn't such a bad idea. This table would be, she thought, an ideal place for a breakup. She said it to Father: "This would be an ideal place for a breakup. So much to look at besides the other person."

Father said, "Are we really not supposed to talk about your defense?"

via sighed. It would have been so easy with Ian. She would have plunged in without king. "I guess it's all right," she said.

They were silent for another minute, which was one reason, really, that it *was* okay to talk about it with Father. How long did he ever dwell on anything, anyway? How much delving did he ever do?

"Of course, I understand why you haven't wanted to tell anyone," he said finally.

"Oh. I'm glad."

"Although it does seem as if your life would have been easier if you had. What with all of us pressing you to get back to work."

"Yes, I could have done without that," Olivia said.

"I was wondering," Father said. He stopped because their wine arrived, and a basket of bread. They waited until the waitress had gone again, then bowed their heads and prayed silently for their meals. Olivia lifted her head first and tore a warm crusty roll in two.

"I was wondering," he began again. "Why *didn't* you tell us? Before now?"

"So you don't understand why."

"I suppose I don't," he said. "But it doesn't seem all that strange either. There's no normal way to behave after—after what happened."

Olivia appreciated this, grudgingly. But she said, "There are a lot of reasons people keep things to themselves. I mean, why do *you* certain things to yourself? Or you and Mc You, Mom, and the others?"

Father said mildly, "I suppose people kec things to themselves if they feel those thing. aren't of interest to anyone."

Only Father would have thought of this.

"Nobody in our family ever thinks their news is not newsworthy except you," Olivia said.

"We were always careful not to tell about Christmas presents," Father said, gently pulling a piece of bread apart, "and birthday presents. That's temporary, so maybe that doesn't count."

"It doesn't," Olivia affirmed. She took a sip of wine and thought again how easy this would be with Vivian. Olivia could have blurted what she'd learned about Ruby, railed about having to learn it from a near stranger, and Vivian would have soothed and apologized or gotten angry herself, most likely some combination thereof, and two hours later the air would have been cleared and every inch of the topic explored.

Father wasn't nearly so satisfying to get angry with. But he was all there was now, and Olivia was angry enough that she wasn't going to let him off the hook just because Vivian was dead. "I was surprised recently," she began. He looked up from his bread. She tried again. "Maybe the most surprising thing about family secrets is learning that they exist at all. When you were one ones who didn't know, I mean. Possibly the one."

ather said, "Yes, I suppose that stands to ason." He seemed to have forgotten that he vas holding a butter knife.

"That's not what I meant to say. I meant to say that I suppose it's natural for people to keep things from the youngest person in the family, however annoying to the youngest that may be, and then it doesn't even seem like a secret to anyone, it's just one more thing kept from the youngest person in the family. But when that person finds things out, especially if it's from a total stranger, it certainly does feel like some dark, horrible secret—" She instantly regretted this choice of words, what happened to Ruby having been in fact dark and horrible. "I mean, it feels, aside from the secret itself, dark and horrible that things had been kept from her. From me. And which I had to learn from a complete stranger."

Father set down the butter knife and the bread. He was not naturally a wary person, the way some people were not math people and had to bring to bear on all mathematical problems an uneasy, effortful force. Father's ears were flushed, and he looked prepared to be miserable. Olivia knew pity, even regret, but it was too late. She pressed on. "I mean, for example,"—this was laughably inaccurate, since it was no mere example but the

entire point, but it softened things, made he
that she was approaching an impossible t
sideways rather than head on—"for exampl
had to hear it from a stranger recently. Abc
Ruby in high school."

One more moment of eye contact, and she
knew he knew exactly what she was talking
about. She dropped her eyes.

The salads had arrived—she didn't know when.
She picked up a fork and poked around in the
greens, skewered a huge homemade crouton. She
put it in her mouth and it hurt her mouth, and she
chewed unhappily, eyes watering from the pain.
She remembered gratefully the bright window at
her elbow and watched a pasta insert being lifted
from a vat of water, silver water streaming back
into the pot, a thick white veil of steam rising
upward. Heat and water and steam, and now the
steaming fettuccine schlooping gloriously into a
large white bowl. When she looked at Father
again, furtively, he was staring at his salad as if
he had never seen one before. His ears were still
flushed, and his face now as well.

Not taking his eyes from the salad, he picked
up his fork. "Who was it?" he said in a voice so
tight Olivia nearly moved her chair back a few
inches. "The stranger who told you?"

"Winnie Kilkenny."

He looked up. The expression in his eyes was
terrible and wounded—Olivia had opened that

d—but he was willing to look up at that
e. "Of course. Winnie Kilkenny."

livia nodded, matching misery for misery.
ey ate their salads in silence, and she realized
he was growing angry again, but not, this time,
with Father. She was angry with Vivian, because
Vivian would have said she'd done wrong to
confront him—Vivian would have said the guilt
that now flooded her was justified. However
Vivian might have fielded accusations against
herself, she would have risen like a valkyrie to
Father's defense and said it was unfair and
unkind to ambush him with this topic, when he
could scarcely bear to think about it then or now.
Protecting him, Olivia thought furiously, *from
engaging in basic communication with his
children.* And to what end? Vivian dies, and the
important things lie dormant until the end of
time.

In her fury she had finished every scrap of
greens, every shred of julienned cucumber on her
plate, with the result that she now had nothing
to do. The bread basket was empty. She lifted
her wineglass and drained it.

The waitress materialized at her elbow, as
suddenly as if Olivia had rubbed a magic lamp.
"Would you like another glass?" she asked.

Olivia would. "Since we're *celebrating,*" she
said, eyes still lowered, and cringed at her own
words. She willed the glass of wine to materialize

as miraculously as the waitress, but the w
picked it up along with Olivia's salad plate,
bore both pieces pedantically back to her stati

Father, as Olivia had done, was plowing throu
his salad. She wanted to warn him to slow dow
or they would both be left with nothing to do
save stare into the kitchen window, which, she
saw now, was much too obvious if they were
both doing it. There were the water goblets; she
supposed they could take turns sipping at those
like a pair of those damn plastic birds that dipped
and rose, dipped and rose. He was down to the
last two slivers of carrot. Olivia watched darkly
while he negotiated this difficulty. They were
too slender to be skewered by the fork, and there
was nothing to push them up against to nudge
them onto the fork bed; even the sides of the
squarish salad plate offered no purchase, barely
sloping as they did to the edge, and entirely
lacking that small vertical rise that usually
bordered the inside base of a plate. *What a stupid
design,* Olivia thought, enraged now at an entire
wing of the dinnerware design industry, the self-
important wing more interested in pretentiously
modern design than in the needs of diners to gain
access to their food. The glass of wine had still
not appeared, and she waited for Father to think
of picking up his knife and pushing the carrots
forth onto his fork—it was the only option as far
as she could see. But then in one fluid motion

she was quite sure he had never made
~~~re in his life, Father approached the carrots
end with the fork alone and swept them up
.th the help of sheer momentum. *Nicely exe-
uted,* she thought bitterly, turning to the window.
She waited for him to realize what he'd done.

There was a very long moment while they both
concentrated on the activity through the bright
glass. Olivia did not try to assign meaning to the
activity but only envied it.

"Here you go," the waitress said, and Olivia and
Father both started. There was her wineglass,
refilled, and a bowl of steaming Italian wedding
soup, and the waitress retreating with Father's
empty salad plate. Olivia gladly relinquished the
window to Father and picked up her soup
spoon.

But Father did not turn back to the window. He
was surprising her in small ways today: the offer
of champagne, the scooping up of the carrots, and
now watching her eat her soup even though it
increased the risk of eye contact. The soup was so
hot she had to blow lightly on each spoonful
before putting it in her mouth. She did this
steadily, doggedly.

Father said, his voice expressionless, "I
imagine Winnie Kilkenny is still upset about
what happened. About what Vivian did."

"I don't even know what Mother did," Olivia
said to her soup, remembering suddenly that she

didn't know. "We never got that far. Winnie
something about nearly losing her grandson
don't know how, or what that could have to
with anything."

"I'll tell you what happened," Father said.

Olivia was so astonished she looked up.

"She was upset about—not just about what
happened to Ruby. We learned there was no point
in pressing charges: lack of evidence. He was
going to get away with it. Vivian went over to
Winnie Kilkenny's to tell her this latest development. It's strange," he said, and he stopped.

Olivia put down her spoon and waited.

"All the people Vivian was close to, and she
chose Winnie Kilkenny. She didn't tell anyone
else anything. We'd agreed not to tell anyone,
not even the aunts; this was very important to
Ruby. But she had told Winnie Kilkenny everything, all along. I've never been entirely sure
why. Maybe because Winnie was unconnected to
everyone else we knew. Maybe because Winnie
herself was so vulnerable. I don't know why that
would help. But I think the real reason she went
there that day was to run into Mr. Kilkenny."

"Why on earth?"

"To provoke him."

"Provoke him—into doing what?"

Father hesitated. "Hitting her," he said finally.

Olivia felt faint: too much oxygen, or not
enough. She took a breath but still could barely

314

out the words: "She wanted Mr. Kilkenny
t her?"

That's correct."

Father was terrible at this. He was so to the
point that you missed the point.

"Why on earth?"

"I think she wanted someone to pay for something. She'd always suspected he was abusive,
and that day she confronted him. She didn't let
up until he did something she could take to the
police."

"How did she—what did she say? How the hell
did she bring something like that up? Was
Winnie there the whole time?"

"I'm sure Winnie was there the whole time. I
don't know exactly how the conversation went."

"You must remember something. She must
have told you everything." Olivia realized she
was waving her hands and wondered suddenly if
she were as visible to the kitchen crew as they
were to her. She wondered but didn't care.

Father said, "I know she accused him of
being abusive and told him she would call the
authorities. He got angry, she pressed her case,
and before long—"

"Are you done with your soup?" the waitress
asked Olivia.

Olivia said, "I don't know." She had forgotten it
was there and looked down at it. It seemed to
be half full. "I don't know."

The waitress melted away.

"He didn't hit her right away. I think he to drag her out of the house, none too gently. resisted; she wouldn't stop talking until he her."

"Once? Did he hit her more than once?"

"I'm not sure."

"How can you not be sure? Was she all *right?*"

"She had a nasty bruise on her head, later that night. Otherwise she was fine. She got right up and went to the police. She called me from there."

"Did she have any trouble getting away from him? Did she have any trouble getting out?"

"I gather he knew he'd made a big mistake the minute he knocked her down. She went on about that later—how he had the self-control to stop, which convinced her he was just a cold, mean man who hit his family because he wanted to."

Olivia looked down, and there was a plate of tortellini in roasted red pepper sauce where her soup had been. The waitress had left a small glass bowl of parmesan cheese and a tiny spoon. Olivia's eyes welled.

"And the police—did they do what she wanted?"

"Essentially." Father cut off a bite of pork tenderloin, which had just as magically appeared. Olivia saw a layer of prosciutto, could smell the sage leaves across the table. "She really wanted them to haul him off to jail that day, and keep

here. They did bring him in, but I can't
mber if he had to stay overnight. But
hen, the grandson, was removed from the
me almost immediately."

"Oh. Of course." She meant, *Of course, Winnie
Kilkenny was upset.* She'd already lost her
daughter; then the grandson, too. *But what a
selfish love,* Olivia thought, *preferring him to be
under the thumb of an abusive man like Mr.
Kilkenny.* Olivia knew she must be oversimplify-
ing, but she didn't care. Vivian had been right to
act as she did. She probably should have done it
sooner.

Although, why hadn't she? Olivia shifted in her
seat, speared a couple of tortellini, and ate them
slowly. Apparently even Vivian had found it hard
to draw the line, until something else compelled
her to act.

"She didn't lose him forever," Olivia said.
"Does that mean things got better in the home?"

"It means Mr. Kilkenny died just a short while
later."

"Really?"

"Within two or three months."

"That's awfully convenient," Olivia said,
meaning it.

"That's what your mother said. She was relieved
when she read it in the paper."

"She and Winnie were not on speaking terms
anymore, I take it."

"That's correct."

"And the grandson was able to return h
and Mrs. Kilkenny continued to raise him?"

"Yes. Mr. Kilkenny did right by them in c
regard, anyway, and that was providing for the⟩
in the event of his death. Mrs. Kilkenny never hac
to work, and they were always comfortable. I
don't remember how Vivian found out the details,
but she did. She wanted to be sure they were
going to be all right."

"Did she ever get back in touch?"

"She wrote to Winnie after the funeral, asking
if she might visit; she never received a reply. I
think she wrote twice and gave up."

The tortellini was tender, and Olivia thought
she detected a note of balsamic vinegar. The tart-
sweetness spread from the tip of her tongue
throughout her mouth; she swallowed, and her
sorrow deepened. It was nonsensical to mourn an
injury done to Vivian years ago and long since
healed, but just as pointless to tell herself this.
She took another slow bite.

"She did the right thing," she said, almost forgetting she was speaking out loud.

"She could have found another way," Father
said. "Something less painful for Winnie. But I
never faulted her. She was under tremendous
stress. If she hadn't confronted Mr. Kilkenny, she
probably would have confronted Coach Sutter,
and that would have been much worse."

ia felt utterly helpless. She remembered
thing Ruby had said. "I thought you and
m did confront Coach Sutter. Even though
u weren't supposed to."

Father cut off another bite of pork. He chewed
for a moment, watching Olivia. "I did. Not your
mother."

This was most unexpected. She put down her
fork and looked at him. Father went back to his
plate, dragged a sage leaf over to one side with his
fork, pushed the remaining morsel of pork and
prosciutto into what was left of the sauce and ate
it. When he looked up again, he seemed to realize
that she was waiting for something. He swallowed
and said, "I never talked about it. Even to Vivian."

That was it, then. She sighed a little and went
back to her tortellini. She was not, strangely, as
disappointed as she would have expected. More
strangely still, as she cleaned her own plate she
became aware that she was even perhaps the
smallest bit relieved. She pushed her plate away
and looked up to see that Father was smiling.
She waited again.

"I doubt Coach Sutter ever talked about it
either," Father said. He wiped his mouth, and the
smile was gone.

"Dessert?" asked the waitress as she picked up
their plates.

"Yes, please," Olivia said. She was still watching Father. "We'll take two of whatever's biggest."

319

• • •

It was not until they were nearly home, jus. red light away, and Olivia was digging in purse for a tissue, that she remembered t photograph of Winnie Kilkenny's grandson. Sh pulled it out of her purse and handed it to Father, pointed out Stephen. "Can you guess who this is?"

He studied it, and when the light turned green handed it back. "No."

"Winnie Kilkenny's grandson." She looked at it again before putting it back in her purse. "I should return it. I left in a hurry last week and didn't realize I was holding on to it."

Father said, "He looks like he's doing well."

"It's just one picture," Olivia said. "Who knows?"

"He's still in her life, anyway. That's good."

"Yes." They pulled into the driveway. "Not the daughter, though. How happy can Winnie Kilkenny be, even with her grandson, when she's estranged from her daughter?"

Father turned off the car but sat for a moment, keys in hand. "That surprises me," he said after a moment, and got out.

Olivia followed. "Why would that surprise you?"

"The daughter moved back to the area, I think. One would think she wouldn't move back here if she wanted distance from her mother."

320

w do you know this?"

vian knew it," he said simply. For a moment
ia thought he would stop there; it almost
unnecessary to go on. Vivian knew it. Vivian
new so much. She made it her business to
know—or sometimes it seemed as if information
sought her out as a resting place, or as a place
where it would be handled appropriately,
expediently, *done* something with, even if that
something turned out in fact to be blundering
and inexpert. Vivian was not without her sins, but
she was not guilty of Winnie's sins of omission.
Rarely that.

They went into the house.

"She found some article in the paper at some
point," he said. "I don't even remember if it was
the *Brookings Register*, or something someone
clipped from the *Argus Leader* and sent to her. It
was about restaurants in this part of the state,
trends in eating."

"And Samantha Kilkenny was in it?"

"One of several new restaurant owners being
featured. She opened up a place in Mitchell, I
think. Or Huron."

Olivia set her purse on the coffee table and
dug out the photograph again, as if Stephen
Kilkenny's face could tell her anything about
his mother. "I'm just sure she hasn't been in
touch with Winnie," she said. "But you know
why she moved back? He's a health inspector

321

for the state. I bet she moved back hopin̲
walk into her restaurant."

Father was settling into his chair with
paper. It was rare for him not to open the pa̲
until after dinner, and Olivia said, "Thank you f̲
dinner. It was delicious." She leaned over an̲
pecked him on the cheek.

"We'll have to celebrate with everyone soon,
you know. You can't avoid it forever."

Olivia nodded, but she was only half listening.
She stood there for several minutes studying
the photograph and wondering which was worse:
separation by death or estrangement. Having
posed the question, she couldn't decide, and that
was the most surprising thought yet.

15

Olivia finally checked her email again the next
day to discover a barrage of messages flying back
and forth between her siblings, with Father and
Olivia copied in. David started them off:

**Sources tell me that our little sister has
snuck off and defended her thesis in the
dead of night, as it were—successfully!!!
Can you believe it??!! Little Livy, a**

If it makes you feel any better, you can take me out for dinner tonight.

They went to Jasper's. Annie requested a table on the dais. Olivia said, as they were being seated, "They do a good Italian wedding soup here."

"You can't seriously expect me not to talk about your defense."

"Remember how thrilled you were to find out you were pregnant? Remember how you didn't want to talk about it?"

"Yes, well, thanks to Aunt Barbara, I now get to talk about it whenever anybody wants to. Although I suppose I was about to tell anyway," she added grudgingly. "Anyway, I don't see why you should get off any easier."

A waitress brought menus. They opened them and started perusing. Ordering with Annie was very different from ordering with Father.

"Shrimp Alexander . . . I'm not feeling very seafoody lately. Pan-roasted Saddle of Venison with blah blah blah and Madeira Jus. Sounds good except for the venison part. I don't remember this Linguini Algonquin. Have they changed the menu?"

"Not lately," Olivia said. "The Pork Saltimbocca is very good."

Annie looked around. The waitress who had served Olivia and Father was walking by, and Annie waved her over.

"She's not our waitress," Olivia said.

"It's no problem," the waitress said. She recognized Olivia and smiled, then turned back to Annie. "What can I do for you?"

"What about this Linguini Algonquin? Do you recommend that?"

"It's very good if you like roasted red peppers and spinach. Actually it's quite spinachy."

"It doesn't sound very *rich*," Annie said reluctantly. "Even *spinachy* spinach doesn't pack much of a wallop, if you know what I mean."

The waitress peered over her shoulder and pointed to something on the menu. "The Spaghetti Carbonara with Dakota Smoked Bacon is very popular."

"And that's rich?"

"Of course, it's rich," Olivia broke in. "It's bacon and eggs on pasta."

"Spinach Tortellini in Roasted Red Pepper Sauce," Annie read.

Olivia said to the waitress who was not their waitress, "Thanks for your help." The woman nodded and left.

Olivia leaned forward. "The tortellini is good but not as good as Mom's. And they use balsamic vinegar in the sauce. It's good but wrong."

When their real waitress reappeared, Olivia ordered the Shrimp Alexander and Annie ordered the Spaghetti Carbonara. Annie also ordered Jasper's Blue Salad with blue cheese dressing and a bowl of cream of potato soup.

"I respect cholesterol as much as the next gourmand," Olivia said, "but you're going to have a coronary right here, and I'm going to feel guilty."

"Cholesterol is good for babies," Annie said. "You're supposed to eat extra eggs and stuff when you're pregnant."

"Uh-huh."

"So Mom knew you were defending, and she managed not to leak it to anyone."

"Looks like it."

"And you never got to tell her you passed."

"No."

Annie lifted her water glass. "To death!" she said. "You won this round, but you're going down, buddy, so don't get used to it."

Olivia clinked her sister's glass with her own and they both drank deeply. A passing busboy gave them an odd look.

"Isn't that a John Donne poem?" Olivia asked, wiping her mouth with the back of her hand.

"If it isn't, it should be."

The salads arrived. Annie said, "So you're really done?"

"I haven't handed in the final paperwork. And, of course, I do have to make some edits. Right now I'm waiting to hear back from Dr. Vitale to see if my extension can be extended. Special circumstances and all."

"Will that be a problem?"

"I don't think so. Dr. Vitale was pretty relieved to hear from me again. He'll probably tell them I had a nervous breakdown, if he has to. I think that's what he believes anyway."

"Well. So what happens next, Dr. Tschetter?"

Olivia looked up from a tomato wedge. "I expect Father to answer when you say that."

"Dr. Tschetter. Can you believe it?" Annie was grinning. "That's three Dr. Tschetters in the family now."

Olivia said, "Two Dr. Tschetters and a Dr. Tschetter-Rodriguez."

Annie lifted her water glass again. "To men who hyphenate, and the women who talk them into it!"

They clinked and drank.

"The hyphenation was David's idea," Olivia reminded her.

"To men addled with love, and the women who addle them!"

Another clink.

Annie replaced her water glass. She added another dollop of blue cheese dressing to what was left of her salad and dug in again. "So does this mean you're job hunting? Looking for a postdoc?"

"No, and I really *don't* want to talk about it."

"All right, what do you want to talk about?"

Olivia said, "Well, I'm almost done with Mom's newsletter."

"Really? I thought it was pretty slow going."

"I got into it again this week. Spent Sunday night doing "Casserole Corner," moved on to "Desserts to Delight You"—ugh, I've never liked Mom's titles. And today at work I had time to wrap up most of those tomato recipes. I wrote up a nice little paragraph introducing Janet, by the way, to go with her Pork Enchiladas recipe. About all that's left is to go back and fake my way through the rest of "Ask Vivian." It's the hardest part of the whole newsletter. Mom could rattle off these wonderful answers without batting an eyelash, but what do I know?"

"You know plenty."

"No I don't. One Lady wants to know whether instant yeast is just as good as regular yeast. I didn't even know there *was* such a thing as instant yeast. Another Lady wants to know why her rhubarb crumble always comes out stringy when she's using her mother's recipe and her mother's rhubarb crumble never came out stringy at all."

"Hmm. That's a good one. You don't peel rhubarb, do you?"

"And the *emotional* questions are worse. You know, when they're asking something food-related, but really there's something else bothering them. Like this one Lady is planning a dinner party for her husband's boss and his wife; she's so hyper about it that she's already got them on the calendar for October. And she's supposedly asking for menu ideas, but then she goes on about what a great hostess the boss's wife is, how she uses fancy china and gold chargers, and glass goblets in all the right sizes, and wine bottle coasters, the works. This Lady is terrified. She's afraid that her grandmother's china is too plain. She's hinting that she might go out and buy a whole new set, just for this dinner."

"Wow."

"Wow indeed. Now, Mom had already starting sketching out some menu ideas—you know, elegant but simple stuff this Lady won't be able to screw up—and I can fill out the rest of the menu, but how do I calm her down?"

"Well, you know what Mom would have said. Mom would have nixed the new set of china and given her a lecture on what hospitality is really about, et cetera, et cetera. We've all heard her hold forth on this."

"I know, but she had a way of putting things . . . advicey, even bossy, but like she was holding the reader's hand the whole time, so it was okay. If I tried that, it would sound—presumptuous."

"Then don't try. You can't be Mom for this Lady, Livy."

"But that's what this Lady *needs*."

"Well, she's not going to get it, is she? She can just join the rest of us who aren't getting everything we need these days."

Olivia looked down and saw a bowl of Italian wedding soup sitting before her. "This restaurant," she said. "The waitresses here are stealth operators."

Annie shrugged. She was already halfway through her bowl of cream of potato.

Olivia ate a meatball. "I do know someone who'd probably be able to answer the stringy rhubarb question," she said. "But I'm not sure I want to ask her. She's on one of the Meals on Wheels routes. Her whole backyard is a rhubarb jungle, and she used to make tons of rhubarb things."

"So why not ask her?"

"I don't know . . . once you ask for advice on a recipe, it implies an ongoing relationship. Don't you think? Come to think of it, I already asked for a different recipe, and it was kind of disastrous. She knew Mom but didn't know Mom was dead at that point. I never did get the recipe. Although I have to go back there anyway," she said to herself, thinking again about the photograph.

"Livy. It's a recipe. You're making too much of it. Ask her your stringy rhubarb question and be done with it."

"But this woman." She wondered, really, how much Annie knew. "She knew Mom so long ago. They talked about cooking all the time, I'm sure. And then I come along, Vivian's daughter, and so talking about cooking with this woman means more than just talking about cooking."

"How did she know Mom?"

She said, a little cautiously, "Do you remember when Mom rear-ended someone, long ago when we were kids?"

"Of course. I was learning to drive on that car. Winnie somebody, strange little woman with a Southern accent?"

Olivia nodded and watched Annie's face. But there was no appreciable change, no shadow crossing her face. "She's still around?" Annie said. "She was the tiniest person then already. I imagine she's shrunk to nearly nothing."

Olivia said, "She *is* strange." She finished her soup just as the waitress arrived to clear their bowls.

"And it's painful to see her," Annie said. "She's talking about Mother a lot, and you find that painful."

"*She* finds it painful," Olivia said. "Well, you know, their friendship sort of fell off."

Annie was watching the activity on the other side of the window. "I guess it did. I haven't thought about her in years."

Olivia looked through the window as well, waiting for something in herself to shift, to give her some clue as to why she was reluctant to tell Annie more. Annie must know what happened to Ruby; Olivia was sure of it. Annie was enough like their mother that she couldn't have gone all these years without either being told or divining what happened on her own. But she didn't know, apparently, what passed between Vivian and Mr. Kilkenny, nor how it affected Winnie—and why should Olivia not tell her?

"Did you say you have to go back anyway?" Annie asked. "You're delivering meals there?"

"I have to go back to return a photograph." She dug it out of her purse and handed it to Annie, pointed to Stephen. "Her grandson."

Annie studied it. "I remember. He was younger —your age, or Ruby's. And the daughter had run off, so she was raising him."

"That's right."

"He turned out all right," she said.

"Yes."

"I mean, he's really good-looking."

"He's pretty good-looking."

"He's no Harry, but still."

Olivia said, "You think Harry's good-looking?"

She realized too late that she had fallen into a trap. She reached for the photograph of Stephen Kilkenny, but Annie pulled her hand away. "You see the resemblance, right?" Annie said. "Harry's hair is darker, his eyes are darker, but that's the same narrow face, just lopsided enough at the chin to make him look like a little boy about to get into trouble."

"You're being ridiculous, and they don't look

anything alike." She knew better than to reach for the photograph again; she tucked her hands under her thighs to make sure she wouldn't. "So I guess if this woman could answer my rhubarb question, I could wrap up the newsletter in about—"

"What do you think of this photograph?" Annie said to their waitress, who had appeared with their entrees. The woman set the plates down carefully and took the photograph from Annie.

"Nice," she said, smiling. She cocked her head in Olivia's direction and said to Annie, "Boyfriend?"

With an effort Olivia managed not to roll her eyes. Annie might as well have handed the woman a script.

"No," Annie said, "but she's got another guy even better looking who'd be jealous if she *did* go out with him."

"Annie," Olivia said.

"You know," Annie said thoughtfully, still addressing the waitress, "that's not a terrible idea. This other guy, Harry, doesn't *know* he'd be jealous because she's never given him the chance. She's been too willing to sit around and wait."

"It never hurts to wake them up," the waitress said to Olivia. "Men don't know what they want until it's gone, trust me."

"I'm not sitting around waiting," Olivia said. "Harry would not be jealous, and I'm not sitting around waiting. We're just friends. And Annie, you're just—bored."

Annie and the waitress exchanged a look. The waitress handed back the photograph.

"I'd like a little black pepper with this," Olivia said loudly.

"Right away," said the waitress, retreating.

"Stop giving her looks," Olivia hissed. "Just once could we eat somewhere without your forming conspiracies with the waitstaff? This is embarrassing."

Annie handed back the photograph.

"Why don't you just admit it about Harry," Annie said. "It's so tiresome. You spend half your breaks together, you've got your weekly little movie night or whatever it is. You do your *laundry* together."

"His building's got laundry, mine doesn't. We're just very good friends, and we've never felt that way about each other."

"You're repressing it."

"We're very good friends *because* we've never felt that way about each other."

The waitress was back, grinding pepper that Olivia didn't want all over Olivia's Shrimp Alexander. "Thank you, that's perfect," Olivia said.

The waitress left, and Annie said, "You love Harry. You love Harry. What's so terrible about admitting it?"

Olivia picked up her knife and began scraping the pepper off the shrimp to the side of the plate. She was going to have to bury it under the rice or the waitress would notice. "I'm not his type," she said finally. "The women he gets involved with are nothing like me." She cut one of the shrimp in half, speared a plump morsel wrapped in bacon and curled tightly around its stuffing of feta cheese. She was afraid she would cry if she put it in her mouth.

"He doesn't need to date women like you, Livy, he's already got you."

She looked up; the room was shining. If she cried, Annie would make her feel better. Her whole life, Annie had been making her feel better. She knew then why she didn't want to tell Annie about Vivian and the Kilkennys, or say anything that would approach the topic of what happened to Ruby: she would not be able to resist Annie's reassurances, and Vivian would slip farther away.

She was so tired.

Olivia said, "If I tell him, it'll ruin our friendship."

"You're going to lose him anyway, Livy. You can't be that close to someone if he's with someone else."

Olivia put the shrimp in her mouth so she wouldn't have to answer.

"Livy," Annie said. "Hey, I'm sorry. Don't do

that. I don't know what I'm talking about half the time. The hormones are making me crazy."

Olivia nodded and kept eating. At first she couldn't taste anything but the feta and bacon, but the texture of the shrimp was perfect, resistant then yielding with a gentle pop. And then she tasted it, mild and pink and sea-salty. She could fall in love with this shrimp. She ate another perfect morsel.

"Please," Annie said. She handed Olivia a tissue. "Harry loves you, he has to. He's crazy if he doesn't. If he doesn't love you, I'll come after him myself. We'll chain him up in that godawful hut Richard uses once a year for ice fishing until he sees reason, feed him on jerky and Aunt Barbara's marshmallow salad and shine lights in his face day and night. Sleep deprivation does wonders; you should see what Richard will agree to after I've talked half the night." She plunged her fork into her plate of spaghetti carbonara.

Olivia nodded. She took another bite. There was a crash in the kitchen and she turned, but the window was too bright and shining. She blinked. More water ran down her face, and white blurred shapes sharpened into people moving to and fro in their usual rhythm; there was no clue as to the origin of the crash.

"Besides," said Annie, while someone on the

other side of the glass began building three salads with admirable rapidity and what looked like a base of radicchio. "By the time we're done with him you won't want him anymore. Either way, problem solved."

"Either way," Olivia said, and for a long moment—while she was still looking through the glass, watching the salads appear—it was as if Vivian were sitting there with them, just out of Olivia's peripheral vision. She was sitting there trying not to give in and have another crusty roll, and she was *happy,* for all sorts of reasons. It took Olivia's breath away; she didn't want to turn her head back. When she did there was only Annie. But the impression remained of her having been there.

"Wherever Mom is," Olivia said before she could stop herself, "do you know how excited she is about this baby?" Annie looked up. Olivia continued, "She's probably going on about it all over heaven to anyone who will listen. She's probably got the Apostle Paul cornered and is telling him all about your fertility problems. I bet she's taking credit because you conceived the night of her funeral."

The waitress was stepping up to the dais. "I'll have another glass of wine," Olivia said, and then, because now it was Annie who couldn't speak, added, "More water for both of us, please."

•••

That night Olivia pulled up "Ask Vivian" and found the letter from LaDonna Wipf of Arlington, South Dakota, that she'd already keyed in. LaDonna had asked not to be identified, so Olivia typed:

Dear Anxious in Arlington,

Then she thought for a long time. When she finally started typing, her fingers could barely keep up with her thoughts.

I'm going to tell you what I think my mother would have told you, though I can't say it as well as she would have. Old Country Roses is a lovely china pattern, but everybody and his brother has a set. The very fact that I, Olivia, who am clueless about china, have heard of this pattern tells you something. My mother's best friend Maureen has a set, our cousins in Duluth have a set, a lady at our church has that exact pattern in blue—it's just one of those patterns that's everywhere, like Blue Willow. So just because your boss's wife entertained you on Old Country Roses doesn't mean she inherited it from the House of Windsor. No, I know my mother would have forbidden you to spend good money on new dishes when you've got a perfectly lovely set handed down from your grandmother.

I don't know if my mother would have said this next part—probably she wouldn't have. One day when I was around seven years old, we got a call from our Toronto cousins. They were traveling around the country, going to all these cat shows, and found themselves in the area; so of course, my mother invited them for dinner.

Now, these particular cousins had given my parents an entire set of china for their wedding, which my mother always insisted was very generous even though they hadn't thought to let her choose the pattern. So naturally Mother wanted to use that china to entertain them. The problem was that we never used this china because it's positively diseased with strawberries: large, red, florid strawberries. Mother had gone through a strawberry stage as a teenager in which she collected all sorts of strawberry things, but she had long since grown to loathe the very sight of them.

(Olivia paused. She was going to have to censor this mercilessly before the final draft. For the moment, though, she indulged herself.)

Of course, the Toronto cousins didn't know this, and when Mother told Ruby and me to set the dining room table, she told us to use the strawberry china from the bottom of the china cabinet.

The meal had just gotten under way when suddenly Annie poked me and pointed to her plate. It was covered with dust, a fine white layer of dust. I looked at my own plate: more dust. It hadn't even occurred to Ruby or me to wipe the dishes before setting them on the table. Annie and I tried not to snicker because Mother came down particularly hard on anyone who goofed off in front of Cousin Bernice. But the food was being passed—it was Annie's Meatballs, which Mother could throw together with her eyes closed—so Annie forked a chunk of tomato from the salad and then sort of swished it around casually on her plate, to clean off the dust. She signaled for me to do the same, and somehow she got Ruby and David's attention and managed to communicate—I have no idea how—that they ought to check their plates, and anyone next to them as well. And as far as we knew, once the reconnaissance reports were all in, Annie and I were the only ones who had dusty plates. This made sense: there had been two stacks of plates in the china cabinet, and Annie and I evidently got the two top plates.

We finished out the meal just fine except that Annie had to keep me from giggling. And later that night when everyone had gone on their way, we told Mother what had happened, and she laughed and laughed and said, "Well, it serves me right trying to pander to Cousin Bernice when she doesn't have the common courtesy to give more than two hours' notice."

I guess I'm not sure what I'm trying to say by all this, except that the next time Cousin Bernice came to town Mother told us to use the everyday dishes. She said the important thing was sitting down with family and friends, not what you ate off of. And the meal was as gracious as if she'd used her best china because Mother so genuinely enjoyed having company, even Cousin Bernice. And that's the secret, I guess: if you can sincerely enjoy your guests, you've done your job.

She sat back and read over what she'd written. She'd edit it later, after Annie had had a chance to read it, but overall she liked what she'd done. She was about to shut down when something occurred to her. She started an email to Ruby:

Would you read something for me? It's for Mom's newsletter. I'll attach.

Then she thought for a long time about the best way to ask what she really wanted to ask. In the end, there wasn't a best way, and she simply wrote:

Please tell me how you're doing.

It was always possible she would. Olivia hit "Send."

Annie's Favorite Meatballs

Here's the recipe you asked for, Bernice. It only serves about four, so I always double it.

simple homemade tomato sauce
    (see box below; I beg you not to use
    store bought)
1–2 slices good white bread
    (I use Italian), crusts removed
⅓ cup milk
¾ lb. ground chuck
¼ lb. ground pork
½ cup grated Parmesan cheese
1 tbls. minced flat-leaf (Italian) parsley
1 or 2 cloves garlic, minced
1 egg
½ tsp. salt
fresh ground pepper
plenty of fine dry bread crumbs
    (at least 1 cup) on a plate
vegetable or olive oil

> **Simple tomato sauce:**
> ⅓ cup olive oil
> 4 cloves garlic, crushed and diced
>   (or leave whole, if you prefer to
>   remove cloves after simmering)
> 2 28 oz. cans whole plum tomatoes,
>   chopped, with juice (I use a hand
>   blender to crush them)
> salt to taste
> 4 tbls. chopped fresh basil (or 4 tsp. dried)
> fresh ground pepper

Before starting the meatballs, make the tomato sauce: heat the oil and garlic in a pan over medium-low heat until the garlic is pale gold. Add the tomatoes, salt, and dried basil (wait if using fresh). Bring to a simmer. You're now ready to add the meatballs, unless you want to use sauce for something else, like lasagna.

When sauce is nearly done simmering, add fresh basil (if using) and pepper.

Heat the bread and milk in a small saucepan on low until the bread has soaked up all the milk. Mash with a fork and set aside to cool.

•❖ Note: instead of bread soaked in milk,
   you can add 1 cup fine dry bread crumbs
   to the meat mixture and increase the milk

345

to ½ cup. This results in meatballs with a firmer, denser texture.

Lightly mix the ground chuck, ground pork, Parmesan cheese, parsley, garlic, egg, salt, pepper, and cooled bread-milk mixture. Use your hands but don't squeeze or you'll toughen the meatballs. When the ingredients are well mixed, shape into 1-inch balls. Roll the balls in the bread crumbs.

Heat vegetable or olive oil over medium-high heat in a pan large enough to hold all the meatballs. (Oil should be about ¼ inch deep.) When oil is hot, carefully add the meatballs. (I use a large spoon or a spatula to slide them in a few at a time.) Brown on all sides. Be gentle when turning them so they don't break up.

When meatballs are browned, remove with a slotted spoon and drain on paper towels. (The meatballs won't be cooked through at this point; they'll finish while simmering in the sauce.)

Add meatballs to tomato sauce, turn gently to coat, and simmer for 20 to 25 minutes, partially covered. (The meatballs do a lovely job of flavoring the sauce.) Serve with hot spaghetti.

●◆ P.S. to everyone: Now that I'm sticking volume numbers on these letters, I hope you'll all still feel free to write back. I don't mean to look so official, but Charlie says I may as well be organized about things. He's right, what with our having a baby in the house again—though she's doing very well, thank you, and not nearly as fussy as Ruby was. We held our breath a bit, now that we knew what a colicky baby was like, but this one's a good little sleeper.

16

By Friday Olivia still had not heard back from Ruby.

It had become a week of severe weather, with green clouds bruising the sky in the west and severe thunderstorm warnings renewing every few hours, and Olivia told herself this could account for Ruby's silence. When she wasn't working overtime to cover the weather herself, Ruby sometimes went along with a couple of storm chasers south of Sioux Falls. She had come back once with footage of a tornado that had upset Vivian terribly though she'd denied it.

"Do whatever fool thing you want, missy," she'd said to Ruby. "Bear in mind next time that we don't particularly need footage of your death."

In vain did Ruby assert that any vehicle properly driven could outrun a tornado.

"And vehicles never break down," Vivian said darkly. "Certainly not when you need them most."

Olivia sent Ruby another email, which felt a lot like stuffing a message in a bottle and setting it adrift at sea:

You still go storm chasing? Remember how that used to upset Mom?

She thought about this a moment after sending the email, half-expecting to find herself worrying just to make up for Vivian's absence. She imagined Ruby in the path of a tornado, watched it scour the earth and blacken the sky until it filled Ruby's whole sky and hurled trees through the air all around her. And the whole time Ruby just stood there, dark hair hiding her face, and wouldn't get back in the truck. But Olivia felt nothing. She couldn't worry about one thing more where Ruby was concerned. Anyway, since Vivian's death it seemed perfectly possible that a tornado might drop from a mild blue sky and pick off one of her loved ones. She might as well *not* worry about it.

She worried about Annie instead, while she entered changes to the directions for one of the routes. Annie's nausea had returned, and more violently than before, which seemed wrong to Olivia. Of course, she had no experience with such things herself—her friends were birthing advanced degrees, not babies—but Annie's morning sickness having finally waned, it seemed strange that it should return with such force, and so out of sync with her previous pattern of nausea alternating with ravenous hunger. There had been no hunger for the past day or so,

349

only vomiting. Annie couldn't hold down even a teaspoon of water. Olivia gave her a call as soon as the new directions were printing.

Richard picked up.

"You're still home?" Olivia said, alarmed.

"Something's wrong," Richard said. "Now she's running a fever on top of everything else. Look, Livy, do me a huge favor. I'm taking her to the hospital. Could you take Abby for the morning? I can call Aunt Barbara if I have to, but—"

"No, I'll take her. I'll leave right now."

Olivia took the updated directions to the kitchen. The morning volunteers were spooning three-bean salad into plastic cups and watching funnel clouds on Channel 5. Tornado warnings crawled across the bottom of the screen.

Doris looked up from a vat of carrot and raisin salad she was mixing and said, "There's been another touchdown near Woonsocket."

Olivia pulled the plastic sleeve for route 3 from the pile on the counter and slid the new directions into it.

"Where is Woonsocket anyway?"

"Northwest of Mitchell," said one of the volunteers.

"Is all that mess moving our way?"

Doris peered over at the tiny television. "They're saying south, at the moment."

Olivia said, "Doris, I have to pick up my

350

niece—Annie's still sick. Any problem if I bring her back with me for the day?"

"Violet's here today," Doris said. "Hiding somewhere with Lydia. She can play with them if she likes."

Olivia looked to the sky in the west when she first stepped outside. It was a washed-out blue, pale and hot; there was no sign of a storm except that the air was so still. When she got to Annie's she forgot about tornadoes: Annie was as washed-out as the sky, gaunt and sallow, her face pinched in misery. Her lips looked dry and old, her eyes dull, and she barely grunted at Olivia; she held a hand at her back and walked like an old woman. Olivia tried to hide her shock for Abby's sake. Richard was distractedly throwing things into Abby's pink backpack, snatched up Annie's purse at the last minute. "Don't worry about locking up," he said over his shoulder to Olivia as he steered Annie out the door.

Olivia smiled down at Abby, feeling false. "She'll be fine," she said brightly. "The doctor'll fix her right up."

"I know," Abby said. Olivia couldn't tell if Abby believed her; she suspected not. Her small triangular face was still creased from sleep, which gave her a cross look, and her fine brown hair was uncombed. She looked tired. Olivia asked if she'd had breakfast. She hadn't.

Olivia took a long detour through the McDonald's drive-through before heading back to MOW and picked up a Sausage McMuffin for Abby and one for herself, so Abby wouldn't have to eat alone. Abby unwrapped her McMuffin right there in the car. She pulled out the slab of processed egg, dropped it in the wrapper, and took a bite of the denuded McMuffin.

"Still not a fan of eggs, huh?" Olivia said, and Abby nodded. Olivia began planning a pot of noodle soup for supper. She could send the leftovers home for Abby's breakfast tomorrow.

They went straight to Olivia's office, where Olivia pulled an extra chair up to her desk. "Let's see what you've got," she said as she unwrapped her own sandwich. Abby unzipped the pink backpack and started pulling things out: a magnetic princess paper doll set, a Tupperware container of beads and sequins, several activity books, half a dozen fluorescent markers. "You could dress up your magnetic princess on my filing cabinet," Olivia said.

Abby pulled a face. "All her shoes are home on the fridge. He forgot them."

"Oh." Even Olivia, with her lack of fashion sense, realized that there wasn't much point without the sparkly shoes. "What about the beads? Are you still making bracelets?"

Abby took a heavy breath. "They're supposed to be for my Jasmine tiara."

"Ooh, that sounds pretty. Let's work on that."

"The tiara part is at home. Anyway I need glue."

Olivia said, "Daddy was in a hurry, wasn't he?"

Abby took up a purple marker and opened one of the activity books, *A-MAZE-ING MAZES*, on her lap. She was taking it easy on Olivia, or maybe just trying not to cry; either way, it broke Olivia's heart. She grabbed Abby's arm and said, "Come quick!" The book slid to the floor; Olivia led her out to the hall and back to the kitchen.

"This is my niece, Abigail," she said to Doris. The morning volunteers were gone; the drivers hadn't arrived yet. "Let's see if Aunt Ruby's doing the weather," Olivia said, pulling a stool up to the counter near the tiny television.

"She's not on today," Doris said. She dried her hands on a towel. "Won't be on again till Monday."

"Is she—she's not sick again, is she?" Olivia tried not to sound concerned.

"Not that I know of. Verna says Ruby says she's got so much vacation leave built up she might lose it if she doesn't take it, so she's taking a few days now."

"Oh." Olivia cast about for some way to ask about Ruby's plans without seeming to ask about Ruby's plans, but Abby spoke up first. "Is Aunt Ruby going to the cabin?" She referred to the

353

cabin near David in the Black Hills that the Tschetter family sometimes rented.

"Not going anywhere that I know of," Doris said to Abby, "except after those summer storms."

"Storm chasing," Olivia echoed, relieved.

"Lord," Doris said. "She's made of sterner stuff. You couldn't get me to go *toward* one of them things for anything."

"I like thunder and lightning," Abby said.

"She really does," Olivia said. "Abby likes being scared."

"I'm talking about tornadoes," Doris said.

Olivia said quickly, "I doubt Aunt Ruby will find one," because Abby did *not* like tornadoes. It was definitely time to find Lydia and Violet, see if Abby could be incorporated into their strange little otherworldly world, but before Olivia could ask where they were hiding, Abby said, "My mother's having a baby."

Doris looked at Olivia, eyebrows high with interest.

"It's a few months off," Olivia said.

"He took her to the hospital," Abby said, looking up at Olivia almost angrily.

"Oh—no, sweetie." Olivia slid her niece off the stool. "I mean, yes, he took her to the hospital, but—excuse us, Doris." She pulled Abby into an empty room across the hall. "Sweetie, I thought you understood. Your mom's not having the baby right now. She's just been feeling sick again, and the doctor's going to make her feel better so the baby stays healthy." *Unless it's already too late*, she thought suddenly.

Abby burst into tears.

"Sweetie." Olivia pulled her in. "She's going to be fine, I promise."

Abby said something incoherent. Olivia pulled a tissue from her skirt (at least she was not without tissues these days) and wiped the girl's face. Abby began hiccoughing. "I thought it was going to be now," she said jerkily.

"Oh, sweetie, it takes months for a baby to grow. It's not going to be born until nearly winter. Didn't they tell you that? November—"

"I know," Abby said. She looked almost cross as she swiped at her eyes. "They *said* that, but now they're calling it Heloise, so I thought it was ready to be born."

"They're calling it Heloise?" When Annie was pregnant with Abby, they'd called the baby Murgatroyd, sure it would be a boy.

"And anyway they don't tell me things, they just surprise me instead, because they think I like that, but I hate it. Like when—" She was seized by a hiccough, and the violence made her cry again; Olivia patted her back until she could talk. "Like one time when we were going on a picnic but then really went all the way to Uncle David's, and they just didn't tell me until we were in the car because they didn't know for sure and I haven't learned to be flexible yet."

Olivia said, "And they're calling it Heloise."

Abby gave a giant sniff and nodded. "Mom says it's a girl for sure."

Olivia pulled her in again. Abby accepted this; she did not put her arms round Olivia because there was an unspoken agreement that it was Olivia's job to put her arms round Abby, and Abby's simply to rest her head on Olivia's shoulder. She exhaled hard in Olivia's ear.

"Well, they never tell you anything," Olivia said, "because you're the youngest in the family. But not for long. Little Heloise will show up soon, or little Herman or whatever it turns out to be, and you will always, always, always know more than she does."

Abby was silent, but she shifted her head just a little.

"And she will do whatever you say for years and years. She will be Jasmine if you want her to, or she will be Jasmine's dog, and you will be the biggest thing in her world." She kept talking in spite of herself, in spite of the uncertainty that now yawned before her like a cave—she talked because she absolutely refused to step forward into its shadow—and anyway Abby was not pushing her away: Abby was absolutely still. "And you will surprise her with things, and she will love it whether she likes it or not, and your mom will make you take care of her, which will be a royal pain. And when she wants to know something she will ask you first, because you will know everything."

Abby took a breath, small and less shaky than before, and pulled herself a little apart from Olivia's embrace. She said, not looking up, "Jasmine doesn't have a dog, Jasmine has a tiger."

"Oh. A tiger, then."

Abby said, still not looking up, "I didn't want it to be now."

Olivia said again, "Oh." She wasn't sure for a moment what to say. "Oh. Well, it's definitely not now, so that's okay."

Abby said, "When your mom has a baby, that's all she does. Everyone says so."

Olivia released her breath. "Not your mom, honey. You've got nothing to worry about. Anyway, she'll be so glad to have your help, you'll be able to name your price."

Abby said, "The baby'll really do whatever I say?"

"Well, you have to be smart about it." Olivia stood. "You have to convince her that she wants what you want her to want, for example."

"How do I do that?"

"Well . . ." She was betraying one of her own, but that one was still unborn, and the small face before her, fierce and messed and blotchy from crying, compelled her. "You help me deliver meals, and I'll tell you how your mom once got me to trade my beloved lavender perfume atomizer for a lousy little roll-on stick."

It was the first time in a long time Olivia had delivered all of route 5. Abby trotted at her side up every sidewalk, importantly carrying the hot pack. Her eyes were still puffy, but there was color in her face, more than when Olivia had first picked her up, and she was talking now, chirping to Olivia about whatever occurred to her. Where there were doorbells, Olivia let Abby push them. The old people, every one of them, looked at Abby as if she were wrapped in a big red bow.

"Your favorite today, Mr. Ryerson," Olivia said, daring him to disagree in front of Abby. "Hot dog and three-bean salad."

He grunted at Abby as he took the meal. "You made the bean salad, did you?"

Abby shook her head, eyes wide. "I just carried it."

"Ah, I don't believe you," he said. "Bet you're in charge of the whole operation."

She shook her head again and looked at Olivia.

Mr. Ryerson leaned down and cupped his hand at the side of his mouth. "Make me a lasagna next time," he whispered hoarsely. "Bet you make a good lasagna."

Abby nodded slowly, still checking in with Olivia out of the corner of her eye. Olivia was careful not to smile. "He was just teasing," she said on the way back to the car, to be sure Abby understood.

"He doesn't smile much," Abby said.

"He doesn't smile at all," Olivia corrected.

Mr. Reynolds answered the door in shorts and a button-down short-sleeve shirt, to Olivia's relief. He silently showed Abby where to set the meal, and Abby said, looking round the tiny house in amazement, "I like your house. It's a fairy tale house."

He said, "I have something for you," and disappeared through a door. He returned with an orange plastic jack-o-lantern full of candy and held it out. Abby reached out, then drew back and looked up at Olivia. Olivia nodded. Abby took a fun-size Snickers bar and said, "Thanks."

"Again," he said. "There's plenty."

Her hand went in again and came out full of lollipops and SweeTarts and a miniature package of red licorice. "And once for her," he said to Abby, jerking his head toward Olivia. Abby went in once more: another Snickers and a hard butterscotch candy.

"Thank you so much," Olivia said when they were back at the door. Mr. Reynolds flushed the color of the pink nightgown he was not wearing.

At Mrs. Carlisle's Abby took a good ten minutes to pay her respects to the cats. Olivia at last had to pry her away from a tabby perched on the sofa arm, to Abby's sorrow and the disgust of the tabby. "Good-bye, kitty," Abby crooned.

"You bring her back soon," Mrs. Carlisle said sternly to Olivia, but she was smiling.

They sat in the car outside Winnie Kilkenny's house. "This lady knew Grandma," Olivia said, wondering what else she should say in preparation, in case—in case what? She sighed and gathered the meals. *Well, they couldn't very well talk about Ruby,* she thought, *with Abby along, which was why it was smart to do this today.*

"That's old sounding," Abby said, when she had pushed the doorbell. "This house has a princess tower. Have you been in it, Aunt Olivia?"

Olivia shook her head.

Mrs. Kilkenny looked up through the mesh of the screen door and saw Olivia, and something in her face quickened; years fell from her countenance. "You've come back," she said.

"Of course," Olivia said, feeling false for the second time that morning. "This is my niece Abigail."

"Abigail." Mrs. Kilkenny searched Abby's face now, intensely enough that Abby shifted from foot to foot.

"Annie's daughter," Olivia said.

360

"Vivian's granddaughter."

"Abby," Olivia said, "let's take the meals inside."

Mrs. Kilkenny stood aside and Olivia led Abby through the foyer to the living room, which was dim today, with the shades down and the TV flickering silently. Olivia showed Abby where to place the hot meal and set the cold sack lunch next to it. Then she began digging through her purse. "Mrs. Kilkenny, I left in such a hurry last time I went off with this." She handed over the photograph of Stephen Kilkenny.

"Thank you," she said, but she hadn't taken her eyes off Abby. When she spoke again it seemed to Olivia that her accent had deepened. "Little girl, you have your grandmother's coloring."

"Abby's been such a help today, but we are running a little late."

Abby said, "Is it a bedroom?"

Mrs. Kilkenny looked at Olivia.

"Oh—Abby, you mean the tower room?" Olivia said. "She calls it a princess tower." Olivia found herself smiling kindly, condescendingly, over Abby's head, and disliked herself for it.

"It was my daughter's bedroom," Mrs. Kilkenny said to Abby. "Would you like to see it?"

Abby nodded eagerly, and Olivia's heart sank. "Mrs. Kilkenny, we wouldn't want to trouble you, and as I said we're running late—"

"Please, Aunt Olivia!"

Olivia stifled a sigh.

The two of them followed Mrs. Kilkenny up the wide front stairs. The cabbage roses tumbled underfoot, somehow all the more splendid for the veil of dust that dimmed their colors. *This will fire Abby's imagination for days,* Olivia thought: *princesses locked in towers, spinning straw into gold, or braiding their own golden locks into ropes* . . . They turned at the landing and walked the rest of the way up in shadow, a shadow that fell the length of the straight hallway from the blinded window at the far end. They passed two closed doors, a cool, shadowy bathroom with tiny white tiles, another closed door, and then they were at the end of the hall. Olivia was alarmed to realize that Winnie was taking in quick, shallow breaths.

"We're tiring you out," Olivia said. "Is there somewhere you can sit down?"

"It's fine," Winnie said faintly, and turned the glass knob of the last door. Light flooded their senses; for a split second Olivia, blinking in its brilliance, thought the light was actually yellow. Then she blinked again, and the room itself was yellow: yellow roses climbing the walls, a white and yellow canopy—of course, a canopy—matching the wadded silk bedspread, braided yellow rugs strewn across the bare wooden floorboards. Abby gave a little cry and ran to the curved

362

windows opposite, where a riot of yellow and pink throw pillows lined the window seat. Abby leaned over the window seat and looked out.

"It's very pretty," Olivia said, although, like the kitchen, it made her sad. The longer you looked at that yellow, the more it faded.

"She thought it was too old-fashioned," Mrs. Kilkenny said. Olivia watched her closely. The eagerness had faded like the yellow wallpaper, and she looked old again, and her face was closed. But she was calm. "When she was older, I mean. We talked about redoing it, just before before she left. But yellow was always her color."

"I like pink and purple," Abby said, playing with the tassels on one of the throw pillows. She looked up with some consternation on her face. "But yellow is good, too." She picked up another pillow and traced the ruching round its edge.

"Our mother wanted us to go with yellow, I mean, the room Ruby and I shared," Olivia said. "For the longest time, though, we insisted on having pink, and of course she let us." She did not want to talk about Vivian, she did not want to think about Vivian or Ruby in this woman's presence, but mostly she did not want to talk about Samantha. "Then Ruby wanted to change everything, so we went with a very pale blue, almost a light aqua, and I think Mother was relieved." She was aware that no one was listen-

363

ing. "Now, of course, everything's white."

Mrs. Kilkenny nodded automatically. She was watching Abby with an expression that Olivia could not bear. "Mrs. Kilkenny, did my mother ever see this room?"

The woman seemed to waken. She turned to Olivia as if just remembering she were there.

"Did my mother ever see this room?" Olivia said again, regretting the question but unable to shut up.

"Oh. Yes, she did. She liked it very much. She said it was a good thing they didn't have a tower room like this, with three girls to fight over it."

Olivia laughed a little, which felt like the first true note she'd struck all this visit. "We would have, too," she said, "but it would have been pointless. Annie would have had it until she left, then Ruby, then me. When we complained, Mother would have said life isn't fair."

"No," said Mrs. Kilkenny, nodding soberly. She was watching Abby again.

Olivia said, "Have you ever seen Samantha since she left?"

Why would she ask this? Why such an intrusive, insensitive question? She caught her lower lip between her teeth and bit down, hard, too late.

Mrs. Kilkenny turned to Olivia again as if she'd been expecting the question, as if it were the next natural thing to say, and intoned, "Not seen, nor heard from. Not once."

"I'm very sorry," Olivia said. "I mean, I should not have asked."

"Why not ask?"

Olivia said, desperately, "I shouldn't bring up something so painful. It was thoughtless of me."

Mrs. Kilkenny smiled, a faint, mirthless smile. "Do you miss Vivian any the less when people don't mention her?"

There was no need for Olivia to reply; Mrs. Kilkenny had turned away again, toward Abby. But Olivia said, "No, of course not," very quietly, to complete her humility.

Abby had arranged the throw pillows into a little semicircular nest, in the center of which she now sat, legs dangling over the window seat. She grinned at the two women, engagingly unprincesslike.

"Abby, we have meals to deliver," Olivia said. "My goodness, but we'll be late. Mrs. Hammond won't mind, but the Walkers will."

Abby unnested herself reluctantly and smoothed the pillows back into place. Olivia half expected Mrs. Kilkenny to invite them again, but she was silent as she led them back down the shadowy hall and round the bend in the stairs to the dust motes hanging in the dampened light of the front hall. It was like descending into a watery world, with the heavy green drapes in the parlor on the left drawn as always against the sun but some light entering weakly through the glass of the front door. Abby stepped carefully on the rose-strewn carpet, her hand skimming the heavy railing reverently, and did not speak again. Olivia said good-bye to Mrs. Kilkenny at the door, and the old lady replied in kind, and Olivia had the terrible premonition that it really was good-bye—that this was the last time she would see Mrs. Kilkenny. Olivia did not believe in premonitions and had no idea what to do with them. Without knowing herself that she was going to, she threw her arms around Mrs. Kilkenny at the last moment—around that small, birdlike frame, surely tinier than Abby's—and said, "I'll be back. Is that all right?"

Mrs. Kilkenny returned the pressure of her arms, though rather weakly, and said something vague that Olivia, caught by fear, was too inattentive to catch. "Does anything ever help?" Olivia said, again not knowing what she was going to say. "Can anyone ever help anyone else?"

"You did help," Mrs. Kilkenny said, looking into Olivia's face as intently as she ever had. "You did help me, Vivian. You brought things to a head that were long overdue. After you had them take Stephen, I poisoned my husband. I did it with rhubarb leaves."

Olivia was on the porch, alone—Abby having danced down the broken sidewalk, swinging the hot pack—she was alone and staring at the heavy door that had closed between them, before she could take in Mrs. Kilkenny's words.

Annie was to stay in the hospital at least overnight. "A double whammy," Richard said when he called that afternoon before supper. "Salmonella to start with—not morning sickness at all—and on top of that they think she's got a kidney infection."

"Salmonella can give you a kidney infection?"

"No, it's coincidental. It's—it's Annie multitasking, as usual." He sounded weary.

"And what about, you know, is everything else all right?" Olivia looked at Abby, who was on a stool at the kitchen counter, drawing castles.

"The baby appears to be fine," Richard said. "They've got movement on the ultrasound."

Olivia let herself take a breath. "Salmonella," she said again, then thought of the Dakota Carbonara at Jasper's: if they made it right, if they made it authentically, then the egg in it wasn't fully cooked. "Wow. But they think everything's going to be okay?"

"They think so," he said, but he sounded more cautious than she would have liked. He talked about fluids, antibiotics, Annie's white blood cell count.

Father went to the hospital that evening. Olivia stayed home with Abby, gave her another bowl of noodle soup at bedtime, and helped her create a pretend princess tower in the corner of Olivia's bedroom using cardboard and an old pink flannel sheet. Then she allowed Abby to stay up late watching *Aladdin* to ensure that she would fall asleep from exhaustion. When Abby was finally asleep and settled in Olivia's big bed, Olivia returned to the living room and said to Father, "How did Mr. Kilkenny die?"

Father looked up from the draft of the gravel manual he was editing. "I don't remember right off," he said. "I know he died in the hospital."

Olivia sat on the arm of the sofa opposite Father's chair. "You don't remember anything unusual about it."

"I don't know that we knew anything about it beyond what we read in the paper, and the paper doesn't usually list the cause of death."

"I didn't know that. That's the most interesting part, isn't it?"

Father lifted one eyebrow and smiled.

"Oh, I'm not being morbid, but really, isn't it newsworthy? Wasn't Mom's cause of death listed?"

Father was riffling through the newspaper piled on the floor beside his chair. "You're thinking of the bulletin at her memorial service. Here, have today's obituaries."

Olivia scanned them quickly. There were no causes of death listed; most of the deceased had died in nursing homes. The closest thing she read to a cause of death was an allusion to a long illness.

Father was attending again to the papers in his lap. "Why does there have to be something unusual about Mr. Kilkenny's death?"

"Mrs. Kilkenny said something odd today."

"She appears to say a lot of odd things."

"She said she poisoned him with rhubarb leaves."

Father looked up at that. "She claims she poisoned him? And that's why he died?"

"She didn't directly say that's why he died, but I'm sure that's the implication. Would that really kill you, eating rhubarb leaves?"

"I have no idea," Father said. "I imagine it would take a lot of rhubarb leaves. Is Mrs. Kilkenny of sound mind at this point?"

"Not entirely," Olivia admitted. "She called me Vivian again."

"Half the time people call you Annie or Ruby."

"But she really thought I was Mother, just at the end. We'd—I think Abby and I stayed too long, taxed her resources, and maybe she just slipped into confusion. But I can't see why she'd make up something like that. Look, wouldn't Mom have saved Mr. Kilkenny's obituary? Isn't that just the sort of thing she would have clipped and filed?"

"If you can call it filing. You'll be looking for a needle in a haystack."

It was, in fact, more than Olivia could face, when she stood in David's old bedroom looking at the piles of papers stacked in uneven towers all along the wide black shelves. There was one actual filing cabinet in the room, which Olivia tentatively opened. She saw hanging files bursting with papers and labeled with the names of each family member, and slammed the drawer shut again. Then she pulled a foot-high stack of papers from the shelf and sat with it on her lap, on David's bed, which was still made up from his and Janet's revelatory visit home. She sat there for several minutes not even thinking anything, just staring down at the papers. On top was a news-paper clipping, a recipe for maple rice pudding, dated February 7, 1994. Over two years old. She knew already that she wasn't going to look through the pile, but it was heavy, pinning her to the mattress, lifting it again suddenly seemed like too much effort.

Why had she thought she could find one obituary twenty-some years old that Vivian may or may not have clipped? Mother was not wildly consistent in her methods; she moved as the spirit moved her. Knowing the man was dead may have been enough—or she may have been compelled to take up a scissors and cut the thing out, if only because Winnie Kilkenny would have been mentioned, if only to make it seem real. If she had cut it out, she may have "filed" it in one of these piles or thrown it out the next week. Or, more likely, she may have put it somewhere that resonated more deeply. Family obituaries often ended up in Vivian's Bible, then migrated to one of several banker's boxes of family memorabilia. Betty Crocker held countless newspaper clippings only marginally related to cooking, and for years one brittle, yellowed letter written by Vivian's favorite grandmother had resided in the china cabinet in a ruby-colored cut glass candy dish handed down from that same grandmother.

Suddenly Olivia realized she knew more than she'd thought. She stood so fast she almost spilled the stack of papers, clutched at it just in time, and piled it back on the shelf more haphazardly than before. There was an enormous cast-iron skillet on a top shelf in the pantry, and she could swear she'd seen papers sticking out of it. Winnie Kilkenny had helped Vivian reseason that skillet, had probably given her recipes for it, and anything having to do with Winnie would be there.

Olivia hurried downstairs to the kitchen and pulled the step stool into the pantry, then hesitated in spite of her pounding heart. This was what Vivian was doing when she had the stroke, the last thing she did before losing consciousness forever. Olivia wondered for the first time what Vivian was reaching for. The thought winded her, and she leaned for a moment against the door frame. She thought that by now she had walked through every detail surrounding Vivian's death, asked every unanswerable question a thousand times, but this was a new one, not significant except that it was fresh, a new wound that hadn't begun to scar over. She pictured Vivian going about her business. She'd been making ravioli that day; there were freshly cut ravioli spread out all over the floury table, stuffed with Olivia's favorite ricotta-spinach filling, more dough wrapped in plastic awaiting its turn at the pasta maker fastened to the edge of the island. Annie had returned later, after the ambulance ride, to freeze the raw ravioli and refrigerate the dough and filling, which a few days later had to be thrown out.

What did she need in the pantry anyway? What did she need with a step stool?

It didn't matter in the least, and yet Olivia missed sharing such mundane things the most, the ordinary details that made up each day. Knowing that Vivian had gone to the pantry for a can of, say, chicken broth and then found the date had expired, because how long had it been since she'd used store-bought chicken broth? And would you believe that the dumpling soup at Aunt Barbara's last week had a salty, tinny edge to it, almost as if she'd added canned broth to stretch things? Aunt Barbara would have denied it, but later, helping in the kitchen, Vivian couldn't help but notice several empty chicken broth cans nestled down in the garbage . . . Such trivia had made up the bulk of Olivia's phone conversations with her mother. She'd have fasted forty days for just one more.

Olivia stepped onto the stool and climbed to the top step. She pulled the cast-iron skillet carefully from the top shelf, disturbing a few cobwebs in the process, and backed down off the stool. The skillet weighed, if anything, even more than Mrs. Kilkenny's. It was full of papers. She set it on the kitchen table.

Olivia riffled through the papers and found that she held a treasure trove of recipes, all credited to Winnie Kilkenny and formatted as if for Vivian's newsletter—and evidently abandoned here. There was Chocolate Puddle, surrounded by tiny cast-iron skillets just as Olivia had remembered, and Sweet Potato Pie, Fried Grits and Sausages, Vidalia Onion Soup. Shrimp Creole! Olivia scanned this last recipe quickly, found the dried juniper berries and thought how happy Stumped in Beadle County would be. Then she thought, *This is what Vivian was doing in the pantry. This is what she was after.* The knowledge changed nothing, yet Olivia felt she'd been given a small gift: one tiny question answered, one thread of conversation continued, briefly, after death.

She looked through the rest of the recipes. There were no newspaper clippings, but there was one photocopy of a clipping, and it wasn't Mr. Kilkenny's obituary. It was dated *August 1988* in her mother's handwriting. Olivia sat down to read:

NEW DINERS STAKING A CLAIM

The restaurant business has always been a risky one, with one in three new restaurants failing, but old-fashioned diners have been a good bet in recent years. With the rising popularity of "comfort food" and the influx of area jobs thanks to Citibank, four diners have joined the Sioux Falls market since 1984.

Now entrepreneurs are testing the waters farther from the state's financial hub. In spite of competition from long-established diners serving a much smaller client base, several new diners have popped up in southeastern South Dakota, and offer customers a twist on the familiar.

Samantha Little, 38, owner of the new Sweet Onion Café in Mitchell, promises home cooking with a distinctly Southern flair. "Southern fried chicken, cheese grits, peach cobbler," says Little, when asked about her specialties. "We also have a lot of Vidalias on the menu: sweet onion pie, baked onion soup, probably the best battered onion rings you'll ever try."

Little returns to southeastern South Dakota after twenty years in the Atlanta, GA, area, where she honed her knowledge of the region's cooking. "It's not for dieters," she admits, "but it's wholesome if you do it right, and it's the best food on earth."

Jonas Stone of Stone's Hamburger Joint in Vermillion touts a national, rather than regional, American favorite . . .

Olivia stopped reading. She knew without thinking that Vivian must have sent Winnie Kilkenny the original clipping. Surely Winnie had acted on the knowledge, had tried to contact her daughter? And the daughter would have known all along that Winnie was right where she left her, but had not come forward on her own or responded to any overtures. "This is how people live," Olivia said out loud, and felt, not for the first time, that her family had not remotely prepared her to grasp the brokenness of the rest of the world.

The doorbell rang, and Olivia started, thought of Richard and something gone wrong at the hospital, but Richard would never ring the doorbell. Almost nobody she could think of, in fact, used the doorbell. Of course, it was eleven o'clock, and the house was locked. She rose from the table, actually afraid, and followed Father's voice to the front door.

"Olivia," said Harry. "Surprise!"

She thought for a moment that he was a vision, a gift from Vivian. She was smiling like an idiot, laughed to cover up the smile, said, "I can't believe it's you," to explain the laugh. She gave herself a hug so she wouldn't throw her arms around him.

Harry laughed, too, gave her a quick, one-armed hug. He dropped his duffel bag on the floor, took off his hat, and shook Father's hand. "Harry," said Father, with more dismay than surprise. "Of course. Nobody called you? Of course not. Annie's in the hospital."

"She is? What happened?"

Father talked about salmonella and kidney infections, and Olivia stared. Harry looked like he'd been traveling for some hours, but if you knew Harry, you knew that's how he always looked: somewhere between rumpled vintage and homeless. Tonight he wore, literally, his grandfather's clothes, the pants and vest from a brown glen plaid suit his grandfather had worn in the thirties, the vest hanging open over an untucked This Shirt Rocks T-shirt. The hat was a brown felt fedora and didn't match the brown of the suit, except that the whole ensemble was so unintentional that it matched perfectly. If Harry had tried a little harder—worn his grandfather's wingtips instead of his worn-out Nikes, had a slightly better haircut—or if the pants hadn't happened to fit as if tailored to his five-foot-eleven build, it wouldn't have worked. Except, again, that it might have, simply because Harry was accidentally good-looking. On Sundays for church he added a pocket watch to the vest.

Olivia thought then that she *should* have hugged Harry; it probably was odd that she hadn't. "Hey you," she said, putting her arms round him briefly and trying to remember how she hugged David.

"I'll take your hat," Father said, then looked at it as if he didn't know what to do with it. He picked up Harry's duffel as well and led the way to the living room.

"I knew something was wrong when nobody was at the airport," Harry said. "I tried Annie's phone number, but no one answered. Then I called a cab."

"You took a taxi all the way from Sioux Falls?" Olivia said. She had never thought about Sioux Falls *having* taxis; it had never come up. She wasn't going to tell Harry that. "That's ridiculous. Why didn't you call us?"

"I figured it could still be a surprise."

377

"It's a surprise, all right," Olivia said.

Father cleared his throat. "Obviously everything had to be delayed," he said to Harry. "I'm sorry about the breakdown in communication."

"What had to be delayed?" Olivia said.

"Please have a seat," Father said, but Harry said, "Actually I could use a bathroom."

"You remember where it is," Olivia said.

"Don't be so happy to see me, it's embarrassing," Harry said, grinning, and left the room.

Olivia and Father did not sit. "What had to be delayed?"

"Your surprise celebration. It was going to be tomorrow night. Harry was supposed to hide out at Annie's until then. We were all going to take you out to the Northland Hearth in Sioux Falls for dinner."

The Hearth was swanky: stone walls, mahogany furnishings, fireplaces large enough to stand in, low heavy beams, chunky brass sconces, crystal chandeliers. Harry would fit perfectly into any party at the Hearth; he would look like a member of the impoverished gentry, patronized for his wit and fine old family name (although in fact his father was an engineer for a heating and cooling company out of Cleveland).

"And you all invited Harry, without asking me."

"He's your closest friend," Father said. "Annie thought of course we should invite him."

"Uh-huh," said Olivia. She wondered when Annie would be feeling better, really better.

"So," Harry said, entering the room again. He shoved his hands in his deep pockets a little diffidently. "Sorry to crash in like this."

"Don't be silly," Olivia said. She sat on the sofa, and he joined her. "Of course I'm glad you're here."

"Something to drink?" Father said. "We have pop, water, orange juice."

"*Soda pop* would be great," Harry said, and Olivia said, "Oh shut up. Bring him a Coke," she said to Father.

"You should be proud of your regionalisms," Harry said.

"Nobody here says *soda pop,*" Olivia said. "It's just pop. And anyway I think they say that in Chicago, too."

"Are you really glad I'm here? I kept asking to come, and you kept saying no, so I figure, you're still having a pretty hard time."

"Well, yes," Olivia said. "You know. The thing is that grief is . . . it's this long, dark, lonely journey." It was the first time she'd said anything like this out loud, and she immediately hated her own words. "Actually it's *not* a journey. I can't stand it when people say everything is a journey. It's more like standing still, except when it's like falling over, and it has this excruciating sameness to it, day after day. I mean, you'd be bored if you had to see me daily since my mom died. It's the same exhausting emotional thing, over and over. Just now, I had to get something from the pantry, which reminded me of her, and it's like I was hit by a truck all over again. I'm sure it must be baffling and boring from the outside looking in."

"I hope I have a better imagination than that," Harry said. "I am an historian."

"Yes," Olivia said. This was true. If anyone knew how to empathize, it was Harry. "And Penelope felt she could spare you?"

"Penelope," Harry said, and ran his hand through his hair. Father returned and handed Harry a Coke. He'd gotten one for himself as well, and sat in his chair opposite them. They all waited for a moment for someone to think of something to say.

"I guess you already know about David being married," Olivia said.

"Yes," Harry said. "That's fantastic. She sounds nice," he said to Father.

"Very nice," Father said. "We look forward to getting to know her better."

And in other news, Olivia thought, *Ruby was molested in high school, developed an eating disorder that she still won't call an eating disorder, and now sneaks a smoke now and then* on my mother's orders *to keep herself from vomiting.* She actually could have said all this to

Harry if they'd been alone, *would* have said it, but they weren't alone. Instead, she said to Father: "Did Richard say when they expect to send Annie home?"

"A day or two," Father said. "She won't be up to anything by tomorrow night, I'm afraid."

"No, of course not."

"You two should find a way to celebrate in the meantime," Father said. "Since Harry's here and all."

"The three of us could go to Jasper's," Olivia said. "Actually four: we should take Abby. You remember my niece," she said to Harry. "We're watching her so Richard can be at the hospital. It all feels so touch and go because of the pregnancy, you know."

Harry sat forward. "Salmonella must be really serious for a pregnant woman."

"It doesn't sound like it passes to the fetus," Father said. "Dehydration is the big concern, and they've got that under control. I think they're more worried about the infection."

Harry nodded. Olivia realized for the first time that he looked tired. His normal schedule had him up until one or two in the morning, but with the hour's time change, and just sitting around in planes and taxis, she supposed he might reasonably be tired. "I'll go see that one of the spare rooms is ready," Olivia said. She stood and reached for his duffle, but he picked it up first.

"I got it," he said.

"Harry, it's a pleasure to have you here," said Father, standing as well, "even if we got you here under false pretenses. Make yourself right at home."

"Thank you, sir," Harry said.

"Charlie's fine," said Father. He always said this early on, whenever he and Harry met.

"Charlie."

Olivia led him upstairs. She hesitated at the top of the stairs, then opened the door to David's room. "The bed in here is all ready," she said, "but the room is cluttered with my mom's papers. The room across the hall is uncluttered but needs clean sheets."

"No, this is just like home," Harry said, hauling the duffle past her into David's room. "I sleep better with piles of papers everywhere." He dropped the duffle under the wide shelf to the left. "Livy," he said. "It's really good to see you. You have no idea—"

"It's really good to see you," she said. Her teeth were suddenly chattering, as if she were cold. "Especially since there's this thing I'm thinking of doing, and I could really stand to run it past you. I'm thinking of butting into some other family's old business, where I have no business to be. In fact, I'm thinking of doing it tomorrow."

"What other family?" Harry sat on the edge of the bed and tried to get Olivia to do the same, but she stood and hugged her elbows and tried not to chatter.

"This woman who's been estranged from her mother for years and years—she ran away as a teenager, left her mother with a brand-new baby and everything. The mother raised the baby, but she's an old lady now, and my mom knew her, back before she was so old. In fact, this old lady sometimes thinks I'm my mother because she's sort of losing it, at least when she gets tired."

"Livy, slow down. I'm not following."

But slowing down was dangerous. "This old lady knows things about Mom, she knows things about Ruby I didn't know until recently." Olivia shuddered, really did feel cold. Cold and a little lightheaded. She wondered, hopefully, if she could possibly be getting sick. "I didn't know anything about what Ruby went through, years ago, and now my mom's gone and I can't talk to her about it, I can't ever get her to tell me why I should believe things are going to be okay, and Ruby is less than helpful when it comes to that sort of thing—"

Harry was standing again. He put his hands on her shoulders, and she started to cry. It was the second time ever she had used her mother's death, just a little, and that made her cry harder. She covered her face. "Hey," he said. "Hey hey hey." He pulled her close and started patting her back. She was soaking his T-shirt, caught the scent of it: a cross between soap and hominy, a warm, human smell. *This will be the best moment of his visit,* she thought miserably, with the same certainty she'd known earlier that day with Winnie Kilkenny. Tomorrow she would find a way to blow it, or he would, because she couldn't go on anymore as she had. She didn't have the energy left to be inauthentic no matter how badly she needed to be. So she clutched the edges of his vest while her shoulders shook, and inhaled him while she could.

17

That night the air was charged with lightning that never struck. Olivia lay awake watching white lights flick on and off across the sky and longing for the storm to gather and spend itself. But after a hot, close night, any brewing storm moved east and a drizzle moved in.

Olivia and Harry headed south through the drizzle. Once they hit I90 west toward Mitchell, the drizzle became a downpour, the downpour became a sluice. Olivia pulled over to wait it out. They could barely see through the curtain of nails slamming into the hood. She shouted, "I'm glad Abby didn't come." Annie had stabilized enough to insist that Richard bring Abby to the hospital for the morning.

While they waited for the rain to lighten, Olivia asked Harry to fill her in on the latest Penelope news. She had to hear it sometime, she thought, and anyway she was nervous about trying to see Samantha Little; Penelope was unpleasant but at least distracting.

The unfortunate thing was that Penelope was the sort of person Olivia might even have been friends with, back in high school. She could imagine her then: naturally and painfully thin, pretty face overwhelmed by a sweep of long, uncut, patent leather hair, and largely friendless because of her belligerent intelligence and a tendency to take extreme positions on everything. Olivia had had one or two friends like that: bright, lonely people who were grateful and surprised that anyone would bother to breach their defenses; they had gone on to blossom in college when they found that they weren't as alone as they'd thought. Olivia knew nothing of Penelope's relationships in college, only that she had swung from ideological extreme to extreme: asceticism to hedonism to all but eco-terrorism. She was now a hardened loner building a name for herself in the St. Anselm political science department. She had learned to accept being attractive, anyway; one of her extremes had involved submitting to a conservative boyfriend who had gotten her her first decent haircut, and she'd kept the haircut and ditched the boyfriend in her Camille Paglia phase. She hadn't dated much between the conservative boyfriend and Harry, because she either offended or terrified most men on sight. But Harry was kind, not needy, and hard to offend. Penelope (as far as Olivia could tell) was thirsty for and suspicious of kindness, and had been circling Harry uncertainly ever since. There was always a reason she was unsure if they should continue the relationship. At the moment, as Harry tried to explain at length, it had to do with a fear of death. Olivia had trouble following this at first, but then, she wasn't really trying.

She pulled onto the highway again as soon as the rain lightened a bit, and fell back on something she'd said to Harry in the past, in response to whatever he had just said. "Penelope is hard to get close to because she's unwilling to be vulnerable, because really she's extremely vulnerable. She's afraid that if she really lets you in, you'll both drown in all her vulnerability. If she says she's afraid of death, it's just another way of saying that she's unable to be close to people. Is that what you want? Someone you have to constantly pry open almost against her will?"

"You're not getting it," Harry said, raising his hands passionately but without anger. Olivia took her eyes off the road briefly, stole a look,

386

and fixed her eyes on the road again. His face was animated, glad. He had clearly missed having her to talk to about Penelope. Talking about the one you loved was the next best thing to being with the one you loved—sometimes better, when the one you loved was not loving you back enough.

She was glad it was dark, that the rain was loud.

"Tell me what I'm not getting," she said loudly.

"She's not saying that *she* fears death. She's saying that *we*—everyone in this country, nearly all Americans, especially American evangelicals who sometimes claim to be above that sort of thing—fear death." He began to talk about a conference Penelope had attended at which a prominent utilitarian philosopher had spoken. Olivia tried halfheartedly to listen but found herself noting, instead, that she feared death less than she ever had—her own death, at any rate. It was a byproduct of having lost the person she loved more fiercely and instinctively than anyone in the world. She wondered if this lack of fear would wear off, and then knew, with an unwelcome certainty, that it would. She knew it because of how afraid she'd been all day for Annie's baby. That was different, of course, from fearing her own death, but the two were messily related: you couldn't desperately want a baby to live without wanting that baby to have

387

the people who it needed most. If Annie had any sense, she was afraid of dying. If Olivia ever got pregnant, she would be afraid, too, and for the rest of her life. It was a trap.

Penelope was right, she thought suddenly: *it was good to be alone.*

"—drives so many of our decisions as consumers, I mean, look at the money spent on the whole pathetic stay-young-forever industry: plastic surgery, outrageous exercise regimens, even just hair dye, for crying out loud. She's right about that, of course, and about the fact that no one is willing to die even when dying would be consistent with those beliefs that we so blithely claim as our own . . ." He had unbuckled his seat belt so he could turn in his seat and face her, a habit Olivia deplored, but for the first time in their friendship she did not harangue him to belt up again, noting instead that she did not, for some reason, fear *his* death, at this moment, anyway, and in spite of the poor driving conditions. She wondered at this, wondered if she could be so cold and selfish as to prefer the thought of him dead to the thought of losing him forever to Penelope or Penelope's next incarnation. (There would be a next incarnation, as surely as things would end with Penelope.)

She began to look for exit 332.

" . . . although, ironically, that's what led to the restraining order," he said.

Olivia said, "What?"

"Olivia," he said, dropping his hands to his lap sadly. "Have you heard a word I've said?"

"Of course," she snapped. "I'm looking for the exit, all right? I can barely see out the windshield and I have to be especially careful not to careen off the road, because if I do, you're pretty clearly flying out the window to your death."

He turned with a sigh and buckled his seat belt.

"What restraining order?" she said again. "A restraining order against Penelope? By *whom?*"

"The utilitarian philosopher, with whom she actually mostly *agreed*," he said. "Actually there was just the threat of a restraining order. Her advisor was there and managed to talk her out of attempting further contact."

"Well," Olivia said. "She's got a useful advisor, anyway. So what was the restraining order for, again?"

He sighed harder this time, and she felt guilty. "I know you're distracted," he said. "I know you're unhappy. Look. The point is, she currently believes that the reason most of us do anything is because we fear death, and that the reason I'm in this relationship with her at all is because I fear death, and that not confronting that would be detrimental to my spiritual health. And she's worried . . ." His hands lifted helplessly. "She's worried that by continuing in this relationship,

389

she is contributing directly to my—to my being unhealthy in this way."

"And why does she think you're only in this relationship because you fear death?"

"Because fearing death is supposedly the only reason I would continue in a relationship with someone who is so uncertain about said relationship."

She could see their exit, tentatively touched the brakes to test the slickness of the road. "So . . . ultimately, *she's* afraid of commitment, and *you're* the one who's unhealthy because you're willing to put up with it?"

Harry said, "Something like that." He wasn't looking animated now. She pulled onto the off ramp and slowed.

The Sweet Onion Café was easy to spot even through the rain: a giant purple onion glowed in neon from the rooftop. Olivia pulled off the frontage road and turned into the lot, parking as close to the entrance as possible. She didn't kill the engine right away; instead, she and Harry sat staring at the brightly lit diner through the sweep of windshield wipers. For some reason, she hated to turn them off—maybe she found the rhythmic creak comforting—but finally she did. Then the rain seemed louder than ever, and the waitresses moving around inside melted and blurred. Olivia sighed. She wished she weren't here, but then she didn't wish she were anywhere else either.

"Tell me again why you think this is a good idea," Harry said.

"Vidalias aren't purple," she said.

"What?"

"Vidalia onions—those big sweet onions. Winnie Kilkenny was from Vidalia, Georgia, where they grow them. That's what the Sweet Onion Café is named for. But they're yellow, not purple."

She could feel Harry looking at her, but she knew he wouldn't tell her what he was really thinking: that she was on a ridiculous mission, that it was the manifestation of a sublimated desire to fix things in her own family she couldn't fix. Harry would not tell her that, no matter how disagreeable Olivia had been about Penelope, because (she could see this in the way he'd looked at her since his arrival) he was a little unsure how to treat her now, since Vivian's death.

"Maybe yellow's not as effective in neon," Harry said, craning his neck to look up at the sign. "Purple's got kind of a film noir thing going, doesn't it? At least when it's raining." They'd gone through a film noir phase a year or so ago. After that it was Bollywood. Penelope hadn't approved of the Bollywood phase; she felt bad taste was bad taste, whether you redefined it as camp or not, so Harry and Olivia had to sneak videos in and out of his apartment for a while.

Poor Harry, Olivia thought bitterly.

Another long moment. "Are we going in?" Harry said, not impatiently.

Olivia turned off the car at last and threw the keys in her purse. They ran the few feet to the door—it was a warm rain, and on a better day Olivia might not have minded getting wet—and stepped inside, gasping. They both pulled at their clothes, trying to shake them dry. This was especially difficult for Harry because today he wore suspenders over his T-shirt.

"Two?" the waitress said, pulling a couple of menus from the pile by the register. They nodded and followed her to a window booth. The overhead lighting was bright, the window dark and streaming; Olivia shivered in the air-conditioning but instinctively liked the place. The pale yellow Formica tabletop held glass bottles of Heinz ketchup and mustard, and another waitress brought them ice water in Coke glasses. Olivia opened her menu.

"Here we go," Harry said. "Pork chops with a side of black-eyed peas and corn bread."

Olivia flipped to the desserts. Pecan pie, peach cobbler in season, sweet potato pie. "She wants to see her mother," she said. "This menu screams nostalgia. Winnie Kilkenny must have made all this when Samantha was growing up."

"If she wants to see her mother, why doesn't she go see her mother?"

"She's proud, she's angry. I don't know. Maybe she doesn't *know* she wants to see her."

"And you're going to tell her," Harry said. Olivia looked up over her menu.

"She wants to see her son," she said flatly, "or she would never have set up shop not two hours from where she deserted him all those years ago. This is South Dakota, Harry. Everyone's connected by like two degrees of separation. And you know what he does, right? He's a health inspector—he supervises *restaurant* health inspectors out of Pierre. He's probably seen her name on lists . . ."

"I can't tell you how not like Penelope you are. You never met a woman who could leave it alone like Penelope."

Olivia stared. "You're joking. I have—let me count—*zero* restraining orders out against me at this moment."

"I meant when it comes to personal affairs."

Olivia slammed her menu shut, but the waitress appeared before she could say anything. Her name tag said Mona and she looked a little harried, blond hair slipping from its ponytail, even though it was early yet. Olivia guessed there must have been a breakfast rush. They ordered, and Olivia asked casually, "Is the owner in today?"

"Every day," the woman said, taking their menus. "Just in case one of us decides to take it

393

easy." She looked at Olivia sharply. "You a friend of hers?"

"No—I know someone who knows her, is all. She's pretty tough to work for?"

The waitress glanced back at the kitchen over her shoulder, then leaned in and lowered her voice. "Personally, I can't stand female bosses. They're always out to prove something." She straightened. "You're gonna love the food here, though. You ordered my favorite," she said and nodded to Harry. "Pork chops."

They watched her walk back to the kitchen, with a swing in her step that was indolent and alert at the same time. Olivia watched the door swing wide, but she didn't catch sight of anyone else. She was nervous enough that she wasn't sure she could eat. She'd only ordered sides— cheese grits and fried green tomatoes—but they were rich, heavyish sides. She said, still watching the door, "Penelope still a vegetarian?"

"Yeah, although she eats chicken now."

Olivia looked at Harry and laughed. "That makes her not so much a vegetarian as a person who eats chicken. Does she still *claim* to be a vegetarian?"

"Sometimes I think you've never liked Penelope. You're ungenerous with her, you know that?"

"Well, Penelope's never liked me." *And why would that be, you idiot?* she thought.

"Penelope likes you fine. She's never said a word about you. See, that's what I mean, she can leave it alone."

"If I were a 'vegetarian,'" Olivia put it in air quotes for good measure, "I don't think I could be with a flesh eater like you."

Harry laughed. "You could no more be a vegetarian than I could."

"Entirely missing the point," Olivia said. "Doesn't she mind when you eat meat in front of her?"

"I don't usually eat meat in front of her," he said—a touch defensively this time, Olivia noted with a small, mean thrill, just as their food arrived. The waitress eyed Olivia as she settled the steaming plates before them.

"You a vegetarian?" she asked.

Olivia snorted. "Goodness, no. His girlfriend."

The woman raised her eyebrows just a touch and lifted one corner of her mouth. Olivia reciprocated with a half-smile.

"What the hell?" Harry said, once the waitress had left. "You guys are bonding because I'm seeing a vegetarian?"

"You're not *seeing* a vegetarian, Harry. You're seeing a person who eats chicken." Olivia sliced into a fried green tomato. A tart smell almost of Granny Smith apples rose, mingled with the scent of Harry's pork chops, and she was hungry in spite of her nervousness. She held up a wedge of tomato and studied it. "Crusted in cornmeal, browned to perfection. I tried this once and it was a greasy mess. I should ask her how she does it before I bring up her mother."

Harry said, his mouth full, "Definitely ask about the pork chops."

They ate in silence. Olivia had ordered the exact right thing: the tomatoes were salted and savory, and the mealy grits slid down her throat and warmed her to her toes. Harry gave her a bite of pork chop. She thought, *I'm like Harry's meat mistress. I'm his culinary other woman.* She was just developing this thought when the kitchen door swung wide again and a woman wrapped in a white apron walked out and stalked to the register, did something with a stack of receipts. Her hair was pulled back in a severe bun that would have suited her, emphasizing the strong, regular bones of her face, if it hadn't been dyed black. She was tall, heavy-boned, not the least bit fat. Olivia could see her on a motorcycle—not riding behind someone, but handling it herself. She looked nothing like Winnie, but Olivia knew this was Samantha, maybe because the two waitresses in her vicinity stood taller and worked faster when she appeared. Olivia felt her heart rate quicken.

"That's her," she said to Harry, quietly. He followed Olivia's glance to the register. "What do I do, ask to speak to her?"

"That's the plan," Harry said. He pushed his plate away and wiped his mouth with his napkin.

The woman left the register and walked to the nearest table, where an older couple and a young boy sat. She spoke to them and nodded, put her hand firmly on the older man's shoulder and laughed at something he said. She moved on to the next table.

"She's going to ask us how our food was," Olivia said, fascinated. "Who does that in diners? Does that ever happen in diners?"

"You sure you want me to wait in the car?" Harry said. "She's kind of formidable. I'm pretty sure she could take you."

"Harry," Olivia said.

"Hey." He reached across the clutter of dishes and squeezed her elbow. "You're going to be fine. You're just asking her a question, right? You'll be fine. Give me the keys."

She pushed her purse across the table, too nervous to dig around in it herself. Harry found the keys and headed off to the restroom. Olivia suddenly realized she needed a restroom, too, but now Samantha was only one table away.

Just asking her a question, she repeated to herself, but then didn't know what the question was. Had she boiled it down to a question? What had she told Harry last night, anyway? This wasn't a matter of one question, it was a conversation, incredibly personal and messy and hardly appropriate to spring on someone at their place of work. She swallowed and knew she was going to chicken out.

"How is everything?"

Olivia said, "Absolutely delicious."

Samantha's eyes—Olivia had expected them to be brown, but they were gray—her eyes darted for a split second to note the remains on Olivia's plate, but she merely smiled and began to move away. Olivia said, "I don't want to finish it because then it will be gone. What's your secret? I tried making fried green tomatoes once and it was a disaster."

Samantha had turned back to face Olivia, hands on hips. "You really want to know?" Her manner was so forthright, so practical, that the force of it seemed warm somehow.

"I'd love to know."

"Wait here." She strolled back to the kitchen, purposeful, not hurried. Olivia released her breath. Did she have a question for this woman? *Do you love your mother? Do you want to see her? Do you know what your mother did? Would you see your son, even if it meant seeing her?*

Please would you see your mother again?

"Here," Samantha said, handing something to Olivia. It was a four-by-six-inch typed recipe card.

Olivia said, "You're really giving me the recipe?"

398

"I have no interest in being mysterious," the woman said. "Anyone should be able to learn this. Anyone should be able to do what I do, if they want to bother."

Olivia tried to concentrate on the card but was afraid the woman would walk away. "Mine fell apart when I tried it. The coating came off, it wouldn't brown evenly, and by the time it *was* browned it was also greasy."

Samantha rested one knee on the padded bench where Harry had sat and leaned against the frame of the booth, arms crossed. "The trick is, you can't turn the tomatoes too early, you can't even check them to see if they're burning. Put them in hot oil and don't touch them for four minutes."

"I probably checked."

"Never check. After four minutes they're a deep crusty brown, you turn them, same thing. No peeking, no fussing. Four minutes."

"I should write this down," Olivia said. Samantha handed her a pen from her apron pocket. Olivia said as she wrote, "And . . . not olive oil?"

Samantha shrugged. "You can use olive oil. Personally I think that's all you taste then, so I use vegetable."

Olivia said, "You're—you're from Brookings originally, aren't you?"

There was the merest flicker of light in

Samantha's gray eyes, like the flickers of sheet lightning Olivia had watched all night. Like the flash of a fish surfacing on a silver pond. Then the pond was smooth again. Samantha said, "Years ago."

Olivia said, "My mother knew your mother."

Samantha dropped her arms, straightened slowly. She was very tall.

"I only know this because my mother just died, and it was after that I happened to meet yours."

For a long moment there was no expression on Samantha's face, although somehow Olivia knew she was breathing a little faster. Then she smiled, a polite smile that didn't touch the eyes. Her earlier warmth was gone, and in its absence her strength was the stark, dangerous strength of a survivor. She said, "I'm so sorry for your loss."

"Thank you," Olivia said, barely above a whisper.

"Good luck with the recipe," Samantha said with a nod, and turned away.

After a few moments Olivia released her breath.

She picked up her fork, put it down, and slid the recipe into her purse with shaking fingers because if she didn't she would surely forget it. Then she picked up her fork again and ate the last two bites of tomato and the last two bites of grits. She looked around and realized they didn't have a check yet, so she rose and took herself and her purse to the cash register up front. The waitress there handed her a check, but while Olivia was rooting in her purse for her wallet, Samantha appeared again and said something to the waitress, who walked away with the register still open. Olivia handed Samantha a twenty wordlessly and was going to return to her table with the tip when Samantha spoke, quietly and without looking up from the register.

"If you have something to say to me, say it in my office."

Then she closed the register and walked back to the double doors of the kitchen. After a few seconds Olivia followed.

Olivia was too distracted to notice anything much in the long galley kitchen beyond two or three large stockpots and someone turning sandwiches at a griddle. Samantha went to a small room at the back and closed the door behind Olivia. She did not sit at the metal desk that took up half the floor space; she stood in front of it, arms crossed, and Olivia had to stand with her back nearly against the door to avoid craning her neck.

"Well," said Samantha.

Olivia swallowed. "I'm sorry if I've been intrusive—"

"Get it over with already."

She took a breath. "I know your mother, just a little. My mother knew her well a long time ago, after—I guess, long after you'd left. They were just connected for a while. Your mother still misses her, I think. I don't know why that makes me feel responsible. Maybe I just can't walk away from someone who cared about my mom."

Samantha waited, her mouth in a tight line.

"When I learned that you're right here, barely two hours away, I wondered why you never got in touch. I thought maybe, if you knew how much she missed you—"

She broke off when Samantha unfolded her arms and stood, if it were possible, even taller. "I will not discuss why I do what I do with a complete stranger," Samantha said, and Olivia murmured, "Of course not."

"I know all about how much a mother misses her child."

"Of course."

"Did she send you here?"

"No. She doesn't know I'm here."

Samantha narrowed her eyes and smiled. "No. Of course not. She was never one to take much initiative."

Olivia wanted to look down, or away, but it was impossible to do so.

Samantha said, "Is there anything else?"

"No. I'm sorry to have troubled you."

"I'm sure you meant well," Samantha said, in too level a voice.

Olivia turned around and put her hand on the doorknob. *Never one to take much initiative.* Winnie's sins of omission, safe sins that lay dormant for years but cast long shadows of regret. Sins that, whatever consequences they incurred, would never incur a restraining order. *Damn Penelope anyway.* She took a breath and turned around. "Actually there are two things. First, you need to know he's not going to come walking in here."

"What?"

"Your son. He's not going to look you up when you're not even willing to have anything to do with your mother. He knows you're here, right? You've made sure he knows? Has he ever shown up? He's loyal to her. I've seen his picture, it's obvious who he is from his picture." She hadn't thought about it before, but she was sure now that she was right: the eyes in the hiking photo were sober, almost stern, the smile intentional. He would sacrifice for what he thought was right. "He's loyal to the only mother he's ever known. Who, by the way, *you* chose for him."

She was braced, almost expecting a physical retaliation, but Samantha stood like a statue. "And second, she poisoned Mr. Kilkenny with rhubarb leaves. When she finally realized what he'd done to you, and they were taking Stephen away anyway, she poisoned him with rhubarb

403

leaves. A little while later he died. How's that for initiative?"

Samantha's lips opened; that was the only change in her expression, but it made her look as if she'd been struck. Then she closed her mouth. After a moment she said, as levelly as before, "That would take a hell of a lot of rhubarb leaves."

Olivia turned the knob and left.

She saw even less on her way back through the kitchen and was only glad she managed not to run into anyone. She passed the cash register and went out to the car where Harry was waiting in the driver's seat. It was still pouring, but she couldn't seem to move quickly. She got soaked.

"Well?" Harry said.

Her teeth were chattering again—*no wonder Harry doesn't know how to treat me,* she thought, *my damn teeth have chattered his whole damn visit*—and she said, "Please find a gas station, I really, really need a bathroom."

He looked at her face another minute.

"I mean, I *really* need a bathroom." She began to cry.

Harry drove into a Sinclair with a big green dinosaur out front. Olivia said, "Fill up the car, here's my card. I can't stand using their bathroom without buying anything."

Harry took the card and got out. When she returned from the restroom, which mercifully was indoors and mercifully not filthy, he had pulled up to the front entrance. Olivia got in and sat.

"You want me to drive?" Harry said.

Olivia nodded.

She had managed to stop crying, but she didn't want to talk, and he didn't make her. Partway through the trip he took her hand and squeezed it, and then she had to concentrate on not crying again. They sat like that for nearly thirty minutes, Olivia the mess and her dear friend Harry who was so patient and so kind that she hated him, and then, before they reached Brookings, Olivia took her hand back and said, "Harry. Penelope doesn't love you."

She didn't want to look at him when she said this, but it seemed unfair: there was some rule that said you must look at someone when saying something terrible about love. So she looked. His face was open, stricken.

"I should have told you this six months ago. Harry, she just doesn't love you. Anyone could see it; probably everyone does. There's no fear of death, there's no excuse of the month. *She doesn't love you.* That's the only problem you two have. I can't—I can't hear about it anymore, because it's not going to get any better."

She finally allowed herself to look away.

She could hear him take a breath—the rain had lightened, was back to a drizzle as they entered Brookings—but he didn't speak. She was miserable, she had made him miserable, but she told herself that people needed to hear the truth. She was telling people the truth today. What people did with it was their business.

What Harry did was leave for the Sioux Falls airport that evening, before dinner.

Annie wanted to know why. Olivia sat on the edge of her hospital bed, looking at the bowl of green Jell-O Annie was supposed to try to eat. "I wanted him to go," Olivia said. "He just wants to be with Penelope. I need to learn to stop being friends with him."

Annie, for once, did not say anything. She took Olivia's hand and squeezed it, but Olivia was tired of crying, and anyway Richard would be back any moment. She said, "I'm going home, I'm making you some strawberry Jell-O with mandarin oranges in it like you like. I'll bring it in tomorrow."

But when she got home she didn't make the Jell-O right away. She went to the deep freezer that sat in a corner of the garage and pulled out the freezer bags of ravioli that Annie had placed there the day Vivian fell. She brought them to the kitchen and put a large pot of water on to boil, put half a stick of butter in another pot to melt, and ran out to the dripping garden to try to find, in the wet and in the gloom, the sage plant in Vivian's herb garden. She pulled a handful of wet sage leaves and brought them inside, cleaned them and chopped them and tossed them in the browning butter. Then she opened the first freezer bag of ravioli. They were covered with crystals and stuck together; Annie had evidently thrown them into the bag raw, all together, instead of freezing them first on cookie sheets and then bagging them. She tried anyway, lowering them into the roiling water for several minutes, then lifting them out with a slotted spoon. She cut into one. It was stiff, with white patches. The texture was worse than the cheapest store-bought frozen ravioli. The filling was okay.

Olivia threw the entire batch, the cooked and the raw, into the trash and turned off the stove. If Abby hadn't been in the house, she would have gone straight to bed. But Abby was in the house.

She found Father and Abby playing dominoes on the floor of Father's study and asked what they wanted for takeout.

18

The three of them were halfway through their Arctic Circle chicken dinners when they heard the front door open and someone holler hello. Olivia made it to the front entrance ahead of Father and Abigail to find David with an armload of fishing tackle and a chubby little boy maybe a couple years older than Abby. Olivia just managed to catch herself and say "Hello" to the little boy before saying to David, "Don't expect me to clean any fish."

"No such luck, sis," David said, kissing her on the cheek (which he never did). "This is my boy, John."

"Hello, John," Father said over her shoulder. Olivia stepped aside so Father could shake John's hand.

"This is your cousin Abigail," David said to John. The two children stared at each other.

Olivia said, "I'm Olivia." She put out her hand. John took it, suspiciously, then gave it back and looked at Father again. His eyes were bright, almost as black as his hair. His olive skin was paler than it should have been, this time of summer, and he looked as if he might start shivering in his green striped tee.

"What've you got to feed a couple of hungry outdoorsman?" David said heartily. Heartily— Olivia looked at him more closely. Heartily meant he was trying too hard, which meant he was feeling awkward. David piled his equipment in one corner and pulled off his sneakers, which were soaked, then kneeled to pull off John's. "We've been camping, haven't we, John, and fishing our way across the state, or trying to. Borrowed Staub's boat at Chamberlain," he looked up at Father. "Got that new outboard motor on it, handles really well. John's not sold on fishing in the rain yet, though. Actually it was coming down a little hard even for me." He stood again, peeled off his windbreaker, and Abby finally lunged at him, hung from one of his fore-arms and tried to swing herself back and forth. David nearly fell over. He pulled himself up and unpeeled her hands from his arm. He said, "Hey, Abby, how about hanging these up for us." He handed her his windbreaker and a wadded-up rain poncho from the floor. Abby wrinkled her nose and let the poncho fall open. It dripped all over the linoleum. It was adult-size; it would have swallowed up the little boy. Olivia took the poncho and the windbreaker from Abby and draped them over an old bench under the window.

"We were going to head down to Platte. I know another guy there with a boat I can always use, but that's where the weather's really interesting. Thought we better take a break." David clapped a hand on John's shoulder.

John stared stolidly ahead at nothing. It was dark in the front entry, and they could hear rain trickling through the gutters. Olivia would have bet money, looking at John's muddied, set face, that he'd been ready for a break from the outset. She said, "John, you like fried chicken? We're in the middle of takeout."

John's face brightened, or at any rate he looked at Olivia again, more eagerly than before. She led him into the dining room and settled him at the table with a plate of drumsticks and mashed potatoes. They were going to run out of food. She saw that Abby was eating again, too, so John wouldn't be alone (although he was so intent on the drumsticks she doubted he cared), and she went back to the kitchen and turned on the pot of water again. She pulled out a package of spaghetti.

"Wash your hands, buddy," Olivia heard David say in the dining room. She went to the doorway. John was in the middle of a drumstick, pulling off the crispy skin first and stuffing it in his mouth, and didn't break form.

"Oh, what's a little dirt?" she said. David sighed and pushed past her to the kitchen sink. She lowered her voice and followed. "Doesn't he need a bathroom, though? How long have you guys been in the car?"

"We've stopped for plenty of bathroom breaks, believe me," David said grimly.

"You're eating spaghetti," Olivia said. "You can't waltz in here and expect to take all our chicken." She turned on the burner under the abandoned browned butter and sage to warm it up.

"Sounds wonderful," David said. "Livy."

She was pulling the milk from the fridge, getting glasses from the cupboard. When David didn't go on, she turned and looked at him. "What?"

"How's Annie?" he said finally.

"She's fine," Olivia said, a little surprised. "Really, she's going to be okay. It looks like the baby will be okay, too. They want to keep her another day or so, make sure the antibiotics are doing their job."

"Good," he said, almost to himself. "I need to talk to her."

Olivia followed him into the dining room, grabbed at him before he sat next to Abby. "She's not back to normal *yet*," she said in his ear. "You can't go upsetting her about anything."

He looked genuinely perplexed. "Why would it upset her to talk to me?"

"You're not going without me," Olivia said.

Father was handing David what was left of his chicken breast. Olivia intercepted it. "David wants spaghetti," she said firmly, returning the breast to Father's plate.

As it turned out, John also had spaghetti, an enormous heaping plate of spaghetti with butter and parmesan cheese. Abby sat with her head in her hands and watched. "You eat a *lot*," she said. John ignored her. "I'm going to watch a video after supper. Do you like *Aladdin*?"

John looked at her and nodded, mouth full of spaghetti, then looked at David. "Sure, whatever,"

411

David said. He took another helping of what John had called the grown-ups' spaghetti, full of suspicious green bits. "This is good, Livy," he said, "whatever it is," but she still didn't forgive him.

The kids settled on floor pillows in front of *Aladdin*. Suddenly they were giggling, best friends united against the vagaries that had brought them together. Father stretched out on the sofa behind them, and David and Olivia's departure was barely acknowledged in the flurry of whispers that rose from the floor.

The rain had stopped, and the sky lightened just in time to fade for the night. They took David's car. It was a short drive, only about eight blocks, and they drove in silence until they reached the parking lot. Then Olivia said, "So. You and your new stepson, on a fishing trip."

"Yep."

"I bet Janet's glad to have a real father figure in his life again, doing things like that. Father-son things."

David sighed. "Yep. Thrilled."

It was past visiting hours, but David said to the night nurse, "I just arrived. Got here as fast as I could." He was handsome and slightly dirt-streaked, and had the air of someone who had fought through the underbrush. Olivia looked away so she could roll her eyes. The nurse mouthed "Go ahead" and waved them through.

Olivia led David round to Annie's room—the rooms were laid out on a wheel around the nurses' station—and then knocked at the open door.

Richard rose from the chair next to Annie's bed, where Annie lay in a limp curl. She looked asleep, and Olivia started to pull David back, but then Annie spoke. Her voice was weak. She had told Olivia earlier that she didn't want to engage her diaphragm or do anything that would remind her stomach that it existed. "You brought my Jell-O," she said, eyes still closed.

"Nothing so exciting," Olivia said "David's here."

Annie opened her eyes a crack and lifted her head. "Hey you," she said, and pulled her lips into a smile.

"Hey," David said. He smiled at Annie, looked at Richard and smiled.

Olivia felt an unaccustomed pang of sympathy for David. Annie looked much better, her skin smooth and elastic again, but she was still pale against the white sheets. If you hadn't seen her yesterday, at her worst, you would think she looked terrible now.

"What brings you here?" Annie said. "Am I dying?"

"He's on a fishing trip with John," Olivia said.

"Walleye?" asked Richard.

"That was the idea," David said. "Not that

413

we've seen any. Nine-year-old boys can't sit still and can't be quiet. I might as well be blasting a foghorn."

"He didn't seem squirmy to me," Olivia said.

"You haven't seen him in a boat. You'd think it was a canoe, the way he had that thing rocking."

"Still," Annie said. She was hoarse, cleared her throat weakly. "Special for him to have time alone with you."

Richard held a cup of water to her lips.

"I've got it," she said impatiently, and took the cup. She drank a swallow or two.

"So," David said. "You're doing better."

"Much."

"And the baby's well," he said.

Richard said, "They think everything's going to be fine."

"Baby may be born dehydrated," Annie said, shifting under her sheets, "and needing to take in fluids every few hours, day and night, for several months. That's the only side effect."

David stared.

"That was a joke," Olivia said. "Not a great joke, but still."

"The nurse liked it," Annie said.

"She has to be nice to you," Olivia said.

Annie reached out and squeezed Olivia's hand.

"Make them leave," Annie said to Richard, "or at least be quiet. I'm missing *Dr. Quinn*."

"We're going," Olivia said, looking sideways at David and daring him to argue. "We'll come back tomorrow, right?"

"Bring John," Annie said. "Don't leave without bringing John."

"Sure," David said.

"Maybe I'll even shower before then. Don't want to scare the kid."

"He and Abby are having a blast," Olivia said. "They're all chummy already."

David squeezed Annie's arm and they left.

On the way to the car, Olivia said, "She's really looking a lot better. You should have seen her yesterday."

"This is nothing," David said as they got in the car. "You want to talk dehydration? We found a guy once, had been missing in the Badlands for three days in the dead of August. We were trying to track these bighorn sheep that were lambing late, which is bad news for the lambs. Anyway we got the bulletin on this guy, and by complete coincidence found him where he wasn't supposed to be—we were in Pinnacles, he was supposed to be in Cedar Pass somewhere. He had crawled under this ledge. The first moment, I thought we were looking at a pile of rags."

"Was he alive?" Olivia forced herself to ask.

"Just. He looked like a vampire had gotten to him. Not a pretty sight."

"But he lived."

"He died in the hospital."

"Thank you for sharing," Olivia said.

David shrugged. "It was years ago."

He crossed Third Street instead of turning left.

"Where are you going?" Olivia asked.

"We're stopping at Zesto's. They still have that Mocha Carmel milkshake?"

"How would I know? They don't send me bulletins on their menu changes." She thought, *I can make him buy me one.* "You have to buy me one," she said. "For showing up unannounced at dinner again."

They got their Mocha Carmel milkshakes and got back into the car, and this time, when David headed west to the edge of town, Olivia didn't have to ask where he was going. She sucked on the milkshake and felt strangely contented. Harry seemed a million miles away—was, by now, a million miles away. And Annie would be all right. People were so easily lost; it was all out of Olivia's control. Vivian was dead, and she had no idea if Ruby was okay, but Annie was all right. That was a gift. David pulled up to the edge of the small airfield and parked with the car facing runway three-zero.

"Aren't you afraid they'll land on us?" Olivia asked, which is what she used to ask whenever they came out here.

David said, as he always did, "If they're that far off course, they've got bigger problems than us."

It wasn't really an answer, but she always found it reassuring. They got out of the car and sat on the hood with their milkshakes. Out of long habit she stayed quiet. Growing up, she used to pay David and Ruby a dollar each to bring her along to the landing lights, but two dollars didn't include talking privileges. Nearly everything out here except the green and white landing lights was some kind of blue. The sky was deepening to a crayon indigo but was still azure in the west, and the taxiway lights were bright fake sapphires. The field lay under the formless blue shadow of night. No one was coming or going. Olivia could smell the grasses in the field, still wet from a full day of rain.

"This fishing trip wasn't John's idea," David said.

"No kidding."

"It wasn't Janet's idea either."

"Really? I would think she'd be all for the bonding time."

"You'd think," David said. He took another long drink; his straw rattled around in the bottom of the cup, and he set the cup down on the hood between them. Olivia prepared for a signal to get back in the car. But David didn't move.

"It came down to this or soccer camp. I wanted John to do soccer camp, and Janet didn't."

"Oh. Why did you want John to do soccer camp?"

"This kid." He threw up his hands. "He wants to spend the entire summer sitting on the couch playing video games. He has no confidence, no experience with sports, he's a disaster in gym class from what Janet says. He needs a little experience. He'll feel a lot better once he has a little experience. I'm not asking him to train for the Olympics, for God's sake."

"Well . . . he lost his dad at a really young age, right?"

"Exactly. So what do you do about it? Janet coddles him, just lets him do what comes easy. She suggests Boy Scout day camp, he bugs out after one afternoon, she lets him. We talk him into this archery class at the Y—archery, for God's sake, little old ladies can do it—and he quits after two days, she lets him. He just needs to finish something. He needs to hang in there and finish, whether or not he's great at it."

Olivia said, "Huh."

She sucked out the last of her milkshake.

"So finally I said, okay, organized sports are out, organized anything is out, I'll take him fishing. He'll spend a little time outdoors, we'll camp, you'll know he's safe with me, we'll get to know each other better. He'll have new experiences, *boy* experiences as opposed to the cyborg crap he spends hours on." He stopped.

"Sounds like a plan to me," Olivia said gamely.

"He's hated every minute. We had to set up

418

camp in the dark the first night, and he trips over the tent peg and lands in the mud. Disaster. He doesn't like being dirty. He also doesn't like eating hot dogs that are dirty, meaning they're not dirty, they're charred from the fire as God intended. Then in the morning there's a daddy longlegs on the tent zipper. My gosh. It was like having you along."

"That bad."

"Worse. I can't even talk about the actual fishing."

"Guess he's not the outdoor type, huh."

Olivia watched the strobe lights flicker from tower to tower.

"Well?" David said.

Olivia, surprised, said, "Well what?"

She could hear him release his breath in exasperation. "What do you think about all this? About this whole failed expedition? Janet's sitting at home biting her nails because John's been without indoor plumbing for the first time in his little life, and in two days she's going to hear what a miserable time he's had. She's going to wrap him in bubble wrap for the rest of his childhood. And the next time I say soccer camp, or softball league, or hey, let's throw a damn football around in the backyard for two minutes, she's going to go deaf. And don't take her side on this," he said snappishly. "I know I'm right about this. Maybe it's understandable, her being overprotective in her situation and all, and maybe I don't know much about kids, but I know I'm right about this."

Olivia thought, *David is asking me for advice.* She repeated it to herself several times: *David is asking* me *for advice.*

"Of course, you're right," she said, to buy time—actually, she meant it. He *was* right: John had been fatherless too long, John needed to be stretched. He needed physical effort, physical pleasure and pain to ground this new relationship in the real world. She thought of Richard tossing Abby over his shoulder, pretending to drop and catch her just in time, swinging her by the ankles, swinging her by *one* ankle until she was soaring overhead and squealing. Annie would order him to stop the whole time, Abby would beg for more. If Abby needed that sort of roughhousing, how much more a little boy like John? "You're certainly right," she said again. "But the fishing trip is over."

The gloom from David's side of the hood was palpable.

"Here's what you do," she said. She knew exactly what he should do. "You start the drive home tomorrow, but you don't drive straight back, and you don't camp on the way. You stay for night at that Wild West Water Park south of Pierre. It's got a great hotel with indoor water slides and everything. We did a church retreat there back when I was in high school. I don't care how sedentary John is, he'll love it, and you'll be doing something together—something easy but extremely physical. If you can get him to go down the Deadwood Drop, he'll think he's really done something, and you can make a big deal out of it. The beauty of it is, he can't fail." She stretched out her hands. "It's a water slide. And he'll think you're great for taking him there."

She looked at David in the dark—it had suddenly become night—and could see him nodding a little.

"And you make up some pseudo-contest for the two of you, a game you also can't lose. instead of catching fish, you tell him you're going to find the perfect hamburger before you get home. Then you eat at every diner you can, start with McDonald's if you have to, and you compare Big Macs to buffalo burgers at Al's Oasis. So your cholesterol level goes off the charts for a few days. Whatever. The point is, he'll have a terrific time, you'll be speaking his language, and he'll get home and rattle on to Janet about all these adventures he had with his dad. You'll have credibility with her next time soccer camp comes up, and John may actually trust you enough to go fishing again sometime. Although probably not in the rain."

After a moment, David said, "It's not a terrible idea."

Olivia said, "If you're lucky, you can get a poolside room right off the water slides. It costs more, but it would wow him."

David said, "I've heard worse ideas."

He slid off the hood. Olivia collected both shake cups and slid off, too. Steam was rising off the wet grass but had nowhere to go; the atmosphere pressed against Olivia, close as a warm damp blanket. She suddenly felt she could go to sleep just standing there, wrapped in that air. They got into the car.

"Here," she said, pulling a dollar bill out of her purse and handing it to David.

He laughed shortly. "Let's call it even this time."

Olivia stuck the bill out farther. "I wouldn't feel right about it. Anyway you can put it toward John's hamburger bill."

David took the dollar bill and slid it into his back pocket.

As he pulled away, Olivia asked, "I assume you tried to reach Ruby first, and failed?"

"Yes."

"Storm chasing, I guess."

"I guess. There were more touchdowns south-east today."

They headed home on Main Street. "You'd think, with Annie in the hospital . . ."

David said, "But you're here, right? She knows that."

Olivia hadn't thought of that, and wasn't sure Ruby would have either. But it was interesting that David had. She was here, and maybe it counted for something.

It was good to have sheets to change in the twin bed room, towels to track down, a bath to run for John. She was so exhausted that these tasks took her last reserves and left no energy for worries or regrets. When she went to bed, she slept hard, in spite of Abby periodically putting her feet in Olivia's stomach. The next morning she rose still tired but with the same welcome sense of purpose: sausage and eggs for David and John before sending them to the hospital and then on their way west, noodle soup for Abby before getting her dressed for church. Olivia ate a little of everything while she moved around the kitchen. Father's sausage and eggs came last, and as soon as she'd set a plate in front of him she went upstairs to dress herself. The phone rang as the three of them were nearly out the door. Olivia stepped to the kitchen and picked up the receiver.

"It's me," a woman's voice on the other end said.

Whoever it was, it wasn't Harry. Olivia hadn't even realized she was hoping to hear from him. "Excuse me?" she said, angry at Harry, angry at herself.

"Samantha Little."

Olivia grabbed a chair, sat down, stood up again immediately, and braced herself against the back of the chair. "Hello," she said.

Father looked around the doorway, pointed at his watch. She waved him away.

"I want to know if it's true," Samantha's voice said. It was flat, to the point.

Fear made her slow. "If what's true?"

"About the rhubarb leaves. If she really poisoned him."

"It's what she told me," Olivia said. "I can't verify it, but I don't think she'd lie."

There was a long silence, which Olivia knew not to break. She waited and tried not to breathe too hard into the phone.

"I have an old friend," Samantha said finally. "A nurse at the Brookings Hospital. I had her look up the records from when he died."

"Oh." *Is that legal?* Olivia wondered.

"He was in for stomach and intestinal pain. They did exploratory surgery, found nothing conclusive, but he got an infection from the surgery. That's what technically killed him."

"Oh."

At last Samantha said, in the same flat tone, "Have you met him?"

Olivia said, confused, "Mr. Kilkenny?"

"My son."

"Oh. I've seen pictures, like I said. She talks about him."

Another long silence. Finally: "I'm coming tomorrow."

"To—to here? To see Winnie Kilkenny?"

"I want you to take me to see her." After a moment, Samantha added, in the same hard tone, "If you're willing."

"Of course," Olivia said. Father appeared, and she waved him off again. *Go without me,* she mouthed. She couldn't think. After a moment she heard the front door close. "Isn't it awfully hard to get away from a restaurant?" *Shut up,* she told herself.

"We're closed Mondays."

"Oh. That must be nice, to have a day off." *Shut up,* she told herself desperately.

"I won't see her alone. I won't do this if you're planning on leaving me alone with her."

"All right," Olivia said. She licked her lips. "I'll stay."

"I'll be there at nine."

"Nine in the morning?" Her mind was racing. "Isn't that awfully early? You'll have to leave awfully early."

"Most days I'm up at four," Samantha said. "Anyway I believe in getting on with things."

"Okay, nine. You'll need my address."

"I'm ready."

"Wait. Can I tell her? I have to tell her you're coming. We can't just show up, without any warning."

There was another pause. The silence on the line roared in Olivia's ear. "I guess you better," Samantha Little said.

"All right then. I'll tell her today." *I have to tell her,* Olivia thought, afraid rather than glad.

After they hung up, Olivia started trembling and sat, staring out the window at the bright day for a long time. She wondered how Vivian had done this sort of thing on a regular basis, without succumbing to nerves, without so much as batting an eye. Olivia wasn't supposed to be doing this sort of thing. She longed, suddenly, for lessons to plan, for research to conduct. She longed to give a lecture on an introduction to transformational-generative grammar, itched to perform the basic act of parsing a complex sentence on a sharply lined, beautifully balanced tree. She knew then that she would accept the postdoc position Dr. Vitale had been holding out. So what if she'd have to share the campus with Harry and Penelope for another year? Vivian was dead, wherever Olivia went, whomever she was with or not with. She might as well do something she loved. She hadn't thought she could love doing anything again. She wasn't even sure she liked the idea.

She would see Winnie Kilkenny first thing, get it over with. Later she'd email Dr. Vitale. And tomorrow morning she would take Samantha Little to see her mother for the first time in thirty-plus years. Then she was finished. She would put Winnie Kilkenny from her mind, for good. She'd give notice and finish out the week at Meals on Wheels. She wanted a few weeks off, if she was really going back to St. Anselm in September. It would take her that long to find the energy to pack. She would take a few of Vivian's clothes; she would figure out how to leave without leaving. She didn't care if that made her a coward.

19

She was going to see Winnie Kilkenny, but first she would buy Winnie a bunch of bright yellow flowers. It would be easier to talk about Samantha while holding a bunch of flowers. She stood in the front entry and counted the money in her purse. Now that she had the idea of flowers, she saw that she should have taken Winnie flowers ages ago. She was glad, too, that she was wearing something nicer than usual, a long, sleeveless summer dress with a brushstroke pattern of blue and purple flowers scattered across pale green leaves. She opened the front door.

Ruby was standing on the other side of the screen door. Her arms hung at her sides. She wasn't rooting for a key or raising a hand to knock. She might have been standing like that for minutes and minutes. Her thick hair was escaping its clip, her tank top and jean shorts looked slept in, and the whole ensemble had a reluctant air that reminded Olivia of John shivering in his green striped tee the night before. She suppressed an unexpected urge to laugh, but her hand at her mouth betrayed her. Ruby looked away in obvious annoyance. Olivia saw, as she did, a small white bandage running parallel to her hairline, maybe two inches long. She stopped smiling and looked more closely.

Ruby said, "I've been in a car the last couple of nights, is all."

"Oh."

Her eyes were heavily shadowed, her jaw not so much swollen as less defined than usual. A long shadow on her thigh was the only actual bruise Olivia could see, but she suddenly knew Ruby was sore all over. She knew it by the way she stood so carefully still. Olivia met Ruby's eyes and saw something smoldering there, a sort of impatient but determined repentance: she was waiting to get the questions over with.

But Olivia found, now that she had Ruby in front of her, now that she had the right to ask what the hell happened (an iron-clad right conferred by Ruby's standing on the front steps for minutes and minutes), that she was done asking questions. She could see Ruby was all right, at least outwardly. She had been neatly stitched and bandaged by a professional; someone had taken care of her. Olivia was grateful for that. Ruby would never tell her anything Ruby didn't want to tell her anyway, whether she were here on the steps or chasing a tornado. Olivia might never know if Ruby were really all right. She realized then—a small, unwelcome, unbidden bit of knowledge—that Vivian had never known either.

But it was the right thing to buy Winnie Kilkenny flowers. It was a relief to know *something*.

Olivia said, because Ruby still hadn't moved, "Are you coming or going?"

Ruby's eyes opened a little wider; after another moment, her expression relaxed. "You going to church?"

"Church is half over," Olivia said. "I have to go buy flowers."

Ruby said, "I'll come with."

Olivia said, "And then I have to deliver the flowers to this old lady who used to know Mom."

Ruby said, "I don't mind."

Olivia took a breath. "If this old lady finds out you're Ruby Tschetter, she's going to want to know how you're doing. I mean, she's going to want to *really* know, starting way back with what happened in high school. She's going to search you with the most earnest blue eyes you've ever looked into, and you're going to feel like the life preserver thrown at a drowning person. Do you still want to come?"

Ruby's eyes had darkened as Olivia spoke. "She knew Mom—back then?"

Olivia said, "Winnie Kilkenny. Way back then."

"Mom told Winnie Kilkenny?"

"Everything."

Ruby sighed, a long, loose sigh of surrender, and her expression relaxed still further. "I'll come."

They got into Olivia's car. Ruby's Mustang was nowhere to be seen, and Olivia didn't ask.

They drove to Hy-Vee because none of the flower shops would open until noon. Olivia and Ruby went to the wall of refrigerators in the florist section containing premade bouquets. Ordinarily Olivia couldn't choose between four or five equally beautiful things in under ten minutes, but now she pointed immediately to a splendid bouquet of yellow roses, Asiatic lilies, and dahlias.

"Shoot," Ruby said when they pulled it out and looked at the price tag. "What did you do, run over this woman's dog?"

"Worse," Olivia said. "I found her long-lost daughter." She took it to the counter. "Guess I won't be paying cash," she said, getting out her card.

"For heaven's sake." Ruby pulled a neatly folded wad of bills from her back pocket. "How much more do you need?"

"Thirty."

They paid the woman and left. Ruby braced the bouquet carefully between her thighs the whole way to Winnie Kilkenny's. When they got there, Olivia parked and sat a moment, as she always did at this address, to gather her forces. "She doesn't know I'm coming," she said. "I hope she's lucid today. I hope she's *alive*."

"Come on," Ruby said. She pushed her door open with one foot and got out bouquet first. She had asked nothing further about Olivia's errand on the way over. Olivia had not asked Ruby whether she'd nearly been flattened by a tornado.

They stood on Winnie's porch, rang the bell, and waited. From time to time Olivia put her face to the flowers and inhaled, and Ruby did the same. The roses were the kind that had very little scent, but something else in the bouquet was spicy. Olivia was lightheaded with the scent by the time the door opened a crack, and Winnie's face showed timidly in the opening. When she saw Olivia and the flowers, her eyes widened, and she opened the door and stepped back.

"Mrs. Kilkenny," Olivia said. "I'm sorry to show up unannounced like this. Do you mind a couple of Sunday visitors?"

"Come in," Winnie said.

She led them not to the living room with the TV and the side table where Olivia always put her meals, but to the watery green sitting room to the right of the foyer. Olivia did not know whether to attribute this privilege to the presence of the splendid yellow bouquet, or Ruby, who had not yet been introduced, or the fact that it was Sunday and Olivia wore a dress. Winnie went to the drapes behind the sofa and pulled a cord, and objects that had been in darkness came suddenly into the light: coffee tables and curio cabinets of fine, dark cherry wood, the sofa and matching settee covered in slippery brown silk, lamps fringed with amber glass beads that glowed. Olivia sat next to Winnie on the sofa, the bouquet balanced on her lap now, and Ruby took the settee.

Olivia said, "These are for you."

Winnie smiled shyly and leaned in to the bouquet, sniffing. She touched the petals of one yellow rosebud.

"You remember my sister Ruby," Olivia said.

Winnie Kilkenny straightened and turned to Ruby, her smile fading, her whole expression taking on a new alertness. "Ruby. Of course. I'd forgotten you don't take after her." She rose, trancelike, and Olivia bowed her head over the flowers, closed her eyes, and breathed. When she opened her eyes again, Winnie Kilkenny was sitting next to Ruby and had taken Ruby's hand between her own. Ruby looked at Olivia but did not draw back her hand; she sat very still. She looked as if she were having her fortune read.

Winnie said, "Sometimes I forget she's gone. I think it's harder to realize it, when I haven't seen her in so many years. She always seems just across town, and not in touch."

"I forget all the time," Ruby said. "Every morning before I open my eyes, I've forgotten."

Olivia looked down into a lily, its petals flung open in astonishment, in joy. Blatant, questioning, frankly appalled. Hopeful and accusing.

"I was angry for a long time," Winnie said. "It's hard to stop being angry with a person when you never see them. It wasn't her fault; she tried to be in touch. I just couldn't, even after I got my Stephen back. I never even thanked her."

Ruby looked at Olivia.

"She doesn't know what our mother did," Olivia said.

"She doesn't know?" Winnie looked at Ruby, astonishment lighting her childlike face. Her next words were almost a gentle rebuke. "You should know what your mother did. It was really because of you."

Olivia could see Ruby's back stiffen.

"You see, your mother was so angry about what happened," Winnie said. "She blamed herself. A mother always blames herself."

"I blamed her, too," Ruby said. "I did everything I could to hide what happened, then I blamed her for not guessing it anyway."

"She would have done anything," Winnie said.

Ruby was studying her hand in Winnie's as if it belonged to somebody else.

"She wanted to go after him and couldn't, of course. I think that's why she went after my husband instead. She called him a wife beater, and a child abuser, and when he told her to leave she wouldn't." Winnie drew herself up suddenly, as if it were she who was being strong. "She stood there like some terrible angel on judgment day, and she wouldn't stop. At first he took it. He'd never hit anyone outside the family. The worst he did, he took her by the arm and tried to pull her to the front door. Until she said the one thing. She wondered about my daughter, Samantha, and why she left. She wondered what he'd done to *her*."

Olivia caught her lower lip between her teeth, gripped the heavy glass vase tighter between her hands. Winnie was nodding. She was terribly pale. "That was the line to cross. She'd found it. That's when he hit her, hard enough to knock her down."

Ruby pulled her hand away from Mrs. Kilkenny, looked at Olivia with a question in her eyes: *Is she crazy? Do we have to believe her?* Olivia nodded shortly.

Winnie said, looking at empty hands, "He knocked her down, and I went to my knees myself. It was the first time that question had occurred to me. I sound like a foolish woman, but I swear I never knew until that moment." She looked at Olivia. "That's why Samantha left: not just because of what he did, but because of what I didn't. Sins of omission." She continued looking at Olivia, searching her face, and something seemed to calm her. "Before Vivian got up, he knew he'd made a mistake. I'd never seen that look on his face before; I'd never seen him scared, All those years I was afraid, and Vivian brought him down in two minutes, *That* was your mother."

Olivia could see Ruby swallow.

"She did it to him because she couldn't do it to that man who hurt you, Ruby. She did what I should have done, years earlier. Then she got up —I was still on my knees, I couldn't have stood for anything—and she said to his face that she was going to the police. He let her just walk out the door because he was afraid. And after that . . . all the rest happened so fast."

"Their grandson Stephen was taken away," Olivia said.

"For nearly three months," Winnie said. She licked her lips, hesitated, and suddenly Olivia didn't want her to talk about the next part. No one should hear it, until Samantha did. Olivia spoke before Mrs. Kilkenny could go on.

435

"And then Mr. Kilkenny died, and Mrs. ilkenny got her grandson back. He comes back ften, doesn't he? He's like her own son."

"I think I remember Stephen," Ruby said. She vas pale but a little more poised, a little more erself. "He was a year behind me in school?"

"It wouldn't have worked out so well for him, without Vivian doing what she did," Winnie said. "She set things in motion—"

"Mrs. Kilkenny," Olivia said. "I have something to tell you."

Winnie Kilkenny looked at her, looked again at the flowers, and then her eyes widened.

"I think it's a good thing," Olivia said. "Samantha wants to see you. She wants to come tomorrow. Is that all right?"

Now it was Ruby who took Winnie's hands, rubbed them hard between her own. "Do you need some water?" she said loudly.

Olivia stood. "I'll get some." She moved to the kitchen quickly, found she was still holding the vase of flowers and set it hard on the counter. She filled a glass with very cold water from the sink and went back to the sitting room—grateful that Ruby was there, afraid at what she might find.

But Winnie wasn't prone on the floor, or lying back motionless against the settee. She took the glass of water from Olivia with both hands like a child and drank. Olivia knelt at her feet.

436

"I saw her myself," Olivia said. "I went to her restaurant and spoke to her. At first she didn't seem—receptive. But she called me, just this morning, and wants to come."

"Is it possible that she's all right?" Winnie said. "I know about the restaurant, she's doing well that way. But is she all right?"

"She looked more than all right to me," Olivia said. "She looked like a very strong woman." She gave Ruby a look, wanted to add, *Actually, she scared the hell out of me.*

"Are *you* all right?" Winnie said, turning back to Ruby. Olivia wasn't sure if she noticed the slight swelling round the jaw, the small neat bandage, or was seeing the memory of a young girl more than fifteen years ago. "Is it possible you're all right?"

"I'm all right," Ruby said, then didn't seem to know how to go on—as if she weren't sure herself if she was thirteen or thirty-two. She actually stammered before saying, "It's just been a hard few months." She shook her head a little, sat taller. "I'm seeing a counselor."

Olivia blurted, "You are?"

"Well, soon. I still have to find one."

"When?" Olivia promised herself it was the last time she would ask.

Ruby leaned forward a little, mouth in a firm line that meant she was becoming annoyed. "This week."

"She doesn't have to forgive me," Winnie said. "It'll be enough just to know she's all right." She looked at Olivia in amazement. "I can tell her about Stephen. She must want to know all about him."

"I know she does," Olivia said.

Winnie looked around her now, at nothing and everything. "She's coming here . . . I need to get ready. The house. I should offer her something. Iced tea. I haven't made it in I don't know how long."

"We'll help you get ready," Olivia said. She was afraid again it would all be too much for Winnie. "I'll dust, it'll take no time. Ruby, you'll run to the store, won't you? For anything we need? And you have the flowers we brought. Everything will be lovely."

They were there for two hours. It was the strangest housecleaning experience Olivia had ever had, bending in her nice dress to look under the kitchen sink, the bathroom sink, for cleaning supplies, choosing a faded bath towel with Mrs. Kilkenny to tear into new rags. They found a canister of Comet, a can of Lemon Pledge, a bottle of blue Windex. Several times a year Winnie had a woman come in to clean, so the corners, the cracks and crevices, were not grimy, merely cobwebby. There was none of the clutter of life to contend with, just months of stasis and disuse to wipe from every surface. Olivia thought as they worked of English country houses shut up for long periods of time, thought of scrupulous maids pulling white shrouds off the furniture and cleaning in preparation for the mistress's return. Ruby worked very hard and without pausing except to run to the store for supplies. She shone the mirrors, rubbed the furniture to life. Olivia pushed a behemoth of a vacuum around and sucked gray dust from the cabbage roses, ran the hose along every crevice in the stairs. She did the upstairs hall but left the closed rooms untouched. Then she filled a bucket and started to kneel on the kitchen floor. Ruby stopped her. "I've got it," she said shortly, eyeing Olivia's dress, and washed the floor on her bare knees with stiff, hard strokes.

Once, stepping out the back door off the kitchen to set a large pitcher of sun tea brewing in a patch of sun, Olivia found herself facing that enormous rhubarb patch. The sea of leaves was deeply green after the recent rains, easy on the eyes, motionless in the bright still air. The thick stalks would be tough and bitter this time of summer. Olivia wondered how Mrs. Kilkenny had done it: adding a few leaves to soup, disguising them with kale? Grinding them up to hide them in homemade sausages?

Winnie wanted to put the vase of yellow flowers on the coffee table in the living room, but Ruby and Olivia talked her into leaving it in the kitchen, on the green metal table. "This is where you'll end up," Olivia said. "People like being in kitchens."

For lunch they had sandwiches from the things Ruby had brought from the store, and then Ruby and Olivia rinsed the plates and wiped up the crumbs. They spoke of the cookies Olivia would make to go with the iced tea. Then they left, Winnie Kilkenny promising to lie down for the afternoon. Once they were finally back in the car, dusty and exhausted, Ruby said, "I haven't even seen Annie yet."

"We can go straight there," Olivia said. "You have to be back for work tomorrow?"

Ruby was watching out the side window distractedly and did not reply.

On the way to the hospital, Ruby pulled at her arm suddenly. "Go this way," she said. She made Olivia take them a couple blocks out of their way to a lot near the railroad tracks, where piles of sand and gravel sat dormant in the summer sun. "Go in here."

Olivia pulled in, circled one of the sand piles and stopped uncertainly. She put the car in park and glanced at Ruby. Ruby was staring at the pile straight ahead. Olivia looked straight ahead, too.

"It's not the same sand, of course," Ruby said. "They use it every year to sand the roads. I don't know how quickly the piles turn over."

"I didn't know that's what they used it for,' Olivia said. "I never thought about it."

She waited. After a moment she sensed movement, and turning her head the merest bit saw that Ruby was shaking. She didn't bother covering her face, her hands in her lap were as helpless as they'd been when Mrs. Kilkenny held them. Tears ran down her dusty face. Olivia ached, did not let herself move, did not let herself ask.

Finally, Ruby took a deep, shuddering breath. She looked at Olivia, her thick eyelashes so wet and matted that Olivia wondered if she could see at all. "I'm glad to be here," Ruby said.

Olivia didn't know if she meant here in this lot of sand and gravel, where years ago she'd broken her own thumb, or here in the town where they'd grown up, or here on this planet. She tried to reach for Ruby but was jerked back by her seat belt. "Damn it," she said, fumbling for the release. She scooted over the bench seat, knocking her purse to the floor, turned awkwardly with one leg under her, and put her arms around her sister. Ruby leaned into her just a little, still shaking. "*I'm* glad you're here," Olivia said. "Whatever you mean, I'm glad, too."

Ruby wept into Olivia's dress. After a time Olivia managed to get the glove compartment open and find a tissue to offer her. Ruby said something into the tissue.

441

"What?" Olivia said. She stroked Ruby's beautiful stringy flyaway hair.

Ruby blew her nose hard. Olivia reached for another tissue, and Ruby took it. She finally pulled back a little. "You get to ask me once a month about the counseling."

"Okay," Olivia said.

"Once a month, no more. If you miss a month, tough luck. Okay?"

"Okay," Olivia said.

"And you've already asked for this month."

"Okay."

Ruby blew her nose a second time. "I guess somebody has to keep track of these things," she said cryptically, and again Olivia wasn't sure precisely what she meant, and again it didn't matter. She drove to the hospital with a glad heart.

In the morning Olivia was compelled to put on another dress, for reasons having more to do with Winnie and the yellow flowers waiting in that newly cleaned house than Samantha, who didn't seem remotely like the dress type. She put on another long sleeveless dress (all her dresses were long, in the hopes that long was slimming), navy with tiny white polka dots. White buttons ran the entire length of the front, and a smart open collar at the neck gave it a slightly more formal feel than yesterday's dress. Olivia had bought it for teaching a class on linguistic analysis a couple summers ago. Ruby had no clothes but the ones she had shown up in, which were now in the laundry. They went through Olivia's things, found a long broomstick skirt, hot pink layered over black, which Olivia hadn't had the courage to wear more than once, and a silky black tee. Once they'd pinned the skirt to tighten it, it looked, as did everything Ruby wore, as if it had been made for her. "It's very peasant," Ruby said, turning in front of the mirror, twitching the skirt. Her clean hair swept over her forehead, completely hiding the bandage.

"You look beautiful," Olivia said. She felt, for once, no trace of envy, only pure admiration, pure gratitude. She didn't know if Ruby was planning to come along again today; she still hadn't mentioned work. Ruby had offered to take Abby swimming in the afternoon.

"I have to call Meals on Wheels, tell them I can't come in this morning," Olivia said as they went downstairs.

"Can they do without you?"

"Easily."

At eight fifty-five Olivia saw a red pickup truck pull into the driveway. At nine exactly the doorbell rang.

Samantha stood in the doorway, her mouth in a tight line, both hands gripping a black handbag. She wore a suit, a navy blue blazer over a pencil skirt, and her hair was pulled back exactly as it was the other day, but slicked down, neater.

She looked as if she were going to a job interview. She looked, Olivia realized, supremely uncomfortable. That realization and the suit gave Olivia the courage to stick out her hand, and they shook awkwardly.

"This is my sister, Ruby," Olivia said, and Samantha shook Ruby's hand as well.

"I just met your mother yesterday," Ruby said easily. "She seems like a lovely person."

"Does she," Samantha said, looking Ruby up and down. Ruby was nearly as tall as Samantha, much lighter boned, but with a confident, easy carriage that could hold its own with anyone. She crossed her arms loosely and returned Samantha's gaze.

"Our mothers had something in common," Ruby said, still as easily as if she were chatting about coupons. "Difficult daughters."

"Really?" Samantha said cynically. "You ran off at fifteen and left a baby behind?"

"There are a million ways to drive your mother crazy," Ruby said.

Samantha's expression softened. "I have a daughter, thirteen. God help all mothers of daughters."

"You have a daughter?" Olivia said, rather stupidly.

Samantha seemed to notice her for the first time all over again. "I bet *she* never gave any trouble."

"Family pet," Ruby said.

Samantha nodded.

Olivia would have choked on her own indignation if she hadn't been grateful that someone could talk to Samantha without nearly genuflecting. Ruby and Samantha chatted for a moment, about Samantha's daughter, about her husband (*there's a husband,* Olivia thought, again surprised). Samantha asked what Ruby did for a living, and Ruby said, "I'm currently unemployed." She glanced at Olivia with the air of having forgotten to mention something of mild interest. "I quit recently."

Olivia said numbly, "She was a meteorologist on Channel Five weather."

"Oh," said Samantha. "I watch thirteen."

"Olivia here just completed her doctorate," Ruby said.

Samantha looked at Olivia narrowly as if she were a very unusual bug. Olivia bit her lip to keep from apologizing for no reason.

"Look, Samantha." Ruby stepped forward and leaned against the door frame confidentially. "Would you like me to come along to your mother's? Since Olivia will be there anyway. Unless you've changed your mind, and want total privacy. That would be *so* understandable."

"No, I'd like that," Samantha said, and now she looked uncomfortable but grateful.

Olivia said, "Maybe . . . I mean, I don't need to come. Maybe you two . . ."

"Yes," Samantha said. She looked at Ruby uncertainly. "If you don't mind? As long as—as long as my . . . do you think she needs Olivia to be there?"

"She remembers Ruby from years ago," Olivia said. "She took to her right away, yesterday."

Ruby scooped up Olivia's purse from the bench. "Keys?" she said. Olivia handed her the Tupperware of almond shortbread they'd made last night. Ruby squeezed Olivia's arm as she followed Samantha out the door.

Olivia released a long breath, watching them go. She was aware suddenly that her armpits were cold with damp, and that J.C. was winding round her ankles, wanting a late breakfast. Olivia shut the door.

She did not go in to Meals on Wheels. She fed the cat and then went to Father's office and pulled up Vivian's newsletter, and that morning she all but finished. She suddenly knew how to handle things that had seemed insurmountable a week before. She told Stringy in Sioux Falls that she had no idea why the rhubarb in her crumble had the consistency of dental floss, and asked any Ladies who might know to contact Olivia so she could pass the information on. When she found she had half a blank page available between two articles, she added a recipe of her own without hesitation: Late Night Fried Spaghetti. From there she put together a few thoughts on spaghetti Westerns, suggestions on what to eat while watching *The Good, the Bad, and the Ugly* for the first time. This was a vast departure from Vivian's modus operandi; Olivia could hardly remember the last time her mother had seen a movie. She sat for a time, lost in thought. The spaghetti Western phase had come sometime before film noir, sometime after submarine movies.

She worked on formatting, leaving spaces throughout the newsletter for Ruby's artwork. If she was really unemployed she'd have no excuse not to provide a few illustrations or at least advise Olivia on clip art; Olivia was confident she could guilt her into that much. She created, for this final issue, a more detailed masthead than had ever been deemed necessary before. She wrote a brief eulogy, carefully unsentimental, and put it in a textbox on the "Letters from Readers" page. She left space in the textbox so she could sign it by hand, once the whole thing was ready for printing.

At eleven she looked at the clock and wondered what was transpiring at Winnie Kilkenny's house. She wondered whether they'd gotten to the almond shortbread, whether anyone was able to eat at all.

At five after eleven she picked up the phone and called Harry, knowing her call would likely wake him. He did not wake easily, was not a uick thinker until after noon. She was counting on this to be true today.

His phone rang about six times, and the answering machine picked up. In the middle of his message ("This is Harry, you know the drill"), Olivia heard the phone fumble, and Harry's unnaturally thick voice saying, "Wait a minute. Wait." She waited. There was a beep, and Harry's voice said, sleepy and resigned, "Hello."

"This is Olivia."

A pause, a heavy exhalation that told her nothing: it could be annoyance, or surprise, or just that he needed to breathe. "Oh," he said finally. "Is it."

"I have to tell you something, Harry."

Another exhalation. He was trying to wake up, maybe coming out of a heavy dream. She heard what sounded like a colossal yawn. "Haven't you told me enough," he said.

"Harry, I'm sorry. I'm really, really sorry."

"Noted." Another deep breath. "If that's it, I'm going back to bed."

She should have planned this better; she hadn't planned it at all, knowing she'd lose courage if she did. She said, urgently, "No, that's not it. I have to tell you something—two things, I mean. I have to tell you two things. I honestly don't know that Penelope doesn't love you. I should never have said that. There's no way I could know something like that and I should

never have said it. Never believe anybody w
tells you something like that."

A long pause. Olivia almost wondered if he'
gone back to sleep, right there on his ratty old
couch next to the phone table. But then he said,
"Apparently you were right. I told her what you
said, and she broke up with me."

Now Olivia sighed. "Harry, I'm sorry. I am so
sorry."

"If that's it—"

"No, that's just the first thing. The second
thing—this one's harder." She said this mostly to
herself.

"I don't want to hear anything hard. I'm going
back to bed."

"Wait—not hard for you, hard for me. And
even for me, maybe not that hard. I mean, there
are worse things." She thought, *There's losing
my mother to a couple of blood clots from some
damn preexisting condition nobody knew about.*
The thought gave her a bitter kind of strength,
and she said out loud, "Actually, all sorts of
things are worse than telling you what I have to
tell you." She looked around Father's office
without seeing anything. "Giving up a baby at
birth. Poisoning someone with rhubarb leaves. It
takes a lot of leaves, you know."

She could hear him shifting, knew somehow
that he was sitting up straighter now. "Olivia, are
you okay? Has something happened?"

No, that's not even my stuff—it doesn't matter. Anyway I'm probably losing you no matter what, given that it's my fault Penelope broke up with you."

Another long pause, which was not encouraging. She took a breath, pictured him sitting there squinting, probably in a pair of striped pajama bottoms, his hair spiky and slept on. Her stomach rose and fell in a perfect swan dive. "I don't know that Penelope doesn't love you. I know that I do."

Not merely a pause: nothing. No breathing. Dead silence. Olivia actually looked at the receiver, wondering if the line had gone dead. She half hoped that it had.

"I'm so sorry, Harry. I'm sorry it turns out I love you. I know it would be so much better if we could just go on being friends, and we can't— even if I hadn't ruined things with Penelope, I mean. We can't be friends. That never works. I'd have to be all careful and brave and pathetic, you'd feel guilty all the time and you'd start being nice in weird fake ways to make up for it." She was starting to cry, but she felt free, she felt relieved as you can only feel when you have wrecked yourself on the rocks and don't have to worry about navigating anymore. "But there's a good part to all this, because this is pretty clearly why I told you Penelope doesn't love you. Of course, I said it out of jealousy, and you should

450

tell her that. Go explain the whole thing, tell her I confessed and it's all my fault, and you guys should really try again."

She was convinced, for ten more seconds, that the line really had gone dead. Finally, Harry spoke. He sounded, at last, fully awake. "This is true?"

"Yes."

"How long?"

"I don't know," Olivia said, somehow irritated by the question. "Maybe since *Das Boot*. I haven't kept track. I'm so tired."

"Olivia, I don't know—"

"That's the front door," Olivia said, in even greater relief. She stood "I have to go see if that's Ruby. I have to find out what happened. Good-bye." She hung up but didn't move for a moment, just stood there leaning against the desk. This wasn't what she had expected. She was as broken as she'd been since Vivian died, but for once, it didn't feel fatal.

The phone had started to ring, and Ruby was calling her name. Olivia ignored the phone and left to find her sister and hear the news.

Late Night Fried Spaghetti

It's fast, it's delicious, and it only uses one pan: perfect for graduate students and other busy people. Don't skip the capers.

approx. 3 tbls. extra-virgin olive oil
1 medium onion, thinly sliced
1–2 cloves garlic, squashed and minced
½ lb. uncooked spaghetti or vermicelli
    (go with imported)
1½ cups water
1 14-oz. can plum tomatoes, chopped,
    with juice
at least ¼ cup black olives, pitted and
    roughly chopped
3 tbls. drained capers
hot red pepper flakes (to taste)
salt and pepper
¼ cup chopped fresh basil
grated Parmesan cheese

Heat 2 Tbls. of the olive oil on medium-high in a large skillet. Sauté onions and garlic until soft, about five minutes. Remove with a slotted spoon and set aside.

Add the last Tbls. olive oil to skillet and hea[...] skillet isn't large enough to hold unbro[...] spaghetti (mine isn't), break the raw spaghetti [...] two. Place spaghetti in skillet. Sauté for abou[...] five minutes, shaking pan and stirring constantly, until some of the spaghetti strands start to brown lightly.

Add the onions and garlic, water, tomatoes (with juice), olives, capers, and red pepper flakes to taste. Season with salt and pepper. Cover and simmer over medium-low heat for about 12 minutes for spaghetti, eight or nine minutes for vermicelli, stirring occasionally and checking for doneness. (Pasta should be tender but firm.) Toss in basil when spaghetti is almost done. (If using dried, add at the same time as other seasonings.) Serve with grated Parmesan.

Serves 2–3 hungry grad students as a main dish.

20

Two weeks later Olivia made ravioli in preparation for her own celebration dinner.

They had asked if she wouldn't rather be taken out. All of them, children too, at the Northland Hearth, or Mendelssohn's, or Dynasty House . . . anything she wanted, and she wouldn't have to do any of the work. But Olivia wanted ravioli, and she wanted to make it herself. She told them to worry about the rest of the meal. Annie would make tiramisu, Aunt Barbara her Marshmallow Salad.

She made the filling first, mashed potatoes flavored with a little Italian sausage. If she didn't work the dough right, if the sheets of pasta turned out a little tougher, less pliable than Vivian's, at least potato and sausage could stand up to it more easily than spinach and ricotta. Olivia had never made ravioli alone before, and it would be a long time before she'd have time to attempt it again. She adjusted the final seasonings—Italian parsley from Vivian's garden, another dash of nutmeg—and turned off the burner. Then she mounded flour on the kitchen island and with one hand hollowed out a well in the middle.

Last week she'd made lasagna for Mr. Ry
The day she gave her notice at Meals on W.
she'd found Doris alone in the kitchen, pc
over her recipe binder. She couldn't think of
elegant way to ask her question: "Is it legal
give food to the clients? I mean, besides th
official meals we deliver?"

"You're not supposed to," Doris said. "Lot of
the clients have dietary restrictions. We can't be
liable for health problems just because some
vigilante of a cook decides to give fudge
brownies to a diabetic. Why?"

"Nothing," Olivia said. "Mr. Ryerson said something once about lasagna, and I thought I'd surprise him." She went back to her office, rolling
around in her mind the concept of vigilante
cooking, but had barely sat down at the computer
before Doris entered. She went to the far filing
cabinet and pulled out a file, placed it on Olivia's
desk. It was labeled with Mr. Ryerson's name.

"Dietary restrictions would be listed at the
back, on the original application," Doris said.
"You also want to check through the file in case
any notes have been added." She started to walk
out.

"Thanks, Doris."

"Don't thank me, I didn't do anything. I don't
even want to know about it."

Olivia made a lasagna, Vivian's recipe, and it
came out well but not like Vivian's. Olivia

455

ained about this to Father while she was
ng a quarter of the lasagna into a plastic
ainer for Mr. Ryerson. Father said, "I don't
nk Vivian followed her own recipe very
osely."

Olivia looked at him, sauce dripping from her
spatula. "That would have been nice to know,"
she said.

"I think she always doubled the sauce, or the
cheese. Something to do with amounts. Sometimes she made her own lasagna noodles."

They had lasagna for supper, and the next day
Olivia borrowed Abigail for the morning. Olivia
handed Mr. Ryerson his usual meal and had
Abby hand him the lasagna. He looked shattered.
Abby looked at Olivia in alarm.

"Young lady," Mr. Ryerson said. He choked up
immediately, cleared his throat. Abby put her
head into Olivia's side, and Olivia ran her fingers
through Abby's hair as if it needed untangling.
"That's about the nicest thing," he got out, before
choking up again. His Doberman appeared and
nosed the container of lasagna.

"The lasagna's for you, not the dog," Olivia said
with a lame, ha-ha laugh. Mr. Ryerson recovered
himself enough to growl at the animal and crack
a smile, and Olivia was satisfied that things
ended well except that Abby could not be talked
out of her disappointment afterward. Surely, if
people were happy, they didn't almost cry?

They delivered another fourth of the la.
Mrs. Kilkenny, who was no longer a Mc
Wheels client as of that week.

Olivia broke the eggs one by one into a b
then poured the contents into the hollowed-
flour well. Why did she find breaking eggs to ͼ
among the most satisfying acts in the kitchen? I
wasn't just the abstract notion of releasing all
that potential, the promise of the deeply orange
yolk. (The Tschetters bought their eggs from the
farm next to Aunt Barbara, and the first time
Olivia saw a store-bought yolk she thought it
came from an anemic chicken.) Nor was it the
sight of each shining yolk cradled in its albumen,
the two parts reluctant to part, held together by
a tenuous integrity. No: it was the sharp crack
itself, the small shatter of a paper-thin, smooth,
infinitely strong shell into two infinitely brittle
halves. It surpassed another of Olivia's favorite
acts, that of crushing a fat clove of garlic beneath
the flat blade of a cleaver. Cooking was composed
of many such minor violences, each of which
released an odor, a potion, a magic ability.

She added olive oil and salt to the eggs and
whisked it with a fork, then began working in a
bit of the surrounding flour a little at a time.

For the others—for Mr. Reynolds, Mrs. Carlisle,
Mrs. Hammond, the Walkers—she'd made bread,
a loaf of oatmeal bread each. The bread was soft
with a fine, dense crumb, almost slightly sweet,

not absolutely require butter to be
d. Annie was home again by then, eating
normally than she had in months, and
ested a loaf herself, and while she was at it
via made loaves for the aunts, for Doris, and
e for Mrs. Kilkenny, just in time for Samantha's
econd visit. For three days the kitchen smelled
of yeast and brown sugar. Father inhaled half a
warm loaf himself, that first lunch. Ruby took a
loaf back to Sioux Falls to eat while she packed
up her apartment.

When the dough was stiff enough, Olivia
abandoned the fork and used her hands. She had
to resist the urge to work in as much flour as the
dough could possibly hold, which is what one
had to do to make *gastel*. Gastel was German
egg noodle dough that you grated instead of
turning into noodles, and even Vivian hadn't liked
to make gastel herself without someone to help
with the kneading. Olivia had theories about
making it with a food processor. She was fairly
sure she was getting a food processor from the
family as a graduation gift.

The dough had nearly enough flour now, was
pleasantly elastic, and Olivia fell easily into the
rhythm of kneading: leaning in hard with the
heel of her right hand, then at once folding and
turning and leaning with both hands, then the
right heel again. Her thoughts fell into an easy
rhythm as well, circling the same topics again

and again. A food processor, hope[...] Cuisinart. She wondered what Harry woul[...] her. He was coming—again—for the celebr[...] dinner. She'd had to answer the phone eventu[...] after all. He thought they needed to talk [...] person. He thought he needed time to let he[...] revelation sink in. He didn't know what would [...] happen, but thought maybe . . . She wondered if he would give her an old, beautiful book. Harry knew used booksellers who called him when certain types of books surfaced. It would be like him to track down a pristine, signed copy of *Syntactic Structures*. Olivia wondered idly if Chomsky ever signed his books.

The dough was sticky, and she added the merest dusting of flour.

But maybe not a book. Maybe not a book. It must be a terrible problem for Harry, choosing what to give a close friend who was no longer exactly a close friend but was not yet and maybe never would be something else. Olivia leaned into the dough, very comfortable with the fact that it was Harry's problem, and not hers.

Maybe a Cuisinart, maybe even an updated version of the one Vivian had.

She wondered if she should have kept Vivian's black cardigan.

She would give Harry the big room this time, and she and Ruby would take the twin bed room again. They wouldn't be housing David's family.

had called Janet specially to invite them—
could manage it easily, with the kids in
ing bags—but John and Maria were too bent
staying at a motel with a pool. Olivia had
nted out that it was summer, and the public
ool was open all the time, but that wasn't the
same, and she understood even before Janet
explained. Anyway, it would be one more place
for the family to congregate between meals. The
cousins could splash in the pool with David
while the adults visited. And Olivia wouldn't be
responsible for so many breakfasts.

She did wonder about the black cardigan, but it
was too late now. Everything that hadn't been
claimed by Olivia or Annie or Ruby had been
taken to the Salvation Army downtown. Olivia
had kept a navy blue cardigan, which came closer
to fitting, and a soft ribbed long-sleeved top in
deep maroon that she already knew she'd grade
papers in, late at night. The fuzzy blue bathrobe
had gone to Ruby. Mostly what they kept were
scarves and sweaters. The jewelry was the
hardest, and they'd finally left it all still spilling
out of the box on Father's dresser, for Father to
decide someday. The hardest part was not, as
Olivia had expected, the sight of Vivian's clothes
bagged up to be donated, but the sight of
Father's closet suddenly half bare. Annie must
have thought so, too: without a word she'd
spread Father's hangers farther apart.

Olivia moving out, and Ruby moving ~~
temporarily, of course, just until she'd ⸳
between Chicago and Minneapolis, but it
keep the house from looking too empty too ⸳
And she'd be gathering grad school appl
tions—she hadn't ruled that out yet, absolutely
dusting off her GRE scores, figuring out whe.
and where to retake them. Father would doubtless
find that sort of activity gratifying. Olivia was
relieved he wouldn't be alone just yet, and
knew Annie was, too. The time was coming soon,
though, and a pang spread like fingers through
her stomach. She kneaded for a moment without
thinking any thoughts at all, until it had passed.

Too late about the cardigan, but she could take
Vivian's cast-iron skillet. Just yesterday she had
made Chocolate Puddle with Winnie Kilkenny,
baking it in the cast-iron skillet she had helped
season. Chocolate, eggs, flour, buttermilk. Winnie
had been nervous because she hadn't baked
anything in so long, but as she directed Olivia
through the steps, she grew calm. Chocolate
Puddle was Stephen's old favorite, she told
Olivia, and now she had so much to tell him.
Olivia had pulled the Chocolate Puddle from the
oven, set out the butter ready to spread on top,
and left before Stephen arrived.

There: the dough was perfect, smooth and
elastic. Olivia kneaded it a few more times for
the sheer pleasure of feeling it spring beneath

…s, then covered it with plastic to let it
…ne was clamping Vivian's pasta maker to
…and when Father walked in.

"…completely forgot about lunch," she said. "I
…n't even hear you come in."

"Mail's here," he said. He handed her a couple
…f letters, stood there absently looking through
the rest of the mail.

Olivia scanned the return addresses—familiar,
but she didn't know why. "Do you think you can
scrounge for a sandwich? I'm about to start
running the dough through the press."

"Sandwich is fine," he said. He pulled one
thick envelope from the pile and said abruptly,
"I'll be right back."

Olivia took a knife and slit open the first
envelope.

Dear Olivia,

*I cook here at St. Thomas' Indian School
for Boys, near Pine Ridge, and I never
met your mother but always felt I knew
her through her newsletter. It was a
shock to get the announcement she had
died, so all the more glad and surprised
when the newsletter arrived out of the
blue several days ago. Thank you for
finishing what she started.*

Thanks esp. for the pork tomatillo

recipe, as suddenly Mexican is all t.
with our boys here and I look for
dishes all the time. Will adapt the re
for a crowd and let you know how
goes!
   I have so much trouble getting the
boys to eat vegetables. Have you thought
of doing an issue of kid-friendly veggie
recipes? Wouldn't have thought of it,
except this last issue was mostly tomatoes.

      Thanks again, I remain a fan,
      Norah Red Grass

A gratifying letter but troubling, too, that the woman hadn't picked up on the fact that this last issue was the last issue. Olivia would have to write and explain. She looked at the waiting dough, then slit open the second envelope: regrets on Vivian's passing and thanks for Olivia's efforts, the spaghetti Western menu ideas were great, and what would she recommend eating during a Hitchcock movie? The reader had found that it was not possible to eat Chinese takeout during a Hitchcock movie without feeling sick afterward, maybe due to some combination of MSG and suspense, and would love Olivia's thoughts on the matter. Also enclosing a recipe for chocolate marshmallow cookies that could be eaten while watching anything.

put the letters aside and cut a slab from
gh, ran it through the machine on the
setting. She was grateful Vivian's pasta
r was motorized. Kneading the dough was
thing; hand-cranking the slabs through a
ilion settings until they were nearly thin
nough to see through was asking for a shoulder
injury. She ran the slab through several more
times, stopping to fold the ragged edges in, before
changing the setting. It was less relaxing than
kneading, too: almost as repetitive but requiring
more attention. You had to guide each pasta sheet
through, stretch it without tearing, cut it down
when it got too long to handle. You had to run it
through each successively narrower setting;
skipping a step would compromise the texture.

It wasn't as if she would have a lot of extra
time to write newsletters in the coming months.

When the first half of the first strip was finally
thin enough, she laid it on the table and began to
drop teaspoonfuls of the filling an inch apart
along the strip. She should have seen this coming
when David, of all people, called last week under
the same misapprehension. David, of course,
never paid attention to details, but Janet had
misunderstood, too.

"You should have amended the title," David
had said when Olivia picked up. It was one of
her bread baking days and she still wore potholders from taking a loaf from the oven. "This is

more accurately *Cooking with Vi.*
Olivia. Although that's a terrible title,
do better than that."

"It's arrived already?"

"Janet likes *Olivia's Kitchen*—very stra.
forward, and then it's clear that it's not jus
legacy newsletter. But I think you should go wi
something more descriptive. We can't improve
on what I came up with years ago: *Cooking with
the Insecure Chef.*"

"You don't have to be obnoxious," Olivia said.

"It's not obnoxious. It's accurate yet whim-
sical."

"There's no need to rename anything anyway,
because this was the last—"

"Janet wants to say hi."

She could hear the phone being handed off,
and children murmuring in the background. One
of the voices suddenly soared: "Hey, David, this
piece got bumped . . ." She envisioned them
sprawled on the floor around a board game, a
puzzle, a set of Tinker Toys, and David bent over
them, godlike in his breezy confidence, his
knowledge of the world, his endless, energetic
flow of ideas. She had felt it, and he was only her
big brother; what must he mean to these new
stepchildren? *He practiced on* me, she wanted
to tell them, as homesickness swept over her.

"Olivia? We love the newsletter."

"I can't believe it got there so fast," Olivia said.

nderful how you handle all that material
ur mother *and* put yourself into it, too.
oice, it's amazing how it resonates with
mother's—how different you are in some
s, Vivian all confident and matter-of-fact,
ɹ sort of earnest and self-deprecating, and how
ɹke in others. Like the way you're both on this
crusade to remind people not to waste money on
boneless chicken breast because they can use
the bones for soup."

"It's just that there's so much you can do with
chicken broth," Olivia said. She shucked the
potholders, tapped the bottom of one loaf cooling
on a rack.

"And those little comments you inserted here
and there, parenthetically, in the middle of her
articles—it was like reading a conversation. It
brought tears to my eyes. I felt like I was meeting
my mother-in-law."

"Well," Olivia said, feeling her breath catch.
"I'm glad it worked. I wasn't sure."

"It's lovely, just lovely. You should have seen
David. He was really moved. He wouldn't even
let me look at it until he'd gone through the
whole thing."

"Really?" Olivia thought, nonsensically, *it must
be the hyphen*. The hyphen had made him go soft.

"Listen, I hope you're going to keep the "Ask
Vivian" column, under a different title, of course.
I've got something I want to write in about, and

I know my mother's going to want
when I read her your question abou
rhubarb. She's a rhubarb expert from wa
She'll probably end up subscribing."

"But this was the last issue," Olivia said. "I r
I was just wrapping things up for my moth
never planned to do another issue beyond that.

"You didn't? I thought—of course, it wa
Vivian's last issue . . . Are you sure?"

"Well, I really can't imagine . . . I just took the
things she had already done and filled in a few
places. I can't imagine starting from scratch. I'm
not the cook she was. I don't have the instincts.
I'm heavily recipe-dependent, and even then half
the time things don't come out the way I expect."

"But I like that," Janet said. "I like to hear from
someone who's had to struggle a little. Otherwise, it's like trying to learn math from someone
who was *born* knowing math. I once had a
semester of calculus from this brilliant professor
who was perfectly useless."

"Well," Olivia said doubtfully.

"What did I tell you?" David's voice rang out
suddenly from another extension. "*Cooking with
the Insecure Chef.* Sure, there'll be some turn-
over in the subscription list, but you'll probably
attract a bunch of new people, too, a sort of
younger, hipper crowd . . ."

"The young hip crowd does not know me as
one of its own," Olivia said.

…er, geekier crowd, then—all your grad
…ums, for example, and all the profs and
…profs—"

…not going to go peddling some weird
…etter with my name on it to the academic
…vd," Olivia said, horrified. "Not to mention
…e fact—"

"Your problem is you don't have vision,"
David said comfortably. "Think of what a PhD in
linguistics could do with a cooking newsletter.
The etymology of *spaghetti*. When and where
the expression 'too many cooks spoil the broth'
developed."

"*Spaghetti* is the diminutive of *spago*—
Italian—and that's pretty much all there is to say
about it," Olivia said. "Besides which I've got
edits to complete before that PhD is mine. And
a postdoc to launch—"

"You've got plenty on your plate," Janet said.
"Don't push her, David. Livy, we just wanted
you to know what a great job you did. And I'm
going to try your recipe for Late Night Fried
Spaghetti tomorrow. I have to say good night
now; it's bedtime on this end."

Groans of protest from afar.

"Good night," Olivia said. "And thanks."

There was a click, and then David said, "We'll
talk more when we're in town for your thing.
You need to work on your formatting."

Now Olivia folded the long side of the noodle

strip over the mounds of filling an
press the dough to seal it. This part w
than it looked: you had to squeeze ou
around each mound and press hard enoug
really good seal, all without tearing the de
dough. She put holes in her first two ravioli
patched them inexpertly with extra dough; th
looked like victims of poor plastic surgery. Wer
she'd get plenty of practice; this was only the
first strip in the first batch, and to have enough
ravioli for the entire family she'd have to make
four batches. She told herself to slow down.

Of course, there was that stack of recipes from
Winnie Kilkenny that she'd found in Vivian's
cast-iron skillet; she wouldn't really be starting
from scratch. Chocolate Puddle, Fried Grits and
Sausages, Vidalia Onion Soup. She wondered if
Samantha would be willing to add a few recipes
—although she'd be good for her own issue, and
might not cotton to a mother-daughter theme
anyway. Things may have moved forward since
that first meeting, but Olivia could not yet picture them in the same photograph. Olivia took the
pizza cutter and sliced off the ragged edge along
the sealed side of the dough. Then she made one
quick slice between each mound.

Father was in the doorway again.

"We could try a couple with lunch," Olivia
said. She was transferring the ravioli to baking
sheets covered with towels. "Just to see how

d out. I'll freeze the rest. Then, the
ne big dinner, all I do is make the ragu,
e water, and voilà—dinner."

r said, "Mm." He looked, if anything,
distracted than before. He was holding
her envelope this time, large and squarish
d powder blue—the kind that was meant to
old a greeting card. Olivia paused, a ravioli in
each hand.

"This is for you," Father said.

"Oh." Olivia lay the two ravioli down with the others and dusted off her hands. She took the envelope. "What's this for?"

"Graduation," he said. "I thought I'd give you my gift now."

She wondered if this meant there would be no food processor, or if this were an extra sort of thing.

"Well, thank you," she said. She slid one finger along a space in the envelope and it fell open easily.

"I suppose I ought to have asked first, but Annie said not to."

"Asked about what? And do we have to do everything Annie says?" She pulled out the card. Graduation caps spangled the front; inside was a folded sheet of paper, and a flowery poem of congratulations that she forced herself to read. Then she unfolded the paper: Olivia's name, and Father's, on a reservation confirmation at the

Casa Ombuto for fall break. She
quickly.

"It's not the same as going with Vivian,
said. His face and ears were flushed. "It'
you, of course, whether you think you'll
the time."

"I'll make the time," Olivia said. She cou
feel her own color rise. "This is Italy." Sh
swallowed, thought ridiculously of Mr. Ryerson
holding his plastic tub of lasagna, shook her
head. "This is wonderful," she said loudly. "This
is—do our fall breaks really coincide?"

"They do," Father said. "It's up to you, though,
whether we go or—or do something else. You
might not want to break stride so soon in your
postdoc."

Olivia hugged her father. When she stepped
back, they both brushed the flour from his shirt.

"It's wonderful," she said again.

Father said, "I think Vivian would be glad."

It would have sounded sentimental coming
from anyone else, but from Father, it was a simple
statement of truth, sober, endowed with gratitude.

"Do I need to change?" he said, looking down
at his shirt again. Olivia took pity.

"You change, then you can make us sandwiches. I have to keep running the dough
through. This is wonderful," she said again. He
was able to return her smile, now that they'd
gotten the most emotional part of the exchange

way, and Olivia saw that it was a
           that he'd done this now, instead of later
         over of the entire family—when the
        could have spoken for him, their high
        cutting his embarrassment. He'd done the
       thing.

Vivian would be glad of that, too.

Olivia placed the paper and card back in the blue envelope and set it carefully on the microwave, out of the way. She reached for one of the envelopes that had just arrived and wrote on the back:

southern U.S. and southern Italian

couscous with golden raisins and The Man Who Knew Too Much

ravioli tutorial for rank beginners

Then she set the envelope aside, put another dusting of flour on the table, and bent over her work again.

Acknowledgments

Thanks to Bill Park, executive chef and dire of Food and Nutrition Services of the Americ Red Cross Greater Rochester Chapter, for lettin, me see the inside workings of the Meals on Wheels program of the Visiting Nurse Service of Monroe County.

A huge thanks to Kim Jones, nutrition director of 60's Plus Dining of the Interlakes Community Action Program; Jeanne Zeigler, site manager of 60's Plus Dining in Brookings; and Dorene Relf, former head cook at 60's Plus, for several days of hands-on experience. Thanks for letting me follow you around, ask a million questions, and sample your delicious food.

Thank you to Phil Schreck, senior meteorologist at KSFY-TV in Sioux Falls, for help and clarification.

Thanks to Timothy Gilbert, Paul Manson, and Dr. Bonnie Swierzbin for Knowing Things.

Thank you to my wonderful friends and sharp readers who read drafts and gave invaluable feedback and encouragement: Laurel Decher, Emily Smith, Delia Ward, and Angela Zale.

A special thank you to my agent, Molly Lyons, for being a wonderful advocate. You are

...ssional, insightful, and a delight to
...n.

... you to my first editor, Trish Grader, for
..., wonderful big-picture feedback and for
...g me my first chance.

...nank you to my editor, Danielle Friedman,
...r whose help, enthusiasm, and sense of humor I
...m most grateful.

Thank you to my teachers, who made a bigger difference than they knew: Marlowe Hovey, Dave Walder, Diane Vreuls, and Joanna Scott.

Thank you to my parents, Gene and Ellen Gilbert, for unconditional love and support.

Thank you to my sister, Ruth Manson, for reading and insisting. You're more than I deserve, wouldn't you say?

More than anything, thank you to my husband, Tim Collins, for listening, reading, encouraging, and occasionally providing the essential shrimp cocktail. I love you.

Reading Group Gui

Starting from Scratch

When her mother dies suddenly, just as she defending her doctoral dissertation, Olivia Tschetter's world falls apart. Upon returning home she must face her father and three older siblings, who, despite all she's accomplished, continue to treat her like a child. Through her passion for cooking—a love she had shared with her mother—Olivia finally begins to confront her grief. Along the way she makes both painful and joyous discoveries that change her perspective on herself, her family, and the many lives touched by her mother. Interspersed with delicious recipes, *Starting from Scratch* is a funny, bittersweet ode to the power of family bonds and the solace of good food.

FOR DISCUSSION

1. Of all of her siblings, Olivia is closest to Annie, yet they are the farthest apart in age. Do you think their closeness is because of this difference?

2. Conversely, Olivia shows frustration and irritation toward her other two siblings,

and David. How does Olivia's relation-
with them change throughout the story?
several instances, Olivia has difficulty
vigating her way around her hometown.
As explained in the book, "Certain members
of Olivia's family had often professed surprise that Olivia could have trouble finding
anything in a town of only sixteen thousand,
and the very town she had grown up in;
Olivia felt that if anything, growing up there
made it more difficult." What, if anything,
does Olivia's inability to navigate through
town reveal about her?

4. While fixing a computer problem at the
   Meals on Wheels office, Olivia thinks, "It
   was strange, after all this time, to be doing
   something someone needed." Why do you
   think she does not feel useful? By increasingly taking on her mother's role as primary
   caretaker, is Olivia trying to improve her
   position in the family somehow? How do
   her feelings about her role in the family
   change by the end of the story?

5. At times Olivia deals with a great sense of
   impatience, including several instances
   when she "stifles a sigh." Do you think this
   restlessness is in truth part of her grieving
   process? How does her grief manifest itself
   throughout the story?

6. Olivia does not attend church regularly

because, as she explains, "the hym
off." The book describes several
denominations within the communi
many of the other characters regularly
church. What role does religion play in
lives of the characters? In their communit

7. When Olivia learns of Annie's pregnancy, s
thinks, ". . . a baby—something that woulc
eventually assert itself as a real person, no
matter how you tried not to think about it . . .
the thought of it was almost offensive." Later
in the story, she thinks "Frankly, the whole
pregnancy thing still seemed unreal to her.
Unreal, and irksome. It was almost hard not
to believe that if Annie would just put her
mind to it, she could set the whole pregnancy
aside for a while and then take it up again
when everyone was better equipped to deal
with it." Why do you think Olivia has such
negative reactions to the pregnancy?

8. When David announces that he is bringing
Janet for a family visit, Olivia worries about
all the necessary arrangements. She tells
him, "Mom isn't here anymore to just do
everything. I'll have to get the house ready.
I'll have to figure out meals—" Here Olivia
seems to resent having to take over her
mother's role as caretaker, but at other times
in the story she seems to enjoy her new role.
Why do you think Olivia feels this conflict?

conversation between Olivia and her ~~er~~ about his memories of Vivian, he says, "~~y~~ou realize there are—events you underwent ~~w~~ith the person who's gone, shared experiences, and then once they're gone, you're it. You're the only one who has those memories. . . . If you remember inaccurately, no one will know. You won't even know yourself . . . I suppose one should write things down more." Considering this and the fact that Vivian's newsletter is, in some ways, a written record of her experiences and memories, why do you think Olivia finishes her newsletter, even though she struggles to get started?

10. Olivia delays telling her family about passing her dissertation defense until very late in the story, even though she has several openings and opportunities to do so and is chided by her family about it throughout the book. When she finally does reveal the truth, it is not in person but through an email. Why do you think she does this?

11. Olivia does not accompany Samantha and Ruby to Winnie's house. Why does she stay behind? What do you think happens during that important visit?

12. What do you think happens between Olivia and Harry after the story ends?

13. What do you think *Starting from Scratch* means to Olivia?

Cheddar Soup with Shredded Carrots and Potatoes

Melt **4 tablespoons butter** in a large pot. Add **cup diced onion** and **10 oz. shredded carrots** and saute for several minutes. Sprinkle about **2 tablespoons flour** over the onion and carrot and stir until blended.

Add **6 cups chicken broth, 1 pound shredded potatoes, ½ tsp. dried thyme, 1 bay leaf, ⅛ tsp. Tabasco** (or more to taste), **½ tsp. Worcestershire sauce** (or more to taste), **¼ tsp. sugar,** and **salt and pepper** to taste. Bring to a gentle boil, then simmer until veggies are tender.

Stir in **1½ cups half and half** (or milk). Remove pot from burner and cool for 1 minute. Add **2 cups shredded cheddar cheese** and stir until melted.

 ➤ Note: You can play with the amount of flour you add. A little more results in a thicker soup.

Center Point Publishing
600 Brooks Road ● PO Box 1
Thorndike ME 04986-0001 USA

(207) 568-3717

US & Canada:
1 800 929-9108
www.centerpointlargeprint.com

ML   V/l